PEARL HARBOR

PEARL HARBOR:
Japan's Fatal Blunder

The True Story behind Japan's Attack on December 7, 1941

Harry Albright

HIPPOCRENE BOOKS
New York

Acknowledgments

I would like to thank the following libraries for the help they provided me in the gathering of information for this book: Pearl Harbor Naval Base Library, Fort Shafter Army Library, Tripler Army Hospital Library and the Aina Haina Public Library.

Hippocrene Paperback Edition, 1991

Copyright © 1988 by Harry Albright

For information, address
Hippocrene Books, Inc.
171 Madison Avenue
New York, NY 10016

Library of Congress Cataloging-in-Publication Data

Albright, Harry.
    Pearl Harbor.

    1. Pearl Harbor (Hawaii), Attack on, 1941.
1. Title.
D767.92.H68 1988   940.54'26   88-4469
ISBN 0-87052-507-7 (hbk)
ISBN 0-87052-074-1 (pbk)
Printed in the United States of America.

To Janet

Contents

*Nothing except a battle lost can be half
so melancholy as a battle won.*

—Duke of Wellington

Part I

Slash swiftly and without warning.

—Samurai precept

1

Fatal Legacy

THE SUN CAME UP RED OUT OF KOREA THAT MORNING OF 25 July, burning its way through a slight overcast down onto the misty surface of the Yellow Sea. A gentle breeze ruffled the waters while small patches of fog moved uncertainly about at the wind's whim.

It was the year 1894, which after a long history of dispute over Korea, found the empires of China and Japan at long last come to the mark, their seamen peering at each other down the barrels of their naval cannon.

The crews of three of these vessels, the swift armored cruisers *Yoshino*, *Akitsushima* and *Naniwa* of the Imperial Japanese Navy, had been mustered to their action stations at an early hour. Under command of Rear Admiral Tsuboi, they had broken off from the main body of the Japanese fleet, scouting towards Korea's west coast port of Asan to intercept any Chinese warships and transports bound for Korea over which both nations were asserting sovereignty.

Close on to 0700 two men-o-war steamed straight at them out of the Asan Strait. They were the steel 2,300-ton Chinese cruiser *Tsi-yuen* and the 1,200-ton gunboat *Kwang-yi*.

Although as yet there had been no declaration of war by either of the nations, all ships cleared for action. At a range of 3,300 yards the battle began. In spite of the fact the Japanese claimed the *Tsi-yuen* fired first, it seems certain the Japanese cruiser *Naniwa* opened the action.

Captain of the *Naniwa* was Heihachiro Togo. He was to gain notice of another sort later that morning.

With all three Japanese cruisers firing on her, the *Tsi-yuen* burst into flame while her secondary guns fell silent. Even so she came on towards the Japanese trio, obscured in mist and cannon smoke, but gradually disappeared from view.

At this moment the small gunboat *Kwang-yi* glided out of the fog. Instantly the *Naniwa* opened on her with all bearing guns. The gunboat staggered out of control, erupting in flame when her magazine exploded while she made for the shallows of the Korean shore. Minutes later the *Tsi-yuen* emerged from the mists, her bow gun disabled and twenty seamen dead, heading westward towards safety. *Naniwa* and *Yoshino* gave chase but lost their target as the obscurity again settled down on the Yellow Sea to hide the Chinese cruiser from the Japanese.

It was then, with the appearance of two other vessels bound for the Korean coast, that the object of the Chinese sortie from Asan Strait became apparent.

They were the British merchant steamship *Kowshing* and her small Chinese naval escort, the gunboat *Tsao-kiang*. The large merchantman was flying the red ensign of the British merchant service.

The *Tsao-kiang*, after signaling the fleeing *Tsi-yuen*, abruptly reversed her course to retreat after her countryman, only to be captured by the cruiser *Akitsushima*. This left *Naniwa* to deal with the oncoming *Kowshing*, apparently relying for her safety on the British red ensign floating at her main.

Owned by the Indo-Chinese Company of London, under charter by its agents, Jardine, Matheson and Company of Hong Kong, to the Chinese government to transport Chinese troops to Korea, her captain Thomas Ryder Galsworthy showed no apprehension about the situation into which he was so confidently steaming. It was now 1008.

Naniwa fired two blank rounds and displayed signals commanding: "Heave to immediately."

Halting near the *Kowshing* with her guns bearing on the transport, the *Naniwa's* signal halyard commanded: "Drop your anchor."

For the first time Captain Galsworthy seemed to comprehend his peril. He obeyed and *Kowshing's* anchor splashed down into the Yellow Sea.

Galsworthy, still hopeful, then signaled: "Can I proceed?"

Togo responded: "Remain at anchor or proceed at your own risk."

Things were becoming clearer to the British master as he surveyed his decks crowded with officers and soldiers of the Imperial Chinese Army, their fourteen field guns and other weapons.

After circling *Kowshing*, Togo lowered a boarding boat with Lieutenant Hitomi in command. Climbing a ladder up the side of *Kowshing*, the lieutenant made his way through the chattering Chinese soldiery to talk with the British captain. After the conference Hitomi was rowed back to *Naniwa* where he reported to Captain Togo that Galsworthy wished him to present his official protest for stopping a British ship in non-Japanese waters.

The stony faced Togo thanked his lieutenant then ordered another signal: "Raise your anchor and follow me."

Kowshing responded: "The Captain wishes to consult you in a matter of importance and requests you to send him a boat."

Togo ordered Hitomi to return to the *Kowshing* with the following instructions: "If the Chinese are unwilling to follow out *Naniwa's* orders, find out the intentions of the captain and the English officers. If they want to come aboard *Naniwa*, bring them with you."

After a shouted conference from his boat with Galsworthy on the deck of *Kowshing*, Hitomi was rowed back to the *Naniwa* without the English officers or a German, Major Constantin von Hanneken, who also was aboard the transport. Hitomi reported to Togo that the situation was out of control on the *Kowshing* with Chinese soldiers proclaiming they would die before being taken prisoner. Guns and ammunition were being distributed aboard amidst wild excitement. The English had shouted down to him in the boat that they were under threat of death if they attempted to leave the vessel, and again asked that *Naniwa* send a boat.

Upon receiving this report Togo ordered another signal hoist: "Crew of *Kowshing* to abandon ship."

The British ship replied: "Send your boats."

This was followed by another signal from *Kowshing* which was hauled down immediately after it had reached the peak: "Neither captain or crew allowed to leave ship."

It was 1300 after a long morning.

His "Abandon ship" signal still flying, Togo had a red flag hoisted to the masthead. It was a warning that *Naniwa* was about to open fire.

The obscurity had again settled over the water so nothing could be seen but the darkling grim cruiser with her single sturdy funnel and the black hulled transport rocking at anchor in the gentle swell of the Yellow Sea. At Togo's quiet command the watch officer brought *Naniwa* into a favorable position with her 10.3 and 5.9-inch guns bearing on the trapped Britisher. The decks of the cruiser were silent, all her crew were at their battle stations.

Togo examined his catch through his glasses. The bridge of *Kowshing* appeared to be deserted while her decks were a scene of wild disorder; some of the Chinese soldiers waved swords at their Japanese tormenters. Sounds of the excitement drifted over the quiet waters.

At ten minutes past one o'clock Togo had made up his mind.

Putting down his glasses he turned to pass the order.

"Open fire."

Two broadsides reinforced with torpedoes flamed from the cruiser, wreathing her in smoke.

Their crashing impact shattered the *Kowshing* in a great explosion. She settled by the stern. Rifle fire erupted on her decks as some of her boats in attempting to get clear, exchanged fire with those left on deck.

At 1315 in the afternoon she was gone.

So were all but a few men who managed to survive. *Naniwa's* boats picked up Captain Galsworthy and his officers while the German major swam ashore. A few of the Chinese clinging to wreckage were rescued by a French gunboat the next morning.

Major Hanneken filed a written report with the British vice consul at Chemulpo, the Korean port which had been the *Kowshing's* destination: "I saw a Japanese boat put into the water, full of armed men. I thought it was coming to pick up survivors. But the men in the boat opened fire on the men who had remained on board the sinking ship."

Later under questioning by Japanese officers at Nagasaki, *Kowshing's* first officer testified: "Two volleys were fired from the *Kowshing* to sink two lifeboats full of Chinese. The Japanese made no attempt to save any of the Chinese."

Captain Galsworthy himself at the Sasebo naval base told his interrogators that the Chinese general aboard *Kowshing* had forbidden him to carry out Togo's orders. When Galsworthy observed that the transport was no match for the cruiser, the general had declared: "Better to die than be taken! Besides I have eleven hundred brave men with me, and there cannot be more than four hundred over there. We can attack them!"

Galsworthy had then proposed that if the general and his troops really were going to fight the *Naniwa*, he and his officers would leave the ship.

"If you attempt to do so, I shall have you shot," the general had replied.

The Chinese government blamed Togo for firing into the

swimming soldiers and for making no attempt to save any of the men in the sea.

After taking the English officers on board, *Naniwa* headed for the Japanese Navy's Korean base where Togo reported to his commander in chief, Vice Admiral Ito. Although a storm of protest arose around the world over his conduct, the silent Togo received no reprimand for the *Kowshing* sinking.

Admiral Freemantle, commanding the Royal Navy's Far Eastern Fleet, sent a curt message to Ito forbidding the Japanese navy to stop British ships on the high seas. The British foreign minister followed with a protest to the Japanese ambassador in London. But in the end nothing came of all the clamor.

In the meantime Togo was becoming a hero in Japan, the first of the Sino-Japanese War.

Official declarations of that war were finally issued by both governments on 1 August 1894, six days after the *Kowshing* had been blown apart.

The first pattern for Pearl Harbor had been set by the man who would become the demi-god of the Japanese naval hierarchy. Heihachiro Togo after successful operations with *Naniwa* in the Japanese victories over the Chinese Fleet at the Battle of the Yalu in the Bay of Korea on 17 September, and the destruction of all enemy men-o-war and the capture of the Chinese naval base at Wei-hai-Wei on 2 February 1895, was promoted rear admiral.

He was destined to lead the Japanese navy to triumph over its first European adversary and in so doing transmit to a young and willing disciple his legacy of swift and ruthless action.

2

The Naked Blade

IN THE YEARS BETWEEN HER VICTORY OVER CHINA AND THE aggravation of Japan's quarrels with Russia over power spheres in the Far East, Togo continued his climb up the naval ladder serving as president of the Advanced Naval College in 1896; being promoted to Vice Admiral in 1899; and placed in command of the naval forces sent to China in the Boxer Rebellion in 1900.

On 17 October 1903 he was requested to appear at the Admiralty. There Admiral Yamamoto, the navy minister, told him there was likely to be war between Japan and Russia. Togo nodded. But the navy minister had other news.

"I have the pleasure of informing you that the high authorities have decided to entrust supreme command of the fleet to you."

The impassively silent admiral bowed his acceptance.

Immediately he set about preparing the Japanese navy to sail against the Russian fleet.

He took official command on 28 December with his flag in the battleship *Mikasa*.

Events were bringing Russo-Japanese disputes over Manchuria and Korea to a climax. Diplomatic negotiations, which had dragged on through the summer and fall in Tokyo, stood at an impasse.

On 5 February 1904 Japan declared the negotiations at an end and recalled her ambassador from St. Petersburg.

Togo moved fast. At 0200 in the black hours of the next morning the *Mikasa's* signal lamps summoned commanding officers of all Japan's fighting ships lying at the Sasebo Naval Base to the flagship. There Togo awaited them at a table on which lay a naked samurai blade. Looking at his silently expectant officers, he spoke softly:

"We sail this morning. Our enemy flies the Russian flag."

He then read the Imperial Order to the Army and Navy of 5 February 1904:

"In consideration of Our profound desire to maintain peace in the East We caused Our government to initiate negotiations with Russia on the subject of the situation in Korea and China. But We now find Ourselves obliged to conclude that the Russian Government is not genuinely desirous of maintaining peace. The territorial integrity of Korea and China has a direct bearing on the independence and defense of Our Empire. We have therefore instructed Our government to break off negotiations with Russia and We have decided that We are free to take action to safeguard our independence. We count on your loyalty and courage to carry out Our decision and to keep the honor of the Empire intact."

The short, sternly handsome admiral paused a moment looking at his assembled officers, before reading his General Fleet Order Number One:

"The fleet will sail at nine this morning and will steer a course for the Yellow Sea to attack the enemy squadrons at Port Arthur and Chemulpo. Rear Admiral Uryu, commanding the Second Squadron, will take command of the Fourth Division, reinforced by the armored cruiser *Asama* and by the Ninth and Fourteenth torpedo boat flotillas. He will attack the enemy ships moored at Chemulpo and will cover the landing to be made at the same place. First, Second, and Third Divisions, and all other torpedo boats, will make directly for Port Arthur. The torpedo boats will go forward in advance and they will attack the enemy on the 8th under cover of darkness. The squadron will follow up the attack on the following day. The salvation of our country depends upon this war. We will work together with all our strength to break the enemy, without losing heart, for the satisfaction of His Majesty."

Supplementary orders were then distributed and the officers dismissed to their ships.

Precisely at 0900 anchors were raised and the fleet prepared to get underway with the torpedo boats first out from Sasebo harbor. Then came Admiral Dewa's light cruisers and auxiliary cruisers. These were followed by Admiral Kamimura's armored cruisers which in turn were followed by the heavyweights, the six battleships with Togo's *Mikasa* in the lead. Admiral Uryu then came with his one heavy and four light cruisers followed by three transports.

The next afternoon the fleet minus Uryu's Chemulpo force halted at Ronde Island, forty-four miles east of the great Russian naval base and fortress of Port Arthur.

This time *Mikasa* signaled all torpedo boat captains to the flagship where Togo's chief of staff, Post Captain Shinamura led them in to the admiral. With charts of the Yellow Sea and Port Arthur Roadstead staring at them from the bulkheads of the cabin, Togo spoke:

"Gentlemen, tonight you will have the chance, in Port Arthur and Dalny, to put the last several months' training to the test of reality."

First he pointed out the position of the Russian men-o-war marked on the charts which were distributed to them. He attested to their reliability for they had been furnished by a Japanese staff officer spy who had just come from inside the great naval base.

He then went over precautions to assure the secrecy of

the attack on the unsuspecting ships, leaving tactical details to be ordered by the individual flotilla commanders.

"Let me remind you," he concluded, "that your attack must be delivered with the greatest possible vigor. For this is war, and only those who act without hesitation can hope for success. Our task, gentlemen, is quite simple, and all I ask of you is be worthy of the trust I am putting in you, and for which I am responsible to His Majesty, the Emperor."

As the young torpedo boat commanders rose, stewards passed among them with champagne with which Togo toasted their success and safe return.

Just before sunset, with clear skies and a light breeze from the northwest, the flagship signaled the torpedo boats: "Proceed to attack according to plan. I wish you success."

As they got underway the senior officer, commander of the First Flotilla, replied: "I answer for our success."

The small but deadly craft then vanished in the twilight.

In the darkness now covering the Yellow Sea, the main fleet units hoisted anchor to set out at half-speed after the torpedo boats.

Obeying Togo's instructions to keep their vessels blacked out, the torpedo boats found the ships of the Russian First Pacific Squadron swinging to their anchors in the outer roadstead of Port Arthur at peace with the sea and the night.

The Japanese moved quietly up to a range of 600 meters from where, about midnight, they loosed their deadly missiles.

In a matter of moments the blackness was torn by a series of explosions followed by flame and the panic-stricken cries of the Russian crews tumbling out of their hammocks to man their action stations. Searchlights stabbed into the night as the surprised men-o-war attempted to spot their attackers.

Two battleships, the *Cesarevitch*, built in France in 1901, and the *Revizane*, built in the U.S.A. in 1900, along with the first class armored cruiser *Pallada*, were heavily damaged. Their attackers escaped with some damage and casualties.

The Russian fleet commander Admiral Stark was not even there, absent attending a party ashore in the fortress.

Meanwhile Togo was preparing the daylight follow-up assault.

With the dawn Admiral Dewa's light cruisers were ordered to lure the enemy seaward out of the range of the powerful seacoast defense batteries of Port Arthur.

The remainder of the main fleet went to battle stations while closing rapidly on the cruisers.

At 0945 Dewa reported he was within 7,000 yards of the Russian squadron but they had not opened fire. Damage to the heavily hit ships in the night torpedo attack was observed. Dewa signaled Togo: "Opportunity for immediate attack favorable."

Togo passed the order: "Formation line ahead First Division, Second Division, Third Division." This put the battleships in the van, followed in turn by the armored cruisers and Dewa's light cruisers.

At 1120 with the Russian squadron milling about in confusion in the outer roads, *Mikasa* signaled: "I am attacking enemy's largest ships."

This was followed at 1126 by Togo's signal from *Mikasa*: "Victory or defeat depends on this first battle. Let. every man do his utmost." It was a signal which would be repeated more than once in the naval history of the Empire.

With battle flags flying, the Japanese fleet steamed west past the fortress of Port Arthur while the Russian ships, which had staggered into line ahead, steamed due east to meet them. *Mikasa* opened the battle at 1155 scoring instant hits as the range closed rapidly from 8,500 to 5,000 yards.

The Russians were now firing from both ships and shore, making consistent hits. *Mikasa* was struck by three shells. Three other battleships, *Fuji*, *Hatsuse* and

Shikishima, also took hits. The Russian fire was hot enough that at 1220 the battleships turned south to allow the armored cruisers their turn. Six minutes later they too turned south in the wake of the battleships with *Adzuma*, *Iwate* and *Yakumo* damaged by shellfire.

Whereupon Dewa's light cruisers entered the fray with all of the ships sustaining damage.

At 1237 Togo instructed him: "Withdraw out of range."

With this surprising break-off of the action, the battle was over. Wrapped in a mood of anti-climax, the Japanese attackers steamed back to join Uryu at Chemulpo where earlier in the day he had sunk a Russian cruiser and gunboat while covering the landing of Japanese army troops.

As a result of the night torpedo attack and the following daylight sea battle before Port Arthur, Japanese spies now reported that out of a squadron of six battleships and seven cruisers, two battleships and five cruisers had been heavily damaged. It was a savage blow, but it was not the total victory Togo had envisaged when he had planned the surprise attack.

The next day, 10 February 1904, both nations formally declared war, the Russians taking note of the surprise attack, stating:

"Without previously notifying us that the rupture of such relations implied the beginning of warlike action, the Japanese Government ordered its torpedo boats to make a sudden attack on our squadron in the outer roadstead of the Fortress of Port Arthur. After receiving the report of our viceroy on the subject, we at once commanded Japan's challenge to be replied to by arms."

The declaration rescript of the Japanese Emperor made no mention of the surprise attacks on the Russians at Port Arthur and Chemulpo.

While the attack did not result in the complete destruction sought by Togo, the First Pacific Squadron was so weakened that it could not challenge the Japanese fleet on the open sea, devoting itself to a series of futile attempts at escape to Vladivostok, until all of the ships were finally destroyed when the Japanese Army overran the land fortifications on 1 January 1905.

The surprise attack was the object of world-wide condemnation, but in Japan, Togo was a hero again.

The climactic naval battle of this war was to see Togo finally achieve his objective of complete destruction of the enemy while at the same time leaving an indelible imprint on the mind of a young Japanese naval officer who, thirty-six years later in similar circumstances, would emulate his mentor's exploits with much graver consequences, both to the hunter and his prey.

3

The Perfect Battle

THE YEAR 1904 WAS A HEADY YEAR TO BE A SENIOR CLASS-
man at the Imperial Japanese Naval Academy at Eta-
jima. The great Admiral Togo had set a seal on the year
with his famed night surprise attack on Russia's First Pacific Squadron at Port Arthur, to be followed by a smashing
sea battle by battleships and cruisers which had left the
unwary Russians trapped in their great fortress.

Every time they tried to escape, Togo had foiled their
efforts, until all of their remaining vessels were lost to the
overland assaults of the Japanese Army which captured
the frowning bastions of the stronghold at the start of the
new year.

Earlier the attention of the entire world had been riveted
on the progress of the Tsar's Baltic fleet which had sailed
from its base at Kronstadt on 15 October 1904 to bring aid
to the beleaguered Russian forces in the Far East.

That world had seriously questioned the proficiency of
the officers and crews of this fleet when on the night of 22
October they blundered into a crowd of British fishing
trawlers in the North Sea, and believing the fishing
smacks to be Japanese torpedo boats, opened fire. With

the entire fleet firing, it was fortunate that not more than one trawler was sunk, three damaged, two fishermen killed and several wounded. To compound their tragic mistake the Russians failed to halt and render aid.

Britain ordered its home and Mediterranean fleets to harrass the Russians until Admiral Zinoviev Rozhestvensky detailed four officers to attend an international court of inquiry to be held in Hull, England. The incident also alienated many of the nations along the fleet's route, which refused harbor and coaling facilities to the Russians on their 18,000-mile voyage to the Far East.

Progress of this demoralized fleet of forty-two vessels was regularly reported by the world press so that its latest position was always well known to the Japanese Admiralty and to Togo who was preparing a reception for the Russians when they steamed into Japanese waters.

One newly commissioned graduate of the Japanese naval academy, Ensign Isoroku Takano who hoped to participate in that reception was extremely pleased upon receiving orders to the cruiser *Nisshin* which served as part of the screen surrounding the great Togo's flagship *Mikasa* when she went into action.

This ensign would himself become a naval co-deity with Togo under the adopted name of Yamamoto. But in the year 1905 he was well content to be a student observer of the great master who had dealt the Russian enemy such a stunning blow at Port Arthur.

The great Battle of Tsushima, or as the Japanese call it, the Battle of the Sea of Japan, began for Ensign Isoroku, as it did for his admiral, at 0500 in the obscure dawn light of 27 May 1905 when the auxiliary cruiser *Shinano Maru* on advanced patrol signaled the *Mikasa* by wireless: "Enemy fleet sighted in square 203 appears to be steering for the western passage past Tsushima."

Preliminary to this message, Commander Narigawa, commanding the *Shinano Maru*, while peering through a cloudless but misty night illuminated by a rising last quarter moon, had sighted a shadowy vessel displaying three vertical lights, blue, white and red, on her foremast. It was 0245.

Ordering *Shinano Maru's* course changed to close with the stranger, Narigawa through his night glasses made out in the faint moonlight a two-funneled, three-masted ship with apparently no guns. As Narigawa steamed off her stern, a signal lamp began winking above the colored foremast lights, questioning the *Shinano Maru*. Narigawa determined she was a hospital ship.

Then Narigawa finally saw more clearly what was before him.

With the mists parting momentarily over the black rolling seas, the ships of the long battle line of Russia's Second Pacific Squadron, the former Baltic fleet, appeared as dark shadows against the night, their tall funnels trailing smoke into the obscurity. Allowing his cruiser to draw back to safety, the excited commander got his critical intelligence off to Togo in the flagship.

The Russians at this time were to the east of Quelpart Island at the mouth of the Korea Strait.

In *Mikasa*, lying in the Sylvia Basin of Chinhae Bay on the Korean east coast, Togo took the message from his flag lieutenant with relief. Rozhestvensky was steaming towards Vladivostok by the very route he had anticipated.

Togo advised Tokyo: "Have just heard of the sighting of the enemy fleet. My fleet will move out to attack and destroy the enemy. Weather fine and clear. Sea very rough."

He then signaled the fleet to get underway to meet the Russians, at that moment some ninety miles to the south.

Clearing the quiet waters of Douglas Inlet, the fleet assumed its formation for battle. Captain Togo Kichitaro, executive officer of the battleship *Asahi* and nephew of the admiral, noted in the log:

"The flagship Mikasa took the lead of the column, and our division formed up in the order of the Shikishima, Fuji, Asahi (battleships), Kasuga and Nisshin (armored cruisers). We proceeded out of port over a tumbling sea, and made for the eastern channel of the Tsushima Straits. . . ."

Free of the land, Admiral Dewa, with his fast division of twelve cruisers, raced ahead to join the protected cruiser *Idzumi* which since daylight had been shadowing the enemy within range of his 12-inch guns while emitting a constant stream of intelligence regarding his movements.

So the tense morning hours passed with the Russian fleet steaming at 12 knots on a northeast course in two parallel "lines ahead" with the more powerful ships in the eastern column, shadowed by the Japanese cruisers on their flanks and rear.

The tall, irritable Russian admiral, weary from his long voyage, was plunging on with no knowledge of his enemy other than the annoying cruisers snooping along his columns. In contrast, Togo knew all about Rozhestvensky and his ships, the constant chatter of the Japanese wireless reporting every enemy move.

"Thus," Togo noted, "though a heavy fog covered the sea, making it impossible to observe anything at a distance of over five miles, all the conditions of the enemy were as clear to us, who were thirty or forty miles distant, as though they had been under our very eyes."

This unremitting surveillance was wearing down Russian nerves.

At about 1100 the battleship *Orel*, without orders and perhaps by mistake, loosed a single shot at four enemy cruisers five miles to starboard. Immediately the entire fleet joined in, water spouts rising about the Japanese ships which prudently withdrew into the mists without returning fire.

Rozhestventsky was not pleased.

From his flagship, the *Suvorov,* he signaled: "Ammunition not to be wasted."

Some time later this was followed by another signal: "Ships companies to have dinner."

So the apprehensive Russian crews sat down to mess, many of them for the last time. As the date was the anniversary of the Tsar's coronation, officers in the ward-rooms supplemented their meal with a toast to His Majesty's health, then with another to the Tsarina, and a third to victory.

Shortly after noon Rozhestvensky again signaled his fleet: "Alter course north 23 east destination Vladivostok."

The order flying from the whipping halyards of the *Suvorov* was in itself the expression of a desperate hope.

At 1340 the two main battle lines came in sight of each other, the dark hulled, yellow funneled Russian ships to the south, the olive gray men-o-war of Japan approaching them from starboard, some seven or eight miles to the north. Togo carefully inspected his antagonists through his glasses before nodding to his chief of staff to fly his battle signal.

The flags crawling up the halyards crackled in the heavy wind. They conveyed a message which made every Japanese heart beat faster. It was a command which would echo down the halls of history to be repeated at a later famous attack:

"The fate of the Empire depends upon this battle. Let every man do his utmost."

To prevent the Russians from continuing towards Vladivostok, Togo first sent his main line boldly westward across their course to then turn southward towards them, his battleships smashing through tumultuous seas. When his ships were coming on the range he then passed the order which marked the decisive point of the battle:

"Ships sixteen points (180 degrees) to port in succession."

This daring maneuver would effect a complete reversal of the Japanese fleet's course so that it would now be steaming to the northward parallel to the Russian battle line. But to achieve this the flagship *Mikasa* would first turn alone, then be followed by each ship in her wake. If the Russians were up to their work, it would present them with a succession of targets as if they were in a shooting gallery.

On the after bridge of the flagship *Suvorov,* the Russian lieutenant Reydkin expressed his disapproval to Commander Semenov:

"How rash! In a minute we will be able to roll up the leading ships."

But Rozhestvensky withheld his fire.

Mikasa made her turn unharmed, to be followed by *Shikishima.*

It was only then, with the enemy four miles distant, the Russian admiral gave the word. The entire Russian battle line opened on the maneuvering Japanese.

They began to score hits. *Mikasa* took several shells but the lucky Togo escaped unscathed.

Three shells forced the cruiser *Asama* briefly out of the battle line but, getting the damage under control, she regained her station.

Ensign Isoroku's cruiser *Nisshin* took a 10-inch shell in her conning tower, injuring Admiral Misu, but the ensign was still untouched.

The *Asahi,* fourth battleship in the line, took two hits amidships, Captain Togo Kitchitaro reporting: "The main plates were twisted and bloody hands and feet and mutilated corpses were lying on deck. I went up to the starboard shelter deck and found the shield of the 12-pounder gun had been pierced."

But still Admiral Togo withheld his fire.

Ship after ship negotiated the turn until the last cruiser *Iwate* brought up the rear of the long column. It was then that the Japanese battle line blazed into flame. It was a little after 1400.

The effect was instantaneous.

Shells fell on the leading enemy ships like rain. At the same time Togo increasing speed, headed off the Russian column, now merged into one, so it had to give way to the eastward, abandoning its Vladivostok course.

Togo had performed the classic maneuver of battleship warfare of crossing the enemy "T" so none but the very foremost Russian ships could bring their guns to bear on the Japanese.

The British naval attache, straw-hatted Captain Pakenham, nonchalantly charting the fall of the shot from his post in the battleship *Asahi*, screwed his monocle more firmly into place to observe that he could look down the entire length of the Russian line.

It was hell in those ships for the new Japanese high explosive shell wreaked such destruction by blast and flame that the Russians could not cope.

In forty minutes the flagship *Suvorov* was a blazing funeral pyre, the badly wounded Rozhestvensky being readied for transfer to a destroyer. The battleships astern of her were aflame with one of them, the 12,000-ton *Osliabia* capsizing about 1500, taking hundreds of crewmen with her and leaving hundreds more drowning in the sea.

Still the Russians fought on attempting to escape the Japanese trap.

At 1630 the heavy cannon smoke mixed with fog to shroud the Russian line, hiding their ships from Togo who then steamed south for an hour before reversing course again to the northward. The move paid off, for at 1830 he sighted six surviving battleships of the Russian First and Second Divisions and immediately reopened the action during which *Alexander III, Borodino* and the wrecked flagship *Suvorov*, were sent to the bottom.

"The main squadron ceased by degrees to press the enemy, "Togo reported, "and at 1928 hours when the sun was setting, drew off to the east."

It was during this part of the battle that Ensign Isoroku was wounded. In writing to his family he reported: "When the shells began to fly above me I found I was not afraid. The ship was damaged by shells and many were killed. At 6:15 in the evening a shell hit the *Nisshin* and knocked me unconscious. When I recovered I found I was wounded in the right leg and two fingers of my left hand were missing. But the Russian ships were completely defeated and many wounded and dead were floating on the sea. When victory was announced at 2 a.m. even the wounded cheered."

Togo left the dark hours to the torpedo boats. They did not fail him, sinking or disabling three more battleships.

The next morning, after a nine minute bombardment, Rear Admiral Nebogatoff surrendered the remnant of Russia's Second Pacific Squadron to Togo, and that afternoon the wounded Rozhestvensky was captured when the Russian destroyer *Biedovy* surrendered to two Japanese destroyers.

The first great sea battle of the Twentieth Century was over.

It was a victory of complete annihilation of Russian seapower in the Pacific.

It imbued the Imperial Japanese Navy with an unshakable belief in its own indomitable strength.

It was the first great victory of the East over the West.

It would leave a legacy of catastrophe to come.

4

The Inheritance

THE GREAT BATTLE, WITH ITS TRADITION OF ANNIHILATION of the enemy, became a dominant force of its own, not only in the Imperial Japanese Navy but in the Empire of Japan itself.

Aging into legend with each passing year, it fostered the deeply held belief in the unconquerable samurai spirit and its divinely bestowed right to victory over lesser men.

In its affirmative display, this spirit was to manifest itself in the self-sacrificing courage and daring of the Empire's armed services; in the reverse, however, a growth of inordinate national pride, irritation with other nations, and arrogance, could be observed.

The irritability with the actions of others was soon displayed. Dissatisfied with what they saw as insufficient reparations for their overwhelming victories over the Russians in the U.S.-sponsored Treaty of Portsmouth of 5 September 1905, mobs rioted in the streets of Tokyo, Yokohama and Nagasaki. On the night of 10 September, while anchored at the Sasebo naval base, Togo's famous flagship *Mikasa* blew up with a loss of nearly six hundred dead and injured. Officially it was termed a spontaneous

explosion of her powder magazine, but this was dis-
believed by many.

Meanwhile Ensign Isoroku spent two months in hospital recovering from the wounds he had received at the
Battle of Tsushima. While his convalescence would be
complete, he would always bear the mark of Togo's greatest day in the two lost fingers of his left hand.

While the navy and the Japanese nation as a whole
would now hold in trust the admiral's legacy of victory, it
would be Isoroku Yamamoto who would become the
legatee and keeper of the shrine, who upon the death of
his parents, was adopted by the prominent Yamamoto
family and assumed the Yamamoto name.

In 1914 upon the outbreak of World War I in Europe,
Japan, both as a matter of self interest and because she
claimed her longstanding treaty with Great Britain required her to keep the peace in the Far East, sent an
ultimatum to Germany on 15 August demanding immediate withdrawal of German warships from Chinese and
Japanese waters, and the surrender within a week of the
German leased territory of Kiaochow on the Shantung
Peninsula.

This time there was a formal declaration of war, for
when Germany refused her demands, Japan proclaimed a
state of armed conflict existing as of 23 August.

On 27 August the Japanese Navy blockaded the Ger-
man-leased port of Tsingtao, and on 2 September ten
thousand Japanese soldiers surrounded the concession
from the land side. It was not until 7 November, however,
that 21,000 Japanese and 1,300 British, supported by Japanese and British warships, were able to compel the 4,000
German defenders to surrender.

It was a cheap and valuable victory, for by late October
the Japanese Navy had occupied all of the German posses-
sions in the Marshall, Mariannas and Caroline Islands,
thus seizing control of a vast portion of the Central Pacific
Ocean. It was a victory that was to give the United States
navy great troubles in the years ahead.

Togo, although he was admiral of the fleet, played no active role in the war, while his disciple Commander Isoroku Yamamoto (his official name now), having married, was a student at Harvard University. There he focused his chief attention on the American petroleum industry and the developing use of aircraft in the Great War. The completion of the world's first aircraft carrier by the British Royal Navy in 1918 was of intense interest to him.

Returning to Japan he was in due course promoted to captain and assigned to be executive officer of the new naval air training center at Kasumigaura, which he promptly transformed. So began his long service in the development of the air arm of the Japanese Navy.

In 1925 he was named naval attache to the Japanese embassy in Washington, renewing his close contact with America. It was during this tour of duty he became an authority on the strengths and weaknesses of the United States Navy.

He put this knowledge to good use as one of the Japanese delegates to the London naval conference of 1930. At this conference Japan began to chip away at the 5-5-3 formula, five ships for Britain and America to every three Japanese, which had been imposed at the Washington naval conference of 1921. The London meeting agreed upon equality for Japan in submarines and light cruisers.

Yamamoto returned to Japan to take over command of the First Air Fleet of the navy. Aircraft carrier training was given first priority.

Then on the evening of 18 September 1931 at 2200 an explosive charge was set off on the main line of the Japanese controlled South Manchurian Railway, not far from the barracks of the 7th Brigade of the Chinese Army. Elements of the Japanese Kwantung Army attacked the astonished Chinese soldiers within the hour, and by morning the large rail center of Mukden was in Japanese hands. Kwantung Army personnel, of course, had planted and fired the railroad charge.

Fighting between Japanese and Chinese troops spread

through Manchuria, spilling over into Shanghai in January 1932. China finally gave in and agreed to the Japanese occupation of Manchuria. But the League of Nations did not, whereupon Japanese delegates stalked out of the League never to return.

So the turmoil continued in Manchuria and North China until it took a more ominous turn the night of 7 July 1937 at the ancient Marco Polo Bridge outside Peking where Japanese of the North China garrison, which had been stationed in China since the Boxer Rebellion, exchanged fire with Chinese Army units. It was the beginning of conflict which would finally envelop much of North China. Japan ordered large elements of her army to invade and sent her bombers against Chinese cities. A new war had begun.

The navy was ready. In the fall of 1934 Yamamoto, now a vice admiral, had been named chief of Japan's delegation to a second London naval conference at which he had torpedoed the old 5-5-3 agreement and launched the world on a new naval armaments race.

Now with China on fire, the Japanese Navy completed its blockade of the Chinese coast in September 1937.

China appealed to the League of Nations which replied with a stinging censure of Japan. President Franklin Roosevelt of the United States joined in, although the U.S. was not a League member, and called for a "quarantine" of aggressor nations.

For the first time Japan and the United States were coming to close grips.

Then on 12 December 1937 American and British seamen felt the full fury of Japanese wrath.

The river gunboat U.S.S. *Panay* was bombed and strafed by Japanese naval aviators as she lay in the Yangtze River near Nanking, her large national ensign in full display to prevent such an incident. The attack was no accident, having been planned in the operations room of the large Japanese aircraft carrier *Kaga* with the attack planes launched from her flight deck.

A week before, the British river gunboat *Ladybird* had

been fired upon by a Japanese artillery regiment from the banks of the Yangtze and then attacked by the Japanese artillerymen. There were casualties in both incidents.

But the Japanese apologized in both cases, pledged indemnification, and the furor blew over. It was not lost upon Japan that neither the U.S. nor Great Britain had done anything but protest.

Yamamoto as Vice Minister of the Navy was prominent in opposing Japan's drift to war with the two great Western powers, but in so doing he made many enemies, mainly in the Japanese Army. His assassination was feared.

Finally the Navy minister Admiral Yonai had his deputy named Commander in Chief of the Combined Fleet, promoted to Admiral and sent off to sea.

Yonai said: "It was the only way to save his life."

5

A Plan Is Born

YAMAMOTO HOISTED HIS ADMIRAL'S FLAG AS COMMANDER in chief in the great battleship *Nagato*, flagship of the combined fleet, in the middle of August 1939.

On 1 September Hitler sent German troops into Poland and World War II began.

Yamamoto responded with stepped-up training activity to prepare the fleet for war. At the same time he proclaimed his policy for the combined fleet:

—Priority for air training.

—Bring the United States fleet to battle at the first opportunity.

These two objectives were to dominate all of his activities and thinking as commander of the gigantic fleet from this time forward.

The air training program was not new ground for Yamamoto. He was one of the greatest living experts on naval aviation and its problems. So the fleet exercised over and over again to perfect its skills in dive bombing, high level bombing, aerial torpedo attack, and in the protection of the large carriers from which these attacks must come.

He drove his flying crews and their support units by day and by night, in fair weather and in foul.

Improvements began to show in accuracy on targets and in all other aspects of aerial warfare.

His major objective of bringing the American fleet to battle at the first opportunity was always on his mind, but as yet he had no firmly developed thoughts.

Meanwhile events in Europe were on the march.

On 27 September the Wermacht captured Warsaw. Russia had invaded Poland on 16 September. Shortly thereafter the besieged nation ceased to exist.

Japan had signed the Tripartite Pact with Germany and Italy in September, so she now had a direct interest in the fortunes of the Fuhrer.

On 30 March of the troubled year of 1940, Japan inaugurated a new government for the conquered areas of China, centered at Nanking under the leadership of the puppet Wang Chingwei.

Germany invaded Norway and Denmark on 8 April for their "protection."

May saw the invasion of Belgium, the Netherlands and Luxemburg by the German Army and Air Force, launching the conquest of all Europe; Paris fell on 14 June.

Japan was later to take her share of the spoils, her army entering Indo-China under an agreement forced on the puppet French Vichy government in September.

By late April and early May Yamamoto had put the combined fleet through an exhaustive series of maneuvers, especially testing the proficiency of the naval air arm. He liked what he saw, so much that in a conversation on the flagship *Nagato* at the conclusion of the maneuvers when his chief of staff, Admiral Shiguru Fukudome observed: "It is beginning to look as if there is no way a surface fleet can elude aerial torpedoes. Is the time ripe for a decisive fleet engagement using aerial torpedo attacks as the main striking power?"

Yamamoto replied: "An even more crushing blow could

be struck against an unsuspecting enemy force by mass torpedo attack."

So the legacy of the Imperial Japanese Navy's past deeds began to emerge in the thinking of Japan's fleet commander as he grappled with the problem of the American Pacific Fleet, which was now based at Pearl Harbor in Hawaii, placed there at the explicit orders of President Roosevelt himself.

It was in the late summer of 1940 that the then prime minister, Prince Fumimaro Konoye, invited the admiral commanding the fleet to visit him at the prime minister's residence at Takigaiso. He put the matter on his mind bluntly to his guest.

If war were to come between Japan and America and Britain, what were the odds?

Yamamoto looked the elegant Konoye squarely in the eyes.

"I can raise havoc with them for one year or at most eighteen months. After that I can give no one any guarantee."

After his meeting with Yamamoto, Konoye made feeble attempts at an understanding with the United States but this only irritated his minister for war, General Hideki Tojo, the "Razor," and he soon dropped his efforts. Shortly after the Luftwaffe's assault on England was blunted by the Royal Air Force in September, Japanese troops entered Indo-China.

Then in November 21 Royal Navy planes were launched by Mediterranean fleet carriers for a night attack on the Italian fleet in their large base at Taranto. It was a great success, sinking three Italian battleships with a loss of two planes.

The news galvanized Yamamoto.

He ordered secret reports on the action from Japan's naval attaches in London and Rome. Under study of the flagship they revealed that the torpedo runs had been made in a harbor with a depth of 42 feet, long considered to be too shallow for such an attack. The Royal Navy had fitted special torpedoes with wooden fins to prevent them from diving into the bottom. The admiral poured over the reports for a long time.

Depth of water in the channels of Pearl Harbor was generally 40 feet.

The assistant naval air attache who sent the London reports on the British part of the operation was Commander Minoru Genda . . . a name to remember.

The Americans were aware of the implications of the Taranto attack, as well. U.S. Secretary of the Navy Frank Knox wrote Henry L. Stimson, the Secretary for War: "The success of the British aerial torpedo attack against ships at anchor suggest that precautionary measures be taken immediately to protect Pearl Harbor against a surprise attack in the event of war between the United States and Japan. The greatest danger will come from the aerial torpedo. The highest priority must be given to getting more interceptor planes, AA guns and additional radar equipment."

But the chief of naval operations, Admiral Harold R. Stark, in writing to Admiral Husband E. Kimmel, newly promoted commander in chief of the U.S. Pacific Fleet, projected a somewhat different view: "Consideration has been given to the installation of anti-torpedo baffles within Pearl Harbor for protection against torpedo plane attack. It is considered that the relatively shallow depth of the water limits the need for anti-torpedo nets in Pearl Harbor. In addition, the congestion and the necessity for maneuvering room limit the practicability of the present type of baffles. . . .

". . . A minimum depth of water of 75 feet may be assumed necessary to successfully drop torpedoes from planes, 150 feet of water is desired. The maximum height planes at present experimentally drop torpedoes is 250 feet. Launching speeds are between 120 and 150 knots. The desirable height for dropping is 60 feet or less. About 200 yards of torpedo run is necessary before the exploding device is armed but this may be altered."

The Americans had different reports than the Japanese, for in the same letter, the chief of naval operations said the depth of water at Taranto, in which the British torpedoes were dropped, was from 84 to 90 feet.

So no torpedo baffles were installed.

In late December 1940 while discussing the Taranto raid with his Chief of Staff Admiral Fukudome on the *Nagato*, Yamamoto first gave voice to his thoughts about "bringing the United States fleet to battle at the first opportunity."

Glancing at Fukudome, Yamamoto said, "An air attack on Pearl Harbor might be possible now, especially as our air training has turned out so successfully." He paused a moment, then continued, "Get me a senior flying officer whose past career has not influenced him in favor of conventional operations. I want him to study this fleet aerial torpedo problem in all its aspects. Keep this matter a secret from all the other staff officers."

After a review of possible candidates, Fukudome presented the name of Rear Admiral Takijiro Onishi, chief of staff of the 11th Air Fleet and an outstanding naval aviator. Yamamoto concurred.

On 26 January 1941 the plan was outlined to Onishi with Yamamoto requesting he make a detailed study of its feasibility. For that study Onishi enlisted the talents of Commander Genda, 36-year-old air officer in the carrier *Kaga*. This was the same officer who had drafted the London report on the Taranto raid. He also was known throughout the navy for his daring concepts in mounting long range mass fighter operations in China.

His report was forwarded to Yamamoto through Onishi in early March. Yamamoto's plan would be difficult to implement. It would entail a high degree of risk. It did have a reasonable chance of success.

Genda further specified all six fleet carriers, which would be available with the commissioning of the new 30,000 ton *Zuikaku* and *Shokaku* in August, must be assigned to the project. Only the navy's best flyers must participate, and complete secrecy must shroud the operation.

This last stipulation might prove most difficult, for on 27 January of the new year, the United States ambassador to Japan, Joseph C. Grew, messaged the State Department in Washington: "The Peruvian minister has informed a member of my staff that he has heard from many sources, including a Japanese source, that in the event of trouble breaking out between the U. S. and Japan the Japanese intend to make a surprise attack against Pearl Harbor with all their strength and employing all their equipment. The Peruvian minister considered the rumours fantastic but he considered them of sufficient importance to convey all this."

The message was duly reported by the Navy Department to Admiral Kimmel at Pearl Harbor with an addendum: "The Division of Naval Intelligence places no credence in these rumours. Furthermore based on known data regarding the present disposition and deployment of Japanese naval and army forces no move against Pearl Harbor appears imminent or planned for the foreseeable future."

So much for secrets.

So much for forecasts.

6

The Instrument

UNDERLYING EVERY SUCCESSFUL NAVAL OR MILITARY OP-
eration there must be a plan. It may be conceived as of
the moment under the spur of necessity, or it may be the
result of months or years of consideration, but the final
design must be feasible and practical, and in the end
achieve the results for which it was conceived.

Above all, in war it must provide for the unexpected so
that in the event of surprise or miscarriage there will be
effective alternatives available to the commander, allowing
him to achieve victory even though threatened by defeat.

With these unspoken tenets bearing heavily upon them,
the planning echelons of the Imperial Japanese Navy set to
work on the task imposed by the commander in chief.

They had as a background the twenty-year-old battle
plans of the Japanese Navy which anticipated that in the
event of hostilities a supposedly superior American fleet
would sortie from Pearl Harbor to carry the war into the
home waters of the Japanese empire in the western Pacific.

The Imperial Navy would then in its turn steam to the
attack and destroy the American invaders.

Curiously this concept fitted nicely with the American Pacific battle plan titled "Rainbow Five" which stipulated:

Navy Tasks.
Prepare to capture and establish control over the Caroline and Marshall Island area.
Defend Midway, Johnston, Palmyra, Wake, Samoa and Guam.
In cooperation with the Army defend Coastal Frontiers (including Hawaiian and Philippine Coastal Frontiers).

So both navies contemplated a major sea battle or battles in the western Pacific after the preliminaries were disposed of.

But the spare, hawk-faced Genda, in making the first evaluation of the projected Hawaii operation for Onishi, had thrown all the old plans over the side. In employing the aircraft of the First Air Fleet which encompassed the six large fleet carriers (two not yet commissioned) he envisaged use of high level and dive bombers, and torpedo planes, all operating under the protection of air cover provided by the new navy fighter, the soon-to-become-famous Zero.

The more he thought about the operation, the more it enthralled him with its technical problems and possibilities. He could hardly wait for developments. They were not long in coming.

Yamamoto had consulted more experts. He asked his senior staff officer, Captain Kameto Kuroshima, to look at the report. Kuroshima, an eccentric but superb naval planner, did better than that. After days of seclusion he came up with a detailed version of the plan which he named "Operation Kuroshima."

To secure better information about the situation in Hawaii, the commander in chief turned to Captain Kanji Ogawa of naval intelligence with the result that a special spy, Ensign Takeo Yoshikawa, was dispatched to Honolulu on the liner *Nitta Maru* ostensibly to join the staff of Consul General Nagao Kita as a consular official under the alias Tadashi Morimura. He would furnish much useful information to Yamamoto and his planners.

Even the title of the contemplated "Operation Hawaii" was obscured.

In April it received the cover designation "Operation Z." Togo's famous signal to the fleet at Tsushima, symbolized by the Z flag, would fly again.

Rear Admiral Ryunosuke Kusaka was appointed chief of staff of the First Air Fleet on 10 April. Before going to his new command he reported to the chief of the operations bureau of the naval general staff, Admiral Fukudome, who had been Yamamoto's first confidant regarding his thoughts on Pearl Harbor.

Fukudome handed the former captain of the carriers *Akagi* and *Hosho* Onishi's and Genda's evaluation, stating: "This is merely a proposal. Nothing has been decided yet. In case of war we need a practicable plan from you. Make it work."

At Hashirajima, Kusaka reported to his new commander, Vice Admiral Chuichi Nagumo in the flagship of the First Air Fleet, the carrier *Akagi*. Nagumo, a stocky, kindly looking man, was not an aviator but an expert on torpedoes and a master handler of ships in formation. He had been astonished by the audacity of Yamamoto's plan and secretly hoped that it would never be approved by the naval general staff. He, instead, was a believer in the general staff's more conventional plan of throwing all of the navy's strength southward for the seizure of the Dutch East Indies oil fields.

But for the moment he had his orders and had to go along.

He informed Kusaka that he would be responsible for Operation Hawaii for the First Air Fleet. Kusaka, although no flier himself, had commanded two large carriers as well as the 24th Air Squadron at Palau in the Caroline Islands. But he would need expert assistance. For this he turned to his senior staff officer, Commander Tamotsu Oishi, and his aviation staff officer, Commander Genda, who unbeknownst to his chief, was already familiar with the Hawaii plan.

As the detailed planning progressed so did Kusaka's doubts, so much so that he would voice his concerns to Admiral Onishi who with Genda had drafted the initial evaluation of Yamamoto's scheme.

He marshalled his objections effectively, for at the conclusion of the conference, Onishi admitted it was really too risky to attempt. Kusaka then suggested they both confront Yamamoto with their reasons the operation be cancelled. Onishi agreed.

After obtaining permission from Nagumo, they boarded the combined fleet flagship *Nagato* in the summer to confront Yamamoto with their arguments. The commander in chief gave them a genial reception but refused to change his mind.

Afterwards, as Kusaka walked away from the interview diconsolate, he felt a hand on his shoulder. It was Yamamoto's.

"I understand why you object," he said, "but the Pearl Harbor attack is a decision I made as commander in chief. Therefore I'd appreciate it if you will stop arguing and from now on make every effort to carry out my decision. If in the future you should have any objections from other people I'll back you up."

So within the fleet, the work went forward.

Kusaka took upon himself the problem of bringing the strike force into position for the air launch. Oishi worked on the details of the entire operational plan, Genda the air attacks.

In getting the ships to Hawaii, Kusaka had two problems: first they must be refueled on the way; second, they must make their long voyage unseen by any unfriendly eyes.

What was the most favorable course?

Instinctively he turned to that cold, wild section of the North Pacific which could be called the "Deserted Sea" for it normally is crossed by no ships of any kind. This is the area lying north of the Honolulu-Yokohama sea lane and south of the great circle course from San Francisco to Yokohama, which reaches northward almost to the Aleutian Islands. In between there is usually nothing but gray seas and cloudy skies.

Because this part of the North Pacific had a reputation for its rough seas, refueling might be difficult, but this would have to remain a matter of chance.

To test his theories, the reluctant Kusaka requested his staff navigation expert to report on the types and flags of ships which had crossed the North Pacific in winter months during the past ten years. Lieutenant Commander Otojiro Sasabe found that no ships, in their attempts to avoid stormy weather, had sailed at latitude 40 degrees north in November or December.

Likewise the take-off harbor for the strike force must be hidden and remote . . . somewhere in the Kuriles no doubt. Oishi considered this along with the make-up of the force and how it should be assembled for the operation.

Genda tested every aspect of the aerial attack. It would come with the dawn. It would involve fighters and bombers to destroy enemy planes on Oahu's airfields; torpedo planes, dive bombers and high level bombers to go after the big ships; and more fighters to provide air cover for the overall operation.

It would come in two waves one hour apart. First target priority would be the large American aircraft carriers, then the battleships and the cruisers.

It would succeed!

It must succeed!

There would be a single commander for the entire air operation. Again Genda's recommendation: Commander Mitsuo Fuchida, outstanding naval aviator and senior wing commander in the carrier task force. He was the one to lead the attack.

Yamamoto approved the plans and the training began.

Throughout June and July the pilots and air crews worked on a round-the-clock basis. They did not know what their objective was going to be but they knew it was going to be a blockbuster.

The fighter pilots performed their tune-up for a great air assault at the Saeki Air Base on Kyushu, the southernmost major island of the Japanese chain, and at the Omura Base, as well.

The dive bombers conducted their exercises at the Tomitaka Air Base, forty miles down the coast, striving for accuracy by using towed rafts with their wide wakes serving as targets. More training went on at the Kasanohara and Oita Air Bases.

High level bombing and torpedo plane training flights roared over the mouth of Kagoshima Bay because the area about Kagoshima City presented similar flying problems as did Pearl Harbor, including confined spaces, buildings, smokestacks. Bases at Izumi and Usa were also used.

Far to the north on Shikoku Island's east coast at Mitsuke Bay, crews of midget submarines, which would be piggy-backed to Hawaii by the Navy's large I class submarines, were conducting secret practice runs.

Admiral Yamamoto and the combined fleet had a secret plan they were preparing to execute.

But it had not as yet been approved by the naval general staff. In early September 1941 all fleet commanders and key staff officers were ordered, along with selected officers of the combined fleet staff, the navy general staff, and the navy ministry to the naval war college in Meguro for the annual war games which had been advanced in date because of the growing tension in the Pacific.

The main room for the table top maneuvers with miniature warships was devoted to the problems of the entire Pacific operation in all of its widespread complexity.

A second smaller room was reserved at the request of Yamamoto for war games which would test his planned attack on Pearl Harbor.

The play of operations in support of the army's assaults

on Hong Kong, the Philippines, Malaya and the Indies consumed three days. When they were over, the hierarchy of the Imperial Japanese Navy, with excitement mounting, turned to the smaller room and Pearl Harbor Operation Hawaii.

With the expeditionary phases complete, the admirals who had commanded the contending forces dropped out, leaving the Hawaii board open for Admiral Ugaki commanding the Japanese forces and general staff captain Ogawa, the American.

The first try went badly for Ugaki with his strike force discovered, one-third of his planes shot down and two carriers sunk. A second try was more successful, however, and umpires ruled the United States fleet had been surprised.

Still the naval general staff and all senior commanders were not convinced.

They favored the conventional sweep to the South Pacific. That alone would draw the Americans out of Pearl Harbor, they argued. Then the climactic battle could be fought in waters closer to Japan and victory achieved.

The arguments went on but Yamamoto's determination never faltered.

Subsequently the staff study on the Pearl Harbor attack plan would appear as Combined Fleet Top Secret Order No. 1's Operation Hawaii section.

Rumblings of the admirals' opposition to the operation even reached the Japanese army, so that Field Marshal Hajime Sugiyama, chief of the army general staff, flew to meet Yamamoto on his flagship. Upon being reassured that a victory at Pearl Harbor could only help the army and that no troops would be needed for the operation, Sugiyama assured his host the army would have no objection.

Then it came to Yamamoto's ears that even in the combined fleet itself there was much criticism of the plan.

He knew that the strike force commander Admiral Nagumo and his chief of staff, Admiral Kusaka, were lukewarm to it, if not actually opposed. Still he could not afford to send the fleet to sea with this undercurrent of defeat rippling through his command.

So ever forthright, the commander in chief summoned more than fifty of his senior commanders to a conference on flagship *Nagato* on 13 October.

Following a review of the actions expected of the combined fleet upon the outbreak of war, Yamamoto hosted a dinner dominated by the spirit of Admiral Togo and the invincible elan of the Imperial Japanese Navy. A feeling of dedicated fellowship swept over his commanders as the admiral gathered them together on the quarterdeck of the great ship, one of the most powerful battleships in the world.

He then asked them to voice their objections to his Pearl Harbor plan. It was to be man to man, no holds barred.

Admiral after admiral expressed his fears. Finally Onishi, who with Genda had drafted the initial evaluation, voiced his doubts. Then the strike force commander, Vice Admiral Chuichi Nagumo, rose. He too was unconvinced. There were so many imponderables. He raised the question of an American ambush of the carriers he would be leading to Hawaii.

Finally Yamamoto spoke. He took up the objections one by one and said they would be considered. Then he brought the full force of his personality to bear upon the assemblage. A handsome, impressive man of great will, it seemed as if he were speaking to each officer individually.

Without the Pearl Harbor attack, he told them, the southern thrust would fail and Japan would face defeat. Without the Pearl Harbor attack, there could be no future for their country. He concluded his emotional appeal as *Nagato's* turrets glowed red in the sunset. "So long as I as am commander in chief of the combined fleet, Pearl Harbor will be attacked."

The conference was over. The fleet had its orders.

But the naval general staff remained.

On 18 October he sent Captain Kuroshima, his senior staff officer, to Tokyo for the final decision.

Arriving in the office of the chief of the operations section of the naval general staff, Captain Sadatoshi Tomioka, Kuroshima wasted no time: "Admiral Yamamoto has ordered me to get immediate clarification on the Pearl Harbor operation. Will it be approved or not? Time is running short. We must have an answer without delay."

Tomioka responded by raising all the arguments of the naval general staff against the adoption of the plan.

When he had finished Kuroshima just as ardently presented all of Yamamoto's reasons why the American fleet at Pearl Harbor had to be attacked.

But Tomioka remained unconvinced.

It was then Kuroshima delivered his thunderbolt: "Admiral Yamamoto insists that his plan be adopted. He has authorized me to state that if it is not, then the commander in chief of the combined fleet can no longer be held responsible for the security of the Empire. In that case he will have no alternative but to resign, and with him his entire staff."

Tomioka stared at Yamamoto's senior staff officer in astonishment. This threat encompassed issues beyond his authority. "We must see Admiral Fukudome," he said.

When Yamamoto's former chief of staff recognized the steely determination behind the fleet admiral's words, he halted further discussion. "This must be put before Nagano, the chief of staff, at once."

Kuroshima was ushered into the office of Vice Admiral Seiichi Ito, deputy chief of the naval general staff. He presented the letter which Yamamoto had given him to deliver: "The presence of the U.S. fleet in Hawaii is a dagger pointed at our throats. Should war be declared, the length and breadth of our southern operations would immediately be exposed to a serious threat on its flank.

"The Hawaii operation is absolutely indispensable. Unless it is carried out Admiral Yamamoto has no confidence that he can fulfill his assigned responsibility. The numerous difficulties of this operation do not make it impossible. Weather conditions worry us most but as there are seven days in a month when refueling at sea is possible, the chance of success is by no means small. If good fortune is bestowed upon us we will be assured of success.

"Should the Hawaii operation by chance end in failure, that would merely imply that fortune is not on our side. That should also be the time for definitely halting all operations."

Ito took the letter and stepped into Admiral Osami Nagano's office. Those outside could hear the two officers discussing the situation.

Finally Admiral Nagano emerged followed by Ito.

He went over to Kuroshima to speak softly: "I fully understand how Yamamoto feels. If he has that much confidence he must be allowed to carry on. I will approve his plan."

Kuroshima bowed his thanks before flying back to the flagship.

The date, 18 October 1941, left just 50 days before the day selected for the attack.

But the two great risks remained:

First, the chance of detection or discovery.

Second, the hazard that the large American aircraft carriers would not be in Pearl Harbor.

The carefully drafted plan did provide safeguards against the first risk.

The second was left to chance and the gods of war.

It would prove a fatal flaw.

7

The Bull's Eye

Pearl Harbor has long held a consuming interest for the United States Navy and for that matter, all of the other navies of major powers throughout the world. But the American navy got there first.

In the Hawaii of old, Pearl Harbor which fans inland from a narrow entrance on the south shore of the island of Oahu into a series of three very large salt water lakes or locks, was known to the Hawaiians as "Wai Momi" meaning "water of pearl." It was believed to be the home of the shark goddess Kaahupahau and at one time was the scene of shark fighting by Hawaiian swimmers.

Because in the early days a coral bar across the entrance barred all vessels having a draft of more than 10 feet, it attracted very little maritime attention, all of the action being centered in the relatively small but deep harbor of Honolulu some six and one-half miles to the east.

Before the start of the American Civil War in 1860, federal naval officers, sent to the islands to construct a coaling station in Honolulu, were impressed with the possibilities of the site. So in 1875 after long negotiations with the Hawaiian Kingdom, the U.S. Navy was granted permission to "enter the harbor of Pearl River" to establish a coaling and repair station.

From that small beginning evolved one of the greatest, if not the greatest, naval bases in the world.

In 1941 it not only was the base for the U.S. Pacific Fleet but also the site of the Pearl Harbor naval shipyard with its graving docks, repair basins and shops, as well as a large submarine base, a wide-spreading oil storage facility, plus all the activities that supported the maintenance of the overall base.

To safeguard Pearl Harbor the U.S. Army maintained its largest offshore establishment, so that in May of 1941 General George C. Marshall, Chief of Staff, could assure President Roosevelt:

AIDE MEMOIRE
Defense of Hawaii

The Island of Oahu, due to its fortification, its garrison, and its physical characteristics, is believed to be the strongest fortress in the world.

To reduce Oahu the enemy must transport overseas an expeditionary force capable of executing a forced landing against a garrison of approximately 35,000 men, manning 127 fixed coast defense guns, 211 antiaircraft weapons, and more than 3,000 artillery pieces and automatic weapons available for beach defense. Without air superiority this is an impossible task.

Air Defense. With adequate air defense, enemy carriers, naval escorts and transports will begin to come under air attack at a distance of approximately 750 miles. This attack will increase in intensity until when within 200 miles of the objective, the enemy forces will be subject to attack by all modern types of bombardment closely supported by our most modern pursuit.

Hawaiian Air Defense. Including the movement of

aviation now in progress Hawaii will be defended by *35 of our most modern flying fortresses, 35 medium range bombers, 13 light bombers, 150 pursuit, of which 105 are of our most modern type. In addition Hawaii is capable of reinforcement by heavy bombers from the mainland by air. With this force available a major attack against Oahu is considered impracticable.

In point of sequence, sabotage is first to be expected and may, within a very limited time, cause great damage. On this account, and in order to assure strong control, it would be highly desirable to set up a military control of the islands prior to the likelihood of our involvement in the Far East.

The U.S. Pacific Fleet in 1941, although it had detached ships to the Atlantic Fleet, which was in a state of un-declared war with the German Navy, and though it was "inferior to the Japanese fleet in every category of fighting ship," according to its commander in chief, still was a most formidable force, counting three large aircraft carriers, eight battleships, and a full complement of cruisers, de-stroyers, submarines and auxiliary vessels of all types.

The major commands, the U.S. Pacific Fleet and the Hawaiian Department of the U.S. Army, had both received new commanders in February of 1941, Admiral Hus-band E. Kimmel and Lieutenant General Walter C. Short. Each in his own way had set about making his command ready for war.

The fleet was organized into five major commands: Task Force One (battleships), Vice Admiral W.S. Pye; Task Force Two (carrier *Enterprise*), Vice Admiral William Halsey; Task Force Three (carrier *Lexington*), Vice Admiral Wilson Brown; Naval Base Force, Rear Admiral W.L. Calhoun; and the 14th Naval District, Rear Admiral Claude C. Bloch.

The army's major commands were: the 24th Infantry

*Due to make a mass flight from mainland to Hawaii May 20th. A number of this type of plane could be dispatched immediately if the situation grew critical. (penciled notation on the typed memo.)

Division, Brigadier General Durward S. Wilson; the 25th Infantry Division, Major General Maxwell Murray, the Hawaiian Separate Coast Artillery Brigade (including both seacoast and antiaircraft artillery), Major General Henry T. Burgin; and the Hawaiian Air Force, Major General Frederick L. Martin.

Upon Short's assumption of command 7 February 1941, General Marshall had written him: " . . . our first concern is to protect the fleet.

"My impression of the Hawaiian problem has been that if no serious harm is done to us during the first six hours of known hostilities, thereafter the existing defenses will discourage an enemy against the hazard of an attack. The risk of sabotage and the risk involved in a surprise raid by air and by submarine constitute the real perils of the situation. Frankly, I do not see any landing threat in the Hawaiian Islands so long as we have air superiority.

"Please keep clearly in mind in all of your negotiations that our mission is to protect the base and the naval concentration and that purpose should be made clearly apparent to Admiral Kimmel. I accentuate this because I found yesterday for example, in a matter of tremendous importance that old Army and Navy feuds engendered from fights over appropriations, with the usual fallacious arguments on both sides, still persist in confusing issues on National defense. We must be completely impersonal in these matters, at least so far as our own nerves and irritations are concerned. . . ."

Kimmel and Short enjoyed cordial personal and official relations. But each had under him complex and varied organizations of two separate armed services. Attempting to mesh them into an adequate defense of the island in the end could only be achieved under the authority of a single commander.

In the War and Navy Departments in Washington another operation, the deciphering of the Japanese diplomatic code, had been in process for some time. It was the result of a joint operation of army and navy cryptographic intelligence experts who had succeeded in perfecting an automatic cipher machine, which in August 1940 began recovering intelligible texts from the Japanese diplomatic code transmissions. It was given the cover name of "Magic."

This breakthrough enabled the United States to read the messages, in the tense year of 1941, between Tokyo and the special Japanese peace envoys to Washington, Admiral Nomura and Ambassador Kurusu, even before the principal addressees had been furnished with their decoded copies. In addition the machine deciphered traffic between the Japanese foreign ministry and its envoys and consular officials scattered around the world. One of these consular officials was stationed in Honolulu. His messages were in time to have great pertinence to the security of the U.S. fleet and the Army's defenses for Oahu.

Because of the need for secrecy regarding the remarkable American intelligence achievement, neither Admiral Kimmel nor General Short was ever advised of this development or furnished with any of the information directly affecting their commands.

This was most unfortunate in its subsequent consequences.

Admiral Kichisaburo Nomura had been named Ambassador to the United States in February 1941 by the then Prime Minister Konoye, in an attempt to secure a peaceful understanding with America. Nomura was a good humored man who had long standing friendships with many high ranking officers of the U.S. Navy. He had become acquainted with President Roosevelt when he was Assistant Secretary of the Navy in the First World War, and Nomura was the Japanese naval attache in Washington.

All through the strife-filled year of 1941 he had been the even tempered buffer between Washington and Tokyo. At times he would call on chief of naval operations Admiral Harold R. Stark, who was an old acquaintance, to complain of the lack of progress he was making with the American Secretary of State Cordell Hull.

His long series of conferences with Hull were marred by constant misunderstanding of each other due mainly to Nomura's fumbling English and Hull's heavy Tennessee drawl. In addition, because he was reading the Japanese reports on their conferences through the Magic intercepts, Hull could not be as natural and candid with Nomura as he normally would have been.

While these talks continued, the Imperial Japanese Navy was overhauling its longtime espionage activities directed at Pearl Harbor, Honolulu, the island of Oahu and all of the Hawaiian area.

First development was the arrival of a new consul general to take over the sprawling Japanese consulate at Nuuanu Avenue and Kuakini Street in uptown Honolulu. When he was selected, Nagao Kita was the consul general at Canton, having served previously in Shanghai and Amoy. He had close ties with the navy which had requested some of his assignments from the foreign ministry.

When the sleek NYK liner *Tatuta Maru* berthed at Pier 7 in Honolulu on 14 March 1941, of all the passengers on board, Consul General Kita was the most interviewed by the Honolulu press.

He was followed by another consulate staff member twelve days later when the newest NYK liner *Nitta Maru* came alongside the same pier in the record time of seven days, five hours and thirty-seven minutes out of Yokohama. It was a crossing which usually took eight or nine days. But this Consulate passenger would have no interviewers, no aloha greeters of any kind other than Vice Consul Otojiro Okuda.

For Consul General Kita had sent this newest man a radiogram while the *Nitta Maru* was still at sea, ordering him to remain in his luxury cabin after the ship had docked. His "name" was "Tadashi Morimura" and he was to become a probationary consul of the eighth rank in Honolulu.

He was, of course, Takeo Yoshikawa, naval reserve ensign on active service with His Majesty's Imperial Japanese Navy. He had been selected for his new post, as had Kita himself, by Captain Kanji Ogawa, chief of Section 5 of the Naval General Staff's Third Bureau, Naval Intelligence. His was the section which handled all espionage matters on North and South America.

It was Captain Ogawa who Yamamoto had summoned to the flagship *Nagato* at Hashirajima on 3 February while Genda was working out the Pearl Harbor attack evaluation of "risky but with a reasonable chance of success." At that conference Yamamoto had requested him to turn all of his major attention to gathering the intelligence necessary to make the Hawaii Operation a victory for Japanese arms.

The erstwhile Morimura waited patiently in his cabin while Vice Consul Okuda made his way through the long corridors of the *Nitta Maru* to welcome him. After a salutation which Okuda thought more military than diplomatic, they left the liner for the consulate.

Once in the consul general's office, Kita locked the door to all others, then turned.

"Welcome to Hawaii, Ensign Yoshikawa. You are Ensign Yoshikawa aren't you?"

Back in Tokyo, Captain Ogawa of Section 5 of the Third Bureau of the naval general staff drew a long breath. At last he had a functioning spy right in the middle of the enemy's lair.

After graduating from the naval academy, Yoshikawa had developed tuberculosis, then retired from active service. He eventually returned to duty on the British desk, Section 8 of the Third Bureau, where he specialized on the movements of the Royal Navy in Far Eastern waters. It was for this background he had been chosen to perform Yamamoto's special task.

He performed it well.

Working entirely alone, this 28-year-old naval officer made himself a walking encyclopedia of facts about Hawaii. He never took written notes, nor attempted photographs. Yet he kept Captain Ogawa in Tokyo minutely informed on naval and military developments on the island of Oahu.

His weekly Pearl Harbor ship movements reports were based on visual observation either from a taxicab, bus, automobile, rented aircraft, or made while trudging along some dusty, isolated sugar cane plantation road.

His name never appeared on a message of any kind, all instructions from Tokyo being addressed to Kita, and all reports cabled back to Japan from Honolulu commercial cable offices in code, being signed by the consul general.

For relaxation he frequented the Shunchoro, an old-style Japanese tea house, high on the hills above Honolulu with a superb view of the waterways of Pearl Harbor and the great naval base itself.

On 24 September Captain Ogawa instructed Yoshikawa, through a message to Kita, to divide Pearl Harbor into sectors, to facilitate speed and accuracy in reporting. The decoded message read:

Henceforth please make your reports concerning the ships (in Pearl Harbor) as follows as far as possible: (1) The waters are to be divided roughly into five subareas. (We have no objection to your abbreviating as much as you like.) Area A: The waters between Ford Island and the Arsenal. Area B: Waters adjacent to but south and west of Ford Island. (This is on the opposite side from Area A.) Area C: East Loch. Area D: Middle Loch. Area E: West Loch and the Channel. (2) With regard to battleships and aircraft carriers, please report those at anchor separately from those tied up at the wharves, buoys and in the docks (but the latter are not too important). Designate types and classes briefly. If possible, we would like to have you mention whenever there are two or more vessels tied up alongside the same wharf.

This message was duly picked up by the army's new Magic monitoring station MS-5 at Fort Shafter, the headquarters of the Hawaiian Department. Here it was bundled together in its encoded form along with other intercepts, and sent via steamship mail to San Francisco on 28 September, finally arriving at the War Department on 3 October. It was finally processed into English and sent to the G-2 Section of the General Staff on 9 October, fifteen days after it had been first intercepted. General Short, of course, did not know of the existence of this new radio station on his own headquarters post because he was not cleared for Magic operations.

In the meantime Yoshikawa on 28 September radioed a proposed amplification of the area code, to Ogawa:

The following codes will be used hereafter to designate the locations of the vessels:
(1) Repair Dock in Navy Yard: KS.
(2) Dock in the Navy Yard (the Ten-Ten Pier): KT.
(3) Moorings in the vicinity of Ford Island: FV.
(4) Alongside Ford Island: FG. (East and west sides will be differentiated by A and B respectively.)

This message was duplicated by Kita to the embassy in Washington and the consulate general in San Francisco. At one of these points the U.S. Navy secured a copy of it. But again there was a long time lag, the message not being translated until 10 October.

Nothing came of this last intercept: it was simply filed.

Captain Ogawa's first area code request for Pearl Harbor ship berthing did however arouse the apprehensions of Colonel Rufus S. Bratton, chief of the Army G-2 Far Eastern Section, who received and processed the Magic intercepts for the Military Intelligence Division of the War Department. However when he took Ogawa's message to Brigadier General Sherman Miles, chief of military intelligence, he was rebuffed with the comment that it was a naval matter and of no interest to the army.

Bratton would not be put off, so he hand carried the intercept to the Office of Naval Intelligence where he again received only polite interest. The Yoshikawa-Ogawa messages remained in their deferred category with the lowest priority in handling. So both the army and navy intelligence sections fumbled badly. All but Colonel Bratton. He put a little flag at Pearl Harbor on a Pacific Ocean map on which he was charting Japan's march to war.

On 23 October the NYK liner *Tatuta Maru* again arrived in Honolulu from Yokohama. Leaving the ship during the day stopover before she resumed her voyage to San Francisco was a foreign ministry official named "Maeda." But this man was in fact not attached to the foreign office but was Lieutenant Commander Minato Nakajima from Ogawa's Americas Section of Japanese naval intelligence, the Third Bureau.

He was bound for the mainland to close out Japan's network of secret agents prior to the outbreak of war. In Honolulu he was taken immediately to the Japanese consulate where he counted out $14,000 in American $100 bills to Kita to pay over to one Otto Kuehn, a German national, who was to be activated as a spy by Japanese intelligence in the ultimate emergency.

Kita employed Yoshikawa and two others from the consulate to deliver the money with Ogawa's instructions to Kuehn to start operating his shortwave radio transmitter and to develop a code and signal system for contacting patrolling Japanese submarines in the event of an emergency. In the end, it was money down the rat hole for the Japanese, and in its delivery Yoshikawa had been dangerously exposed to discovery by American intelligence. But nothing came of this opportunity either, so another American chance to uncover a vital Pearl Harbor attack connection failed.

Things went along for the Japanese spy on a routine basis until another NYK liner, the *Taiyo Maru,* arrived in Honolulu 1 November 1941 on a strange voyage from Yokohama.

But no one but the ship's officers knew how strange a voyage it was because the passengers were told nothing.

The usual daily plot of the course of the ship across the Pacific, a fixture in all passenger liner lounges, did not appear once during the passage. The *Taiyo Maru* was on a secret naval mission. She had in fact just traversed the course laid down by Admiral Kusaka for bringing the Pearl Harbor strike force secretly across the North Pacific to the launching point for flying off the attack planes against Oahu.

Two ship's officers aboard the *Taiyo Maru*, on this bob-tailed voyage to Honolulu and back carrying repatriates in both directions, were not NYK officers at all. One was Lieutenant Commander Suguro Suzuki, carrier air expert of the naval general staff's Third Bureau; the other was Commander Toshihide Maejima, the bureau's ranking submarine officer. Each would check the latest intelligence from Pearl as it affected his special areas of the attack plan. A third undercover officer aboard was Sublieutenant Keiu Matsuo, midget submarine expert.

They had spent the entire voyage on the bridge at all hours, searching for passing ships, studying the weather encountered, and observing the *Taiyo's* performance in the sea conditions along the route. They did not see another ship during the voyage, while the weather, although dull, gray and windy, was passable.

Forewarned of the officers' coming by Ogawa, Kita met secretly with them away from the eyes of the many under-cover operatives who were watching the ship. In a tiny ball of rice paper which Suzuki pressed into Kita's hand were listed 97 questions concerning the army and navy forces at Pearl Harbor and on Oahu.

When Kita returned with Yoshikawa's answers to the detailed questionnaire the first answer was the most revealing.

Q. On what day of the week would the most ships be in Pearl Harbor?

A. Sunday.

After a five day layover the *Taiyo Maru* cast off her lines, and going astern into Honolulu Harbor until she was abreast the world famed Aloha Tower, swung bow on towards the channel leaving the surf-lined shores of Oahu on either hand.

Hers was to be last commercial passenger voyage between Hawaii and Japan by a liner under any flag, for many years.

Part II

Their fatal hands intend no second stroke.

—John Milton

8

The Lighted Fuse

IN ARIAKE BAY IN SOUTHERN KYUSHU ON 3 NOVEMBER AD-
miral Nagumo assembled his task force commanders
and their staffs on the flagship *Akagi*. Ushered in to the
office of chief of staff Admiral Kusaka they saw to their
astonishment a large and detailed model of Oahu and a
mock-up of Pearl Harbor and its waterways. Here they
were to learn for the first time what their targets would be.

Using the models, Commanders Genda and Fuchida
then outlined the various aspects of the attack plan in
relation to the terrain features of the island, Pearl Harbor
and the major flying fields. Most of the officers listened in
silent amazement.

Then their weeks of intense training were put to test
over the next two days when the combined fleet moved
out into the Pacific where it became the U.S. Pacific Fleet,
target for Nagumo's attacking forces. The first day's effort
rated only passable, but the second day's rehearsal was
almost letter perfect. As Nagumo's carriers moved back to
their anchorage, combined fleet flagship *Nagato* winked its
approval in code: "The attack was splendid."

On 5 November from the *Nagato*, Yamamoto issued

Combined Fleet Operational Order No. 1. Classified top
secret, its one hundred pages were thick with details of the
entire Pacific attack including Wake, Guam, the Philippines, Hong Kong, Malaya, the Indies (Operation Hawaii
was only included in the original copy). Its preface declared: "In the East the American fleet will be destroyed.
The American lines of operation and supply lines to the
Orient will be cut. Enemy forces will be intercepted and
annihilated. Victories will be exploited to break the enemy's will to fight. . . .

". . . when the decision is made to complete overall
preparations for operations an order will be issued establishing the approximate day Y-Day for the commencement
of operations. . . . the time for the outbreak of war X-Day
will be given in an Imperial Headquarters Order."

This order in turn was followed by Combined Fleet
Operations Order No. 2: "The task force, keeping its
movements strictly secret, shall assemble in Hittokappu
Bay by 22 November for refueling."

Hittokappu Bay is a wide anchorage at Etorofu Island in
the remote snow covered Kurile Islands stretching northward from Japan to the Kamchatka Peninsula. Hidden by
snow, sleet and fog, it was the ideal roadstead from which
to launch the thunderbolt.

Yamamoto had won the army's agreement to a week's
delay in the start of all operations, so Imperial Headquarters secretly decided hostilities would begin at 0830 Sunday 7 December Hawaiian time.

Meanwhile in Washington Ambassador Nomura, who
had become increasingly suspicious that he was merely a
screen, used the replacement of Prime Minister Konoye by
General Hideki Tojo to complain of the role he was assigned to play. Magic read the plea to Tokyo by the old
admiral to let him retire with the Konoye government,
with these revealing words: "There are some Americans
who trust this poor novice and say that things will get
better for me, but, alas, their encouragement is no solace
for me. Among my colleagues here there are those who

profess compassion for me but, alas, they are but deluded souls. . . . I do not want to be the bones of a dead horse. I don't want to go on with this hypocrisy, deceiving other people. No, please do not think that I am trying to flee from the field of battle, but as a man of honor this is the only way that is left for me to tread. Kindly allow me to return to Japan. Most humbly do I beseech your forgiveness if I have injured your dignity and I prostrate myself before your Excellency in the depths of my rudeness."

His was one of the few honest voices crying from a well of intrigue and duplicity. Instead of relief, he got a helper by the name of Saburo Kurusu.

This diplomat, who as ambassador to Germany had signed the Tripartite Pact with Hitler, boarded a Pan American clipper in Hong Kong to arrive in Honolulu on the afternoon of 12 November, obtaining a fine view of the American fleet as the big Boeing flying boat settled onto the waters of Pearl Harbor. Distracted by the hullabaloo of a noisy reception by the American press, he took refuge briefly in the ladies room of Pan Am's old Pearl City air depot, only to be photographed as he emerged for a news photo which hardly soothed his dignity.

After spending a day with Consul General Kita, he resumed his flight to San Francisco and on to Washington. While he was on his way, the foreign minister radioed Nomura that Ambassador Kurusu was being sent to assist him "to make a show of our Empire's sincerity."

During the same week, on 10 November Admiral Nagumo issued his first operations order for the mission from his flagship. The carrier *Akagi* then steamed to Saeki Bay on the northeastern coast of the island of Kyushu, which opens into the Bungo Strait, one of the entrances to the Inland Sea. The order to the thirty ships of his command gave specific instructions on individual sailing times, routes, and the anchorage positions the vessels of the force would take upon arriving at Hittokappu Bay in the Kuriles no later than 22 November.

In a flaming fight talk, Yamamoto's new chief of staff of the combined fleet, Vice Admiral Matome Ugaki, at a meeting on the *Nagato* addressed the flag officers of the fleet: "A gigantic fleet has massed at Pearl Harbor. This fleet will be utterly crushed at one blow at the very beginning of our hostilities. Should these plans fail at any stage our navy will suffer the wretched fate of never being able to rise again.

"The success of our surprise attack on Pearl Harbor will prove to be the Waterloo of the war to follow. For this reason the Imperial Navy is massing the cream of its strength in ships and planes to insure success.

"It is clear that America's enormous heavy industry is being immediately converted to the manufacture of ships, planes and other war material. It will take several months for her manpower to be mobilized against us. If we ensure strategic supremacy at the very outset by attacking and seizing all key points at one blow while America is still unprepared we can swing the scales of later operations in our favour. Heaven will bear witness to the righteousness of our struggle."

On the afternoon of 17 November the commander in chief's barge pulled away from *Nagato* and made for *Akagi* which was getting ready for sea.

Looking somewhat grim, Yamamoto mounted the gangway to meet with Admirals Nagumo and Kusaka, key members of their staff, and the captain of *Akagi*.

His speech was short and blunt, warning them that they should be prepared for "terrific American resistance."

Afterwards the group adjourned to the carrier's ward room for a farewell party. It was quite formal, even gloomy, until Yamamoto said: "I expect this operation to be a success."

His assurance heartened his officers immensely.

Raising their glasses in a toast to victory for the Emperor, they all shouted: "Banzai! Banzai! Banzai!"

With night coming on, *Akagi*, blacked out, headed seaward with two darkened destroyers for escort. At about the same hour other elements of the force began sailing from other ports, all bound for the same cold, lonely rendezvous.

This silent sailing was followed by even more obscure ones as the far ranging fleet submarines began slipping from their moorings in the large naval bases of Yokosuka and Kure, making for sea, leaving in groups of threes and fours over the next several days. Nine had already sailed for the Marshall Islands in the Japanese Mandate for they were bound for Hawaii by the southern route. Eleven others would take the great circle course to the north.

Their mission was to blockade Pearl Harbor to prevent any ships from escaping from Nagumo's attack, to cut off Hawaii from the American mainland, and to furnish the task force with intelligence. Five more boats would delay their departures, for they were to carry Japan's new secret weapon, the midget submarines.

Three other fast scouting boats made for Hittokappu Bay for they were to precede the strike force through the "deserted sea."

Japan's fleet submarines were large vessels with a displacement of almost 2,000 tons, and a length of 320 feet. They had a cruising range of 14,000 miles at 10 knots, with a top speed of almost 24 knots. With four 21-inch torpedo tubes in the bow and two in the stern, and mounting one 4.7-inch and two 13mm deck guns, they were formidable indeed.

Eleven carried small scouting planes abaft their conning towers. Some of the boats could act as submarine transports carrying landing troops.

The small two-man midget submarines would ride piggy-back, clamped to the deck of their fleet class mothers. Their mission was to get inside Pearl Harbor where after resting submerged throughout the raid, they would deliver their own attack after sunset, torpedoing suitable targets. They would then escape in the darkness to be recovered by the big submarines.

But this plan was changed at a party hosted by fleet

submarine commander Admiral Mitsumi Shimizu aboard his flagship *Katori* on 14 November when Lieutenant Iwasa, senior midget submarine officer, pleaded with the admiral to allow the midgets to attack either during or just after the first air raid.

At first the admiral would not hear or it, but gradually Iwasa convinced him that an all-day wait would be too much of a nerve strain on the midget crews. So at last Shimizu agreed that once the raid had begun the midgets could fire their two torpedoes at targets of opportunity, preferably aircraft carriers or battleships.

The gray shapes of the gathering men-o-war glided silently into the loneliness of Hittokappu Bay letting go their anchors into the chill northern water, sullen under the sleet and snow squalls which swept the island from time to time.

Earlier the gunboat *Kunashiri* had impounded all communications from the one forlorn fishing village which boasted three fishermen's huts, a post office, a signal station and a small pier. Smaller boats patrolled the shoreline to assure absolute secrecy.

Nagumo's deadline for assembly, 22 November, was met with the arrival of the aircraft carrier *Kaga* which had delayed her sailing so as to bring the last of the specially fitted aerial torpedoes modified by boxing in the fins so they would run shallow in the confined waters of Pearl Harbor.

At last through the snow flurries, sleet and mist, the still fearful Nagumo could be sure that his task force was all there. It was a most powerful array:

Dominating the formation were the black, coffin-like hulls of the six largest aircraft carriers in the Japanese Navy: *Akagi, Kaga, Hiryu, Soryu, Shokaku* and *Zuikaku*. In contrast to the shapeless flat-tops were the two battleships *Hiei* and *Kirishima* with their exotic towering pagoda superstructures and their ugly main batteries.

Swept-back funnels and four forward gun turrets marked the two heavy cruisers *Tone* and *Chikuma*, while the squat Oriental design of three-funneled *Abukuma* represented the lone light cruiser present.

Interspersed amongst the heavier ships were the peak-bowed twin-funneled destroyers *Urakaze, Isokaze, Tanikaze, Hamakaze, Kasumi, Arare, Kagero, Shiranuhi,* and *Akigumo.* Nearby were three slim-hulled submarines I-19, I-21 and I-23. Completing the assemblage of thirty war vessels were the oil tankers *Kyokuto Maru, Kenyo Maru, Kokuyo Maru, Shinkoku Maru, Toho Maru, Toei Maru,* and *Nihon Maru.*

The fleet would be organized into a strike force of the carriers, a screening force of the battleships, cruisers and destroyers, the advanced patrol unit of three submarines, and the fleet train of oilers.

While the work commenced of loading drums of oil aboard the ships to augment that which they would take aboard in refueling operations, Nagumo called a staff conference in the guarded room housing the Pearl Harbor mock-ups. Opening at 8 o'clock the night of 22 November, Lieutenant Commander Suzuki, who had made his espionage voyage to Hawaii disguised as a purser aboard the *Taiyo Maru,* briefed the staff officers on the latest intelligence from Pearl Harbor.

Nagumo sat silently attentive to every word. When Suzuki asked for questions, the force commander then voiced all of his concerns: Would the task force be discovered? Would the enemy counterattack? What ships would be in Pearl Harbor?

Genda and Fuchida posed questions about the whereabouts of the American carriers. Suzuki admitted he could not say. The two airmen were disappointed.

The next day of the stay at anchorage a general briefing on the attack was conducted on the *Akagi* for some five hundred flying officers from all the carriers. When Nagumo opened the meeting with the announcement that the target would be Pearl Harbor and wished them all "Good fight and good luck!" their cheers reverberated from the steel bulkheads. Chief of Staff Kusaka then sketched the overall plan of the mission before turning the conference over to Commander Genda, Commander Fuchida and the fliers.

All phases of the planned two-wave attack were reviewed in greatest detail. A giant sake party climaxed the briefing session.

During this day, *Akagi* received Yamamoto's sailing orders:

1. The task force keeping its movements strictly secret will leave Hittokappu Bay on the morning of 26 November and advance to a standby position on the afternoon of 3 December speedily to complete refueling.

2. The task force keeping its movements strictly secret and maintaining close guard against submarines and aircraft will advance into Hawaiian waters. Upon the very opening of hostilities it will attack the main force of the U.S. Fleet in Hawaii and deal it a mortal blow. The first air raid is planned for the dawn of X-Day exact date to be given by later order.

Upon completion of the air raid the task force, keeping close co-ordination and guarding against the enemy's counterattack, will speedily leave enemy waters and return to Japan.

4. Should negotiations with the United States prove successful, the task force shall hold itself in readiness forthwith to return and reassemble.

In the very early morning darkness of 26 November the fateful task force hoisted anchors and got underway at 0600. It was a departure marked by *Akagi* fouling one of her anchors for a time and the loss of a seaman who fell into the icy waters of the bay.

First out were the three submarines nosing into the sullen waters of the North Pacific. Their slim hulls were soon lost in the mist. Next came the lean two-funneled destroyers to establish the security perimeter. They in turn were followed by the cruisers and battleships of the screen.

Each of the big ships test fired their guns as they cleared the bay. The roar and flame of the guns, followed by geysers of snow as the shells impacted on Etorofu's lonely hills, furnished a warlike prelude to the mission.

Then in a grim parade came the carriers led by the flagship *Akagi*. It was a spectacle of might.

Last out came the tankers, the grimy ships of the train.

As *Akagi* rounded out to meet the open sea, a patrol craft signaled: "Good luck on your mission!" The big flagship responded with a curt "Thanks."

Soon all were swallowed into the obscurity, their cargo the fate of the ancient Empire of Japan.

Yamamoto's sailing orders had been met.

In Washington Secretary of State Hull handed the Japanese special envoys, Nomura and Kurusu, a note. It demanded Japan withdraw all military and naval forces from China and Indo-China and recognize Chiang Kai-shek's government. In exchange the U.S. would normalize trade and financial relations and grant far-reaching economic concessions. The two Japanese were stunned for they knew Tokyo could not accept this.

Nevertheless the note was forwarded to Tokyo where it shocked Tojo and his government who looked upon it as an ultimatum.

The next morning when Secretary of War Stimson inquired into the status of the negotiations, Hull told him: "I have washed my hands of it and it is now in the hands of you and Knox—the Army and the Navy."

With reports of Japanese troop and naval movements all over the Orient, an alarmed Stimson demanded the American commanders in the Pacific be alerted to their danger.

On 27 November Admiral Kimmel at Pearl Harbor and Admiral Thomas C. Hart, commander in chief of the U.S. Asiatic fleet with headquarters in Manila, received this dispatch from the chief of naval operations:

This dispatch is to be considered a war warning. Negotiations with Japan looking toward stabilization of conditions in the Pacific have ceased and an aggressive move by Japan is expected within the next few days. The number and equipment of Japanese troops and the organization of naval task forces indicates an amphibious expedition against either the Philippines Thai or Kra Peninsula or possibly Borneo. Execute an appropriate defensive deployment preparatory to carrying out the tasks assigned in WPL 46. Inform District and Army authorities. A similar warning is being sent by War Department. SPENAVO* inform British. Continental Districts Guam Samoa directed take appropriate measures against sabotage.
*Special Naval Observer London

Lieutenant General Walter C. Short received a similar War Department warning the same day:

Negotiations with Japanese appear to be terminated to all practical purposes with only the barest possibilities that the Japanese government might come back and offer to continue. Japanese future action unpredictable but hostile action possible at any moment. If hostilities cannot, repeat cannot, be avoided, United States desires that Japan commit the first act. This policy should not, repeat not, be construed as restricting you to a course of action that might jeopardize your defense. Prior to hostile Japanese action you are directed to undertake such reconnaissance and other measures as you deem necessary but these measures should be carried out so as not, repeat not, to alarm the civil population or disclose intent. Report measures taken. Should hostilities occur you will carry out the tasks assigned in Rainbow 5 as far as they pertain to Japan. Limit dissemination of this highly secret information to minimum essential officers.

signed MARSHALL

The same day the War Department G-2 radioed Colonel
Kendall J. Fielder, the Hawaiian Department G-2:

Advise only the commanding general and chief of
staff that it appears that the conference with the
Japanese has ended in an apparent deadlock. Acts of
sabotage and espionage probable.

Earlier that day Kimmel had held a conference of ranking officers of the Fleet and the naval base with General
Short present, to consider air reinforcements for Wake and
Midway Islands. It had been decided to send the carriers
Enterprise to Wake and *Lexington* to Midway with marine
planes. Kimmel did not receive his "war warning" until
after Short had left for Shafter from where he advised the
War Department that: "Department alerted against sabotage. Liaison with Navy."

He received no directions to do otherwise.

In Tokyo on 29 November three days after Nagumo's
ships had slipped out to sea in gloom and fog, eight
former prime ministers of Japan met with Premier Tojo
and four of his cabinet officers to discuss the impasse
between the U.S. and Japan. Tojo told them that he held
"no hope for diplomatic dealings" and that diplomacy
should be used "to facilitate operations." After an in-
conclusive discussion, they all lunched with the Emperor.
None of those present knew that Nagumo's ships were
well into the approach voyage for the Hawaiian attack.

Later that afternoon at a conference with military leaders, Tojo learned from the chief of the naval general staff,
Admiral Nagano, and his deputy, Ito, that the war would
start on 8 December. Foreign Minister Togo asked if the
Washington envoys or the naval attache had been informed. Nagano had to admit they had not been told.

"We're going to make a surprise attack," he replied.

Vice Admiral Ito explained: "We do not want to termi-
nate negotiations until hostilities have begun—in order to

achieve the maximum possible effect with the initial attack."

On 1 December the Imperial Conference opened before Hirohito seated on his dias. Tojo went into great detail concerning the negotiations being conducted in Washington. Admiral Nagano spoke for the navy, General Teiichi Suzuki, for the army.

After a summing up by Tojo, the Emperor retired to the bows of all those gathered at the palace meeting. The documents were then signed and taken to the Emperor who after some time placed his official seal on them. The decision for war with the United States, Great Britain and the Netherlands had been affirmed.

During the morning conference Admiral Ito had told Foreign Minister Togo he had no objection to Japan's advising the U.S. of the termination of negotiations at 12:30 P.M. on 7 December Washington time. The attack would go in at Pearl Harbor at 2 o'clock, an hour-and-a-half later.

This had raised objections from some who held that Admiral Togo's Port Arthur attack without warning had set a precedent. So a compromise was effected, the envoys would deliver their notice at 1:30 P.M. There would thus be one-half hour notice before the attack.

But meanwhile there had been some changes in the situation at Pearl Harbor.

In spite of all of the most modern communications aids being ready to hand, Admiral Kimmel and his staff in the Pacific fleet headquarters at Pearl Harbor were operating in a dense fog of war, their problems accentuated because they did not realize how dense the fog really was.

The Navy Department and the chief of naval operations in Washington supposedly were keeping Kimmel informed of the developing danger in the Pacific. Actually they were not. Because of the acute sensitivity of compromise in the handling of the Magic translations of the Japanese diplomatic communications between Tokyo and Washington, and the rest of the world as well, none of the very great dangers to American security revealed in this traffic were relayed to Hawaii.

Apparently no thought was given to sending a specially designated officer to Hawaii, or calling Kimmel to San Francisco where he could have been fully briefed away from listening ears.

Although the war warning message had been radioed to major Pacific commanders on 27 November, the impact of both the Navy and Army alerts was watered down immensely by subsequent actions of Navy and War Department officers.

The Navy Department message flatly advised Kimmel that the Japanese-American talks had ceased. Two days later the department radioed Kimmel an excerpt of the War Department's 27 November warning to General Short which stated: "Negotiations with Japan *appear* to be terminated with only the barest possibility of resumption." (In fact there was a public resumption of the Hull-Nomura negotiations widely heralded in the American press.)

The Navy Department did not advise him of the American note of 26 November demanding Japan get out of China which the chief of naval operations and his staff believed imposed conditions so drastic that Japan could not accept them. As a result, although the Department knew that the subsequent negotiations were nothing more than a charade, Kimmel was not warned of the deception.

The Department's dispatch of 29 November quoting the Army warning to General Short closed with two directives to the commander in chief of the Pacific Fleet: "W.P.L. 52 is not applicable to Pacific Area and will not be placed in effect in that area except as now in force in South East Pacific Sub Area and Panama Naval Coastal Frontier. Undertake no offensive action until Japan has committed an overt act. Be prepared to carry out tasks assigned in W.P.L. 46 so far as they apply to Japan in case hostilities occur."

W.P.L. 52 was the Navy Western Hemisphere Defense Plan No. 5 which gave shooting orders to naval units meeting Axis vessels in the Atlantic, with the same orders to apply on the West Coast of South America. This dispatch withheld any shooting orders from the Pacific Fleet within the areas of its responsibility.

The Navy Department's war warning message of 27 November to Kimmel in Hawaii and Hart in Manila included a direct order to the commanders of the Pacific and Asiatic fleets: ". . . Execute an appropriate defensive deployment preparatory to carrying out the tasks assigned in WPL 46."

For Kimmel this meant he had to so position the fleet that it could, upon outbreak of war, launch an immediate attack on Japanese installations in the Marshall Island atolls of the Japanese Mandate. The name of the plan was the Marshall Reconnaissance and Raiding Plan.

The plan called for the fleet to send three task forces westward to attack selected islands in the widespread Marshall's group. The attacks had to be delivered with speed in order to draw off Japanese battle strength from British Malaya and the Dutch East Indies. They were to commence one day after war with Japan had begun.

At the time of the fall of the Konoye cabinet in mid-October, Kimmel in response to a Navy Department order to take "due precautions," had sent submarines to conduct war patrols off Wake and Midway Islands. He had reinforced Johnston Island and Wake with more Marines, ammunition and stores. He sent more Marines to Palmyra Island and ordered the commandant of the Fourteenth Naval District at Pearl Harbor to direct the outlying Pacific islands to go on alert status. Six submarines were held in readiness at Pearl for dispatch to Japan; fleet units on the West Coast were put on 12-hours notice, and one battleship due for overhaul was held in Hawaii. Twelve patrol plane flyingboats were sent to patrol off Midway and additional security was imposed in fleet operating areas.

These measures were approved by the chief of naval operations.

So Kimmel believed that he had taken proper precautions in line with Navy Department evaluation of the perils.

There was still another more alarming gap in the intelligence picture as it was developing in Washington and at Pearl Harbor. This was in the handling of Magic translations of traffic between the Japanese foreign ministry in Tokyo and Consul General Kita in Honolulu.

In mid-November Captain Ogawa of the Third Bureau messaged Yoshikawa in the Japanese consulate in Hawaii: "As relations between Japan and the United States are most critical make your 'ships in harbor' reports irregularly but a a rate of twice a week. Although you already are no doubt aware, please take extra care to observe secrecy."

Yoshikawa complied with alacrity, filing his first report to Tokyo 18 November:

(1) The warships at anchor in the Harbor on the 15th were as I told you in my No. 219 that day:
Area A—A battleship of the Oklahoma class entered and one tanker left port.
Area C—3 warships of the heavy-cruiser class were at anchor.
(2) On the 17th, the Saratoga was not in the Harbor. The carrier *Enterprise* (or some other vessel) was in Area C. Two heavy cruisers of the Chicago class, one of the Pensacola class were tied up at docks KS. Four merchant vessels were at anchor in Area D.
(3) At 1000 on the 17th, 8 destroyers were observed entering the Harbor. Their course was as follows: In a single file at a distance of 1000 meters apart at a speed of 3 knots, they moved into Pearl Harbor. From the entrance of the Harbor through Area B to the buoys in Area C, to which they were moored, they changed course five times, each time roughly 30 degrees. The elapsed time was one hour. However, one of these destroyers entered Area A after passing the water reservoir on the eastern side.

During the following eighteen days ending on the evening of 6 December, the ensign spy filed 24 radiograms to Tokyo.

However the Magic messages dealing with the Nomura-Hull negotiations held center stage. The Japanese consulate radiograms to Tokyo were processed on a deferred basis and when they were read, their mass of detailed naval information about the status of the fleet inside Pearl Harbor failed to impress their U.S. Navy readers who dismissed them as routine consular service reports.

Admiral Kimmel at Pearl Harbor would have been impressed.

But he was not advised.

There was one avenue of intelligence over which Kimmel did have some degree of control, only to find that his enemy had moved to shut this off to him also. This was the shadowy, uncertain world of radio traffic analysis.

This operation attempts to identify the call signals of the vessels, commands or other units which go to make up an enemy fleet. Once identified, radio direction finders ascertain the location from which the signal was sent.

In the Pacific the American Navy had such stations at Pearl Harbor, Manila, Guam, Dutch Harbor, Pago Pago, Midway and Bainbridge Island in Puget Sound. It is a trying and painstaking business with the payoff many times far off the mark in accuracy. Usually it is coupled with a code breaking effort, but in 1941 the Japanese naval codes were secure except those of very low level rating.

So Admiral Kimmel and his staff went over the daily traffic analysis with great care.

On 1 November the Japanese fleet changed all its call signals which had been in effect since 1 May 1941, so all previous work by communications intelligence units went out the window and they had to start again from scratch. In addition, the Japanese, undetected by the Americans, were transmitting a blizzard of fake messages to cover the departure of Nagumo's strike force from Japan and its assembly in Hittokappu Bay.

After monumental attempts to solve the problem the intelligence units were compelled to admit defeat—there was no reliable information on the Japanese aircraft carriers or submarines.

On 1 December the Japanese navy changed its call signals again. These changes were recognized at Pearl as a prelude to war, but when? Where?

At the conference Kimmel held with his task force commanders at Pearl Harbor on the day of the famous war warning message from the Navy Department, 27 November, when it was decided to reinforce Wake and Midway Islands with Marine fighter and scouting planes, Vice Admiral William Halsey, commander of Task Force 2, was directed to lead off in the *Enterprise,* sailing the next morning for Wake Island with twelve F4F fighters aboard. Vice Admiral Wilson Brown was charged with having his sub-Task Force 12 under Rear Admiral John Newton, ferry eighteen Marine scout bombers out to Midway in the carrier *Lexington,* leaving Pearl 5 December, while he took the remainder of Task Force 3 down to Johnston Island for exercises with landing boats.

Worried about the outbreak of war, Halsey asked Kimmel what he should do if he encountered any Japanese ships or planes.

". . . . use your common sense!" the commander in chief replied.

With these instructions, Halsey sortied from Pearl at 0800 on the 28th with *Enterprise,* three battleships, heavy cruisers and destroyers. But once outside, Task Force 2 was divided with Halsey taking the *Enterprise,* three heavy cruisers and nine destroyers off on the Wake mission, Task Force 8, with Rear Admiral Milo Draemel leading the remainder of Task Force 2, the three battleships, a light cruiser and eight destroyers, headed for the fleet's drill areas south of Oahu because the 17-knot battleships would only delay the 30-knot *Enterprise* on her voyage to the westward.

When well clear of the other ships, Halsey had *Enterprise*

Captain George Murray issue Battle Order No. 1 beginning:

1. The Enterprise is now operating under war conditions.
2. Any time, day or night, we must be ready for instant action.
3. Hostile submarines may be encountered. . . .

Halsey then ordered Task Force 8 to be prepared to destroy any ships or planes sighted, so the secrecy of the mission would be preserved.

The departure of Task Force 2 had been noted and reported to Tokyo by the naval spy Yoshikawa who, of course, had no knowledge of the division of the force or the special *Enterprise* mission.

With Halsey's planes searching out to 300 miles as they steamed toward Wake, Kimmel ordered the big PBY flying boat patrol planes to begin search missions on the outer perimeters with one squadron taking off from Midway for Wake 28 November. Once at Wake they were to conduct searches out to a distance of 525 miles.

On 30 November another squadron of patrol planes left Pearl for Johnston Island en route to Midway, charged with conducting searches of the ocean areas over which they flew. While at Midway they too were ordered to search the ocean areas off those tiny islands.

So Kimmel took what actions he could to prepare for war, blinded as he was partly by the enemy and partly by his own Navy Department.

In Tokyo on 2 December at 1030 the chiefs of staff of the Imperial Army and Navy, General Sugiyama and Admiral Nagano, bowed their heads and requested the Emperor's divine permission to commence war on 8 December (7 December at Pearl Harbor). He nodded his assent.

The X Day warnings went out to the forces that afternoon.

Admiral Yamamoto's combined fleet order was flashed to all the fleets:

"Climb Mount Niitaka 1208" meaning "Attack as planned 8 December." (Mount Niitaka at 13,599 feet on the island of Formosa, was the highest peak in the Japanese Empire.)

The Pearl Harbor Strike Force, now seven days into its voyage, received Yamamoto's order while steaming at a modest 14 knots over calm seas with four of its destroyers patrolling in the van.

With the carriers steaming in parallel columns of three, the battleships astern, the heavy cruisers held position as flank guards. Led by the light cruiser *Abukuma*, the destroyers were scattered about the task force like sheep dogs around the flock. Silent and invisible, off *Akagi's* starboard, the submarines slid through the cold, sullen waters searching sea and sky—searching and listening—but nothing did they find.

Admiral Kusaka, Nagumo's chief of staff, felt relief. The task force would deliver its devastating blow to the American fleet, then vanish into the wastes of the North Pacific. He and his commander were still wary of their mission, still distrustful of their own success. Secretly he wished the whole operation was over and done with.

Not so the Japanese naval ratings, however, who, when informed by their ship captains for the first time of Operation Hawaii and the coming attack on Pearl Harbor, were caught up in the overwhelming emotion of patriotic zeal for the Emperor and the Empire.

Far to the westward in Yokohama harbor, the pride of the NYK fleet, the big liner *Tatuta Maru* was making ready for sea, her destination San Francisco. Hers was to be the third special voyage authorized by the United States for the exchange of American evacuees from the Far East for Japanese nationals desiring to return home from the U.S.

Shortly before sailing time Commander Toshikazu Ohmae of the Imperial Navy boarded the big liner to make his way to the captain's cabin. Here he handed the master of the *Tatuta* a sealed box which he was to open at 0000 hours on 7 December. Inside were twenty loaded pistols and an order to return to Yokohama at top speed in radio silence and in blackout.

At Pearl Harbor Pacific Fleet headquarters, fleet intelligence officer Lieutenant Commander Edwin T. Layton faced his chief, Admiral Kimmel, in a sunlit room overlooking the waters of the naval base, now crowded with all types of men-o-war. They had just received reports from the commander in chief of the Asiatic Fleet that his patrol planes had spotted a total of nine submarines in the South China Sea, all heading south. Twenty-one Japanese transports, huddled under an air patrol, were lying in Camranh Bay on the eastern coast of Indo-China above Saigon. Layton identified this assemblage of shipping as part of an expeditionary fleet.

After a discussion of this data the two naval officers then turned to Layton's estimate of the present locations of major Japanese naval units. Painstakingly they went down the long lists of fleets, commencing with the First Fleet in the Kure-Sasebo area in home waters.

Third Fleet—China Fleet—Second Fleet—Fourth Fleet—South China Fleet—Carrier Division Three—Carrier Division Four—Expeditionary Force—Submarine Force Commander at Saipan. In great detail the memorandum covered the best possible information the American Navy had been able to gather on their probable antagonist—the "Orange."

Kimmel looked up at his intelligence commander quizzically.

"What! You don't know where Carrier Division 1 and Carrier Division 2 are?"

"No, Sir," Layton replied, "I do not. I think they are in home waters, but I do not know where they are. The rest of these units I feel pretty confident about."

Admiral Kimmel looked at Layton sternly, yet his eyes twinkled.

"Do you mean to say that they could be rounding Diamond Head and you wouldn't know it?"

"I hope they would be sighted before now," his intelligence chief replied.

Carrier Divisions 1 and 2 in company with Carrier Division 5 of his Imperial Japanese Majesty's Navy at that moment were steaming in battle formation through sullen Pacific seas far to the northwestward of pleasant Pearl Harbor, the two battleships *Hiei* and *Kirishima* with their tall pagoda-shaped fighting bridges clustered about their foremasts, moving grimly in the wakes of the six big carriers with the rest of the attack force spread about the whole.

A sailor standing on the fantail of one of these steel monsters watching her wake disappearing into the distance might well ponder the irrevocable destiny enwrapped in the mission of the ships about him. All of the mighty traditions of Japan gathered from the mists of antiquity were moving at a constant 14 knots through a dark sea. Every thrust of the glistening shafts working in the oily sweat of the engine rooms far below, every turn of the great propellers was moving the destinies of Nippon and all her millions toward a single throw of the dice of Mars.

But there was no time for philosophy on *Akagi*. Nagumo and his officers spent hours pouring over the latest intelligence on the situation at Pearl, relayed to the attacking force from the Imperial General Staff.

Across Honolulu at the old Japanese consulate, Kita handed Yoshikawa a radiogram from Captain Ogawa of the Third Bureau: "In view of the present situation, the presence in port of warships, airplane carriers, and cruisers is of utmost importance. Hereafter, to the utmost of your ability, let me know day by day. Wire me in each case whether or not there are any barrage balloons above Pearl Harbor or if there are any indications that they will be sent up. Also advise me whether or not the warships are provided with antitorpedo nets."

But as Honolulu intercept traffic was in a deferred status in Washington's Magic operations, this message was not decoded and translated until after the attack.

For Yoshikawa however, it was top priority. The next day he radioed three ship movement reports to Tokyo.

On 3 December the Nagumo force reached the standby position for the task force as set forth in Yamamoto's battle orders, 42 degrees north and 170 degrees west. When the refueling operation was rendered impossible by heavy weather, cutting speed to 12 knots, the fleet commenced its ever more dangerous run down towards Hawaiian waters.

Now with the force setting a new course towards the southeast, Nagumo and Kusaka got a jolt from the Combined Fleet when Yamamoto warned them that a radio interception had been picked up, probably from an American submarine in their vicinity. A tense exchange of blinker signals between ships failed to uncover any radio interceptions.

So the ships steamed on unseen by any foe, the force commander and his staff chief still unsettled by the fleet warning which had come to naught.

In Tokyo the argument concerning the time of presentation of the negotiations break-off note to Hull continued to rage within the Navy, some officers violently opposing any warning time whatsoever.

The foreign ministry meanwhile labored at drafting the long recitation of American wrongs to Japan which would precede the final note declaring diplomatic relations at an end. It would consist of thirteen parts which would be cabled to Washington on 6 December along with a set of instructions to the embassy. The final section giving notice of the break in relations would arrive in Washington very early in the morning of Sunday 7 December.

As it was being prepared, Vice Admiral Ito dropped in on foreign minister Togo to tell him the note should not be presented to Hull until 1 P.M. instead of at 12:30 P.M. When Togo asked why the change, Ito said Chief of Staff

Nagano's previous calculations were in error, but that the new deadline would still provide advance notice of the attack.

Togo asked him how much advance notice, but Ito would not tell him because of "fleet security."

In Honolulu spy Yoshikawa, after a survey of Pearl Harbor, messaged Ogawa in Tokyo: "The following ships were in port on the afternoon of the 5th: eight battleships, three light cruisers, sixteen destroyers."

Earlier he had reported the movements of Rear Admiral John H. Newton who had cleared Pearl Harbor for Midway Islands with Task Force 12 consisting of the large aircraft carrier *Lexington*, three heavy cruisers and five destroyers. Likewise Vice Admiral Wilson Brown, commander of Task Force 3 of which Task Force 12 was a part, had steamed out of the naval base to conduct operations with cruisers and destroyers at Johnston Island.

Vice Admiral Halsey in *Enterprise* was returning with Task Force 8 after launching Marine fighters for Wake Island.

Yoshikawa could see with his own eyes, however, that the carriers had gone.

For Nagumo's force still steaming on a southeast heading at fair speed, the weather had turned cloudy with 20 knot winds and heavy seas crashing against the ships. From time to time mist or fog enveloped the vessels so they had difficulty maintaining station in their formation.

The wet slanting decks were dangerous to negotiate, and one petty officer was swept over the side.

Although the bad weather did provide some cover against enemy eyes, it still did not assauge Nagumo's fears. The long stealthy voyage was building to its climax.

Far to the south, off the southern shores of Oahu, the Japanese flotillas of big fleet submarines were slipping into their assigned stations. Some of the blockading ring would close off the Molokai Channel, others would patrol off the Pearl Harbor channel and five would launch their midget submarines to deliver an attack within the harbor itself.

Two other fleet submarines were to check the U.S. fleet rendezvous in Lahaina Roads off Maui.

Two more alarms closed out the day for Nagumo. An alert from Tokyo brought six fighter planes onto *Kaga*'s flight deck during the afternoon with a report that there was a Russian ship in the vicinity of the task force. But nothing further developed and the planes were returned to the hangar deck.

Then early in the night a light was seen over the formation. Crews went to general quarters prepared for action, but the light turned out to be a weather balloon launched from *Kaga* herself and quiet prevailed again.

On Oahu 6 December found the sun breaking the eastern horizon bright and clear. There was considerable cloudiness in the Hawaiian area with some shower activity on the windward slopes. The great cloud caps were not yet formed on the sky-reaching volcanoes but their beginnings were already hovering over the torn craters in misty tatters. In the lowlands and along the beaches, the day promised fair.

Honolulu airport reported moderate winds from the east northeast with temperatures in the seventies at eight o'clock.

On the outlying islands, the plantations had been astir for hours serving the needs of the sugar and the pineapples. Waking Honolulu prepared for the abbreviated half-day of work and the coming weekend.

Headlines in the morning *Advertiser* proclaimed: "America Expected to Reject Japan's Reply on Indo-China," "Japanese Navy Moving South," "Detailed Plans Completed for M-Day Setup."

The city, however, exhibited the calmness of nature in the complete harmony which marks the Hawaiian sunrise. If there was any excitement over the early morning coffee, it tended towards discussion of the relative strengths of the University of Hawaii Rainbows and the Willamette University football Elevens scheduled to meet on behalf of the island's crippled children in the annual Shrine game that afternoon. For those who could not go to the stadium there would be a radio broadcast of the game, a broadcast which would be much more historic then even the most enthusiastic football fan could conjecture.

Far to the northwestward out along the Hawaiian chain, out beyond French Frigate Shoals and Necker Island, on the tiny coral islands of Midway, the big Pan American flyingboat, the *Philippine Clipper,* was being readied to resume her transit of the Pacific. She had a long flight ahead of her that Saturday and her crew was about early making preparations. She was scheduled to sit down that night in the lagoon at Wake Island.

Sentries on alert duty at the forts and airfields on Oahu greeted the dawn with relief. Soon steaming coffee would erase the stiffness of the long night hours. In the Fleet the crews began stirring to for another day. Admiral Kimmel checked over his "Steps to be taken in case of American-Japanese war within the next twenty-four hours" prior to beginning a morning and afternoon given over to a complete review of the Pacific situation with his staff chiefs. General Short nervously resurveyed all measures he had taken to guard against sabotage. Were they adequate?

By seven o'clock in Hawaii with the sun but a half-hour old, it was Saturday noon time in the crowded government offices and broad boulevards of Washington. As the weekend throngs poured homeward bound into the streets, significant events were beginning to unfold themselves before the watchful eyes of officials in the innermost seats of power and authority.

At 1040 a message marked "Triple Priority and Most Urgent—Personal and Secret to the Secretary and the President" had been received from Winant, Ambassador to the Court of St. James in London. It read: "British Admiralty reports at 3 A.M. London time this morning, two parties seen off Cambodia Point sailing slowly westward toward Kra, 14 hours distant in time. First party 25 transports, 6 cruisers, 10 destroyers. Second party 10 transports, 2 cruisers, 10 destroyers."

This message indicated a Japanese attack on Thailand, the isthmus of Kra, and Malaya within hours. Only a handful of the very highest American leaders knew that they had already committed the nation to go to the armed assistance of the British and the Dutch if their colonies were attacked. Now they had warning that that attack was about to be unleashed.

Shortly thereafter at 1150 the Navy intercepted through Magic, a pilot message to Nomura and Kurusu alerting them to the fact that the Japanese government's answer to the American ultimatum of 26 November demanding Japan get out of China, recognize Chiang and abandon the Axis, would begin coming into the embassy shortly and that it would be in fourteen parts.

The two envoys were further advised to withhold presenting the Japanese reply to Secretary Hull until they had received a separate "pilot" message which would set forth the specific time it was to be handed to the American Secretary of State.

Now the whole picture was clearing rapidly for Washington: Japanese assault forces steaming to attack Malaya. Japanese embassies and consulates ordered to destroy their codes. The finally reply to the U.S. ultimatum on the way with a specific time set for its delivery.

Yet no more words of warning were dispatched to the anxious commanders at Hawaii!

Far to the north of the Islands the dawn of Saturday 6 December brought painful tension to the flagship *Akagi*.

The strike force began the day by refueling every ship to capacity. The fleet oilers then dropped away to head for a prearranged post strike rendezvous.

Then in the early hours Yoshikawa's Friday ship status report was handed by communications officer Commander Kenjiro Ono to Nagumo and Kusaka. It created a stir of disappointment in the fact that none of the American aircraft carriers were inside Pearl Harbor. Where were they? Would they return by tomorrow morning?

For the first time flaws in the supersecret Pearl Harbor

attack plan began to appear.

All of the planning had been presaged on the presence of the American battle strength being present in the harbor when the blow fell. Now the main power would be gone along with the other very sizable elements of heavy cruisers and destroyers.

Then ensued a spirited discussion amongst Nagumo's staff as to whether any of the eight battleships moored at Pearl would leave that day or whether any of the missing carriers would return. After much talk in which the air officers repeatedly regretted the absence of all the carriers from Pearl Harbor, Chief of Staff Kusaka declared it unlikely the battleships would sortie on Saturday or Sunday or that the carriers would return.

Up until now the Japanese effort had been shaped to hit and run. But with the main targets missing, what then? The argument raged on in the flag spaces of *Akagi*. In the end, it was Kusaka who summed up the situation.

"The carriers are not there," he said. "It is unlikely they will return before we attack. Still eight battleships with light cruisers and destroyers are quite a prize. We have come so far with so much danger, the attack must go in."

The flying officers were forced to agree, there was no other answer. But the planning, the planning—

At 1130 all ships' crews were mustered to hear the reading of the Emperor's rescript for war.

It was followed by a message from Admiral Yamamoto, commander in chief of the combined fleet: "The rise or fall of the Empire depends upon this battle. Every man will do his duty to the utmost."

So the ghost of the great Admiral Togo stalked Nagumo's ships as they executed a wide, foaming turn to starboard and a new heading—180 degrees, due south to Oahu. In spite of the heavily rolling seas, speed was increased to 24 knots and the run down to the launching point began.

The radio rooms in the ships continued to grimly monitor the airwaves for any sign of alarm on Oahu. All they heard, however, was the light-hearted chatter of the two Honolulu broadcasting stations KGU and KGMB with incessant frivolous music. All was peaceful in the Islands.

At 1903 *Akagi* received more exciting material: "American Fleet is not in Lahaina Anchorage."

This vital if somewhat disappointing intelligence was radioed by submarine I-72 which had carefully inspected the sparkling waters of the wide roadstead between Maui and Lanai Islands that peaceful Saturday morning. It ruled out any chance that the missing carriers might be in this fleet operating area.

Early in the evening Tokyo advised Nagumo that the ships in Pearl were guarded neither by torpedo nets nor by barrage balloons. Then late in the night Yoshikawa's last ship report was relayed from Tokyo: "The following ships were observed at anchor on the 6th: 9 battleships, 3 light cruisers, 3 seaplane tenders, 17 destroyers. In addition there were 4 light cruisers and 2 destroyers lying at docks. It appears that no air reconnaissance is being conducted by the fleet air arm."

When he read the dispatch Commander Genda shook his head sadly. The big prizes were gone.

Out to the westward the *Tatuta Maru* to the consternation of her American passengers would reverse her course and head back towards Japan with 20 unused pistols.

Close on to midnight about six miles south of the Pearl Harbor channel entrance, the five fleet submarines went about launching their midgets for their great attempt. In Hawaii the weather was clear with a moon three days past the full. The submarine crews working on the midgets' shackles could see the bright lights of Waikiki whenever a surge brought them out of the wave trough. It was a lovely night in the Islands.

To the northward however, it was a grimmer ocean with Nagumo's ships pitching and rolling heavily in the black seas.

Nagumo gathered his staff in *Akagi's* operations room to give them his battle estimate:

Enemy strength in the Hawaiian area consists of nine battleships, two carriers, about ten heavy and six light cruisers. The carriers and heavy cruisers seem to be at sea but the others are in harbor.

There is no indication the enemy has been alerted but that is no reason to relax our security.

Unless an unforseen situation develops, our attack will be launched upon Pearl Harbor.

Afterwards the Admiral resumed his incessant pacing the bridge of *Akagi*, staring into the night, peering at the binnacle, then rechecking the attack plans laid out for him in the operations room.

With all hands at their duty stations at 0300 the ships smashed through the heavy seas toward the launching point two hundred miles north of Oahu.

In the flagship *Nagato* in the Hashirajima anchorage, the man who had conceived the plan waited out the tense hours. With the combined fleet ready to sail if needed, Yamamoto devoted part of his time to a game of Japanese chess.

Like Togo at Port Arthur, he had his ships bearing down on an unsuspecting foe.

Like Togo at Port Arthur, he had his spy within the fortress.

Like Togo at Tsushima, he would have the old *Mikasa's* "Z" flag hoisted to the masthead of *Akagi*.

He also had a most carefully detailed attack plan.

But it had only two options: Go or No Go.

He also had two timid commanders directing the most important strike in all the wide Pacific war.

The enemy carriers were somewhere at sea. Would there be any way to reach them?

9

The Fury Bursts

THERE WERE OTHER TIMID MEN.
In Washington on 6 December all through the afternoon and early evening Magic was revealing piece by piece to the waiting eyes of Army and Navy communication intelligence officers, the reply of the Imperial Japanese Government to the American ultimatum of 26 November. Ironically the Japanese were instructing their ambassadors Nomura and Kurusu to hold the reply in strictest secrecy until presentation to Secretary of State Hull at a time to be specified by Tokyo in a subsequent message.

Even to uninformed eyes the reply was not a friendly one. Phrased in diplomatic yet forceful language it defended Japan's actions in the Far East while accusing the United States and Great Britain of enveloping her with a ring of force. It flatly stated that Japan was bound to observe her pledges to Germany and Italy under the Tri-Partite Pact, charging that America was plotting an extension of the European war to the Orient. It then bluntly rejected Hull's ten-point note of 26 November in its entirety.

By 9 P.M. Eastern Standard Time, thirteen parts of the

101

message had been decoded and translated in the War and Navy Departments. Neither "Part Fourteen" nor the "Pilot Message" with directions for time of delivery, had as yet appeared.

Deciding the material they had was too hot to hold, officers in charge began distribution of this most secret and vital information. Lieutenant Commander Alwin D. Kramer, with his wife at the wheel, was driven to the White House where he turned over a locked pouch with the message inside to the President's junior naval aide for immediate delivery to Roosevelt himself.

While the commander and his wife waited to deliver copies to Navy Secretary Knox as well as a select other few on the Navy distribution list, the naval aide sped the message to Roosevelt who was closeted with his assistant, Harry Hopkins, in the second floor study of the White House.

With the lieutenant and Hopkins waiting, Roosevelt read Japan's final answer to the American 26 November ultimatum: ". . . . the proposal menaces the Empire's existence itself and disparages its honor and prestige. Therefore, viewed in its entirety, the Japanese Government regrets that it cannot accept the proposal as a basis of negotiation."

He handed the message to Hopkins. When Hopkins had finished reading it, the President looked at him with excited eyes declaring: "This means war!"

At this moment it was just past 5 P.M. in Honolulu. There were still a few minutes of fading daylight before the sun would sink beneath the Pacific at 1719.

Admiral Kimmel had completed a long afternoon of consultations with his War Plans and Operations officers, checking fleet dispositions and readiness to react to an emergency, unaware that the most dangerous peril he faced was revealing itself to the President even as he took leave of his staff officers in the dusk of Pearl Harbor. The unwarned admiral, not realizing that now each tick of the clock was heavy with history, said goodnight to Captains McMorris and DeLany before going to his quarters.

Back in Washington, Roosevelt phoned Admiral Stark from the White House but when told the chief of naval operations was at the play "The Student Prince," he did nothing more.

Meanwhile Commander Kramer with the Magic messages had delivered a copy to Knox who likewise did nothing. Then on through the night the commander's wife drove him across the Potomac to Arlington where he showed the Magic message to the chiefs of army and navy intelligence gathered at a dinner party. Upon learning that the final segment, the fourteenth part of the message, was still to come, they both agreed to let the matter ride over until the next day.

While Roosevelt and the Navy Department let destiny take its course with the fate of the nation and the lives of thousands of Americans discharging their duties in the fleet and the fortress, the Army was finding it equally difficult to act.

When the Navy's Magic had completed decoding and processing the first thirteen parts of Japan's fourteen part reply to the United States, copies were turned over to Major Harold Doud of the Army Signal Corps code and cipher section for delivery to those officials for whom the army had assumed responsibility. Doud in turn gave them into the hands of Colonel Bratton, chief of the Far Eastern Section of the intelligence branch of War Department G-2, who had been made directly responsible for handling and distributing all Magic messages received by the department.

Bratton, like his opposite number—Captain McCollum in naval intelligence—immediately grasped the terrible import contained in Japan's truculent reply to the United States. Consequently he was extremely anxious when he brought the fateful message in a locked bag to Colonel Bedell Smith, secretary to the General Staff.

"This is very important," he told Smith. "General Marshall should be informed at once so he can unlock the bag and read the contents."

Colonel Smith took the locked bag but General Marshall, the chief of staff, so far as history knows, did not learn of the existence of the message until late the next morning.

From the War Department Colonel Bratton took the last of the locked messages to the darkened State Department where it was delivered to the secretary's duty officer at about half-past ten o'clock. His work was now finished except for receipt of the fateful fourteenth part whenever it should be intercepted. He had delivered the Japanese retort. He had called the attention of the most responsible officers to the importance of the message. There was nothing further he could do.

Wearily he sought some sleep.

Night was now deepening over Honolulu. Lovers in parked cars at Makapuu Point overlooking Rabbit Island and the booming surf far below had a fine view of the swollen golden moon just three days past the full, when it showed the top edge of its disc above the eastern horizon line of the ocean at five minutes after eight o'clock. Rising rapidly out of the great depths it began its ascent of the night sky.

There was gaiety and dancing in Honolulu. The University of Hawaii had beaten Willamette 20 to 6 in the Shrine football extravaganza and party crowds thronged the beach spots at Waikiki. Ukuleles and guitars strummed favorite Hawaiian tunes under the coconut palms edging the surf in front of the Royal Hawaiian Hotel where lei-bedecked women and white-dinner-jacketed men laughed and toasted each other in the beauty of the tropic night.

Solid jazz was favored at other beach rendezvous while in downtown Honolulu soldiers, sailors and Marines on weekend liberty thronged the honky-tonks and dives of the Hotel-River-Street section.

Hamilton Field in California was an Army air strip just

beyond the city of San Rafael, north of the Golden Gate. That evening of 6 December pilots and navigators of thirteen B-17 Flying Fortress bombers were checking wind and weather between the continental mainland and Hawaii. The weather was good and the winds were favorable. Shortly after, the long graceful ships began their takeoff runs, rising one after the other into the stars, outbound for the Islands.

These aircraft were destined for the defense of the Philippine Islands, and General Hap Arnold, commander of the Army Air Force, was himself at the edge of the runway to see them safely in the air. Because of the 2,400 miles of flight before them, they were loaded with gasoline instead of ammunition, their guns peacefully stowed away, unmounted inside each ship.

The early monotony of the flight was broken when one bomber developed a fretful engine, forcing her pilot to turn back to the American coast. The other twelve droned onward through the starry skies with the late moon riding on their wings.

One of the pilots told his flight diary he had never seen such a beautiful night.

At about this time General Short, who had gone to an Army charity event at Schofield Barracks with his G-2 Colonel Fielder and their wives, was preparing for the long downhill drive back to Fort Shafter. Admiral Kimmel, after enjoying a quiet dinner with Rear Admiral H. F. Leary at the Halekulani Hotel at Waikiki, was back in his Pearl Harbor quarters ready to turn in. It was about ten o'clock.

Some three hundred fifty miles to the north, the Japanese hit-run squadron was coming hard due south for Oahu. The black ships on the moon mottled ocean were making heavy weather; the building seas hissing inboard from time to time under the whipping wind.

Admiral Nagumo watched out the anxious hours from *Akagi's* bridge. He had carried a heavy load these past few weeks, the fate of the ancient empire hanging about his neck like an iron collar. Now he was within hours of breaking that collar, of delivering his attack successfully on order or seeing it spill up against the mouth of American cannon in devastating failure. He stared out at the nasty, hissing sea. He set his face calmly in a stern Oriental mask, making his slow spoken observations while his lieutenants marveled at his iron control. Behind that mask his heart was pounding with every straining beat of his engines, with every nervous thrust of the screws. He wished it were all over. He wished the night would end.

Outside the entrance to Pearl Harbor an ancient vessel named for the first naval officer killed in the American Civil War, the four-piper destroyer *Ward* of the inshore patrol, was steaming back and forth over the black waters south of the great naval base. Around midnight she was to receive company in the clumsy shapes of two minesweepers bearing the unlikely names *Condor* and *Crossbill*, which poked their blunt noses out of the narrow channel to take up their menial task of sweeping the entrance areas clear of any secretly planted mines.

Within the long, darkling reaches of Pearl Harbor itself with "Condition Three" in effect on the sleeping decks of those forbidding masses of steel, the battleships of the fleet saw two five-inch antiaircraft guns and two heavy machineguns ready for instant action on each man-o-war. Not that anything was expected. . . .

As one bluejacket assured his mate in the lonely watches of that night: "Nothing ever happens. It just gets colder on towards morning."

In the Navy's Magic center in Washington, the white-faced clocks marked out 0730 Eastern Standard Time. Officers who had waited all night for it could now read the ominous words of the fourteenth and final portion of Japan's reply to the American ultimatum for peace in the Far East. They were belligerent. They read:

> Obviously it is the intention of the American
> Government to conspire with Great Britain and other

countries to obstruct Japan's efforts toward the establishment of peace through the creation of a New Order in East Asia, and especially to preserve Anglo-American rights and interests by keeping Japan and China at war. This intention has been revealed clearly during the course of the present negotiations. Thus, the earnest hope of the Japanese Government to adjust Japanese-American relations and to preserve and promote the peace of the Pacific through cooperation with the American Government has finally been lost.

The Japanese Government regrets to have to notify hereby the American Government that in view of the attitude of the American Government it cannot but consider that it is impossible to reach an agreement through future negotiations.

Alongside the diplomatic message which when decoded read out in English lay another dispatch awaiting translation from the Japanese. It had been intercepted by the lonely naval radio intercept station on fir-tree-lined Bainbridge Island in Puget Sound, then relayed to the Navy Department by teletype.

The faithful navy commander courier who had caught a few hours sleep after delivering the first thirteen parts of Japan's retort the night before stared at this added enigmatic note with irritation.

He voiced his impatience.

But impatience would not reveal the hidden meaning and he must begin his rounds of the "Very Important Persons" with "Part 14 of 14" immediately. This he did about 0900 including Roosevelt at the White House, Admiral Stark, and the duty officer at the State Department.

When he returned to the Magic center, the commander courier swiftly glanced at the translation of the Bainbridge Island relay. His eyes widened when he read the Japanese instructions. It was the pilot message for which they had been waiting all night:

From: Tokyo
To : Washington
December 7, 1941
Purple (Urgent—Very Important)
No. 907 To be handled in government code.
Re my No. 902 (the fourteen part message)
Will the Ambassador please submit to the United States
Government (if possible to the Secretary of State) our
reply to the United States at 1:00 p.m. on the 7th your
time.

The commander looked at his watch. It was now 10:20
A.M. in Washington, 4:50 A.M. at Pearl Harbor. The time
set for delivery of the Japanese reply at 1:00 P.M. Washington time would be about an hour after dawn in Hawaii
and late in the night in the Philippines.

A second decoded message lay with the first. It instructed the embassy: "After deciphering Part 14 of my No.
902 and also my 907, 908 and 909, please destroy at once
the remaining cipher machine and all machine codes. Dis-
pose in like manner all secret documents."

The alarm bells were clanging urgently now. The commander set out to see their danger signal was heard. He
had two hours and forty minutes before the deadline.

At the War Department, military intelligence Colonel
Bratton was making frantic efforts to reach the chief of staff
but General Marshall was galloping his horse over the
rolling Virginia hills. All action on the Army side was
halted waiting his return.

Although the night was dying it still lay black on the
waters off Oahu. Only the late moon gave some faint
illumination. Suddenly the lookout in the ungainly
minesweeper *Condor* sighted something in the moonpath.
He stared hard. There in the defensive sea area off the
Pearl Harbor entrance buoys was a periscope moving silently toward the channel into the naval base. It was about
100 feet from and on a collision course with the *Condor* but
suddenly it turned sharply to port. The *Condor* imme-

diately turned to starboard well knowing that American submarines were prohibited from operating submerged in this restricted area. It was 0342 Hawaiian Time.

The *Condor's* signal man blinked the alarm to the patrol destroyer *Ward:* "Sighted submerged submarine on westerly course, speed 9 knots."

The destroyer immediately commenced a sonar search for the intruder.

For well over an hour the *Ward* continued her diligent but unsuccessful search for the unknown trespasser. Finally at 0520 the *Ward* radioed *Condor:* "What was the approximate distance and course of the submarine that you sighted?"

Condor replied: "The course was about what we were steering at the time 020 magnetic and about 1000 yards from the entrance apparently heading for the entrance."

With this further information the destroyer captain realized he had been searching in the wrong direction. He changed the search pattern but again with no result. The radio conversations between the minesweeper and the patrol destroyer were overheard and transcribed in the log of the Bishops Point section base at Pearl, a radio station of the inshore patrol net, but since the conversation was between two ships with no request for relay, it was not reported to higher authority.

The *Condor* did not consider the identification positive enough to report to other than the *Ward* while Lieutenant Commander Outerbridge, captain of the *Ward,* thought the *Condor* might be mistaken in concluding it had seen a submarine.

The *Condor* and the *Crossbill,* their night's sweeping concluded, now stood in. It was 0532 when the minesweepers glided noiselessly into the channel.

At this same moment in the predawn darkness due north of Oahu, the heavy cruisers *Chikuma* and *Tone* were launching Zero float planes for preliminary reconnaissance of Oahu. On the pitching, rolling flight decks of the carriers, the warplanes were massed ready for takeoff, their crews making final adjustments to their craft and equipment.

Under the faint illumination of the battle lamps in the briefing rooms, the pilots were receiving last minute instructions for the attack. In the flagship *Akagi*, Nagumo clasped the hand of the air strike commander Fuchida as he reported: "Ready for the mission."

"I have confidence in you," the admiral replied. The two of them then made their way to the ready room where *Akagi's* Captain Kiichi Hasegawa gave his order to the airmen crowded in the shadows of the room: "Take off according to plan."

A blackboard with the latest positions of the American ships at Pearl Harbor chalked on its black surface glowered at the backs of the pilots as they rushed out to man their planes.

Fuchida made his way down the tumbling deck to the commander's plane with the red and yellow striped tail. His senior petty officer helping him up into the cockpit, presented him with a white *hachimaki*, a cloth headband, requesting that for the sake of the plane crew he wear it as a talisman over Pearl Harbor. The air commander obligingly fastened it to his flying helmet.

Along the deck pilots were being boosted into their planes, the "victory" *hachimakis* streaming from their helmets as they entered the cockpits.

Slowly the big carrier turned to port, into the teeth of the easterly wind which was kicking up dirty spots of white on the blackness of the sea. One by one the planes began to warm up, roaring out their powerful blasts into the dying night. Lamps swung crazily to the pitch and toss of the ships, while over all crackled the Japanese battle flag and Admiral Togo's "Z" signal of victory.

A green lantern swung in a tight circle from the darkness at the bow of *Akagi*. In answer the first plane started slowly down the deck gathering speed. It seemed to hang for an instant over the plunging end of the flight deck, then it was airborne. A cheer went up in the darkness from the sailors massed in the gun galleries along the sides of the carrier. A second plane made her precarious run. Then she too was safely in the air.

So from the six big carriers the 183 fighters, bombers and torpedo planes of the first attack wave swarmed up into the darkness. It took fifteen minutes to launch them, the ships' crews watching their signal lights glowing against the morning sky. It was 0615 and Oahu was bearing South 230 miles distant.

The shadows of Pearl Harbor were reaching out to engulf the bright Sunday noon of Washington. General Marshall, finally warned of the momentous events upon his return from his gallop through the winter woods, was at his desk in the War Department, scrutinizing the Japanese challenge to America's terms for peace in the Pacific when the G-2 of the Army, Brigadier General Miles, and the alert Colonel Bratton entered with the "1 P.M. delivery message."

Waiting silently while the chief of staff read the intercept holding the key to all Japan's designs against Pearl Harbor, Brigadier General Gerow of the War Plans Division, Miles and Bratton were now unanimous in advising that the overseas commanders in the Philippines, Hawaii and Panama be warned without delay.

Marshall picked up the phone and called Admiral Stark in the Navy Department. What did he think? Although Stark had had the messages before him for two hours, the chief of naval operations acted like a man with a bad dream. He couldn't move. Finally he said he thought further warnings were unnecessary.

This statement was made in spite of the fact that his attention had been called to the delivery time of 1 P.M., which would be close after dawn in Hawaii.

In the War Department Marshall took up his pen and wrote: "Japanese are presenting at 1 P.M. Eastern Standard Time today what amounts to an ultimatum also they are under orders to destroy their code machine immediately. Just what significance the hour set may have we do not know but be on alert accordingly. Inform naval authorities of this communication. —MARSHALL"

The chief of the Army added the last sentence following an interruption caused by the ringing of the telephone on his desk. It was Admiral Stark. He had changed his mind. The army overseas commanders could pass on the alert to their naval counterparts. It was a most unusual way to notify the fleet commanders of the proudest navy in the world that war was on the way.

Now ensued an ironic discussion between the generals as to how the warning should be sent. The first thought was to use the scrambler telephone on Marshall's desk. But that was ruled out because of "security" reasons. It was decided to send it by radio to MacArthur at Manila, Short at Fort Shafter, McAndrews at Panama, and DeWitt at the Presidio of San Francisco.

In the War Department message center, facilities were checked and because transmission between the department and the small station at Fort Shafter was uncertain in the early morning hours, it was decided to send it by commercial radio. The message was then teletyped to Western Union which in turn would send it through RCA radio facilities from San Francisco to Honolulu. The transmission was completed to Western Union at 1217 Eastern Standard Time.

Four minutes earlier the sun had broken the rim of the eastern horizon for the start of another perfect Hawaiian day.

At this moment outside the entrance to Pearl Harbor the plodding naval cargo ship USS *Antares* patiently began its slow entrance into the channel, its progress made slower by the 500-ton steel barge it had towed all the way from Canton and Palmyra Islands. Checking back on the tow, one of her officers noticed a curious object off her starboard quarter. It was good light and even at fifteen hundred yards the observer thought it a small submarine. *Antares* immediately asked the *Ward* to investigate.

The destroyer came up at a rush, almost immediately

sighting a submarine's conning tower following *Antares* into the channel. It was 0640. Clanging "General Quarters" and with engines "Full Ahead" the *Ward* boiled her speed up to twenty-five knots. Tensely her gun crews stood to their posts tracking on the dark object.

Closer raced the *Ward.*

"Fire!"

Guns One and Three opened. The first shot, fired from Number One at 100 yards range, passed directly over the conning tower. The second shot, from Number Three gun at fifty yards or less, ripped into the submarine's hull at the base of her conning tower. A navy patrol bomber from Kaneohe Naval Air Station began dropping bombs on the spot. It was 0645.

The submarine, heeling over, began to sink. *Ward* held her fire to commence depth charging her victim. Large oil slicks streaked upwards to the surface to mark the place of action. The submarine was down in 200 fathoms.

The action over, Outerbridge, commanding the *Ward,* notified Commandant 14th Naval District: "We have dropped depth charges upon sub operating in defensive sea area."

To make sure there would be no mistake about it, this message at 0651 was followed three minutes later by a more detailed dispatch:

"We have attacked, fired upon and dropped depth charges upon submarine operating in defensive sea area."

This message went rapidly to the officer in charge of the net and boom defenses of the inshore patrol as well as to the ComFourteen duty officer. The naval district chief of staff was informed at 0712 and the Pacific Fleet staff duty officer three minutes later.

The ready-duty destroyer *Monaghan* was ordered to get underway to race assistance to the *Ward* while the stand-by destroyer began to get up steam. All of this, including verification of the *Ward's* messages, consumed precious minutes. It was not until 0740 that the fleet staff duty officer put in his call to notify Admiral Kimmel.

Unaware of the sea action off the Pearl Harbor entrance, Fuchida watched the sunrise from his position at the head of the Japanese air armada flying directly on Oahu over a heavy carpet of clouds at an altitude of 9,800 feet. At 0700 and about an hour out from the target, he corrected his course on music broadcast from Honolulu radio station KGMB, the same music which was guiding the twelve American bombers from the coast into Hickam Field.

As the alert Japanese commander listened casually to the melody, he suddenly heard the overtones of more important information. Adjusting his radio he caught the tail-end of a weather report for Oahu: ". . . averaging partly cloudy with clouds mostly over the mountains. Cloud base at 3,500 feet. Visibility good. Wind north 10 knots."

Fuchida smiled grimly. Perfect attack conditions. The gods were good.

The sunlight glittered off the many wings of the formation. But the deadly objects in the bomb racks were lusterless in the morning light.

Dead ahead of the Japanese formation, but still many miles away, two army privates sat watching the screen of their radar at lonely Opana Station in the Aircraft Warning Service chain of installations. They were set back on a remote ridge nose behind the Kahuku sugar plantation on the north tip of Oahu.

Since the black hour of 0400 the two soldiers had fussed with the new instrument, Private Lockard explaining to Private Elliott, his pupil, the methods of proper operation of the set. Ostensibly such findings as they could make would be flashed to the information center at Fort Shafter from where interceptor fighter planes could be ordered off the ground to hunt down and destroy intruders in the air spaces over Oahu. But this reaction was real in theory only. The vital information center was still in the setting-up stage with one lieutenant of the Air Force assigned to training and observation duty daily from 0400 to 0800. The men manning the station were all in training so it was in reality no information center at all.

Still it could and did receive reports from the chain of radar observers scanning the sea and sky about the island. At 0700 all activity ceased on order . . . all but at the lonely Opana outpost where Elliott badgered Lockard into keeping the set operating so he might take instruction until their truck came to pick them up for breakfast. At the information center all the men filed out for early morning chow with the exception of the phone operator and the duty lieutenant.

In switching the set back on and adjusting it, Lockard immediately saw a large blip appear on the oscilloscope. Because of the great number of planes the dancing blip depicted, he began to check the machine for error, but everything was in order. Finally the excited pair decided they had picked up a large formation of aircraft coming in on Oahu from a direction three degrees east of north. The flight appeared to be about 132 miles away. At Elliott's prompting, Lockard called the information center. It was two minutes past 7 A.M.

After some delay they got the duty lieutenant on the line and reported their discovery. The puzzled lieutenant had no information on planes coming in other than the B-17s from Hamilton Field in California. Could these be the same? He was confused but he had to give an answer. It was a short one. The two excited soldiers were told not to worry about it.

Dutifully they went back to their radar where they followed the large flight in until the aircraft entered the set's dead space near the coast, not far from their station. They then flicked off the equipment to wait the appearance of their chow truck.

At this time north of Oahu, Fuchida was anxiously scanning the cloud layers ahead. It was time for the landfall. Then there it was! The surf-splattered foreshore of Kahuku Point shone through a break in the clouds. Below the

Pacific rolled onwards toward the land in long blue lines. The air commander waited, the pulse in his blood beating out the seconds. Now came the report from the pre-strike reconnaissance planes. Cruiser *Chikuma's* plane painstakingly detailed the locations of the American men-o-war trapped in the calm waterways of Pearl Harbor. *Tone's* scouting plane signaled "Enemy fleet not in Lahaina Anchorage."

Fuchida, leaning out of the canopy, raised his signal pistol. His finger pulled the trigger and the "Black Dragon" signal flashed in the air. Immediately the dive bombers climbed to 12,000 feet, the level bombers dropped just below the clouds, while the torpedo planes plummeted down until they were barely clearing obstructions on the ground. When the fighters failed to respond to the "surprise achieved" signal, Fuchida fired a second shot. This alerted them but confused the dive bombers which took it to mean "no surprise." As a result they dived into their attacks when they should have followed the torpedo plane assaults.

The attack force was now flashing over the lush green fields of Oahu. Through his binoculars Fuchida could see the battleships and cruisers moored in Pearl. He counted carefully. The big ones were there all right. Turning to his radioman he ordered the attack to begin.

Immediately the code signal flashed through the air.

"To, To, To. . . ."

It was 0749.

Washington's frantic morning by this time had run its course. Like men afflicted with mass hypnosis, the chiefs of the government, of the Army and Navy, sat in muddled chaos waiting for the blow to fall.

The one o'clock deadline had come and gone. Still the clock ticked off the fateful minutes. Ambassador Nomura's request for a one o'clock appointment with the Secretary of State had been amended to 1:45 P.M. Secretary of War Stimson went home to lunch; Knox, the Secretary of the Navy, to his office in the Navy Department.

General Marshall and Admiral Stark waited in their respective headquarters for some break in the ominous maze in which they found themselves entrapped. Marshall's belated warning message sent by the slowest means as proved by circumstances was even then en route to General Short from the RCA offices in downtown Honolulu in the dispatch bag of a motorcycle messenger boy—a loyal young American of Japanese descent.

President Roosevelt had shut himself off from the world in the White House where he was alone with his stamp collection.

At Pearl Harbor thousands of Americans were now unknowingly in the center of the bullseye.

The blow fell with the blood showering smash of a meat cleaver.

At five minutes until eight o'clock Sunday morning, the long runways at Hickam Field seemed deserted of humankind, only the fat bellied B-18 bombers left clustered together while lone sentinels walked their anti-sabotage alert.

Up in the middle of Oahu at Wheeler Field, the more modern pursuit planes were likewise grouped in neat coveys while bored sentries watched the growing sunlight shifting over the multi-colored greens of the overhanging Waianae mountains to the west.

Ford Island in the center of Pearl Harbor had the great PBY flyingboats of the fleet, drawn up on the base concrete shore ramps in sleepy weekend respite from their long patrols. Overall hung the American spirit of relaxation and enjoyment which marks the lazy weekend hours.

The clatter of mess gear could be heard from the kitchens and dining halls. Plans were for fishing and golf and swimming—and with the hour for religious service near— many thoughts were of home. For a moment the stiff discipline of the armed services mellowed. It was that kind of a day.

Then in the swift arcing fall of one bomb from the first plunging warplane with the ugly red spots on its wings, the quiet of serenity vomited upwards into a thunderous inferno of destruction. Men at the mess tables turned staring skyward in disbelief then ran scurrying like rats for their posts of duty.

On the great ships lying in the placid waters at Pearl, the first warning of battle did not reach into their innermost parts for a few moments. Then to the harsh clangor of alarms ringing through their steel corridors, and the voices of the "talkers," their crews responded.

"All hands, general quarters! Air raid! This is not drill! All hands, general quarters! Air raid! This is not drill!"

The first rattling rounds cleared the barrels of the .50-caliber and three-inch guns. In another moment could be heard the heavy pound, pound of the five-inchers. Wicked looking splotches of high explosive detonations began to checkerboard the skies from Diamond Head to Barbers Point.

Communications officers and men were furiously shrilling out the news.

From the spider-legged platform of the signal tower high above Pearl Harbor the word flashed out: "Air Raid Pearl Harbor X This is no drill"

Admiral Kimmel was still receiving reports on the *Ward*'s sinking of the midget two-man submarine when the Japanese talons ripped into the fleet and the fortress. He stepped out of his quarters to see the first torpedo run on the battleships across the channel. The antiaircraft guns of the fleet were throwing up a tremendous fire above the harbor.

General Short, his face set in grimness, hurried to the old headquarters at the head of the Shafter parade ground from where he ordered Alert No. 3 into effect. This started the 24th and 25th Divisions deploying into their battle positions. The field artillery began drawing ammunition and moving units of fire to the guns. Portions of the seacoast artillery and antiaircraft command were already in action against the Japanese planes.

High in the air above Pearl, Commander Fuchida had unleashed his vultures on the unready foe below. Lieutenant Commander Takahashi already had screamed his dive bombers down on the runways of Hickam and Ford Island while Lieutenant Sakamoto plummeted his planes down on the long lines of fighters at Wheeler Field. Great fires were burning and the cries of the wounded were smothered in gigantic clouds of smoke and flame.

Already the Americans were fighting back as best they could. Machineguns spit hard at the Japanese strafing from treetop level at Wheeler and Hickam fields.

Now the hard months of training of the Japanese torpedo plane crews were coming into fruit. Lieutenant Commander Murata, who had swung wide to the southeast towards Honolulu, brought his torpedo planes low over the roofs of the already burning hangars at Hickam. There was a sharp wingover before the deadly craft, swooping in down over the submarine base, launched their fish into the calm waters of Pearl Harbor.

Meanwhile another group was bombing and strafing at the Kaneohe Naval Air Station and the Army's Bellows Field on the eastern shore of Oahu.

Fuchida, watching the devil's work unfold below, now led the level bomber group in the path of the torpedo planes around the western shore. Through his glasses the battleships still appeared to be sleeping. The surprise of the attack was assured.

He ordered the code word sent *Akagi.*

"Tora . . . Tora . . . Tora"

The Japanese word for "tiger" split the ether in all directions. Not only the tensely waiting officers in *Akagi* got the flash, but through some freak of transmission, it was picked up by the flagship of the combined fleet, the *Nagato* in Hashirajima anchorage. Now both Admirals Nagumo and Yamamoto could know the glorious news!

It was time for Fuchida to lead the bombers in. There lay the American base, spread out below him in all its detail, just as it lay spread out for Genda and him on the mock-up in *Akagi*. Real waterspouts were now rising alongside real battleships. The raiders were getting in their deadly work.

The commander's plane banked sharply to the left. Soon all ten squadrons of the formation tailed into the long column of death. The level bombers now would make their run. It was 0805—barely ten death-filled minutes since the first bomb had burst into orange flame on Hickam Field.

The air was rocking with antiaircraft fire. No longer did the battleships seem asleep. Some of the Japanese bombers were torn by fragments. The planes held to their run. Clouds streamed past below between the lead squadron and its target. It had to wing out over Honolulu for a second try.

But others had better luck. A tremendous explosion occurred at the inshore end of the row of battleships followed by a fountain of flame and smoke a thousand feet high. It was the death stroke of the battleship *Arizona*. Already hit by an aerial torpedo and seven bombs, the heavy ship then suffered the frightful misfortune of having a 1,763-pound bomb plunge through her deck to flash off her main magazines. She erupted like a volcano.

Huge pillars of smoke were billowing up from Pearl to mark the death pyre. Fuchida's formation made its turn, coming back to attack the battleship *Maryland* lying inshore of the ill-fated *Oklahoma*. From watching his bombs fall home, he turned to a close inspection of the damage done by his initial stroke.

Battleships *West Virginia, Oklahoma, Arizona, Maryland, California* and *Tennessee* were hit and burning. *Nevada* was underway attempting to escape the fate of her sisters while the fleet flagship *Pennsylvania*, cradled with two destroyers in the mammoth drydock, was giving battle from her exposed position.

West of Ford Island the target vessel *Utah* and the light cruiser *Raleigh* had sustained torpedo hits. Light cruisers *Helena* and *Honolulu* in the navy yard repair basin were also hurt. Destroyers as well as the capsized *Oglala* were sinking or damaged.

On the runways of the flying fields, burning debris scattered out in all directions. Some planes had taken off to offer combat but for the most part they had been shot down out of hand.

The attack was indeed a success.

The disbelief and astonished shock of Hawaii's half-million people centered on their radio sets.

"Civilians must get off the streets and stay off the telephone. All military and naval personnel are ordered to report to their posts immediately."

Out went the Army's orders to the radio stations which were now broadcasting intermittently.

"Oahu is under sporadic air attack. The attacking planes have been identified as Japanese."

This was the bare framework of the announcement which marked the end of one era and the beginning of a new.

In downtown Honolulu the Army-Navy counterespionage nets, the FBI and the police began to round-up known Japanese agents, Kita was caught in his consulate burning his papers. But most of them had gone up in flame by the time the officers arrived.

High above the noise of battle and confusion, Fuchida dispatched the last of his first wave back to their carriers to re-arm and await orders. He had lost five torpedo planes, three fighters and one dive bomber. The surprise had been bought cheaply. Now he could wait with professional calm for Lieutenant Commander Shimazaki to lead in the second wave of 167 aircraft.

Below him the battleship *Oklahoma* had capsized trapping hundreds of her crew in her topsy turvy decks. *Arizona* was a blasted burning hulk with 1,102 officers and men entombed in her flaming wreckage. *California* was hidden in black smoke from blazing oil. *Tennessee*'s crew was fighting fire. *West Virginia* was sunk with *Maryland* hit and damaged. *Utah* was bottom up with 58 crewmen inside. The destroyer *Shaw* had exploded in her floating drydock in one great skyrocket burst of flaming destruction.

Shimazaki crossed Kahuhu Point at 0840 just as the last elements of the first wave were leaving the island. Fighters, dive bombers and high level bombers, they began their carrion's work at 0854, bombing and strafing those targets left to them by the first attackers. Fire from the ground and the ships was very heavy now, making it more difficult for the Japanese to thread their way in to their victims. Cruisers and destroyers got more attention. The battleship *Nevada*, making a gallant effort to clear for the open sea, was finally bracketed with five bombs. When she could proceed no farther without danger of her sinking and blocking the channel entrance, she was run aground on the beach opposite Hospital Point.

By 1000, their work of destruction completed, the raiders turned back for their carriers. Fuchida took one last look at the burning ships and airfields. Four battleships sunk, four damaged, cruisers and destroyers hit, scores of planes destroyed—the American Pacific Fleet immobilized.

Japanese losses: twenty more planes in the second wave for a total of twenty-nine. A sad price, but a cheap one.

Fuchida went over and over his impressions of the damage during his return flight. When he bounced down on *Akagi's* rolling flight deck, he went immediately to where Nagumo awaited him on the bridge.

The air commander saluted and reported the staggering success. He asked permission to lead in another attack.

By 0900 order was coming out of chaos in the Army's command system as it was coming out of the confusion in the actual areas under fire. The city of Honolulu was reacting well and bravely. There was no panic. Military orders were being obeyed promptly. Pearl Harbor and the posts around the island were fighting back with everything they had.

Gone now was all concern about security of the trans-

Pacific telephone. Short talked twice with Marshall while Fielder talked with Miles, War Department G-2.

Pearl Harbor had given immediate notice and battle directions to all its small outlying bases and to the fighting ships at sea.

In the G-2 Section at the Army's Shafter headquarters, officers and men were settling into the routine of handling matters of great urgency in the matter-of-fact manner demanded by combat. War was now a fact.

This was underlined in many little things: by the dumping of pistols and .45-caliber ball ammunition on the floor of headquarters sections for all to have; by the lavish issue of scores of minor items previously hoarded lovingly by the quartermasters; by the gas masks and the 1918-style tin hats which magically appeared; by the sandbags which began to build up around Army and Navy installations.

At 0930 Mars made his bloody appearance in the Army's G-2 Section, with the casual entrance of a sergeant struggling with the heavy folds of a mass of greenish colored khaki. Bearing his burden with an anguished expression, the sergeant stood in an open space.

"Well, where do you want it?" he asked no one in particular.

Getting no reply he dumped his burden uncermoniously on the floor. The folds of green khaki fell open. A long, sticky stream of scarlet coursed slowly over the coarseness of the foreign cloth to spill out upon the floor.

"Jap aviator shot down over Fort Kam," the sergeant said, saluting the G-2. "We let nobody get their hands on the goddamn things. We brought them right to you."

"Good," Fielder replied. "Let's have a look."

From a sort of muzette bag, the same shade of khaki as the canvas flying gear, he drew forth a worn wallet. When it fell open a gasp of surprise went up from the watching officers. There on a crude map was Pearl Harbor with the outlines of the ships at their moorings. The pilot's course of attack was lined with solid red. What appeared to be an alternate plan was designated with a broken red line.

About the entire diagram were Japanese characters. The pilot evidently had done his best.

"Well, they knew exactly what they wanted," someone observed.

"And how to get to it," came the retort.

No one at this moment knew that a young American motorcycle messenger of Japanese descent lay pinned down by enemy fire on a highway close to Shafter. Neither the messenger nor any of the staff officers at the headquarters could know that in his dispatch bag lay General Marshall's "last chance" warning of impending war, a warning which now would not be placed in the hands of General Short until nearly noon.

There was no time at Pearl Harbor and Shafter for recrimination or regret. Now the concern was only for control and mitigation of the damage and preparation for subsequent assaults. Every action was predicated on the assumption that things would shortly get much worse.

Out there beyond the sea rim, most officers suspected, Japanese transports with their covering naval forces must be preparing for the big try. Oahu at the first grab!

About this time Washington added some remote control irony of its own.

"They say we have been authorized by the War Department to return hostile fire," one officer reported.

"My God! Don't they know by now the guns have been in action since before eight o'clock?"

If the out islands should fall—Maui, Hawaii, Kauai, Molokai, Lanai—and the great assault on Oahu should succeed, what then? The entire Pacific Coast from Alaska to Mexico would be laid wide open. Even now Japanese invasion formations might be en route to those hundreds of miles of undefended beach line.

Wounded, both military and civilian, were now pouring into hospitals in Honolulu and around the island. Volunteer surgical teams made up of Honolulu doctors were reporting for duty at the Army's Tripler General Hospital across the street from Fort Shafter. Queen's Hospital in downtown Honolulu was receiving the maimed bodies of men, women and children—many of them American Japanese—wounded or killed by enemy bombing or strafing, or worse by the explosion of American antiaircraft shells which, improperly fused, arced to their apex then plummeted back to shower city streets with their splinters of steel.

At Wahiawa near Wheeler Field the Japanese pilots amused themselves with spraying the village streets with machinegun fire. One flier, becoming too eager, misjudged and crashed into a roof, setting fire to two houses. The pilot was cremated in the flames.

The buff colored consulate on Nuuanu was the scene of a strange drama played out against the discord and noise of aerial bombardment.

Burning secret papers in an overturned washtub, Consul General Kita, his vice consul Okuda and an aide were snatching documents and files out of the consulate safes for the fire when FBI agents and police flung in upon them. One of the Japanese cursed the intruders, but things went quietly after the officers took over.

Kita calmly told his captors he knew nothing of what was going on. "I thought the bombing was maneuvers by the United States," he said. "I was lazy this morning and didn't get up till late. I will have to reserve comment until I can find out what this is all about."

Okuda said he was even more surprised than his chief. Everyone was surprised.

Yoshikawa, the spy, said nothing as they all were hustled off to jail.

Troops in the field had been digging while the bombing and strafing went on around them. By 1000 the outlines of these field fortifications were appearing all around the island to bolster the fixed defenses.

In *Akagi*, flagship of the raiding squadron, debate raged on the bridge. Should another strike be launched at burning Pearl or should the formation turn and run for home? Fuchida and Genda held for another attack. There were many targets left they said. But now caution was reacting to the reckless cunning which had flown off the planes at dawn. Nagumo stroked his chin and looked out at his fleet.

Was the stake worth the risk?

Part III

There is a tide in the affairs of men,
Which taken at the flood, leads on
to fortune.

—Shakespeare

10

The Lost Hours

FOR THE STRIKE FORCE COMMANDERS, NAGUMO AND HIS chief of staff, Kusaka, the first cheering words of the long night and early morning had been the radioed message: "To-To-To!" the first syllable of the Japanese word "Charge!" sent by the air commander Fuchida at 0749. Shortly after, Fuchida sent them an even more heartening message: "Tora! Tora! Tora!" for "Tiger! Tiger! Tiger!" the code word chosen to report complete surprise of the enemy.

So to the great relief of the two admirals and Commander Genda, who had plotted the main plan of the operation, it had been known since as early as a little after 0800 that a very great victory was in the making. Each bit of detail overheard by *Akagi*'s radio operators, or reported to the flagship, added to the picture of great battleships capsized or sinking in flame and explosion, of aircraft burning or shot to pieces on airfields with their hangars ravaged by fire and bomb.

There was also evidence that other than the quick response of American antiaircraft guns, there had been relatively light airborne opposition from enemy army or navy planes.

The great successes reported by Japanese torpedo planes and bombers had done much to dispel some of the gloom of the early hours when it had become certain that none of the large American aircraft carriers were in Pearl.

Rapidly preparations for a third attack were begun on each of the six carriers, the planes being refueled and rearmed.

Arguments for successive attacks followed fast, led by Genda who urged Nagumo to launch a third strike to destroy the great bases and any other targets which had escaped the first two onslaughts.

The need for a third attack was being argued with some heat on the bridge of *Akagi* when Fuchida's plane jerked to a stop on the flight deck. He was immediately summoned by the admiral for his report.

The keen-eyed Fuchida faced the stocky admiral flanked by his imposing chief of staff.

"Four battleships definitely sunk," he said. "One sank instantly, another capsized, the other two settled to the bottom of the bay and may have capsized. Four battleships damaged."

A pleased Nagumo broke into his report.

"We may then conclude that anticipated results have been achieved."

Fuchida moved on to detail damage at airfields and air bases. He concluded: "All things considered we have achieved a great amount of destruction, but it would be unwise to assume that we have destroyed everything. There are still many targets remaining which should be hit. Therefore I recommend that another attack be launched."

Three vital targets still untouched by the morning raids included the Pearl Harbor tank farm holding 4,500,000 barrels of oil to fuel the fleet, the invaluable machine and tool shops for servicing and repairing the ships and planes, and the submarine base from which the first attacks on Japan itself would eventually be launched.

The volatile Genda entered the debate arguing that the two big carriers, which were known to be in the Hawaiian area, should be hunted down and destroyed.

A staff officer pointed out that the fleet tankers had already withdrawn to a prearranged refueling point on the return course to Japan.

From the second carrier division a blinkered message to *Akagi*, from Rear Admiral Tamon Yamaguchi advised Nagumo he should launch a third attack wave at once, signaling his carriers the *Soryu* and *Hiryu* were ready and standing by:

"All is ready for another attack."

Still Nagumo and Kusaka were hesitant. The attack had succeeded beyond their dreams. The strike commander was tired after the long nervous night and the traumatic morning hours. His chief of staff gave no support to another attack. He held great fears of a land based aerial counterattack although his own flying officers felt this was not within the capabilities of the wrecked American air forces.

Aboard the combined fleet flagship *Nagato* at Hashirajima off Kure in the Inland Sea, Yamamoto, the only man who could have changed the course of events that fateful afternoon, would not act, leaving the decisions to the man on the spot, Nagumo.

Yet he had grim premonition that Nagumo had had enough.

In *Akagi*, Nagumo looked to his chief of staff Kusaka for counsel.

"We should retire as planned," Kusaka advised.

When an air officer interposed, Kusaka spoke firmly: "There will be no more attacks of any kind."

With those words Japan was committed to four long years of agony. The greatest sea battle of history, Midway, would be fought and lost by the Japanese with their main objective that of bringing their big carriers to the spot where they now were that critical Sunday afternoon. Later Nagumo outlined his reasons for withdrawal in a short memorandum he left as justification for his decision:

1. The first attack had inflicted practically all the damage that we had anticipated, and a further attack could not have been expected to augment this damage to any great extent.

2. Even in the first attack, the enemy's antiaircraft fire reaction had been so prompt as virtually to nullify the advantage of surprise. In a further attack, it had to be expected that our losses would increase out of all proportion to the results achievable.

3. Radio intercepts indicated that the enemy still had at least 50 large-type aircraft in operational condition, and at the same time the whereabouts and activities of his carriers, heavy cruisers, and submarines were unknown.

4. To remain within attack range of enemy land-based planes was distinctly to our disadvantage, especially in view of the limited range (250 miles) of our own air searches and the undependability of our submarine patrol then operating in the Hawaiian area.

The strike itself had been immensely successful. By 12 NOON all planes had returned to their carriers except for those lost: 9 fighters, 15 dive bombers, 5 torpedo planes, out of a total of 353 aircraft. Fifty-five officers and men were missing.

By contrast all of the eight battleships of the U.S. Pacific Fleet had been sunk, or damaged. Nagumo's intelligence listed *Arizona, California* and *West Virginia* sunk; *Oklahoma* capsized; *Maryland, Nevada, Pennsylvania* and *Tennessee* damaged. Sunk were the minelayer *Oglalla,* one-time flagship of the fleet's mineforce, and the target ship *Utah.* Other ships damaged included the light cruisers *Helena, Honolulu* and *Raleigh,* the destroyers *Cassin, Downes* and

Shaw, the repair ship *Vestal* and the seaplane tender *Curtiss*.

Scores of American aircraft had been destroyed and although the officers, compiling the results at the reporting table set up on *Akagi's* flight deck on which the outline of Oahu was boldly chalked, could not know it, 2,403 American servicemen had been killed and 1,143 wounded.

But still the flying officers persisted. They wanted the American carriers. Fuchida contended another air strike would draw them in to defend where they could be dealt the same devastating blows that had sunk the battleships.

It was to no avail. Nagumo and Kusaka were adamant. The decision had been made.

Kusaka turned to Nagumo. "I will order the signal to retire."

The force commander replied: "Please do."

At 1330 in the afternoon when there no longer was any chance of stray aircraft returning, a flag signal climbed to the yardarm of the flagship. It ordered the strike force to retire at full speed, course north northwest.

At the same hour the aircraft carrier USS *Enterprise* was approaching Oahu returning home from her plane delivery voyage to Wake Island. The other big carrier, USS *Lexington* with her escorting cruisers and destroyers, was some two days out of Pearl on her way with a plane delivery which had been scheduled for Midway that evening. Both, of course, were now available for immediate action in the Hawaiian area.

The third Pacific Fleet carrier, USS *Saratoga*, was in San Diego after refit. When she sailed west she was due to pick up two escorting destroyers from Pearl after she crossed the 150th meridian of longitude, so she was far from the scene of action.

Long after the war was over, Fleet Admiral Chester W. Nimitz who directed the cross Pacific assaults which ultimately defeated Japan, wrote: ". . . the consequences of the Japanese attack could very easily have been devastatingly greater.

"Had our commands received timely warnings of the approach of the enemy, there is no doubt in my mind whatever that our fleet would have been at sea maneuvering to intercept the attacking force and striving to bring about a fleet action.

"In such a case, our battle line—slower by at least two knots—could never have closed to ranges where we might have exploited our skill in gunnery. Our one old carrier probably would have been hopelessly overwhelmed by the six Japanese carriers that accompanied the attacking force. Our battleships and cruisers would have come under heavy air attack by greatly superior forces and might have been sunk in deep water with 100 percent loss of life. Our destroyers would have made heroic efforts to torpedo the enemy carriers, but with inadequate air cover, would have suffered great losses.

"Such an action probably would have occupied most of the day of December 7, 1941.

"Our forces ashore would have had ample information of the course of the battle at sea and could have taken steps to prepare for the blows to be expected the following day. Some of the Army Air Corps planes might even have joined the sea battle if the Japanese commander had chosen to accept battle within the range of Oahu's shore-based planes. Despite this, the greatly superior Japanese fleet could have returned on December 8 to complete the destruction of all American air strength and then, methodically and leisurely, proceeded to destroy the repair facilities of the naval base and to burn—with explosive machinegun fire—4,500,000 barrels of fuel oil stored in a completely exposed tank farm.

"What a shocking loss that would have been! The destruction of the repair facilities would have forced our Navy all the way back to the West Coast of the United States.

"The loss of that great fuel supply would have been well-nigh irreparable. The campaigns against the Japanese would have been so much delayed that they might have established themselves so strongly in the Western Pacific that years of effort would be needed for their expulsion.

"We might be fighting out there to this day! (December 7, 1958).

"What happened instead was perhaps the greatest boon and good luck to our Navy to come out of our misfortune at Pearl Harbor. Because we were caught by surprise, our fleet was in a relatively shallow port. This fact enabled us to salvage most of our outdated ships and greatly reduce the loss of our trained officers and men.

"Fortunately, too, for the Allied cause, a great underground bomb-proof fuel storage was nearing completion in the hills behind Pearl Harbor. Into this vast storage, rushed to completion in 1942, was dumped our precious reserve of fuel. This important storage—to this day, and for the predictable future—is perhaps our greatest strength factor in the Eastern Pacific. Atomic power may replace in a small way our dependence on petroleum fuels, but such will not be the case for many decades.

"Another such underground bomb-proof fuel storage in the Western Pacific—in Guam, which we control—would so strengthen American control of the Pacific for years to come that it is surprising that such is not now under construction.

"The object of the Japanese attack on Pearl Harbor was to inflict sufficient damage to our naval strength to give their navy a free hand to expand and consolidate its holdings. For this purpose, they could have chosen better targets at Pearl Harbor—the destruction of its fuel!

"The Japanese attack left our submarine base at Pearl virtually untouched. Its destruction by bombs would have been easy and it would have greatly hampered our most effective—and only—available weapon, our submarine force, which, incidentally, was the only force we had which could operate unsupported in Japanese waters from the earliest days of the war. The effectiveness of those submarines in cutting down Japanese naval strength and their merchant marine, is too well known to require retelling.

"Just why the Japanese Navy failed to complete the havoc and destruction at Pearl Harbor, which was easily in their power, must be left to another story.

"But the attack shocked our country out of its apathy about the World War already under way in Europe. All the arguments for and against entering the conflict ended and America, as one man, joined the fight against aggression.

"Can anyone doubt that, during those momentous years of World War II, an all-seeing Divine Providence was guiding and protecting our nation as, indeed, it had from the days of our Revolution?"

Nagumo led his victorious force back to Japan and a tumultuous welcome. On the return, Carrier Division 2 with the *Soryu* and *Hiryu* under command of the eager Admiral Yamaguchi, along with the heavy cruisers *Tone* and *Chikuma*, plus two destroyers, broke away from the strike force to help salvage the Japanese attack on Wake Island whose U.S. Marines had repelled the first invasion attempt on 11 December. Beset with all this added might, Wake had to haul down its colors on 23 December.

In Tokyo, Nagumo and the leaders of the two attack waves, Fuchida and Shimazaki, reported on the operation to the Emperor.

But praise was not forthcoming from everyone.

Yamamoto's unpredictable operations officer, Captain Kuroshima, who had tried to get Yamamoto to order a third attack on Pearl, was particularly outspoken. He recommended to his chief that Nagumo be transferred to another command.

But Yamamoto refused on the grounds it would break Nagumo's spirit.

His refusal was to cost him dearly when Hawaii was again the ultimate target at the great sea fight at Midway Islands.

11

The Bloody Target

THE GUNS ABOUT THE ISLAND FELL SILENT WITH THE DIS-
appearance of the Japanese war planes from Oahu
skies. But they roused themselves at the slightest alarm so
that the occasional rumble of artillery punctuated the day
as the morning wore on into afternoon. The staccato chatter of small arms fire would break out from time to time in
various sections of the city as if in warning of what was to
come.

In army headquarters at Fort Shafter the tempo increased with the cessation of actual attack. Now people—
and all the people were involved—had time to ponder and
to fear. The weary hours of listening to a radio which was
silent except for short messages given at long intervals,
were not easy ones.

And the messages. . . .

"Prepare your homes for blackout tonight. No lights
must be shown on penalty of arrest."

"Fill your bathtubs and all other receptacles with water
in case there should be a failure of the water supply."

"Provide flashlights for convenience in the blackout.

These flashlights should be blacked out with colored paper."

"Stay off the streets. No one is allowed to travel except on military business."

The hands of the clock crawled slowly around. Americans, heartsick over the disaster, fought flame and smoke to halt the destruction at Pearl and at the airfields. Doctors in every hospital were working over the operating tables. Hour after hour. There was no surcease.

Already the collection of the dead—more than twenty-four hundred—had begun but the orders were not to move the bodies until after nightfall. The island had held up bravely but there was a limit to what it might endure.

By ten o'clock Territorial Governor Joseph R. Poindexter had proclaimed a state of emergency. By afternoon martial law would be proclaimed and the Army would govern the territory.

Army and navy aircraft, what few were left, were hurriedly gotten into the air to commence searching both to the northwest and the southwest. But the Japanese surface squadron could not be found.

A flight of Army P-40s, which had been lucky enough to be weekending at the makeshift airstrip at Haleiwa on the north shore and consequently completely overlooked by the Japanese, got into the air to make a quick killing of the unwary intruders. But the damage of the second wave had already been done. Nothing anyone could do would undo the work of destruction.

With thousands of troops moving into the field, the intelligence section of army headquarters was a maelstrom of fact and rumor.

"Paratroopers are landing on Tantalus." Tantalus is a two-thousand-foot mountain rising behind Honolulu.

The officer on the telephone found this hard to believe but anything could be true.

"Are you sure?"

"They have blue coveralls with red discs on their shoulders."

So another alarm had to be run down by flying squads of soldiers and police.

After noon the calls increased.

"The Japanese are landing at Kawela Bay."

The officer on the phone knew that no military observation post had reported enemy surface craft off the northern shores.

"Are you certain of your information?"

The answer came back with pitying condescension. "Hell man, I can see the sunlight flashing on their bayonets!"

One by one the reports proved untrue. One by one the battle positions were filled with troops. Censorship of press, radio and mail was established. The mainland U.S. knew nothing of the terrible magnitude of the disaster at Pearl; Oahu but little more. Now a close curtain was to be drawn to keep the truth from the American people until their anger and sorrow had ebbed or had been diverted to other things. This blackout of the facts did not mislead the Japanese who had closely observed the damage and had a pictorial record of the action on motion picture film. It was better than anything the Americans could produce because it was taken from the air.

As dusk settled over Honolulu it seemed a city of the dead. No one was in the long silent streets except the gathering night. Not a light showed in the stony faces of buildings and stores. Outwardly there was no indication of the sorrow and anxiety which were seeping through the town like a deadly mist. Here or there would be joy as word came from some loved one, but in other homes there was nothing but the silence of suspense, hour after each terrible hour with each succeeding one grimmer than the one before.

It was now night. A black night damp with the promise of rain showers and warm with the breath of the enemy. Officers and men who had been at their duties without a break stood up to stretch. Some went out to chow. In the blacked-out dining room in the officers club at Fort Shafter, the commanding general and his chief of staff ate a quick meal. Short's usually ruddy face was even redder with the strain of the day, but no emotion showed.

Here was a man whose life had been built to fit him to grapple with and overcome great crisis. Now that crisis had burst upon him to find him trapped. Time was ashes in his mouth. There would be no second chance.

A major and a captain talked while they ate their first food in eleven hours.

"How's your wife and family?"

"I don't know," the major replied. "They are going up into that big tunnel the quartermaster has back in the hill. I'm afraid they're in for one hell of a night."

The sound of machinegun fire came into the room but no one took notice.

"I expect we all are," the captain said. His voice became sterner. "What do you really think the chances are? Do you think the Jap fleet is out there with their transports?"

"They sure as hell ought to be," the major answered. "But you never can tell. The hottest spots in my opinion are the outside islands. Take Kauai with that long runway at Barking Sands. One Jap heavy cruiser with a battalion of marines could seize the place in a flash. Same thing goes for Hawaii or Maui."

He caught the flash of concern on his companion's face. "Sorry, didn't mean to upset you."

"It figures," the captain, who came from Kauai, said bitterly, "and not a damn thing we could do about it."

"Not much," the major admitted. "I understand they had hoped to get some B-17s in from the West Coast tonight but now I hear that the weather is unfavorable and the enemy danger too great. You heard that a flight of twelve crash-landed all around the island in the middle of the Japanese attack this morning?"

"I heard something but I wasn't sure it wasn't another rumor."

"No, it's true enough. They came in from Hamilton Field

to land at Hickam. It was just as the Japanese were making their first attack. Our planes saw the smoke but they thought it came from burning sugar cane. Then when they called the Hickam control tower they got the word fast enough. One of them started to tangle with a Jap fighter but when a crewman shoved a camera out of the waist opening, the Japanese sheered off. You know they were sent down here with their guns in their bomb-bays. They were on their way to the Philippines."

"How did they make out? Did any of them get in safely?"

"I doubt if any of the planes came through undamaged, what with landing on golf courses, bombed runways and so forth. However some of the crews got down and are okay." His voice changed slightly. "Others however were not so lucky. I understand one bomber coming in to Hickam was followed right down by a Jap who shot him to pieces just as he was feeling for the runway."

"The bastards."

"Yes, the casualties are running very heavy. There were a considerable number of civilians killed."

"And if they try to come in tomorrow. . . ."

"There will be a lot more."

"What do you think the chances are?"

"If we get through tomorrow without getting the business, then we're going to have a little time to prepare— maybe days, maybe weeks."

"You think though that they're going to try?"

The major turned to him face on.

"If they don't they're fools. The Japanese will never get a better chance to take Hawaii."

One of the prime targets for Nagumo's strike force, the large fleet aircraft carrier *Enterprise,* was approximately 150 miles off Oahu approaching from the westward as the attackers were coming down from the north on Pearl Harbor that fateful Sunday morning.

The "Big E," as she was known even before she had left

her indelible mark on the great Pacific War, was returning to Pearl with the three heavy cruisers and nine destroyers of her task force, after delivering Marine Fighting Squadron 211 with their Grumman F4F Wildcat fighters to a fly-off point for Wake Island. Now on 7 December shortly after 0600 she was preparing to launch her own Dauntless SBDs of Scouting Six for Ford Island in the middle of the huge naval base.

Her first planes would arrive off Oahu about 0820 with the rest of the flight following on in. The ships of the task force were still eight hours steaming time from Pearl when the operations began.

Commanding the task force was Vice Admiral William F. Halsey with Captain George D. Murray in command of the Big E.

Leading plane off the flight deck was that of the carrier's air group Commander Brigham Young, closely followed by his wingman. It was an uneventful flight until when closing Oahu, Young noticed a covey of planes above the Marine Corps air station at Ewa. Puzzled by black puffs of antiaircraft fire over Pearl Harbor itself and the planes circling the air station, Young received a shock when he came under fire from a Japanese Zero fighter.

The two SBDs took violent evasive action and moments later the dive bombers landed safely at Ford Island. Some minutes afterwards other SBDs from Scouting Six followed them in. But not all.

A number of the planes were shot down, their pilots and gunners killed.

First hint of disaster came out of the Big E's speakers when a voice call was picked up from pilot Ensign Manuel Gonzales somewhere west of Oahu urgently pleading: "Please don't shoot! This is an American plane." There was a pause. Then: "We're on fire. Bail out!" Gonzales and his gunner were never heard from again.

Next over the radios came the calm voice of Lieutenant Earl Gallaher, Scounting Six executive officer: "Pearl is under attack by enemy planes! May be Jap planes."

At 0812 came a message from the Fleet: "Pearl Harbor is being attacked by enemy planes X This is no drill." This was followed at 0823:

From: CINCPAC
To: All ships present
Alert X Japanese planes attacking Pearl and air fields on Oahu.

Then again at 0903 from CINCPAC to all ships present: "Hostilities with Japan commenced with air raid on Pearl."

Finally at 0921:
From: CINCPAC
To : Task Forces 3-8-12
Rendezvous as CTF-8 directs X Further instructions when enemy located.

Meanwhile all ships able, were ordered to sortie from Pearl and rendezvous with Halsey, giving him command of all the forces at sea. These ships, an assortment of cruisers and destroyers escaping from Pearl, were designated Special Task Force One with Rear Admiral Milo Draemel in command.

At 1105 a signal hoist ran up to Enterprise's yardarm. "Prepare For Battle" Whereupon every ship in the force hoisted their largest national battle flags.

If Nagumo was not searching for the *Enterprise*, Halsey was hunting for him.

Torpedo planes and bombers stood ready for action while the combat air patrol searched the areas surrounding the task force.

Nothing.

Towards noon Halsey signaled Vice Admiral Wilson Brown, commander of Task Force 3 in the heavy cruiser *Indianapolis* with five minesweepers off Johnston Island to the south, setting up a rendezvous for the two task forces at 1330 Monday 8 December at latitude 22 degrees north and longitude 162 degrees west.

Lexington Task Force 12, which was part of Task Force 3, would conform to the rendezvous order to bring the two large American carriers together with their supporting heavy cruisers and destroyers, at a point some 140 to 150 miles due west of the Barking Sands on the island of Kauai. This was some 330 miles south and west of where the Nagumo Force was then taking its attack planes back onto the decks of its six carriers that Sunday.

The proposed Monday American rendezvous would concentrate all the U.S. Navy's strength in the Hawaiian area including carriers *Enterprise* and *Lexington,* heavy cruisers, light cruisers and destroyers. With this force Halsey intended to seek out and give battle to the Japanese.

On the morning of 7 December at the time of Pearl Harbor's warning: "Air Raid Pearl Harbor X This Is No Drill," the second big Japanese prize, the giant carrier *Lexington,* was less than 400 miles southeast of Midway Islands, steaming towards her launching point from where 18 Marine scouting planes were to fly off for Midway.

But Pearl's distress signal cancelled all plans. The Marine planes were hurriedly returned to the hangar deck while the task force prepared for battle, reversing course back toward Oahu.

All searches during the day sighted nothing more than a solitary merchantman with a "K" on her stack, and flying a red burgee with a blue margin. Unhindered she was allowed to continue her perilous, lonely westward way. *Lexington,* her heavy cruisers and destroyers continued to drive southeast towards Halsey, her planes searching as they went. They found nothing.

On Ford Island the Big E's surviving scout bombers took off to search to the north. Same result, except for some oil slicks on a deserted sea.

Late in the afternoon an enemy force was reported

south of Oahu. Halsey ordered an air and sea strike but the searchers instead found American cruisers and destroyers out of Pearl, seeking to join up with Halsey. In the first night landing ever made on an American carrier by planes carrying live torpedoes, the strike force came back aboard. All but the fighters, which because of low fuel readings had to fly on into Pearl, and for some a fatal reception from the fleet- and shore-based antiaircraft guns.

In the chaotic hours of the first evening of the war, *Enterprise*, over boldly or not, was steaming with her cruisers and destroyers near Kaula Rock some fifty miles west southwest of the Barking Sands, closest American approach to the early morning launching point of the Nagumo force.

Of her squadrons, Bombing Six and Torpedo Six were safely aboard. Scouting Six had planes at Ford Island, Ewa and Kaneohe Naval Air Station. Fighting Six, less casualties lost over Pearl Harbor, was at Ford Island. *Enterprise* had lost at least four Wildcat fighters and five Dauntless dive bombers.

All unknowingly, the two main antagonists at the battle of Pearl Harbor, the Japanese carriers and one large American carrier, had tangled in air combat on the opening day of the war. It was an action which would be repeated many times in the days ahead.

All through Sunday night while *Enterprise* with her cruisers and destroyers maneuvered in the darkness awaiting dawn, Halsey considered the odds.

"Suppose that the enemy was located," he wrote later, "and suppose that I could intercept him: what then? A surface engagement was out of the question, since I had nothing but cruisers to oppose his heavy ships. In addition, we were perilously low on fuel; the *Enterprise* was down to 50 percent of her capacity, the cruisers to 30 percent, the destroyers to 20 percent. On the other hand, my few remaining planes might inflict some damage, and by the next forenoon the *Lexington*'s task force would reach a position from which her air group could support an attack. If only someone would give us the straight word!"

But there was to be no carrier battle developing out of the Pearl Harbor attack.

Near 1100 Monday morning dropping fuel gauges forced Halsey to order a return to Pearl. Entrance was made through the narrow channel just after nightfall. *Enterprise* then eased her cautious way into the harbor passing the battleship *Nevada*, run aground off Waipio Point. On she went slowly in the darkness picking her careful way.

It was a melancholy tour of destruction which could be felt and smelled rather than seen in the blackness. Finally the Big E was at her moorings and the night's tasks of refueling and restocking supplies began.

The nervous work was finished by 0315. Under a faint moon obscured by rain showers the fleet oiler *Neosho* got underway from alongside *Enterprise* at 0353 and other attending smaller craft cleared away. With her captain, executive officer, navigator and pilot on the bridge, the great carrier got underway from her F-9 berth at 0420. Five minutes later her assisting yard tugs cast off and she was in the stream.

With Captain Murray conning she eased slowly through the dark towards the channel. At 0556 she passed channel buoy No. 1 abeam to port, and at a speed of 20 knots she was in the open sea to begin the marvelous career which would make her the most famous fighting ship of the great Pacific War.

Several days later *Lexington* put into Pearl for the same replenishment.

So the two great American carriers which Yamamoto had hoped to destroy were again both at sea bearing the wrath which was to come.

With the approach of Monday dawn's first light, gunners in the artillery positions around Oahu checked their pieces to be sure the guns were ready. Machinegun crews fiddled nervously with belted ammunition. Infantrymen, who had not believed they would ever see a war in their lifetime, felt the edges of their bayonets, as if they could not really believe these crude blades of steel had been made for actual use.

All eyes were peering through the darkness, lying heavily on the water, now only faintly illumined by the dying moon.

Soldiers feeling the chill of the damp night were acutely aware of all the small things which would have passed without notice twenty-four hours before—the sound of the wind in the trees, the beat of the surf, the night smell of the mountains and the rain, the chattering of the waking birds. All of these things which before had held no meaning now became important of themselves. It was good to stretch, to wiggle toes into the warmness of socks. It was good to be living.

The false dawn came and passed. Planes droned nervously unseen above the overcast. The first light began to spread. Then with the suddenness of the Hawaiian sunrise, the fingers of the day commenced to chase the shadows out of the hills and valleys. The vast horizon of the sea began to reveal itself until finally it stretched outward to the bulging of the earth line. Men searched the sea and sky and waited.

There was nothing.

As the brightening minutes swept by it became apparent there would be no fighting on the beaches that morning. The tension temporarily eased; one first sergeant sent his charges tumbling to hard labor.

"We can't all be actors in this drama," he told his men. "Somebody has got to build the props."

So the sandbag building began. Around gun positions, command posts, observation posts and strong points, the bags began to rise. Along the shores, sandy or rugged with slabs of lava rock, the nasty-pointed barbed wire began to string its way. Camouflage nets went up. And hour after hour the ammunition rolled into the positions.

Infantry, artillery, anti-aircraft, ordnance, quarter-master, engineers, signals, medical corps—all the myriad sections of the ground army pushed their alloted tasks. All with the expectation that before the sun sank again, the Japanese heavy ships would be blasting these positions with shells of great caliber all the way down to the stinging fire of the smaller guns. But first must come the planes. So all the morning eyes stared skyward and seaward for the first tell-tale aircraft bringing its message of the fury to come.

One by one, the 19th, 21st, 27th and 35th Infantry Regiments of the Regular Army, and the 298th Infantry Regiment of the Hawaii National Guard, reported their field fortifications strengthening hourly. Generals Murray and Wilson, commanding the 24th and 25th Divisions, told Short they would give the Japs a bloody time if they hit the beaches now. General Burgin had the seacoast and antiaircraft gunners standing to their armament. The ground army was as ready as it could be. Now all it could do was dig and wait.

For the air, it was a different matter. Long before first light the airmen had sent patched-up planes of all types racing in takeoff down the littered, blood-soaked runways. If the Jap was coming back he would not find them on the ground a second time. In pitifully small numbers, army and navy, they ranged into the black morning air searching for an enemy they could not find. The airfields themselves began the noisome job of salvage, picking through the charred water-flooded remains of planes, guns and men.

"Look at that," one pilot at Hickam pointed to a score of planes inside a blasted hangar, "cooked like a bunch of fried trout."

And indeed they were.

Far out over the Islands ranged the American planes, north, east, south and west. But no enemy could they find. This proved little, however, for the ocean expanse was so vast and the planes in the air so few, that flotillas of ships could have been steaming steadily on to Hawaii without being discovered.

Still nothing happened.

In mid-morning the Army G-2 sent one of his captains on a mission to Pearl Harbor. It was then the captain, who had sat in the nest of army command communications throughout the night, began to see the physical aspects of the defense. His car passed a tank drawn up under trees in front of a small house, the tank men busily perfecting the camouflage above their ponderous weapon.

Machineguns poked their snouts down ugly fire-lanes hastily cut through the thickly growing cane. Infantry outposts showed here and there on the hillsides. Signal Corps wire trailed its way along the highway. Through all the lush landscape of palms, monkeypod and cane, the suntan sinews of the army had interlaced themselves, braced for the shock of threatened onslaught.

The car turned a sharp curve in the highway to give the captain his first distant view of Pearl Harbor. He gasped as if he had been punched in the belly. There, over the waving tips of the cane, he could see the fighting-tops of the battleships, lurched drunkenly from their disciplined vertical positions as the hulls beneath them had settled into the turbid waters of the harbor. Shocked by the weird appearance of the mastheads, he waited with tense expectancy for a view of the ships themselves.

Another turn of the highway and the hulls were in sight, only for some of the great ships, they were not there. *Oklahoma* lay mastheads deep in the muck of the harbor, her whale-like bottom turned indecently to the sky. Water lapped over the main deck of *West Virginia* while *Arizona* lay astern, a crumpled wreck of torn steel. *California*, scorched and burned, rested on the bottom at her moorings, with *Tennessee* and *Maryland*, scarred with the violence of the assault, mute and helpless at their inshore berths which had protected them from the full fury of the torpedoes.

The captain gaped in disbelief. Inside the main gate, the

navy yard was filled with strangely silent activity. Men were methodically picking at the wreckage, an atmosphere of nightmare enshrouding their efforts. The great naval base was one vast morgue. Americans working dazedly through the destruction, averted their eyes from one another. It was a shameful thing. A disgrace. It should not have happened. Yet there it was.

In Washington, the blame for the attack was being placed, and rightly, on the duplicity and treachery of the Japanese nation.

The blame for failure to repel or destroy the attackers before they had wrecked the fleet was being prepared as the eternal burden of Admiral Kimmel and General Short. No outward sign was given that the attack had not been the complete surprise it was held out to be. No sign was given that the commanders at Hawaii had never received clear orders to get to their battle stations. No sign was given that the Japanese had unwittingly revealed to the American top command their plans and that the simple deductions to be drawn from those revelations had been denied the commanders charged with defending the United States' most important military and naval base.

No, the blame for the disaster was conveniently shrouded in obscure denunciations of the enemy and in the ruthless dismissal of the field commanders while the real facts were covertly consigned to the dump heap of history.

In addition it was becoming apparent that the Japanese had made a great mistake at Pearl in not destroying the shore installations as well as the ships and planes. This talk had the cheerful effect of making the whole affair seem not quite such the total disaster that it was. It even implied some sort of reverse intelligence on the part of the Americans in this negative misjudgment by the enemy.

The truth however, was told straight out to the captain by a naval commander while they were inspecting the burned out hulks of the battle line from a small boat in the middle of Pearl Harbor.

"We will win in the end," the grim-faced officer promised, "but this will add at least a year to the war. It should not have happened."

The captain returned to Fort Shafter proud of the many-storied acts of bravery displayed in the fleet and the yard on that awful Sunday, but heartsick at the death and destruction which had been wrought.

What he could not know was that in spite of Roosevelt's claim that the attack was a surprise, the United States of America would never again be so forewarned of an impending hostile assault as it had been during the weeks, days and hours before the devastation fell upon Pearl Harbor.

12

The Storm's Edge

O AHU, SITE OF HONOLULU AND PRINCIPAL CENTER OF commerce in the Hawaiian Islands, is but one of six major islands in a chain which extends more than 1,500 miles to the northwest of the largest island, Hawaii. The islands in order of size are Hawaii, Maui, Oahu, Kauai, Molokai and Lanai. There are two relatively minor islands of Niihau and Kahoolawe, and scores of rocks, reefs and shoals terminating at Midway Islands and Kure, closest to Japan.

The major islands of the group have a coastline of almost a thousand miles, much of which is inaccessible except from the sea.

These "out islands," as they were termed, had long been seen by the U.S. Army and Navy as potential dangers to the military integrity of Oahu itself. But until the development of the airplane, naval force based on Pearl Harbor would preclude any aggressor from using them as bases from which to launch assaults against the main fortress of Oahu.

Development of longer ranged military aircraft heightened the potential of attack from airfields on the "out

153

islands" immensely. Because of costs involved, however, there was little could be done to strengthen the defense of these islands other than to provide a shield of protection by sea and air forces stationed on Oahu.

This problem had long been uppermost in the minds of army planners charged with the defense of Pearl Harbor, Oahu and the other major islands, with or without the aid of the U.S. fleet. So battle plans for Oahu were predicated on the absence of the fleet, granting an enemy unfettered freedom to hurl a seaborne invasion at the island.

To repel such a thrust, the Army had lavished War Department funds over the years to install 127 fixed coast artillery cannon of all sizes up to the largest firing 16-inch shell. In addition there were 211 antiaircraft guns plus more than 3,000 artillery pieces and automatic weapons for defense of the island's beaches. Fighter and bombardment aircraft were assigned for air defense operating off the main bases at Hickam and Wheeler fields. Air superiority over the island was essential for its retention in American hands.

Manning this mighty array were 35,000 soldiers organized in two infantry ground divisions, a separate coast artillery and antiaircraft command, plus all the quartermaster, engineer, signal, medical, transport and other units necessary to maintain the fighting capacity of the defense. The Hawaiian Air Force guarded the skies.

Chief of Staff of the Army, George Marshall, was fully justified when he advised President Roosevelt that: "The Island of Oahu, due to its fortification, its garrison, and its physical characteristics, is believed to be the strongest fortress in the world."

Its main mission, other than to hold the island for the United States, was to provide a safe base for the U.S. Pacific Fleet.

The two infantry divisions divided the island in halves with the 24th Infantry Division responsible for the North Sector with its initial operating headquarters at Schofield Barracks, and the 25th Infantry Division defending the

South Sector including Pearl Harbor and Honolulu, with its headquarters close to the island battle command post deep inside the shell of an ancient volcano, Aliamanu Crater.

Beach defenses were closely coordinated with the coast and antiaircraft artillery, while mobile infantry formations were held under centralized control in general reserve.

The coast artillery was a marvel of observation, communication and coordination of fire. Major fire control points included world famed Diamond Head with a multistoried maze of observation posts and operations rooms where intricate computations aimed to assure a direct hit on a ship with the first shot. Heavily protected by friendly aircraft, the big cannon were formidable weapons. Without air protection they would become extinct.

So even with the loss of a great portion of the fleet, Oahu still had many teeth.

Not so the out islands. Their defenses on 7 December 1941 consisted mainly of elements of the federalized 299th Infantry Regiment of the Hawaii National Guard.

The big island of Hawaii had the bulk of these troops stationed near the island's main city of Hilo with other units at Waimea and Kau in the north and south areas of the island.

Kauai had about six hundred troops at Mana at the Barking Sands, Hanapepe and Wailua while Maui had a lesser number. Molokai had an infantry company. Lanai and Niihau had no troops at all.

Considering the wide areas of mountainous terrain and long stretches of beaches they were charged with patrolling, even the islands with troops were virtually undefended. Hawaii, Maui and Kauai all had airfields, none with any real defenses. Lanai's short airstrip lay wide open.

A quick assault by a Japanese landing party would have been almost assured of a lodgment with an excellent chance, particularly on Kauai and Hawaii, of capturing an operational airfield.

Such a move would have forced the U.S. Army and Navy to attempt recapture of the ground with whatever air, sea and land elements were available.

As it did happen, the isolated island of Niihau was the site of a crash landing by a Japanese pilot early in the afternoon of 7 December when he brought his damaged fighter down on a rocky field.

Niihau, about twenty miles west of the island of Kauai, has been held by a single family since it was first purchased from the Hawaiian King Kamehameha IV in 1864. Maintained as a sanctuary for Hawaiians with no outside visitors allowed, on 7 December its people had no knowledge of what was taking place at Pearl Harbor.

Nevertheless, a Hawaiian who lived near the crash site disarmed the pilot and took his papers when he climbed from the plane. He then sent for two Japanese who lived on the island to act as interpreters. Through them the pilot admitted he had been in the attack on Pearl Harbor.

The islanders then placed him under guard to await the arrival of the weekly sampan from Kauai on Monday. When the sampan, Niihau's only link with the outside world, failed to arrive on schedule, the puzzled islanders waited.

By Friday with no sampan, a large bonfire visible to Kauai was set ablaze as an alarm signal. With time running out, the naval pilot persuaded one of the Japanese to help him escape. They removed two machineguns from the plane and set them up in the island's only village of Puuwai, threatening to kill everyone unless the pilot's papers were returned.

During the afternoon a 51-year-old Hawaiian, Benehakaka Kanahele, with the help of a fellow islander, crawled into the machinegun nest and removed the ammunition. After a night of terror on the island, the Japanese pilot, now armed with a pistol, and his accomplice in searching for the lost papers, captured Kanahele and his wife.

He then sent Kanahele looking for the first Hawaiian

who had taken his military papers, while holding Mrs. Kanahele as hostage for his return. But Kanahele, fearful for his wife's safety, made only a pretense at a search, quickly returning to his wife.

Waving a pistol at them, the Japanese flier threatened to kill the Kanaheles as an example to the islanders. Kanahele reached for the weapon but missed whereupon the flier shot him three times.

This was too much for the large Hawaiian who picked up the pilot and smashed his head against a stone wall, killing him instantly. Kanahele later said that he just "got mad."

All the while a boatload of islanders had rowed their way to Kauai taking sixteen hours to cross the stormy Kaulakahi Channel. They returned late Sunday on a U.S. Lighthouse Service tender along with an Army contingent of fourteen men led by a lieutenant of American-Japanese ancestry.

So the "Battle of Niihau" ended in an American victory, but a Japanese naval pilot had held U.S. territory under his control for almost a week.

It was a lesson not lost on those military officers charged with the defense of the Hawaiian Islands.

13

The Ripest Plums

O F ALL THE HAWAIIAN LANDS OPEN TO JAPANESE ATTACK that evil Sunday, the three areas most difficult to defend from a seaborne raid were the southern end of the Big Island of Hawaii and the north and west shores of the island of Kauai.

All of these areas are remote even on their own islands. All are accessible only by a single deadend road. On 7 December these roads were narrow two-lane surfaced highways, little traveled by visitors. All have terrain configurations which confine passage to the road corridors.

First plum was the southernmost tip of United States territory, formed by the outer flanks of the long, tall Mauna Loa volcano, one of the largest in the world.

Sloping south into the sea Mauna Loa enters the Pacific at Ka Lae or South Point, in the form of a bold, high plateau which falls away in a sharp cliff towering above a wild surf breaking on huge rocks far below. On top of the plateau which was sparsely inhabited by a few Hawaiian ranchers, there was a rudimentary airstrip used chiefly by planes of the Hawaiian Air Force commanded from Hickam Field on Oahu by Major General Frederick L.

Martin. No planes were stationed there, the strip being used mostly by B-18 twin-motored bombers on flights around the Big Island.

It served as an emergency landing strip for any plane in trouble south of Mauna Loa. Landings were tricky affairs, the planes approaching from the west in the teeth of the very strong trade wind blowing from the northeast. As the pilot approached the strip from the ocean, he had to set his plane down fast once it had cleared the edge of the escarpment to assure himself of enough length of field before he flew off the other side. The strip itself was bumpy but usable.

On 7 December 1941 Morse Field, as this primitive airstrip was known, was guarded by Company G of the 299th Infantry Regiment of the Hawaii National Guard. There was also a small detachment of the Air Force responsible for the air operations at the field.

The infantry company mustered about one hundred ten officers and men armed with the M1 rifle, light machineguns and 60 mm mortars. For the air detachment the Colt 45-caliber pistol was the main armament. Ammunition issue was approximately forty-five rounds per man.

These troops were housed near the runway on the plateau escarpment. To secure supplies other than by air involved a truck haul of some seventy miles from the island's main port of Hilo along the Hawaii belt road to the turnoff for South Point. The trucks then had another ten mile downhill run into the airfield area.

Nearest reinforcements in case of attack would have to be provided by rifle Company E in Hilo or by the heavy weapons Company H guarding the island's main airport at Hilo.

Company G and the Morse Field air detachment were in fact on their own.

Landings on the rocky beach below the escarpment could be effected by a determined enemy even in the face of fire from above. Attack on the airfield would then involve a difficult approach with the odds favoring the attackers if they had selected the best routes into the defensive position.

If surprise landings could be effected in darkness and the defending company be caught unawares, it would be even more difficult for Company G to protect the integrity of the airstrip or its own ability to survive.

So stood matters on the morning of 7 December on the southernmost military airstrip in the Hawaiian Islands.

Of little comfort was a 15 May 1941 memorandum from Lieutenant General Walter C. Short, commanding the army in Hawaii, to Lieutenant General Delos C. Emmons in the War Department for relay to the chief of staff, detailing a request for funds to prepare Morse Field as a base for two bombardment squadrons. This request rested in the War Department through the summer with no action forthcoming.

Some three hundred forty miles to the northwest there were two other ripe plums waiting to be plucked, both on the beautiful "garden island" of Kauai.

One of these was the long airstrip at Barking Sands made famous when it was used by the Australian Sir Charles Kingsford Smith on the first trans-Pacific flight from Oakland, California, to Brisbane, Australia. It was then mostly underdeveloped scrub grassland, flat and long enough to allow a heavily loaded aircraft to take off with some chance of getting into the air. It, however, provided a very long runway when there was nothing on Oahu to match it.

The beach itself affords easy landing areas with plenty of room both north and south. Across the Kaulakahi Channel is the island of Niihau where the only Japanese land seizure was made on 7 December but which, because of the isolation of the island, was not discovered for a week. National Guard troops of Company I of the 299th Infantry and a small Air Force detachment were stationed at Mana at Barking Sands on the morning of the attack. Another company of the 299th, M Company, was quartered in the armory in the small village of Hanapepe twenty miles down the island belt road to the southeast. One of this company's assignments was to protect the commercial airport, Burns Field, at Port Allen.

Like Morse Field on Hawaii, Barking Sands had been designated to the War Department as the future home base of two bombardment squadrons, but as at Morse Field, no work had gotten underway.

While both of these potential landing sites had the advantage of adjacent airstrips available for carrier plane use, there was still another possibility, but with no airstrip nearby. This was the wide-mouthed Hanalei Bay deeply inset into the north coast of Kauai.

There were no troops other than outpost patrols within twenty-five miles of Hanalei Village, these being provided by the 299th Regiment's 3rd Battalion Headquarters Detachment and Company C units stationed near Wailua on the eastern coast of the island. Their position was twenty-two miles from Hanapepe armory and M Company, and forty-two miles from Barking Sands and Company I, in those days hours away by car or truck.

Hanalei Bay had a fine sand beach at its head and was free and clear of obstacles. A landing party could expect to maintain its lodgment with little interference from anything but random aerial or surface bombardment for several days.

This time factor as at Morse Field and Barking Sands would be long enough to force the large American carriers to come to battle, for from the moment it became known that United States territory had been captured by a Japanese invading force there could be no holding back.

Of the three possible sites for an intrusion, Hanalei Bay perhaps held the greatest advantages because of its remoteness from any attacking troops. Although it had no airfield, it was possible to land float planes on the bay.

All three landing sites were exposed to ship bombardment as well as aerial attack, but this, of course, would be the object of the landing for no cruisers or destroyers could shell them without air cover, and that cover after the Pearl

Harbor attack would have to be provided mainly by the American carriers.

Well aware of the vulnerability of the outside islands to this type of attack, General Short's battle orders charged: "The District Commanders of Hawaii, Maui (includes Molokai) and Kauai Districts, assisted by the air corps detachments present within the districts, will:

"Defend the air fields against acts of sabotage, hostile attacks and maintain order in the civil community."

Short specifically commented on the exposure of the out islands in a review of defenses from air attack on 15 March 1941 when he wrote General Marshall:

"Plans have been made to provide gas and bombs at all emergency landing fields on outlying islands and for the stationing on Kauai, Maui and Hawaii of the battalions of the National Guard which came from these islands for the protection of the air fields from sabotage and small landing parties. Incidentally these battalions would serve to prevent local disorders. Unless there is an emergency these troops will not be sent to the other islands until the camp buildings for one company have been provided at each airfield. Part of each battalion can be quartered in existing Armories on these islands usually at some distance from the air field."

While these plans looked somewhat comfortable on paper, they were in fact pitifully inadequate. Troops and weapons assigned might possibly put up a creditable defense of the airfield perimeters themselves, but they could not in their understrength condition deny enemy landings nor enemy access to main island roads or centers of population.

From the Japanese viewpoint while all of the islands other than Oahu were vulnerable to landing attacks from the sea, their choice for an out island target would have eventually come down to the Big Island or Kauai.

Of these two, Kauai most certainly held forth the greater advantages.

It lay directly southward of the line of aerial attack by

Nagumo's big carriers as they came down on Oahu from the north, so any initial operation on Kauai could easily be supported by planes from the carriers.

Any submarines or surface craft involved would also be much closer to help from the Pearl Harbor attack force in case of need.

But most important, any lodgment on the island would necessitate retaliatory action by American forces including the carriers, pulling them north into the areas where they would be exposed to attacks from the Nagumo Force.

This would have brought the American carriers and the remaining cruisers and destroyers of the Pacific Fleet into the battle of decision which Yamamoto was to seek off Midway Islands six months later with the greatest sea armada ever assembled up to that time.

On 7–8 December, Nagumo could have forced this battle with a much greater margin for victory than in the Midway operation, saving Japan the certainty of the agonies of death and destruction of the next four years of the Pacific War.

What had happened?

14

Cocked Dice

IN WAR WHERE SO MUCH DEPENDS ON THE HAZARDS OF chance, a commander's plans must provide for all of the shifts or turns of fortune that can be foreseen or anticipated, so that workable options are provided for instant execution if victory is to be achieved. Above all the commander must not fall into the trap of self-delusion where his plans may be based on desirable but false assumptions.

So was it at Pearl Harbor for both attacker and attacked.

All great powers have plans of some sort for almost any situation they may be called upon to face within their spheres of interest.

In the development of the planning for the Pearl Harbor attack, this first surfaced when it was decided that there would be no land attack on Oahu in the course of the raid.

Support for such a landing action was voiced in the naval general staff with the proposal for an amphibious force to move against Oahu and seize the island and the naval base in connection with the air attack. But the deputy chief of naval staff, Vice Admiral Seiishi Ito, was opposed because he said there were no oilers or transports to spare for such a major effort.

Admiral Yamamoto concurred because the addition of such vessels would so expand and slow down the progress of the attack force that the element of surprise would be seriously imperiled.

Commander Genda who drafted the first plan has since said: "If the attack went well, I advocated that we land troops on the island of Oahu. We should then proceed to the California coast and spread demoralization by bombing installations there."

"After the Pearl Harbor attack I felt more than ever that we had to seek out the American aircraft carriers and sink them. I was in favor of heading for California or Midway. But our tankers had already withdrawn to a designated refueling position on the way home and we had to rendezvous with them."

Commander Fuchida who led the air attack on Pearl Harbor has written:

"Related to, but certainly less logical than the queries concerning Admiral Nagumo's decision to retire, is the speculation so frequently indulged in since the war as to why Japan did not seize Hawaii outright instead of merely delivering a hit-and-run attack on Pearl Harbor. In the first place, this speculation arises only because the Pearl Harbor attack turned out to be such an unexpectedly great success. At the time the attack was decided upon, we were by no means so confident of success; indeed we felt very much as if we were about to pull the eagle's tail feathers. Naturally nothing so ambitious as the conquest of Hawaii had even entered our calculations.

"Furthermore . . . the primary objective of our initial war strategy was to secure oil resources. The Pearl Harbor attack itself was conceived purely as a supporting operation toward that objective. As our military resources were limited and oil was our immediate goal, there was no reason at this stage to contemplate the seizure of Hawaiian territory.

"All in all, the Pearl Harbor operation did achieve its basic strategic objective of preventing the U.S. Pacific Fleet from interfering with Japanese operations in the south. But the failure to inflict any damage on the enemy carriers still weighed heavily on the minds of Admiral Nagumo's air staff and flying officers as the task force cruised back toward home waters. We immediately began laying plans for subsequent operations to achieve what we had been unable to accomplish at Pearl Harbor."

Above all the other prizes desired by the Japanese at Pearl Harbor were the large American aircraft carriers. There were three of them in the Pacific: *Enterprise* and *Lexington* in Hawaiian waters, and the third, the *Saratoga* out of immediate reach in San Diego on the American West Coast.

It would not have taken a major invasion effort against the island of Oahu to bring these carriers to battle. The temporary seizure of any Hawaiian soil would have forced them to attack the Japanese task force.

As a matter of historical record, Admiral Halsey in the *Enterprise* task force did come up on the island of Kauai on that fateful Sunday night of 7 December seeking out the Japanese. The *Lexington* force under Rear Admiral John Newton was flogging its way back at top speed to join Halsey off Kauai to do battle. *Saratoga*, a few days away on the Pacific Coast, would have come racing down on Hawaii in this hour of need, which indeed she did, bringing reinforcing aircraft to Oahu, arriving at Pearl on 15 December, eight days after the attack.

So the Japanese navy could have brought their enemy to bay if their plans had provided the options that were needed.

Why was this not done?

Primarily because in their planning the Japanese only envisaged an all-out attack on Oahu as an alternative option. They were, of course, correct in rejecting this as a practical course of action. Apparently, however, no thought at all was given to temporary seizure of other Hawaiian territory for use as bait to draw enemy counteraction.

Rather, this great striking force put to sea on the chance of destroying all American seapower in the Pacific while it lay peacefully unaware of its danger at Pearl Harbor. If by chance the American ships were not in Pearl Harbor, then the attack would be cancelled and the Nagumo force would reverse its course back across the Pacific.

So, faced with a "Go!" or "No Go!" decision, Nagumo ordered the run-in to begin, knowing the carriers were not there.

American defense plans for the Hawaiian Islands were in themselves flawed.

While Oahu with its heavy armament and its thousands of troops was as formidable as a peacetime America could make it, the out islands were in fact wide open to surprise attack from the sea with little or no counterforce available to the defenders once the aerial umbrella based on Oahu airfields had been shut down.

The requirement of the commanding general of the Hawaiian Department to his three out island district commanders to defend the airfields while maintaining order in the civilian communities was not within reach of their capabilities.

The outlying islands were defenseless on their own, so that any determined enemy, once Oahu had been shut down, could have landed almost anywhere he pleased.

If planners of the Japanese naval staff had but considered this problem they could have found means to deliver such an attack without compromising the surprise so necessary to the success of the primary mission of the Nagumo force.

The status of American defenses on the out islands could have been easily ascertained by any one of the many consular agents the Japanese maintained on these islands before the strike against Pearl Harbor. Undoubtedly the war and navy ministries already had this information as it would have been forwarded to them in the Honolulu consulate's reports to Tokyo, as a matter of course.

Positions of National Guard units on the out islands

were well known throughout these island communities as a matter of common knowledge so no special espionage effort would have been necessary to ascertain the status of the defenses.

If local intelligence was available to the Japanese Navy so also were the means of delivering a shore attack.

First option would have been the assignment of destroyer-transports to the Nagumo force, combat-loaded with units of the Special Naval Landing Forces, their mission to go ashore and capture American soil at Hanalei Bay or Barking Sands, or both.

These destroyer-transports were officially designated Patrol Boats 1 and 2, and 31 through 39. Patrol Boats 1 and 2 were actually the old destroyers *Shimakaze* and *Nadakaze* which had been drastically modified in late 1941 to convert them to fast transports. Originally constructed as twin-funneled fleet destroyers, their stern sections were raked down to the waterline and rebuilt to provide launching ramps for two 46-foot Daihatsu landing craft. Forward, the destroyers were completely remodeled so they could each transport and land 250 naval troops.

Of 1,390 tons displacement, they were 336½ feet long, 29 feet in the beam, with a 10 foot draft. Mounting three 4.7-inch and ten 25mm guns, they had a speed of 20 knots.

Patrol Boats 31 through 39 were also former destroyers but of a smaller size. Of 935 tons displacement, they were 280 feet in length and 26 feet in the beam. They had a draft of 8 feet. Raked down to provide a launching ramp at the stern, they each could transport and land 150 naval troops, carrying one Daihatsu landing craft for this purpose. They were armed with two 4.7-inch and eight 25mm guns, and had a speed of 18 knots.

Two of these transports, Patrol Boats 32 and 33, were purposely stranded on Wake Island in the second and successful attack which captured this American outpost on 23 December 1941. They had earlier on 11 December been a part of Rear Admiral Sadamichi Kajioka's original assault force repulsed by the tiny island, which had included the flagship light cruiser *Yubari*, six destroyers, and the two destroyer-transports, Patrol Boats 32 and 33 carrying a landing party of 560 sailors of the Special Naval Landing Forces.

This attack, three days after the Pearl Harbor raid, was repelled by the United States Marines defending the island. Holding their fire until the Japanese were within 4,500 yards, the Marines then opened with their 5-inch guns, scoring immediate hits on the *Yubari* and sinking a destroyer.

The shore guns then hit two more destroyers and one of the destroyer-transports. Kajioka called off the invasion attempt after 45 minutes of action when Marine Captain Henry Elrod, flying one of the few Grumman Wildcat fighters which had survived the four days of preparatory aerial bombardment which began on 7 December, dropped a 100-pound bomb directly on depth charges stored near the stern of the destroyer *Kisaragi*. The *Kisaragi* blew up with a tremendous explosion and sank with all hands.

Patrol Boats 32 and 33 returned in the second attack on Wake 23 December with Kajioka bringing an immensely stronger force beefed up by the aircraft carriers *Hiryu* and *Soryu* which had attacked Pearl Harbor on 7 December. He also had with him the two heavy cruisers *Chikuma* and *Tone* plus two destroyers of Nagumo's task force which were deflected from their return voyage to Japan with the carriers, to add the weight of their fire power to the Wake Island attack.

It came at 0200 in the morning of 23 December with the dive bombers from the Pearl Harbor attack carriers pounding the defenses of the little island into rubble. In the action the two destroyer-transports were purposely run aground on Wake's coral reefs to send their naval troops ashore. After hours of bitter fighting, Major James Devereux was forced to surrender with his Marines and some 1,200 civilian construction workers who had been strengthening the island's defenses.

The Daihatsu landing craft, carried by the destroyer-transports, were 46-foot long open boats with beach landing ramps enabling field guns to be wheeled onto the shore. The coxswain and engine were protected by bulletproof plating. With a beam of 11 feet and a 2½-foot draft, they could carry seventy fully equipped troops, one tank or 10 tons of cargo. Admirably suited for their work, they had a speed of 8 knots, were armed with two 7.7 mm or two 13 mm guns, and were manned by crews with long experience in landing operations beginning with the war in China in 1933.

The Special Naval Landing Forces were highly trained specialists in amphibious operations much like the U.S. Marines. Organized into rifle companies with supporting machinegun and mortar units, they also had field artillery and when the situation warranted, tanks and armored cars.

The destroyer-transports had been designed especially for them and their commando-type missions.

Hanalei Bay or Barking Sands on Kauai would have posed no unusual problems for them on 7 December or the following day, if they could have been delivered to the shore to effect their lodgment.

There still was another delivery system available to the Japanese Navy if the planning had provided for it.

This would have been by submarine.

Large I Class fleet submarines could have done the job. By removal of some of their torpedoes they could have been transformed into transport submarines with room for transporting detachments of the Special Naval Landing Force for special tasks on the north and west shores of Kauai.

The transfer of the naval troops into rubber assault boats would have entailed more difficulties than the landing craft transfer from the destroyer-transports, but it could have been effected easily in Hanalei Bay although the operation off Barking Sands would have depended on the state of the sea and surf at the time.

Such actual remodeling of two big I Class submarines was effected early in 1942 when I-71 and I-74 were modified by removal of their 4.7-inch guns and some torpedoes so they could perform as transport submarines carrying one 46-foot landing craft.

So a little more forethought in 1941 could have resulted in their use in actions which would have brought the U.S. Pacific Fleet carriers to battle on Japanese terms.

15

Calling the Shots

EVENTS ARE SHAPED BY MEN. FATE DETERMINES THEIR conclusion.

The Pearl Harbor drama illustrates this as a varied cast of characters take their places before the footlights of history.

First there was the creator and the impelling force behind the attack on Pearl Harbor.

Admiral Isoroku Yamamoto, commander in chief of the combined fleet, was cast in the Napoleonic mold. Of short and upright stature, he was a realist who brought a brilliant yet practical mind to the command structure of the Imperial Japanese Navy. Of aggressive, at times almost arrogant nature, he almost always had his way.

Opposed to war with America at the beginning, he planned and carried forward the Pearl Harbor operation. His mutilated hand a constant reminder of Japan's great naval victory of Tsushima, he was a faithful devotee to the memory of the great Admiral Heihachiro Togo and the proud traditions of the Imperial Navy.

If there were any faults in this commander, it may have been his inability to accept or consider other views, once he had made up his mind.

There is also the evidence that he was slow or unable to remove a commander even though that commander had accomplished less than might have been expected of him.

Next in the Pearl Harbor attack command chain was Vice Admiral Chuichi Nagumo, commander of the First Air Fleet, who would be the tactical commander of the strike force. A stocky, kindly man, he strangely enough was not an aviator but one of the Navy's top torpedo experts and ship handlers. Because aviation was not his specialty he placed great reliance on his staff.

Of a conservative nature, where Yamamoto was a gambler for high stakes, he at first had opposed Yamamoto's planned attack on the American fleet at Pearl Harbor. However, reluctant though he might be, he would do his duty with the strike force. How far that enthusiasm would carry was left to the future.

Nagumo's chief of staff was Rear Admiral Ryunosuke Kusaka. Although he too was not an aviator he had spent a lot of time with the air arm, having captained the carriers *Akagi* and *Hosho*, as well as the 24th Air Squadron based in Palau.

He was of robust, erect figure and possessed of rock hard will. Conservative and cautious, he was a skillful planner and fighter. He it was who had tried to talk Yamamoto into abandoning the Pearl Harbor operation.

Nagumo rested so much dependence on his judgment that Kusaka became his alter ego, the actual commander of the Pearl Harbor Strike Force.

Under the two admirals on the *Akagi*, served the two preeminent airmen, Commander Minoru Genda, aviation staff officer for the First Air Fleet, and Commander Mitsuo Fuchida, air commander of the strike forces air attack groups.

These two younger, hawk-faced men, the planner and the air leader, had none of the conservative approach to war of their two senior officers. They were the spearheads in the attempt to get Nagumo to hurl a third attack on Pearl Harbor, that fateful Sunday afternoon north of Oahu.

They had been involved in the planning and training for the Pearl attack almost from its inception.

Both airmen were highly disciplined Japanese naval officers, however, so were very conscious of the limits to which they could go in pressing their combat recommendations on the senior flag officers commanding the force.

The U.S. Pacific Fleet was commanded by a sturdy, energetic Admiral Husband E. Kimmel who regarded his major task the preparation of the fleet for war.

He had taken over command under rather unsettling circumstances in January of 1941 when the commander in chief of the fleet, Admiral James O. Richardson, had been summarily removed at the insistence of President Roosevelt because he did not agree with Roosevelt's decision to keep the fleet in Hawaii instead of on the Pacific Coast where Richardson felt training and preparation for war could be carried out far more effectively and efficiently.

Upon taking over command Kimmel had devoted himself to the reorganization and training of the fleet which, because of the uncertainty as to where it was to be based, was not ready for war. These pressing tasks in the course of events deflected the focus of attention of the fleet to the training tasks, rather than to the unseen dangers developing within the Japanese Empire some thirty-four hundred miles to the westward.

So Kimmel, an earnest hard-working admiral, depended heavily upon the Navy Department to keep him aware of perils developing beyond his ken.

During this time of building crisis he maintained a close relationship with the top army commander in Hawaii. That commander, Lieutenant General Walter C. Short, had assumed direction of the Hawaiian Department at about the same time Admiral Kimmel was taking over the fleet.

Short was a tall, ruddy faced soldier who, like Kimmel, was dissatisfied with the condition of the command he had been called upon to lead. He devoted his days to spurring on the training of his troops and the improvement of the materiel defenses of his command. Like Kimmel he was

restive under any restraints or requirements which inter-
fered. He relied completely upon the War Department and
the Navy to keep him alert to any outside threats which
might appear. And when he did receive such a warning he
misread it.

So for the Japanese a daring and unconventional attack
plan which was executed with superb skill failed to achieve
ultimate results because ultracautious leadership made no
effort at exploitation of a great success, and the very plan
itself failed to provide optional actions which would bring
its most desired targets into the bombing sights.

For the Americans the need to ever improve the quality
and performance of the sea and land commands dulled
the awareness necessary for the safety of the fleet and the
fortress.

If there were two reluctant admirals on the bridge of the
flagship *Akagi* that fateful Sunday afternoon, there was
another admiral who just could not wait to get at them.

Task Force 8 commanded by Admiral Halsey spent Sunday afternoon and night searching for the Japanese, with
plans for a rendezvous with all available American ships to
continue the hunt the following day.

So the two large American carriers, *Enterprise* and *Lexington* with their heavy cruisers and destroyers, were offering battle to the Nagumo force but because of the caution
of the Japanese commanders it was not to be.

So too Nagumo and Kusaka had the opportunity to
engage what they regarded as their greatest prizes, but
overwhelmed by the success of their first two air attacks
and beset with fears for the safety of the carriers of the
First Air Fleet, they flew the withdrawal signal, and retired.

It was a decision that would cost their nation untold
suffering.

Yet it all could have been much different. . . .

Part IV

Our surprise attack . . . will prove to be the Waterloo of the war to follow.
—Vice Admiral Matome Ugaki to flag officers of the fleets in flagship *Nagato*, 13 November 1941

16

The Third Attack

WHEN AIR ATTACK COMMANDER MITSUO FUCHIDA'S bomber landed on flagship *Akagi's* rolling flight deck with the last of the raid planes about 1200 Sunday afternoon, he found the discussion of a third attack well underway with Admiral Nagumo and his chief of staff Admiral Kusaka already carefully weighing the risks.

Fuchida plunged into the conference giving his summation of the results of the first two attacks, concluding: ". . . All things considered we have achieved a great amount of destruction but it would be unwise to assume that we have destroyed everything. There are still many targets remaining which should be hit. Therefore I recommend that another attack be launched."

Nagumo appeared undecided although it was apparent Kusaka would be adamantly opposed to a third strike. He was very impatient to clear out of the area and be on the way back to Japan.

History could have been so different!

Patrol Boat 1 with her special naval landing force troops aboard would have been hours into her run down on Kauai, having cut loose from the strike force as soon as cruisers *Chikuma* and *Tone* had launched their pre-strike scouting planes at 0530. She would have arrived in Hanalei Bay sometime after full dark which would come about 1730. But her mission which both Nagumo and Kusaka deplored could be easily scrubbed and the destroyer-transport ordered to a rendezvous to the westward where she would not disclose the homeward route of the Nagumo force, if the admiral so opted.

The same conditions held for the big fleet submarine I-74 which was scheduled to land a smaller party at Barking Sands after dark. Both such cancellations would relieve the two admirals a great deal.

Kusaka was commanding the signal officer to run up the signal for retirement when the chief radio officer thrust a message into his hand. Drafted by his impetuous operations officer Captain Kurishima, it was from Yamamoto aboard the *Nagato* in the Inland Sea. Holding it in front of him so both he and Nagumo could read, they received their new orders: "Exploit victory. Seek out American carriers. They must be destroyed."

The "retirement" signal was never flown. Instead the carriers were instructed to be prepared to launch a third attack on Pearl Harbor at 1400 hours.

A buzz of anticipation ran through every ship of the strike force.

Genda and Fuchida busied themselves organizing this third strike while all of the carriers swarmed with activity. Priority targets would be the Pearl Harbor oil storage tank farm, the machine shops and repair facilities at Pearl and Hickam Field, the Pearl Harbor submarine base and, of course, any undamaged men-o-war or fighting planes encountered.

Promptly at 1400 the carriers swung into the wind once more. The sea had abated somewhat so the take-offs were easier than in the morning attacks. Fuchida was again to lead the attack which would carry no torpedoes but depend on level and dive bombers protected by their fighters to complete the destruction of the Pearl Harbor and

Hickam installations while keeping watch for the absent carriers. Torpedo bombers would be held on the carrier flight decks ready for this contingency.

The baiting actions by Patrol Boat 1 and submarine I-74 would receive no air support that night but it was anticipated that their operations would lead to direct contact with the big American carriers the following day.

With the Zero fighters spearheading the way, the planes rapidly reflew their route of the morning attack only this time they would come in high for surprise and security, then plummet down upon their stricken targets. The fighters would suppress all air-borne opposition.

Wide open to visual observation in the bright afternoon sunlight, Fuchida led the formation more to the eastward than it had flown in the morning attacks, reasoning that the Americans by now would be concentrating whatever planes or ships they had available out towards the northwest and southwest sectors. No ships nor planes did they see, only a completely vacant ocean.

The island of Oahu again came into view an hour-and-one-half into the flight with no incidents or enemy contact of any kind. Fuchida, focusing his binoculars over the center of the island, could see smoke still rising from burning Pearl Harbor on the south shore.

He overflew the northern sectors of the island and Wheeler Field at great height then dropped steeply down upon the great oil tank farm at Pearl Harbor. Other planes were falling like stones on the navy yard section of the base with its crowded buildings housing the machine shops, repair basins with their tall cranes, the long Ten Ten Dock and the countless smaller structures devoted to fleet support activities. A third thrust would center on the concentrated area of the submarine base.

But now they had been discovered. Puffs of black anti-aircraft bursts were checkerboarding the sky. Two bombers caught in the fire screamed flaming into the cauldron.

Now, too, some American planes were winging their way into the melee which spread out over the whole Pearl

Harbor area. It was about 1530 when the first bombs blasted the oil tanks into flame. They erupted in great fountains of fire, followed immediately by long columns of smoke.

Orange fireballs soared into the sky speckled with the blossoms of high explosive shell. Most of the ships, even the damaged ones, were returning fire as best they could, while the Army's antiaircraft batteries were shooting as fast as they could load the shells.

Japanese fliers caught brief glimpses of the huge battleship *Pennsylvania*, flagship of the American fleet, fighting back from her watery berth inside the great graving dock with two sunken and wrecked destroyers, the *Cassin* and the *Downes*, just forward of her massive bow.

Some fire seemed to be coming from several of the other battleships hit in the two morning raids. It was evident to Fuchida that his force was taking heavy losses from the fierce counterfire. All formations were under orders to clear the Oahu area and return to their carriers once they had dropped on their targets.

This they were doing although many of them would not get back.

Pearl Harbor was now one great bowl of smoke erupting from the burning gasoline tanks and fed by other fires in the industrial navy yard buildings and the submarine base. Fuchida, himself, his plane's bombs long gone, drew off from the Pearl Harbor crucible to survey the destruction.

When all planes had cleared the area, he flew on to his rendezvous point where picking up a lone fighter, the flight back to the carriers began. The third attack had consumed less than thirty minutes. Even so it would be a race with daylight.

Landing on *Akagi* in the last rays of the setting sun, Fuchida reported to an apprehensive Nagumo on the bridge of the flagship. In a muted discussion, in view of the substantial losses inflicted by the enemy, the flight leader reported all objectives achieved.

The admiral glanced at his chief of staff.

"All but the carriers. We have seen no sign of them."

"That is true. But they must come to us now."

Kusaka glanced into the gathering dusk where the faint shapes of the other vessels of the force were growing more indistinct by the minute.

Genda, who had been a listener through much of the discussion, now spoke up.

"Yes. We cannot steam too far off. We must be ready to attack as soon as we can locate their carriers."

Kusaka stared out at the shadows of the force vessels, all planes in, now assuming their night battle formation.

"Nevertheless we must not risk our own destruction," he said. "We shall do the best we can."

It would be a nervous night.

17

A Firelit Hell

INSIDE PEARL HARBOR ON THE SHIPS AND THROUGHOUT THE navy yard, most rescue and salvage efforts were now turned to the staggering task of fighting fire.

Fire apparatus from the navy yard was joined by Honolulu Fire Department companies, many of which had already been engaged in assisting the military and naval fire units in attempting to suppress fires started by the first two morning raids. Some Honolulu pumper engines bore scars from bullets and shell fragments sustained in performing that duty.

Added to the din of the bomb bursts and the antiaircraft fire were the wailing screams of the fire engines attempting to pick their way through the confusion of debris which littered the streets of the great base. Towering high over the burning chaos, the giant crane mounted on railroad tracks of the Ten Ten Dock would be obscured for long moments by black, billowing smoke.

The rescue crews attempting to cut trapped men out of the capsized hull of the battleship *Oklahoma* were forced to flatten themselves against her steel bottom plates, completely exposed to attack from the air.

Most of the fighting ships, the cruisers and destroyers which were to escape Pearl Harbor that day, had long before stood to sea, negotiating the narrow channel almost plugged by the valiant battleship *Nevada* in her thrilling transit of the bomb-swept harbor during the morning raids.

The old battlewagon—she had seen service in World War I in the Atlantic—performed the miracle of the day when she got underway from her berth astern of the stricken *Arizona*, headed out into the harbor, glided past the *West Virginia* and *Tennessee*, the *Maryland* and upside down *Oklahoma*, and finally the great *California* bow down and burning opposite the Ten Ten Dock.

Her guns flashing and wreathed in smoke from Japanese bombs, she was the embattled spirit of the United States Navy, making her defiant sortie. With a clear shot at the channel, *Nevada* drew Japanese war planes like honey draws flies. Yet she stood on.

But it was too much of a chance. The navy yard signal mast atop the tall yard tower had burst into a flurry of signals: "Stand Clear of the Channel." Reluctantly her gallant crew had pushed her massive bow into Hospital Point at the inshore end of the channel. Here wind and water swung her full about so she was left heading back into the harbor. During the morning raids, she was pulled off the shore and run aground across the channel on Waipio Peninsula.

Now she joined the fire fight against the third attack, her guns barking as vigorously as when she had been making her epic run.

This afternoon mass raid by the Japanese bore heavily on the nerves of the overburdened staffs of Oahu hospitals already flooded with the dying and the wounded. Pearl Harbor Naval Hospital, Hickam Field and Schofield Barracks hospitals, and the Army's old, wooden-built Tripler Hospital were overflowing. In downtown Honolulu Queen's Hospital was receiving wounded civilians and resupplying the vital blood bank supplies with hundreds of donors.

The new onslaught seemed more than flesh could bear yet the people carried on.

Then it was all over as quickly as it had come.

Men and women came out of their holes, looked up into the blue Hawaiian sky, then resumed their duties of mercy or rescue or salvage as if there had been no deadly interference.

While the sun sank behind the jagged peaks of the Waianae Range, long shadows spread across the devastated island. But Oahu toiled on.

Remarkably there had been no panic, no civilian hesitancy in speeding the work of resistance to the attackers.

Honolulu responded magnificently with all her many races, including the Japanese, delivering more than was asked by the armed forces in their defending actions against the raid.

While the darkness crept over Oahu, all of the areas outside of the stricken military and naval bases were abandoned to the coming night. In Honolulu there were no automobiles on the deserted streets, no lights in the buildings or houses, no people to be seen. Radios had to be left on for emergency broadcasts but these only came on the air at infrequent intervals. There was no information as to the attack itself, only warnings to stay off the streets, stay off the telephone, show no lights, and keep bathtubs filled with water.

During the afternoon the Army had assumed control of the Hawaiian Islands as territorial governor Joseph E. Poindexter, upon the recommendation of President Roosevelt, had declared martial law with Lieutenant General Walter C. Short the military governor.

Silently Honolulu waited for full dark like a city of the dead. Where before there had been life and gaiety and hopes, now there was nothing.

Far out to the westward the American task forces were racing back towards Pearl seeking battle regardless of the odds.

18

Kauai's Peril

PATROL BOAT NO. 1, THE CONVERTED OLD DESTROYER *Shimakaze*, crowded with the sea soldiers of her special naval landing forces, had cut loose from the Nagumo force in the pre-dawn darkness of 0530, the morning of 7 December, to head straight for Hanalei Bay on the north shore of Kauai at her best possible speed permitted by the very heavy seas whipped by a howling northeast trade wind.

Her departure was timed to the catapulting of the first Pearl Harbor scouting mission, two Zero float planes, by the heavy cruisers *Chikuma* and *Tone*.

To port she left the powerful task force of six carriers, two fast battleships, two heavy cruisers, one light cruiser and nine destroyers, with the carriers already preparing to turn into the wind to launch the first Pearl Harbor air attack wave at 0600. They quickly faded into the darkness.

In her tiny radio room receivers were tuned to the strike force channel, but one set picked up the Honolulu commercial broadcasting station KGMB which had been on the air all night broadcasting music so the incoming B-17s from Hamilton Field in California would have a radio fix to

189

aid them in their landings at Hickam Field, scheduled for 0800.

At 0615 the sound of aircraft in the clouds overhead told the crew of Patrol Boat 1 that the first wave of the air attack had launched on time and was now on its way to the target. The night was just beginning to give way to the dawn.

With the coming of full light over the tossing waves, those aboard the old destroyer began to feel very much alone.

The command was at its battle stations as daylight took over the hostile seas, with the full armament of the three 4.7-inch and the ten 25mm guns ready for instant action. But there was nothing other than the lonely seas and the constant wind.

The sailors of the landing party began to review their assignments for the Hanalei attack but in a lackluster fashion for all aboard the destroyer-transport were interested in only one thing, news of the Pearl raid. So as the old *Shimakaze* sliced her way southward through the heavy seas, the chief duty became one of waiting while scanning the empty sea and sky.

Just before 0800 the captain of Patrol Boat 1 advised the crew and the landing party that Fuchida had signaled *Nagumo* "Tora! Tora! Tora!" The surprise of Pearl Harbor had been achieved.

Knowing that their mission was now on beyond recall the landing parties began again rehearsing their missions and objectives once they were put ashore on the enemy island that night.

In the pilot house the navigator kept a constant check on the course while the helmsman had his hands full with the smashing seas. The day had now turned bright with tropical blue skies and white puffed-up clouds.

The radio operators kept constant ears to their channels but other than picking up station KTOH on Kauai, which along with the Honolulu stations had gone off the air after announcing the Oahu attack, they could learn little other than the instructions to the civilian population to stay off the streets and off the telephones.

For the first day of war the hours dragged their way at an uneventful but apprehensive pace for Patrol Boat 1.

Things were different in the big fleet submarine I-74 which was working her way, submerged, slowly eastward through the Kaulakahi Channel towards the western shores of Kauai.

She had made her way up to Hawaii from Kwajalein Atoll in the Marshall Islands with sixty specially trained officers and men of the Special Naval Landing Forces who were to execute a commando-like raid on the American air field at Barking Sands.

Unlike the unit embarked in Patrol Boat 1, which was planning an invasion lodgment of at least two days at Hanalei, the I-74 sea soldiers were to do their work in a single night before withdrawing in the submarine the following morning.

When the overall Pearl Harbor attack plans had been drawn, the two Kauai landings had been added to be used in the contingency that the American carriers or other major fleet units were absent at the time of the raid. It was expected that the seizure of American soil at Hanalei and a destructive raid on the Barking Sands area would make it necessary for the missing carriers to provide air cover for combat elements dispatched to the aid of the island.

Depending upon how the actions went it was hoped that the big U.S. carriers would be destroyed and perhaps Kauai Island itself might be captured. This in turn would furnish an exploitation base from which greatly expanded forces from the homeland could launch an all-out invasion attack on Oahu itself. To this end additional units of the special naval landing forces were distributed amongst the ships of the Nagumo force.

But the long voyage up from the Mandates had proven wearing on both the crew of I-74 and her naval landing party. Lack of adequate space was the main irritant so all hands were eagerly awaiting completion of the mission.

As the day wore on I-74 began closing Kauai's western coast, coming to periscope depth from time to time to look around. It was an uneventful approach for no air nor surface craft were in sight.

The commando band began to bestir themselves for their night's work. Guns were loaded and checked. Where the landing party at Hanalei would go comfortably ashore in their Daihatsu landing craft, the I-74 unit would use heavy rubber surf rafts.

Late in the morning the submarine did sight an aircraft which seemed to be taking off from Barking Sands for a flight along Kauai's coast. But then it vanished from view and did not reappear.

While I-74 was now closing her target, it was well into the afternoon before the destroyer-transport began lifting the green-coated cliffs of Kauai's north shore out of the sea. Her captain was satisfied. He did not want to bring her in too close before sunset for while he knew that the attack on the big naval base had been successful, he had to be most careful that some vagrant enemy did not spot him in that empty ocean.

Above all he desired nightfall so that the darkness would hide him from any hostile eyes.

But he had been seen.

All day long the keepers of the great Kilauea Lighthouse, towering high above the surflined cliffs on the northeast corner of Kauai, had been scanning the northern and western horizon with their glasses searching for enemy ships or planes.

Some planes were seen, but friendly or hostile could not be determined. Nevertheless they had phoned their sightings to the army's district commander in Lihue, Kauai's largest town.

Now for the first time the two keepers felt they had really something to report.

Through their glasses they quickly identified the vessel as a twin-funneled destroyer. But friend or foe? She was still too far out to determine.

One of the keepers picked up the phone to alert the island command.

For Kauai realization of a state of war had come slowly. Anyone listening to Honolulu radio stations KGU and KGMB would have heard special bulletins calling all military and naval personnel to duty. These announcements would be followed by one at 0832 asking all Honolulu police and firemen to report to their posts.

The first official announcement of the attack came from the Army at 0840: "A sporadic air attack has been made on Oahu. . . . enemy airplanes have been shot down. . . . the rising sun has been sighted on the wingtips."

Still the word spread slowly.

Civil defense meetings were being held later in the morning when confirmation of war was received and the participants were confronted with the "real McCoy," as announcer Webley Edwards had termed it over station KGMB.

During the morning the national guardsmen of the 299th Infantry were alerted at their posts at Mana near Barking Sands, Hanapepe near the Port Allen airfield, and at Wailua beyond Lihue.

Yet what to do?

Placing movable obstacles on the island's airports was the first obvious reaction to the Pearl attack. At Barking Sands they were removed temporarily to allow the navy plane, the I-74 sighted, to take off and circuit the island looking for enemies. The pilot found none.

During the morning guardsmen under command of the 3rd Battalion Headquarters at Wailua began to move into their defense positions and in cooperation with the Kauai Police Department to set up traffic control posts at certain points along the island's main highways.

There were far too few soldiers for so many miles of coastline. Company C with the battalion headquarters and special units was responsible for Lihue, the Nawiliwili port area, and for all points northward along the road to Hanalei Bay some twenty-five miles away.

Company I spread itself about the Burns Field airstrip and Port Allen dock areas on the south shore twenty miles from Company C.

Company M was guarding the Barking Sands area and airstrip, another twenty miles down the main island road along the western shores of the island.

These perimeter dispositions did not allow for a defense in depth. As the day grew older the commanders of these widely spread units could only anticipate nightfall with apprehension.

All of Kauai's ears were attuned to its radio station KTOH with its infrequent but vital advisories to the island.

At nightfall all of the island along with the rest of its sisters in the Hawaiian chain would be blacked out in anticipation of enemy air raids.

During the afternoon it was only human that the rumor mills began to grind with false reports of enemy landings and hostile actions. So with tension rising with each hour, the picturesquely beautiful island awaited the coming of the night.

Till now all of the action had been centered on Oahu. But now with the approach of nightfall the out islands were fearful that their turn had come.

Meanwhile, their sighting phoned in to the island command post, the two lightkeepers at the top of the Kilauea Light resumed their watch on the incoming stranger. Because of the glare of the setting sun on the empty vastness of the Pacific, it was hard to distinguish details. This was made more difficult by surface squalls moving across the face of the ocean, giving promise of a rainy night.

Finally Patrol Boat No. 1 emerged into the bright light of the dying sun. For one moment all of her superstructure stood out like a silhouette before she was hidden by another squally patch.

"Something strange about her," said the keeper who had once served aboard a Lighthouse Service buoy tender. "She doesn't quite look like one of our destroyers."

"She has a well deck forward of her bridge. Does seem different somehow," his companion agreed.

"That's it," said the former buoy tender man. "She's Japanese. We had better get on the horn."

Leaving his companion keeping watch from the gallery and running around the lantern room at the top of the light, he went down the circular iron stairs to the telephone.

"I want the Army District Command," he told the operator.

A soldier answered.

"I want the district commander," the keeper asked.

"He's very busy."

"I think you had better put him on. This is Kilauea light calling. We have something important for him."

"Okay. Wait a minute."

A voice came on the line. "Hullo, District Command."

"District Commander?"

"No. He's tied up right now. This is the assistant D.C."

"This is Kilauea light. We have sighted what we think is a Japanese destroyer."

"You have?" The assistant D.C.'s voice was incredulous.

"Yes. We phoned the first sighting in about twenty minutes ago but couldn't tell much about her. Whether one of ours or not."

"But now?"

"We just got a good look at her against the sun. She has a strange appearance forward. We think she is Japanese."

"Just a minute. Let me get the chart." The voice faded then came back into the phone. "All right. What direction is she from you and how far out is she?"

"I would say she is bearing west-northwest from Kilauea light. She must be six to eight miles offshore."

"Can you tell where she is headed?"

"Could be Hanalei or maybe around the west side of the island. Hard to make out."

"Is she still in view?"

"You will have to wait a moment. I am in the office at the

bottom of the shaft. Hold on, I'll find out."

His voice came back on after several minutes. "No. We've lost her. Its getting squally out there. Hard to see."

"Okay, I'll pass it on. Call me back in ten minutes."

"Its getting dark out there now but we'll call back."

The assistant took his notes into the district commander's office.

"We may have our first enemy," he said.

After hearing the report, the district commander said: "You check the 3rd Battalion. They ought to have a motor patrol out that way somewhere. Maybe you can rouse somebody in Hanalei. I'll pass the dope on to Oahu but I may have a hard time getting in to Fort Shafter. Are the light keepers still watching her?"

"They can't see her now but they are going to call back in ten minutes, one way or the other."

The assistant D.C. told the operator he wanted the 3rd Battalion's command post, and just like that, he had it.

"Give me the C.O. or the operations officer," he asked.

The harried S-3 answered.

"We may have some trouble brewing out on the north shore," the assistant D.C. said.

"We've had nothing but trouble all day," the S-3 responded. "The C.O. is out in the field so you better tell me."

The assistant D.C. passed on the report of the Kilauea light keepers.

"Wow!" came the response. "What do you think she is up to . . . if she is the enemy?"

"Hard to say. The district commander is warning Fort Shafter. They will alert the navy. Only thing I can see is that she must be headed for a landing somewhere. Have you got anything out around Hanalei?"

There was a pause.

"We ran a motor patrol—one jeep—out there earlier to look around but they haven't reported back yet. They were going all the way to the end of the line at Haena. . . . must have been there hours ago. I would imagine they will be in shortly."

"Any way to get hold of them?"

"I'll try but our communication with a vehicle is not so hot at that distance. I'll phone you if I can make contact. What about the lighthouse men?"

"They're going to call back in a few minutes, but the visibility was fading when I last talked with them and it's getting dark now."

"Okay. Let me know and vice versa."

The assistant went in to the district commander who was just hanging up his phone.

"I was lucky," he said. "After some trouble I got the G-2 section at Shafter. They will alert the Navy. Just the kind of news they need. What have you got?"

He relayed the information about the motor patrol.

A corporal called the assistant who went to the phone. It was Kilauea.

"Not much to tell," the lighthouse keeper said. "The Jap got lost in the mist and the squalls. It's real rainy out here," he paused, "and dark too."

The assistant D.C. had been too busy to notice.

"Stay in touch if you get anything more," he said. "I'll be here all night. I guess you people are out of business for the duration."

"We wont be showing any lights if that's what you mean. But we'll keep watch."

He turned to the D.C.

"That was Kilauea Light. They have lost track of their sighting."

The phone rang again. It was the 3rd Battalion S-3.

"My patrol came in from Haena," he said. "They report everything is quiet out that way. People are very uncomfortable. They don't know what to expect. We're going to run another patrol out there with the police, leaving here at 1800. I'll keep you informed."

The assistant D.C. stepped out of the closeness of the blacked-out office into the cool night air. He stopped to inhale the beauty and the scent of the evening. Not a light was showing anywhere.

Pearl Harbor added the Kilauea sighting to all the others that had accumulated during the morning and afternoon but there was not much that could be done other than pass the information on to the task forces and the other ships in the area hoping someone would get a chance to check out the report.

Hiding under the skirts of night the Japanese destroyer-transport with her two hundred and fifty landing party personnel now prepared to go ashore, headed directly for the wide mouth of Hanalei Bay with its gently sloping two-mile-long sand beach at its head. The two 46-foot Daihatsu landing craft were already loaded with the landing party's machineguns and small mortars. This party would take no artillery ashore depending on the armament of the patrol boat if it was needed.

During the morning and afternoon hours, the commander of the shore expedition had carefully reviewed the tasks assigned to the three combat units into which the force would be divided, with his three lieutenants who would conduct the operations.

The officers of Patrol Boat 1 had also participated, so all elements of the attack would know exactly what each of them was expected to achieve.

"Force Village will lead the attack on Hanalei Town," he pointed out on their rough field maps, "assisted by the other units if necessary in the opening phases of the operation. After the capture of the village it will be responsible for the security of the beach including the concrete pier here, and become the reserve under my direct command. This force will send a small detachment to secure our western flank."

His pointer moved to that end of the bay.

"You know that because of the mountains and Na Pali cliffs here, this portion of the island is impassible around the coast." The heads of his listeners nodded. "This wild region runs on towards the southwest for about twenty miles where it ends at the Barking Sands which will be attacked tonight by the I-74 party."

The Force Village lieutenant posed a question.

"How far in from the beach shall we penetrate?"

"Just far enough to secure the town and the main road," the commander answered. "Of course all of us must be prepared for any unforeseen events as they occur."

He turned again to the field map.

"Force Lookout will follow in trace of Force Village then move out to the east along the main road, climb these heights to the lookout and dig in a defensive position with emplaced machineguns and mortars, strong enough to hold off any attackers from penetrating our positions until darkness tomorrow when we expect to commence our withdrawal."

He looked at the Force Lookout lieutenant.

"You understand? You must hold."

"I will hold," the lieutenant replied.

The commander then turned to his third lieutenant.

"Force Valley will advance eastward in trace of Force Lookout and deploy to secure the main beach road from any attack from the valley. As the valley widens out considerably along the Hanalei River, you may have to make most of your adjustments after daylight tomorrow when we must be prepared for attacks from the east."

The lieutenant nodded his understanding.

"How far should I advance up the River Road?"

"No farther than necessary to prevent rifle fire on the shore road. Our command will be spread out as it is. I want as much unity as we can achieve and still discharge our mission."

All heads nodded.

"Oh yes," the commander added as an afterthought, "Force Lookout will be responsible for the Lookout Road from the top down to where it leads into the Hanalei River bridge in the valley. The base of this road will be the responsibility of Force Valley. Understand?"

All of his unit leaders affirmed.

"Headquarters will be in the village area. Captured vehicles may be used where useful," he added. "Patrol Boat No. 1 will remain in the bay unless driven out by aircraft when she will cruise off the Na Pali Coast where the high cliffs and peaks will afford some protection."

He turned to the captain of the destroyer-transport.

"That's right," the captain responded. "We will leave the landing boats with their crews on the shore so in an emergency they will be available. After the action starts I hope the I-74 landing at Barking Sands will be helpful to us."

"Any questions?"

These were veterans of similar landings in China so the operational routine was familiar to all.

They all understood they were acting as bait for the carrier operation and that the risks would be high, but they accepted them.

"Force Village will go ashore first, followed by Force Lookout and then Force Valley. It is imperative that Force Lookout seize and hold the escarpment so there can be no interference from outside."

With the breakup of the conference, the leaders returned to their troops to insure that their soldier-seamen understood exactly what they were to do.

The destroyer-transport was close in now, within the enveloping gloom of the island whose cliffs and mountains etched their outlines against the starlit night.

There were the sounds of movement throughout the vessel as the first troops went to their places in the landing boats. Then all was silent as the old *Shimakaze* slid silently through the calm waters of the bay towards the darkness where the surf could be heard breaking gently on the sand.

Twenty miles down the coast to the southwest, past the wild cliffs and spires of the impassible Na Pali Coast, with their feet in the surf-lashed sea, the fleet submarine I-74 which had surfaced shortly after nightfall was slowly approaching Kauai from the westward. Nothing could be seen in the blackness but the I-74 had been able to obtain some fair shore sightings through her periscope in the rays of the setting sun.

Now she was attempting to come in as close to the beach as she safely could so the landing parties would have the least distance between them and the shore after they had embarked in the rubber landing rafts. Once they had crossed the 100-fathom line the seas abated quite markedly until as they neared the gloom of the island it became quite calm.

From the conning tower I-74's captain examined the surfline through his night glasses. He turned to the landing party commander who stood beside him.

"Here, have a look."

He handed him the glasses.

The shore party lieutenant examined the surfline carefully.

"It may be a little high but we'll have to chance it."

"I'll bring you in as close as I dare. Signal when you want me to bring you off."

His companion nodded.

"I also will signal you when we are all ashore."

The submarine captain shook his hand. They then went down to the deck where the raiders were preparing to launch the surf rafts.

The battle plan for the Barking Sands attack was starkly simple. The Japanese would land at the northern end of the miles-long beach then advance south in a column of two bob-tailed platoons deployed in line with the lieutenant and his messengers leading behind a sparse line of scouts.

Expecting it would be slow going through the heavy beach sand, they would continue their march until they came within range of the airfield. At this point they would get in as close as they could without alarming the sentries, where they would deploy their machineguns and mortars, opening up on whatever targets they could find. Intending nothing more than an intense fire fight display to confuse the defenders into believing they were the objective of a much larger attacking force, they would after expending most of their ammunition withdraw back up the beach to their landing rafts where they would signal the I-74 to come in to take them off.

As the operation was more to cause alarm than to inflict major damage, the troops were armed with light machineguns, small mortars, rifles and grenades. It would be important to get plenty of ammunition ashore which they would pull across the sand in light wooden sleds.

Preparing to board the surf rafts, the landing party could see the darker loom of the Na Pali cliffs against the night sky to the north while the high mountains of Kauai rose up quickly in dark shadow behind the surfline.

The hour had come for both Kauai landing operations to begin.

It was a time of anxious waiting in the Nagumo task force which spent the night hours steaming holding courses well to the north of Kauai, keeping off the island while they waited for the bait to draw the quarry.

During the same hours Task Force 8 with *Enterprise* was steaming out the clock west of Kauai while Task Force 12 with *Lexington* was racing southeast towards Halsey's rendezvous point.

Pearl Harbor was pressing rescue and salvage operations, the fortress of Oahu was standing to its guns, and the out islands were simply sweating out the hours of darkness.

In the mainland United States there was anger and apprehension for the safety of not only Hawaii and Alaska, but also the security of the West Coast states of California, Oregon and Washington.

In the nation's capital President Roosevelt had read to his cabinet the war message he proposed to deliver to the Congress at noon the next day. Later his son, James, a captain in the Marines, found him alone reviewing his stamp collection.

Without looking up, he said: "It's bad. It's pretty bad."

19

Baited Trap

THE 3RD BATTALION'S MOTOR PATROL TO KAUAI'S NORTH shore hauled in to the darkened headquarters while the night patrol and its police escort were waiting for them. The Battalion S-3 and Company C commander who was furnishing the patrol, received the sergeant's report.

"Nothing at all from here to the north side," he said. "The people are anxious but nothing at all."

"You went to the end of the road?"

"All the way. Down into Hanalei and on to Haena. Talked to the people in Hanalei. All quiet."

"How about the blackout?"

"Coming back black as a sock. No cars on the road."

C Company commander turned to the new patrol and the police. "We have a report of a Japanese destroyer off Hanalei or the Na Pali coast. It may be false. Kilauea Light saw it."

"What time?"

"About half-past four o'clock. She was some ways out and they could not see her distinctly. She may be one of ours."

"What do you want us to do?" the sergeant asked.

"You had better go directly to Hanalei and patrol the beach." He glanced at the policeman. "If you can't reach us by radio, call us by telephone from Kilauea village. You can get one there. That way we'll know where you are before you go on to Princeville and down from the Lookout into Hanalei."

"Okay," the sergeant nodded. "How long do you want us to stay out there?"

The S-3 looked at C Company commander.

"Maybe all night," the captain said. "We will have a better reading when you call us. It will be six o'clock when you leave and it's about twenty miles from here to Kilauea."

"Can you make it in an hour blacked out?"

"Pretty close, unless we're held up somewhere."

The S-3 stared at the sergeant in the blackness.

"I don't want you to get held up. I want you to get to Hanalei. Understand?"

"Yes, sir."

"From Kilauea you will have another eight miles on to Hanalei and another six beyond that to the end of the road. It will be very black out there."

The company commander spoke up. "You have plenty of ammunition?"

"Yes. We have three M 1s and an automatic rifle with lots of rounds."

The S-3 had the last word.

"We have to hear from you before you go into the valley."

"Yes, sir."

With that the four soldiers and two policemen in a blacked-out jeep and patrol car moved quietly into the night.

The S-3 and the company commander walked to battalion to report on the patrol.

They found the battalion intelligence officer with the C.O.

"The island started to get spooked as soon as the sun

went down," the S-2 said. "We're getting the same damn fool reports that I hear Oahu got during the afternoon."

"What's that?"

"Oh, you know, paratroops landing, beach landings and so forth."

"We'll just have to check them out the best we can. You never know."

The battalion commander put on his helmet and his pistol belt. "I'm going to check the airfields. First Burns Field then Barking Sands. I will contact you from each company command post. If you want me, leave messages. I don't know how well the radios will perform from the vehicles."

"I'll keep a close watch," his S-3 assured him.

The assistant district commander took leave for his own headquarters where the island district C.O. looked up as he came in.

"That patrol get back okay?"

"Yes, but they had nothing to report of any moment. It's quiet out there."

"I phoned Shafter our 1800 report. They seem satisfied. I guess they have had a busy day," the district commander said. "They had nothing for us."

"Any word on the Japanese?"

"Nope. Not a thing. They have had plenty of reports like our Jap destroyer, but nothing has come of any of them."

"The 3rd Battalion has a night patrol with a police car on the way to the Hanalei side now," the assistant said. "Left at 1800. They will call battalion headquarters from Kilauea. I will check it out. Incidentally how is the medical situation?"

"The civil defense people have been working like beavers," the district commander said."Each of the towns and plantations should be in pretty fair shape." He shrugged his shoulders. "It's been a long day."

His assistant nodded.

"Had chow?"

"Yes, while it was still light."

"I should have but that Kilauea sighting got in the way. I'll get some now, then drop in on the 3rd Battalion. I'll call from there."

Before he stepped out into the darkness he glanced at his watch. It was a quarter to seven. That patrol should be well up the island by now for in spite of the blackout the soldiers and the police knew the island main road like the backs of their hands. Yet they couldn't get going too fast. That would be dangerous. There could always be other vehicles, or cattle or horses in the road.

The mess was hot and bright after he stepped in from the night. Few soldiers were around but the cooks took care of him, so feeling replenished he made his way back to the 3rd Battalion. It was now shortly after 7 o'clock.

"How's your Hanalei patrol doing?" he asked the S-2.

"No word yet. May be a little too early for them to get to Kilauea."

The S-3 chimed in. "We did hear from the C.O. All quiet."

"He's going to Burns Field at Hanapepe?"

"Yes. He's on his way. But travel is slow. It really is pitch black out there."

"A little drizzle too," the assistant D.C. confirmed.

The telephone rang shrilly on the S-2's desk. He answered looking up at the S-3. "It's the sergeant. He's at Kilauea now. Do you want to talk to him?"

"Yes, when you're through."

It was twenty minutes after seven o'clock.

"Sergeant, how are things?"

The voice came to him in a muffled sound.

"Quiet and black all the way. We didn't see nothing but a few stray cattle."

"You're going on to Hanalei now?"

"Yes. We're calling from the Kalauea store."

"Take a good look at Hanalei beach and give me a call from there."

"Yes, sir."

The S-3 looked up at the assistant D.C. who had joined them.

"Everything is quiet along the north shore."

"And all around the island too," the S-3 responded. "I hope it stays that way. I would have liked to have put some people out there but we just don't have enough to go 'round."

At this moment the two Daihatsu landing craft were preparing for launch from their destroyer-transport. Patrol Boat No. 1 had swung around to face the open end of the bay and the gentle swells from the ocean. Hanalei was in absolute blackout and as yet there was no moon. Slight rain mist moved across the bay from time to time but it was no hinderance to the operations which for the most part were conducted with little sound.

On shore there was no indication of any movement or activity. Dogs would bark at intervals but mostly there were only the sounds of the big trade wind and the easy surf on the shore.

Suddenly this all changed. The two landing craft started up their motors and headed for the beach each with about seventy men apiece. They would make two trips to land the entire force.

To most of the houses at Hanalei, being back from the beach along the island road which served as the main street in the village, the sound of the motors on the landing craft did not appear to create an immediate stir. Apparently all fishermen had been discouraged on this night by the air raid warning broadcast by Honolulu earlier in the day.

But now a light showed here and there in the trees as a door was opened and shut quickly. Sounds of voices could be heard by the sailors in the landing craft as they prepared to enter the surfline.

Jumping down onto the sandy bottom, the first ashore ran well beyond the beach to take up defensive positions to cover the landing operations. With the two landing craft quickly discharging their loads, the beach perimeter built up rapidly so the Force Village commander began to organize his men for the advance inland against Hanalei town.

A voice hallooed in the night. The words were in English.

"Who is there? Who is there?"

Immediately a response came back in English from the landing party.

"Patrol! Patrol! Stand clear!"

Several shadows could be seen moving on the foreshore. Then the voice cut through the night again.

"Who are you? Who are you?"

Then a louder voice shouted out of the darkness much closer at hand.

"They are Japanese! They are soldiers!"

With surprise lost, the landing party commander ordered Force Village to seize the town. The three groups comprising the force ran across the open fields towards the houses.

Then from their left flank came a burst of automatic rifle fire.

C Company's patrol at last had something to report.

A voice on the road yelled out: "Clear the town! Go to the mountain!"

Now a burst of fire from the landing party replied.

It was answered by another volley from the left. The party began to take some wounded, one man's screams cutting through the night.

Sounds of quick departures were coming from the village now with a baby crying while a multitude of dogs set off a constant howling and barking in alarm.

But still the landing party had not clearly seen a single individual.

Several shots came from the darkness up the beach to their right.

Again hits were scored on the Japanese, several sailors crying out in pain.

The shore party replied with another fusillade. But it

was just at shadows.

"Hold all fire!" the commander ordered.

The residents of Hanalei town, confronted with their worst fears, were now slipping away into the night, into the mountains which rise sharply off to the west of the village where they knew they would be safe at least until daylight.

The stray shots from the Japanese right flank were from some hunters who lived west of and back of the town. Masters of Hawaiian mountain craft, they were taking advantage of cover and the night to harrass the invaders.

C Company's patrol which had opened from the eastern side of the beach now withheld all fire while, sending the police car ahead to phone the alarm to Lihue, they drove their blacked-out jeep at full speed up the sharp grade back to the top of the lookout.

With all firing halted the valley settled into an uneasy silence, the landing party bringing ashore the rest of its men, and its scouts probing the shadows of the buildings of the town.

Once atop the escarpment, the four guardsmen chose firing positions which would allow them free fields of fire on the road down into the valley from which they had just come. Below them they could hear shots from the village area but what was happening they could not discern.

Actually the landing party was entering a ghost town from which all the inhabitants had fled. But the fire fights had made the sailors nervous, jumping off shots at every alarm.

And now they had a fire.

It was one of the single story wooden buildings next to the town's only gas station, which soon caught on fire to spread the conflagration. The village was set blazing with light against which the Japanese figures made excellent targets for the boar hunters who apparently had collected reinforcements, for fire from the western edge of the town was now increasing.

The Force Village flank guard advancing west along the

narrow two-lane highway ran into trouble, pinned down by the guerrilla fire.

Suddenly there was a large explosion in the village as the service station with its supply of gasoline and oil was reached by the flames.

Through the firelight the landing party commander dispatched his lookout and valley forces along the highway to the east.

Up until now, with the exception of the early fire fights, the situation had been developing favorably for his party, so he expected he should be able to maintain his grip on the town and the bay area without too much fear of being expelled.

Still in war?

Finding a home with a phone in a darkened cluster of buildings beyond the lookout, the policemen phoned the alarm directly into the island district command center. With his assistant at his elbow the district C.O. took the call. The first words were chilling.

"Japanese are landing at Hanalei Bay. They have shot up the town, starting some fires. The town people have gone back into the mountains. We don't know if anyone has been hurt."

"What time did this happen?"

"A little after half-past seven. There is a blacked out vessel in the bay which put them ashore."

"What about C Company's patrol?"

"They fired on the landing party on the beach. Then after an exchange with the Japanese, the sergeant asked us to go back up the hill and phone you."

"Thanks. Where are you now?"

"Near Princeville."

"Keep this line open while we call headquarters of the 3rd Battalion."

The district commander repeated the information to his assistant asking him to get the battalion on the line.

He turned back to the phone. "Stay with me. We're calling the 3rd Battalion now."

The battalion executive officer listened carefully to the report.

"The C.O. is at Burns Field. We'll pass the info on. In the meantime I will instruct C Company to get two platoons on the road. You say our patrol is at Hanalei lookout?"

"Yes. They will try and hold that point."

There was a moment of silence while the battalion exec conferred with C Company's commander.

"Have the police officer tell the patrol to hold on. Two platoons will be on their way in a few minutes. We will be sending some machineguns and mortars. They will come just as fast as they can."

"Okay. Oh yes, the patrol asked for more grenades."

"Roger. Will send."

The district C.O. turned back to the Princeville call.

"Officer?"

"Yes."

"Tell the sergeant to hold on. C Company platoons are on the way. Two of them. They are bringing grenades. Ask someone to standby your phone for more calls."

"Okay. Call the chief. Let him know what's doing."

"Will do."

Just shortly before, the submarine I-74's landing party had taken to their rubber rafts heavily loaded with men, weapons and ammunition. The transfer from the submarine's deck to the rafts had been executed with not too much difficulty in spite of the seas which were running higher than expected.

It was when the rubber rafts neared the surf line that the lieutenant commanding the operation sensed difficulty. Although he had expected possible heavy surf, he was surprised by the boom of the waves as they fell upon the long sand beach.

Inshore he could see nothing but darkness, but the seas would be a hazard in themselves.

Speaking his orders directly into the ear of the coxswain who was steering the raft, he conned him through the outer swells. Seeing that the surf would be relatively short with a steep drop to the sand, he ordered his men, all wearing life jackets, over the side, leaving the heavier weapons and ammunition in the raft.

Then catching a wave just right, the rubber raft surfed shoreward to suddenly drop upright on the sand. Quickly the stumbling sailors regained their feet, and fighting the heavy drag of the outgoing wave, held their footing in the sand. The following wave crashed down upon them but they held their own and suddenly they were safely on the beach. Not a man nor a weapon lost.

It was a masterful job.

Then in came the second raft in like fashion. But the third misjudged, forcing the men ashore to mount a quick rescue effort. For the most part it succeeded, but a light machinegun and a grenade discharger were lost as were two seamen who could not be located in the waves.

Shortly thereafter another raft flipped over in the surf setting off a mad, wet scramble to recover her load. One man was lost.

While his party sorted itself out, the lieutenant faced seaward and carefully shielding his flashlight, signaled I-74 that the landing had been made. Then taking his second-in-command with him, he crossed the sands toward the cliffs which came down close at this point. Advancing a short way into the night they stumbled on to a sort of unimproved road which would assist in the advance of the left flank. But the commander did see that the area would widen out considerably as the party went south towards the airstrip.

He would not have enough men to spread even a skirmish line across the open places. No matter, the walking would be good, so their direction of approach would be guided with their left on the road. The beach area would simply have to be bypassed except for one scout who was assigned to walk the shore.

With the depth of the sand making it rather heavy going for the first hour, although little could be seen in the inky blackness, the lieutenant figured that they must have covered the better part of two miles. Because of the spread of the land, he judged they had passed Nohili Point out to their right flank and were drawing in close to the airfield, but as yet they had encountered no guard posts nor patrols.

He halted the advance.

In a whispered consultation with his two platoon leaders, they decided that although they must be close to the enemy outpost line, the advance could continue if conducted with utmost care.

The advance resumed.

Shortly the scouting line could hear the murmur of voices from the direction of the airfield. Then someone to their front dropped an object to the ground, then more muffled voices.

It was the airstrip outpost line.

The landing party halted while the scouts went forward. The night stayed quiet although now the sound of a motorcar could be heard off to their front. But no light broke the darkness.

With the starlight furnishing some illumination, the scouts began to come back.

At another whispered conference it was estimated that they must be about a hundred yards from the outpost line with the end of the airstrip another hundred or so yards beyond.

It was time to prepare the attack.

Quietly the lines moved forward.

Suddenly there came the sound of rustling in low bushes to the left front, there was a gasp, then silence.

One outpost had gone down.

Over on the right came the clash of arms, then firing broke out in front of the leading platoon. All of the darkness erupted in front of the landing party with flashes of rifle fire outlining the trace of the American outposts.

As yet there had been little fire from the Japanese but the lieutenant could wait no longer.

Harsh commands split the night as the attackers moved

in on the surprised and unnerved outposts.

First two mortars shot flares blossoming brightly into the black sky. An eerie light shown down on the American positions with the faint outline of the airstrip to the south. A machinegun began to chatter until Japanese counterfire silenced it.

It was apparent the Americans were not prepared for the realities of battle, that the outposts were falling back on the main defense line.

Moving forward the Japarrese landing party continued to bring fire down upon everything that moved.

Then abruptly the lieutenant broke off the action. All Japanese fire ceased with only American weapons firing at intervals into the night. He did so because he would have to conserve ammunition although the party had left two caches behind them on the line of withdrawal they would follow back to the I-74.

Finally the American guns ceased their fire and an uneasy calm settled over the Barking Sands.

But there was no calm in island command centers as word of the two landings worked their way upwards.

The Kauai district commander didn't wait on such niceties as coded messages. He got on the inter-island phone for the army's G-2 Intelligence Section at Fort Shafter behind Honolulu.

"I want the G-2 himself, none other."

"Just a moment."

The G-2 came on the phone.

"Yes?"

"This is the Kauai district commander calling. We have a report of a Japanese landing at Hanalei Bay."

"No!"

"Yes. They brought a destroyer into the bay after nightfall. Japanese are ashore in the village after a firefight with 299th troops. Reinforcements are now on their way to Hanalei."

"Give us all the details." The G-2 beckoned to some of

his officers. "Time of attack, strengths if you know them. Current objectives."

Carefully the Kauai commander went over all the details he had assembled. "We will need more troops soon," he said. "The 3rd Battalion of the 299th is spread out all over hell."

"See what we can do. Keep us up to the minute. I'll get to the general and the G-3."

"Okay. Be back to you shortly."

Meanwhile the 3rd Battalion headquarters got the word on the Barking Sands fight from their own C.O. himself.

"I just arrived here from Burns Field," he told his astonished executive officer, "when all hell broke loose north of the airstrip. We really don't know what is out there but it looks as if they are advancing."

The exec broke in to tell him about the Hanalei landing.

"I've sent two platoons of C Company to reinforce their motor patrol which is entrenched in a strongpoint on the bluff at the Hanalei lookout. We hope they can hold till C Company's platoons get there."

There was silence at the Barking Sands end.

"Well I'll be damned! Does Shafter know about this?"

"The district commander has just talked to them. We tried to get you at Burns but missed you."

"I am going to stay here with M Company until they repel this attack. We will alert I Company at Burns but no matter what we do we will not have enough. Ask the D.C. to tell Shafter we need more troops right now."

"I've already asked."

As soon as the D.C. got the Barking Sands alarm, he was back with the G-2 Section at Shafter.

"Is the G-2 there?"

"He's with the general."

"We have more hot stuff breaking on Kauai. Barking Sands is under attack."

"Just a minute."

The Assistant G-2 came on the line.

"Give me all the dope, I'll get it to them fast."

The Kauai D.C. then repeated the report of the C.O. 3rd Battalion of the 299th as received from the M Company command post Barking Sands.

"He's calling for reinforcements and I concur," the D.C. said. "We need them fast or else the whole island might go down."

"I'll get to the G-2 and the G-3 immediately. We'll see what can be done."

News of the Kauai attacks hit the operating sections of the joint army-navy battle command post deep inside Aliamanu Crater between Shafter and Pearl Harbor, like a slug in the belly.

"Japanese ashore at two points on Kauai!" It was electrifying.

"It must mean that their carriers are hanging around out there," one Army staff chief surmised. "The Navy better know."

"The admiral and the general already have the word. The 3-Section is talking to the divisions to see if we can scrape up some support forces."

"How will we get them there?"

"Must be some cruisers or destroyers somewhere that could carry them over, that is if they can get any air cover on the way."

There was no delay along the line.

The word already had gone out to Halsey who was now weighing the developments with his staff high in the flag plot of the blacked-out *Enterprise* steaming impatiently, awaiting daylight and her late morning rendezvous with *Lexington*.

In Washington, D.C., the news posed new problems. How do you explain to the American people that Japanese troops are ashore at two points in the territory of Hawaii? It was a difficult matter so no announcement was made during the night hours, everyone including the President waiting to see what would happen next.

20

With Fire and Sword

WHILE FORCE VILLAGE WAS CONSOLIDATING ITS GRIP ON Hanalei Town, the other two components of the landing party were moving steadily east along the main island road, toward the base of the Lookout escarpment with Force Lookout in the lead. Following the first burst of automatic rifle fire from the eastern edge of the bay there had been no hostile activity to their front.

The lieutenant leading Force Lookout, knowing the need for speed, flogged his troops along the road, gradually pulling away from the Valley Force in their rear. Soon his point men sent back word that they were across the Hanalei River bridge and beginning the ascent of the steeply climbing road to the lookout and out of the valley.

Then his whole troop of some seventy-odd men were moving swiftly across the wooden floored bridge, still with no opposition to their fore. The road began to ascend rapidly now, slowing the pace of the advance markedly. With exhortations to his noncoms to keep the column moving, the lieutenant sweated his way up the bluff until he was with the very point men of the column.

They were not far from their objective now, the lookout

which would seal off Hanalei from any outside relief, the key to their grip on the entire Hanalei position.

But there were four other men who had much different intentions as to the progress of his advance.

After their initial burst of fire into the landing party on the beach, C Company's patrol sergeant ordered his men to dash for the jeep. Once in, they careened down the beach road back across Hanalei bridge and up the cliff road to the top.

There the sergeant marked off a rough position from which their fire could sweep those portions of the road not defiladed from the top. Rapidly he assigned the tasks and the digging began. Below them the valley and the town were marked by new bursts of enemy fire.

"Keep digging," he shouted. "This is where they're going to make their real push. This is the place we have to hold."

Driven by the whip of impending combat, the firing points took form rapidly. The ammunition was cached about within arm's reach with the grenades being accorded the priority of place.

"If anything is going to stop them it is these babies," the sergeant said.

After a short while the police car drove up in their rear.

"I got the island commander. He passed the word to C Company," the officer told the sergeant. "Two platoons are on the way with plenty grenades."

"I hope they step on it," the sergeant replied. "I don't think we are going to get too much more time."

The two police officers pitched in to help with the crude fort complex being thrown up above the crest of the lookout road.

"Say, you know we have a supply of highway flares in the car," he told the soldiers. "Why not use them to mark the road at the proper time?"

"Good idea," responded the sergeant while there came a volley of shots far below them. "Sounds like they are beginning to come up. There must be a bunch of boar hunters down there. They have been potshotting the Japs since they first came ashore."

"Not much time now. We have to watch on all sides whether the cliff looks climbable or not. As soon as they know we're here, they will try to surround us."

Some of the cowboys from the Princeville Ranch rode into the rough position, each carrying a rifle and his own ammunition.

"We're the first," they told the sergeant. "There are more on the way."

"Grab a shovel and start digging in. I'll show you where."

Still more *paniolos* rode up. When they were assigned digging spots, one of them took the horses back along the road, out of the danger area.

"This could turn into quite a fight."

One of the policemen held up his hand. "Quiet. You can hear them on the road."

Work ceased while all listened. In the silence the soft sound of movement came to them from far below.

"Who has the best sight?" the sergeant asked.

A young paniolo was thrust forward by his rangemates. "He's the hunter. He has eyes like a cat."

"Ever throw a grenade?"

"Nope."

"All you do is pull this ring keeping your thumb on the firing pin. When you see them clearing that bend in the road, let them come on until there are enough of them around the bend so we'll have some targets. Okay?"

"Okay. Can I open fire after I've thrown the grenade?"

"You'll be facing their advance point. Take cover first, then you can fire."

Taking three grenades the young cowboy went softly off into the darkness.

Now all settled down into positions from which they could bring fire onto the road and the crest.

Only the sound of distant firing in the valley marred the silence of the night.

But now again came the rustling on the road below them. All of the men in the lookout post froze in position. The Japanese were very close now. The patrol would have to hold them with the help of the paniolos and the two policemen.

Then it happened.

Below them sounds of movement could be heard more clearly. Suddenly a grenade lobbed from a shoulder of the road exploded in the midst of the attack party. A flare went up followed by shooting from all directions.

They were not going to force the road on this try.

The "night sight" cowboy had accomplished his task—it was now up to the rest to exploit it. Automatic and rifle fire swept down the road like rain forcing the Japanese sailor troops to seek shelter wherever they could find it.

But none of the defenders of the strongpoint believed this would be the end of the matter. However a period of quite did ensue.

At Barking Sands a like period of calm which had followed the initial attack on the airfield was finally broken by American fire both on the seaward and mountain flanks of the Japanese line.

Sensing that they were attempting to envelope both of his flanks at once, the Japanese commander had a barrage of grenades dropped on the northern end of the airfield with some of the white phosphorous charges setting fires in the dry grass areas.

Having been ashore more than four hours with local time edging up to midnight, the landing party commander ordered his first platoon to withdraw through a line set up by the second platoon, to begin his retrograde movement over the route they had come.

Orders were now passed that the first major stand would be made in the area of the second ammunition cache they had dumped on their march route.

This in itself deceived the M Company attackers, who believing they had the enemy on the run, delivered an uncoordinated assault all along the line only to be thrown back with losses.

The lesson learned, the pressure was renewed after a lull in the fighting, with the Japanese again resuming their withdrawl movement until they arrived at their ammunition cache.

Whereupon, the naval landing party delivered a stunning volume of fire on the Americans, allowing them to slip rapidly up the sands toward their first cache where a longer holding action would have to be undertaken to give the I-74 time to begin taking the troops off the beach.

But the Americans, taken aback by the ferocity of the last fire fight, did not renew their pursuit for a long time.

The shore party lieutenant, surmising they were waiting to bring up support elements, decided that the second platoon should proceed directly to the embarkation area, leaving himself and the first platoon to conduct the delaying action at the last ammunition cache.

But he had reckoned without the surprise element being turned against him until to his dismay he found his first platoon force being attacked from the rear by a unit which had flanked his line from the mountain edge of Barking Sands and was driving a wedge between him and his second platoon now well on its way to the I-74.

With nothing for it but to cut their way out, the first platoon engaged their tormentors in a fire fight gradually extricating themselves from the enveloping action.

The second platoon observing their predicament held up its withdrawal, set up a base of fire to provide cover for the first platoon's retreat, then on signal silently moved back on their final resistance line by their first ammunition cache.

Faced with these delays, the party commander ordered the second platoon to collect its wounded, contact the I-74 and begin returning to the submarine while he pulled the first platoon into a loose semi-circular formation with orders to drive off any enemy attempt to interfere with the embarkation.

Both combatants were in a state of semi-exhaustion after the long fight, allowing the Japanese some surcease during which they collected their wounded and sent the first rafts off through the surf to the I-74. The dead would have to be left behind.

Making only a few feeble attempts to interfere, the American fighting line was now restricted to fairly long range rifle and automatic-rifle fire which was not of much effect.

The naval landing party demolition experts then exploded the remaining ammunition as a fiery barricade behind which the last of the team left the beach, ending the operation.

Designed as a fake invasion attempt, it had succeeded in all of its objectives, particularly in influencing the actions of the American forces which now were planning desperately to free Kauai from the enemy invaders.

The last raft was pushed through the surf with a satisfied lieutenant climbing aboard.

He had done what he had been ordered to do.

It was more than the Hanalei force commander could claim at this hour of a wild night.

His Force Lookout unable to take its objective on its first try was now strung out on the road up the escarpment with an apparently strong American outpost holding the lookout position which would threaten all of the Japanese forces and Patrol Boat No. 1 itself when daylight came.

He could not understand how it had happened. His ears, long tuned to gunfire in China combat, had told him the unit which had opened the firing from the eastern side of the bay was a weak one. Where had the additional strength come from?

As more volunteers arrived, the sergeant posted them along the rim of the bluff to guard against infiltrators crawling up the sides of the lookout.

At the same time he prayed for the arrival of C Company's two platoons and a new defense commander. For while he had done everything just right up until this time, he was in dread that there was some action he had left undone which would permit the Japanese to break through his outpost ring. If that were to happen, he knew it would be quickly over.

But C Company's reinforcing platoons were coming fast.

They had not been many minutes out of Wailua when the lieutenant commanding ordered the vehicles to turn on their lights.

"If they see us, they see us!" he shouted. "If we get to Hanalei too late it won't matter, black-out or no black-out."

So with a cheer of approval the jeeps and trucks assigned to the mission barreled up Kauai's main highway at breakneck speed. The Wailua River bridge and the town of Kapaa flashed past, then Anahola Bay with Kilauea right ahead.

At Princeville lights were darkened while the column felt its way forward to its beleagured patrol.

Approaching the lookout, they found their patrol surrounded by enemy fire from all but the road approach side which the defenders had managed to hold open. Dismounting his force with as much speed as the need for quiet permitted, the lieutenant outlined a rapid battle plan for a frontal attack straight down the road. He would take the first platoon on the left with his right flank on the road, his second in command would take the second platoon on the right with his left flank on the road.

Quickly tasks were assigned. There was an irrepressible yell along the line as it charged forward with fixed bayonets, then a volley of fire aimed short so it did not endanger the outpost more than necessary. Then all were engulfed in a general melee.

Caught short by the swiftness of the assault which he had feared from the time his seamen had climbed over the escarpment, Force Lookout commander tried to rally his units but it was too late. The fury of the charge carried the

Japanese back over the edge of the bluff when they ran to avoid the fire from their rear.

Some of the fighting spread out onto the plateau but here the surge was with the new attackers. Force Lookout was beaten off their objective. The best the commander could hope for was support from the destroyer-transport which still lay silently within the bay below.

Patrol Boat No. 1 responded within a matter of moments. But it was of little use because of the height of the lookout, most of the destroyer-transport's fire scoring only along the edge of the position although after experimentation the ship managed to drop some fire on the plateau area. It was not effective, however, so after a while Patrol Boat No. 1 returned to its darkened, silent vigil.

The destroyer-transport captain mulled over this newest problem.

If the landing party could not control the heights of the eastern shore of the bay, he had to assume that the defenders would bring artillery to the position sometime after daylight. This fire would make his position inside the bay untenable so he must make preparations to pull out into the open sea. He sent his exec officer to the beach to so advise the landing party commander of his intentions. These were that he must be clear of Hanalei Bay by daylight. He would hold station close in to the high line of the Na Pali cliffs to the west, taking advantage of whatever protection their elevation would give his ship against low flying air attack.

The landing party commander should advise the exec how long he intended to keep his party ashore and when he would be ready to reembark his forces once night had fallen and Patrol Boat No. 1 could reenter the bay. The exec saluted, tumbled into a small boat and headed for the beach.

He found the landing party commander in the midst of changing his plans for the battle of Hanalei. Force Valley had had an easy time in thrusting its nose up into the valley and in holding onto the road, Hanalei Bridge and other points vital to the advance of Force Lookout to the heights.

Now that this force had been repulsed, Force Valley must furnish the muscle which would push the enemy off the overlook and chase them a safe way back down the island from whence they had come. But the only ready means of access was the road out of the valley on which Force Lookout had met defeat. Other ways might be to stage a general assault on the heights, or to ascend Hanalei River then climb up onto the Princeville plateau and put in the attack from the south. This would take much time, however, maybe more time than the landing party could afford.

Still the commander's instructions were clear: to achieve a two-day lodgment of the invasion forces on Kauai by capture of the Hanalei area. By daylight they would have been ashore twelve hours. That would leave thirty-six hours to go.

It would truly be a stiff Monday with a stiffer Monday night and Tuesday morning to follow.

In the relief of the embattled Lookout position, all control had been lost in the savagery of the charge. Now it was imperative for the guard platoons to regain order and prepare for counterattack.

The lieutenant called for the sergeant of the patrol. There was no answer.

After some searching a voice cried out:

"Here he is!"

The lieutenant ran over with words of praise. They never passed his lips.

Stunned he looked down on the big Hawaiian with blood seeping out of his suntan shirt where the bullets had ripped across his chest. He was dead.

Silently he and his guardsmen touched their helmets in salute. Then the body was placed in a weapons carrier.

He had held the fort.

Part V

To find a fight
—Vice Admiral William Halsey
USS *Enterprise*
7 December 1941

21

To Find a Fight

A FLASH MESSAGE FROM PEARL ON THE KAUAI STRIKES came in to *Enterprise* shortly after 2000 hours while the big carrier was tensely waiting the return of nineteen planes of Torpedo Squadron Six with six smoke planes from an aborted mission against a supposed Japanese carrier south of Pearl Harbor.

Enterprise had launched them with six shepherding fighters but they had found nothing. With the fighters directed on into Pearl where four of them were shot down, the remainer of the flight was now due home. For the torpedo planes it was to be their first night landing carrying armed torpedoes.

Now came the Kauai invasion flash adding to the complications of Task Force 8 commander Vice Admiral William Halsey who had had a most frustrating day.

"The confusing and conflicting reports that had poured in on us all day had succeeded in enraging me," he was to write later. "It is bad enough to be blindfolded, but it is worse to be led around the compass.

"I waited all night for the straight word, and all night I reviewed my situation. Suppose that the enemy was located, and suppose that I could intercept him, what then? A surface engagement was out of the question, since I had nothing but cruisers to oppose his heavy ships. In addition, we were perilously low on fuel; the *Enterprise* was down to 50 percent of her capacity, the cruisers to 30 percent, the destroyers to 20 percent.

"On the other hand, my few remaining planes might inflict some damage, and by the next forenoon the *Lexington*'s task force would reach a position from which her air group could support an attack. If only someone would give us the straight word!"

Meanwhile, this Kauai attack. The shaggy-browed admiral looked at his chief of staff, Commander Miles Browning.

"What do you make of it?"

"It's a come-on for us," the lean faced aviator replied. "But I think it does tell us one thing for certain."

"What is that?"

"This attack came out of the north. Their carriers must be hanging around out there waiting for us to make our move with *Enterprise* and *Lexington*."

"You said carriers not carrier. Why?"

"The destruction which has been accomplished at Pearl must have been delivered from two or more carriers. One couldn't have done it."

"True."

"I suggest we make our rendezvous with *Lexington* as soon as possible. Then by pooling our forces for both defense of the ships and attack on the Japanese, we can strike with greater strength."

"Maybe we had better edge a little west and north of our original point to speed up this marriage."

"It would be better."

"Now what about Kauai?" Halsey addressed this question to the flag plot in general, expecting no answer. "I suppose the army will be asking for help to save the island."

"They have some flyable aircraft I presume," Browning replied. "They should get them over there at first light."

Halsey rose as the carrier stirred to begin preparations to receive her homecoming warbirds.

"Get the word to Task Force 12, Pearl and whoever else should know."

Browning nodded.

"Also you had better warn George Murray that the vultures are rustling out there in the night."

Captain Murray was the commanding officer of *Enterprise*."

"Will do."

With that Halsey went out on his bridge to await the arrival of his planes.

So all the intricate planning for a Monday strike against the Pearl Harbor raiding force got underway with no information as to the enemy's position other than the two landings on Kauai.

But Miles Browning knew a baited trap when he saw one.

22

Unwilling Warriors

WHILE FRUSTRATION ENVELOPED THE *ENTERPRISE*, A higher tension could be felt in the operations room of *Akagi* where preparations were underway for a dawn search and strike against the American carriers.

Where the flying officers in the flagship could scarcely conceal their eagerness to get at the enemy, Admirals Nagumo and Kusaka could not hide their reluctance in mounting the new operation. Both of the commanders believed that they had fulfilled the letter of their original orders and that to press further was to invite disaster to the ships which were the core of Japanese naval might.

They wanted to take their winnings and run rather than hazard everything for more gain.

Nevertheless the work of preparation went forward. Planes were fueled and armed while the flying crews tried to get some rest in readiness for the morrow.

In the operations room Genda and Fuchida with officers of the staff were plotting the search missions which would take off just before the dawn. They were in agreement as to what must be done.

"They must be somewhere to the west of Kauai," Genda

said with a sweep of his hand over the broad expanse of ocean extending out from the garden island. "Our planes can spread out in a giant fan. I am sure at least one of them will sight the enemy."

"How far out should they go?"

"Three hundred miles is about our limit. It would be difficult to do more."

Huddled over the chart they designated the search patterns and the ships from which the planes would come.

Although they had no way of knowing, their search areas included the present position of *Enterprise* and the rendezvous point where she was due to join up with *Lexington* in the forenoon of the next day.

In spite of the risk from enemy submarines the search orders were transmitted to the carriers and cruisers by blinker signals.

Then the air staff in the flagship turned its efforts to the strike plan against the American ships.

All action, of course, would have to await a confirmed sighting of their prey. When they came in everything would have to go out at once: fighters, dive bombers, torpedo planes.

At the insistence of the two admirals an ample force of Zeros would have to be retained as combat air patrol over the Nagumo Force. A brief argument regarding the number ensued but the high commanders prevailed.

Now the pilots and air crews were directed to sleep if they could while the hangar deck crews checked on the arming and servicing of the strike craft. Much of this task had been accomplished immediately after the third raid on Pearl Harbor with only the last minute fine tuning of the planes remaining.

With these tasks finished, the rest of the night was left to the navigating officers as they held the formation together throughout the dark hours. Although it had come on to rain intermittently, the seas were diminishing so the strike launch should be a fairly easy one.

The search planes would go out at 0545, fifteen minutes later than the initial Pearl Harbor scouts on Sunday's attack, for the Japanese now could take no chances that the American ships might be close in to their formation.

At 0300 hours on 8 December 1941 the Nagumo Force went to battle stations for the action of decision.

Only the lucky ones had been able to catch any sleep. But now the impending events caught up everyone in their portent for the destiny of the Empire.

The attack on Pearl Harbor had turned into one of the great naval victories of the ages. Admiral Togo's triumphs had been equalled. Now the attack on the American carriers would be the climax, the devastating slash which would destroy the hated, arrogant enemy. Every rating, every officer was carried up to martial heights by the electricity of emotion which ran through every ship in the fleet.

The briefings in the ready rooms had been short. "Fighters would take off first, then dive bombers, then torpedo planes." There was a single mission: "Sink the carriers!"

The deck crews were now bringing up planes from the hangar decks in each of the six big carriers. There were fewer now than on Sunday morning for as Nagumo had feared, the third raid on Pearl had taken a heavy toll. Still when the planes were launched they would form a most formidable air armada, certainly much greater than could be launched by *Enterprise* and *Lexington*.

During the night Genda and Fuchida had discussed the possibility that there might even be a third carrier in the Hawaiian seas, the *Saratoga* most likely. But Admiral Yamamoto's spy had given no indication of a third, so they felt they would put in their attack when it came, with the odds of six to two.

The air crews had gone to breakfast, the planes were ready, it was now simply a question of waiting out the clock.

Curiously no one in the flagship had given too much

thought to what had happened to the bait that the special naval landing parties had tossed before the Americans on the island of Kauai.

The flagship knew from the messages received that both parties had gone ashore, that opposition had been encountered, so the alarm must have spread through the American command structure.

There had been a late message that the I-74 had taken her party off the beach. This had been followed by a garbled radio dispatch from Patrol Boat No. 1 which, although unclear in details, indicated the Hanalei operation had encountered difficulties.

But there was nothing *Akagi* could do to help. Every plane would be needed for the carrier attack. Not a single one could be spared.

The special landing parties were on their own.

23

Hold the Fort

I N THE FLAG PLOT OF THE *ENTERPRISE* THE PROBLEM WAS
coming clearer by the minute. With attacks on Kauai
delivered to draw American assistance to that island, there
must be a Japanese naval force hiding beyond, waiting to
pounce on American ships bringing such aid. Men-o-war
warranting such action could only be *Enterprise* and
Saratoga. Therefore the Japanese force lurking in the night
must be of such power that it felt assured of victory in
offering battle to the two carriers.

If they could be destroyed in detail so much the better
for Nagumo.

So Halsey's problem was how to avoid battle with what
must be a vastly superior force until *Lexington* had come
up. Even then the two American carriers would be out-
weighed but the two together would greatly increase their
chances in a fight.

Task Force 8 would run the reverse course of *Lexington* as
fast as it could to move up the time of rendezvous before
the Japanese could find *Enterprise* alone.

Orders went out to the force, courses were changed and

speed increased. *Lexington* and her force were ordered to pour on the coal as the meeting of the two task forces was now vital to the survival of United States naval power in the Pacific.

Out to the northwest *Lexington* got the word. Newton, with his carrier, cruisers and destroyers, was already coming fast, but speed was pushed up even more.

The time of the rendezvous was moved to 1000 hours Monday 8 December bringing the two carriers together much earlier than had been thought possible.

The rendezvous itself was moved to the west and north.

This would not only speed up the juncture of the two task forces but with every turn of the propellers increase the distance between *Enterprise* and the Japanese carriers which most likely would launch their search planes with the dawn.

In *Lexington* preparations for Monday's battle were going forward as they were in *Enterprise*.

Pilot talk in the wardroom centered on the meet-up with the *Enterprise*.

"She's in a bit of a spot," one fighter pilot said. "If we don't get there she may be up against it two to one."

"Or three to one or maybe more," another chimed in.

"Maybe we should send her a cheer-up message."

"Like what?"

"Well how about 'Hold the fort for we are coming!' for a starter?"

"That belongs to the U.S. Cavalry," somebody commented scornfully. "This isn't the Wild West."

A dive bomber pilot on his way to catch some shut-eye responded over his shoulder.

"After all that has happened today, I am not so sure."

The few night owls in the wardroom could feel the giant carrier trembling with her increased speed.

This indeed was a race for all the marbles.

On the hangar deck the plane maintenance crews were checking and rechecking their birds. Everything must be just right.

Down in the engine rooms it was another world. Bright with electric light and noisy with the beat of machinery, the men who made her go knew *Lexington* was coming on hard, about as hard as she could go. Somebody needed her, and fast.

In the Army command posts on Oahu, after all that could be done had been done, it was a time to watch and wait.

In the G-2 Section of the headquarters of the Hawaiian Department, the lights were harsh and glaring in contrast to the total blackness outside. Someone had tuned up a shortwave radio so its blatant noisiness filled the room.

"Why don't you shut that damned thing off?" a voice asked.

A listening sergeant turned around.

"That's Tokyo direct. They're bragging about what they did to us today."

Fascinated, the entire section focused its attention on the irritating nasal boasting of the Japanese announcer speaking in flawless English. He was then followed by a female voice even more arrogant. But nevertheless when you had taken a licking and the enemy was bragging about how he did it, and how he was going to give you some more, you sat and listened—and hated.

The noise of gunfire, big guns, roared interruption.

Officers and men jumped to their phones. Some dashed downstairs and out into the night to scan the skies. The crash of detonations grew in volume.

"Antiaircraft fire. They must have some intruders on target."

The roaring of the guns lasted about ten minutes then gradually muttered out into a sullen silence.

About midnight the G-2 Section got some indication of what the fight was all about when a dazed pilot from the carrier *Enterprise* made his way slowly into the section.

"What's the matter, son?" the G-2 asked kindly."I am an

ensign in the *Enterprise*," the dazed flier responded. "I was over the island about eight-forty-five trying to get into Pearl when everything on Oahu opened up. I flew around in a dark space back of Barbers Point but my plane was hit and losing fuel. Finally I got out and jumped, landing in a cane field. When I found a road, a car came along and picked me up. The driver said I should report to G-2 so here I am."

Questioning quickly revealed that a number of *Enterprise* planes had probably met a similar fate. Reports from various stations swiftly confirmed this. Oahu's skies were now a deadly place.

At Pearl Harbor lights from ships still burning in the channels glowed with subdued and everchanging glare. Truck convoys were moving at creeping speed with only tiny blackout lights to guide them. Several of the longest convoys held the bodies of the dead—those dead not interred in the twisted steel or flooded decks of blasted ships.

Isolated bursts of gunfire shattered the silence around the black island—nerve jarring blasts bringing to taut attention those thousands who had been waiting out the tense hours for the invaders to smash ashore. Gradually the night fell away to the cold hours before the dawn.

Huddled in a dim corner of the G-2 Section a small group of officers and men laughed and joked in tired, nervous voices. They knew no more than others what might come but they had done all they could. About the long room on cots others slept in their clothes where they had lain down to shut lids on burning eyes. Even the telephones went silent as the great fortress waited. Waited for every anxious minute to crawl by.

Four o'clock came and went. At this time yesterday there had been peace where now was only anguish and women weeping for their dead. At this time yesterday there had been dreams of sunny hours in sleeping heads that now were cold and bloody. At this time yesterday there had been time for warning. Now all was regret and recrimination.

Suddenly from a small radio turned into the Interceptor Command's aircraft warning net came a voice that brought every ear in that room to attention: ". . . . aircraft approaching Kaena Point from northwest. . . ."

There was silence for a moment, then the voice continued. ". . . . unidentified aircraft maintain approach. . . ."

A soldier moved uncomfortably. "I suppose this is the way they would begin. . . ."

"Shut up!" a voice commanded while other voices muttered imperceptibly.

There was a long silence, then the impersonal radio voice began again. ". . . . aircraft nearly over Red Dog. . . ."

Around the island gunners were standing to their guns, staring up into the bottomless well of night.

Seconds slid into the shadows.

Then the voice was back. ". . . . aircraft still approaching. . . ." The voice took on a new note, almost of joy " . . . aircraft identified as friendly . . . friendly. . . ."

An exhalation of relief was audible in the shadows.

"What time is it?"

"Almost five o'clock."

"More than an hour until dawn."

"That's right—doesn't seem like Monday though."

"No—seems like years since yesterday."

So the black islands waited in the night for the enemy and the dawn, waited with every stroke of the pendulum of time. Everywhere men were at their weapons. In thousands of homes other men and women listened to the quiet breathing of the children and waited and wondered. It would not be long until the dawn.

So the islands lay in sorrow and death waiting the rising of the sun.

Of that shock-filled day and alarm-ridden night, Halsey

was later to write: "Well the milk was spilled, and the horse was stolen; there is nothing to be done about it now. I am sure I made mistakes in judgment during the four years that followed, but I have the consolation of knowing that, on the opening day of the war, I did everything in my power to find a fight."

24

Battle for the Beach

SPECIAL TASK FORCE I, COMPRISED OF THE ESCAPED
cruisers and destroyers from the Pearl Harbor debacle,
was moving through the darkness north of Oahu towards
Halsey's rendezvous when Admiral Draemel was ordered
to send a destroyer to Hanalei Bay to engage an enemy
surface vessel which was landing troops on Kauai.

This was done, with the detached destroyer under orders to rejoin the Special Task Force after disposing of the
Kauai threat. So even while the defending Americans were
locked in battle with their attackers on Hanalei's heights,
assistance was on the way.

Meanwhile the captain of *Patrol Boat No. 1* was anxiously
awaiting the outcome of the renewed assault on Hanalei
Lookout and the return of his executive officer who he had
sent to the beach to confer with the landing party commander.

Unless that attack succeeded in capturing the brow of
that frowning bluff which seemed to hang over his ship in
the night, the captain knew he would have to get out of
the bay. If this were to be done, then every moment
increased the dangers. Somehow, somewhere the Amer-

icans must be preparing a counterattack either by air or by sea.

Nervously he paced the confined space of his bridge. He could not wait too long.

Ashore, Force Valley was already advancing up the Lookout road in trace of the route the first Japanese attack had taken. Once near the crest, the landing party commander, who was now directing the operation, intended his combined forces would reinforce the firing line which by now almost completely enveloped the enemy position. After a build up of fire on the Americans, he would then order a general assault to capture the Lookout.

Minutes were passing rapidly while Force Valley struggled up the Lookout road, its progress punctuated by short bursts of fire from both American and Japanese positions. But no general fusillade had burst forth after the melee which had seen the American rescue platoons deliver their driving charge on Force Lookout in its attempt to capture the crest.

More time crawled by as the troops were fed out to both flanks to crawl along the steep slope of the hill to strengthen the Japanese lines. Then when he felt that Force Valley had deployed its strength as best it could within the time constraints he faced, the landing party commander raised his pistol and fired a flare which dropped its fiery light over the American position.

With a fierce cry the second Japanese attack went in.

Now the national guardsmen were hard put to it to hold their line. Slowly they were forced back but going to hand-to-hand combat, they blunted the Japanese thrust.

The invaders' charge sputtered to a halt. Heavy firing flamed along both battle lines. The Americans had held.

Savagely the Japanese commander tried to get the assault restarted, but his men were professionals, they knew when they had been stopped. It was no use. Nothing more to do but hold on.

Patrol Boat No. 1's executive officer saw that it would be

a long uncertain night. He passed the word on to the landing party commander, the destroyer-transport would leave the bay to return at nightfall.

The landing party would be on its own until then.

Climbing into his small motor launch he went back to the vessel to find the captain already preparing to get underway.

He had accurately assessed the results of the firefight.

"They cannot get the Americans off the bluff?"

"No," his exec answered. "Both sides are pinned down along the crest. Our attack will be renewed at daylight."

The captain glanced up at the moon sailing out from the shadow of a huge trade cloud.

"We have been here too long as it is. Keep all hands at their stations and be prepared for anything."

"Aye, Sir." The exec touched his cap while the orders to get underway were passed.

The departure of Patrol Boat No. 1 from Hanalei Bay was an unobtrusive one, the quiet sound of her engines barely audible amid the firing and explosions which rimmed the edge of the Lookout. Once outside, the patrol boat headed west toward the Na Pali coast and the shelter afforded by the mountain flanks dropping sharply into the sea.

Shortly after this silent departure Special Task Force 1's destroyer dispatched to Hanalei came sliding through the dark seas around the northeast corner of Kauai, her officers anxiously searching the black island with their glasses.

Soon they could see the sparkle of gunfire on the heights over Hanalei Bay, but who was friend and where was the foe?

At the entrance of the bay, the destroyer, knowing she would be silhouetted for any lurking submarine, fired flares over the beach line. Instantly the Japanese landing craft were illuminated in the harsh light.

But before they could fire, the destroyer's guns were in action, hammering at the two landing craft. The enemy responded with heavy machineguns and mortars, only to have the powerful armament of the destroyer turned against them.

With the landing craft in flames and their mother craft gone, the landing party was indeed alone.

The brief battle for Hanalei Bay over, the American destroyer cut for the open sea, the jitters of the Pearl Harbor attack still plaguing her crew. Speeding westward to rejoin their formation of Pearl Harbor survivors in Special Task Force 1, her lookouts kept careful watch on the dark seas for submarines and the sky for hostile aircraft.

It was almost by accident they picked up the darker shadow of Patrol Boat No. 1 hiding in the loom of the Na Pali cliffs. But the Japanese were more watchful. Recognizing the enemy immediately, the patrol boat captain ordered all bearing guns to fire on the unexpected intruder.

She erupted in a blaze of flame, her gunnery proof of the Japanese proficiency in night operations.

The American, stunned by the suddenness of the onslaught, took a moment to respond with her four five-inch guns answering the 4.7-inch and the 25mm guns of her attacker. Hits began to be scored by each side with small fires breaking out here and there on both vessels.

His mission calling for him to protect his landing party, the Japanese captain suddenly broke off the engagement to reverse his course 180 degrees bringing him onto an easterly heading. Before the American destroyer could match his maneuver, he was lost in the night. Now the American had to be most careful not to come between the Japanese and the burning fires of Hanalei Bay.

So at cautious speed she headed north, her captain knowing that the Japanese were tied to the landing party on Kauai. But when she again approached Hanalei from the northwestward no sign of her antagonist could she find.

The engagement ending in a draw, the destroyer headed west and north to regain her station with her special task force while the Japanese destroyer-transport looped around off the northeast corner of Kauai to wait out the night.

On Kauai the fight for the heights of Hanalei had fallen off into a sullen struggle for small advantages as the Japanese continued to press the defenders.

Intelligence of the sea fight was electrifying to command groups in the *Akagi* and the *Enterprise.*

The two fleets had now made contact the significance of which could be easily misread by either side.

In *Akagi,* Nagumo and Kusaka were somewhat unnerved by this appearance of American surface power on their southern flank when all of their efforts were directed towards the westward. If an American destroyer was in action off Kauai to the south, would the American carriers also be in that area?

But the airmen felt not, correctly guessing that the destroyer was a stray from Pearl which had been deflected to handle the Kauai situation.

In *Enterprise,* drawing away to the northwestward from Kauai, it was a reminder that the Japanese attackers were spraddled over a great deal of ocean with their exact position unknown to the Americans.

So the night dragged on with the *Enterprise* force drawing off to the northwest and a convergence with the *Lexington* task force racing down the southeast course from Midway.

Following far astern of the *Enterprise* force came the Pearl Harbor escapees which carried formidable power with them in their cruisers and the swarm of destroyers in their train.

Far out to the northwest, Midway Islands had beaten off a bombardment attack by two Japanese destroyers, *Ushio* and *Sazanami,* aimed at the air base. This supplementary force to the Nagumo fleet had sailed from the vicinity of the Yokosuka naval base November 28 as a decoy operation with its support vessel, the fleet tanker *Shiriya Maru,* commanded by Captain Minoru Togo, son of the great Japanese victor at Tsushima. But Midway's Marines knocked them back with a loss of four dead and ten wounded Americans.

25

Seek and Find

WITH ALL ACTIVITY NOW DIRECTED TOWARD PREPARING the search planes and the strike forces for the impending battle, both sides worked feverishly against the coming of the dawn.

Halsey had already alerted Pearl to the need for all the air help it could muster, while Special Task Force 1 was instructed to concentrate as best it could to aid the two beleagured carriers repel the Japanese attack when it came in. This was proving a difficult task with ships spread all over the ocean just beginning to shake themselves into a cohesive battle force after the alarms and excursions of the afternoon and evening.

Draemel's staff in the light cruiser *Detroit* was beginning to bring order into the destroyer formations of the fleet so they would present a coordinated array of surface power when they joined up with Task Forces 8 and 12 during the coming day. As the clock's hands crept towards 0500 *Enterprise* and her attending heavy cruisers *Chester, Northampton* and *Salt Lake City* held ready to launch their scouting planes.

It would be a slim search, indeed, directed from the northwest to the north-northeast while to the south Pearl would take over the areas immediately north of Oahu and Kauai with what planes could be gotten into the air. The *Enterprise* search would be launched earlier than the Japanese for the Americans had more assurance that the waters they had covered during the night were free of the enemy.

Halsey wanted his searchers to be far out at first light so that if the enemy were seen he would have earliest warning.

Because it was vital that each plane perform its search mission leaving no blank spaces of ocean in which the Japanese task force might hide the thunderbolt which the Americans knew they would launch at *Enterprise* and *Lexington* that coming day, each air crew had been specially briefed by their commanders on their task and the special situations they might encounter during the search.

Just before 0500 *Enterprise* swung into the wind and increased her speed for the critical launch. The four scout bombers roared down the flight deck to become airborne in the darkness while at the same time the three heavy cruisers each launched a plane. Seven planes to find an enemy who until now had remained hidden but for the destruction he had inflicted on Pearl Harbor and the American air squadrons!

On Oahu the Navy had rounded up planes which would search the air space to the north of Oahu and Kauai. With this reinforcement it was hoped the search planes would find the enemy unless he had flown.

Now Task Force 8 would await the dawn and its convergence with Task Force 12 and the *Lexington,* and the other surface forces steaming towards a juncture with the carriers.

For the searching planes it was a miserable morning, flying over a dark ocean made darker by the incessant rain squalls, maintaining a constant procession from the northeast off to the southwest. With such a high value placed on the need to sight the enemy before he could spot the task force, nervous tension in the planes became a tangible companion pressing in upon the fliers already beset with fatigue from the interminable hours of Sunday and Sunday night.

So the American air search droned on through the darkness of the late night, the air crews wishing for the dawn even though the greater visibility would multiply their perils.

In the Nagumo force the excitement in the carriers rose by the minute as time approached for the launch. This should be the day when the final harvest of Pearl Harbor would be reaped in flame and death.

Although it was too much to expect a tactical surprise, it was the general feeling in the great carriers that the whip-hand belonged to the Japanese, assuring the destruction of the American carriers and an almost certain promise of victory in the Pacific War now not quite a day old.

With confidence as their companion, the Japanese reconnaissance pilots cockily took their planes off their carrier decks promptly at 0545 over moderate seas speckled with rain squalls. Their take-offs were made amid cheers of the airmen and seamen of the six carriers, for this was surely the day of ultimate triumph.

Fifteen minutes into their flight, the Japanese were greeted by the first streaks of dawn which came up red from the east, promising more rain throughout the day. But no weather could quell the ebullience of the carrier pilots as they winged their way on to the final act of the Pearl Harbor attack. The fever of the hunt would sustain them through their 300-mile outbound flight during which they would be searching, searching for the long black rectangles on the sea which would be the American carriers.

The enthusiasm of their crews could not calm the fears of Nagumo and Kusaka, however. Secretly the two reluctant admirals almost hoped that their search efforts would fail.

Nagumo had been unable to sleep during the night so was approaching the edge of physical exhaustion, requiring all the reassurance Kusaka could give to sustain him through what was sure to be a long and troubling day.

In his flagship *Nagato* in the Inland Sea, Yamamoto, spurred by the need for physical movement, dragged his reluctant operations officer Captain Kurishima up and down the decks of the great warship. While Nagumo, Kusaka and even Yamamoto might have doubts of the outcome of the battle, Kuroshima seemed to have none, leaving all to the gods of war. But he gamely matched stride for stride with his restless admiral who now sensing the kill could hardly restrain his impatience.

In the flag plot of *Enterprise,* Halsey matched him stride for stride as he mentally computed the positions of Task Force 8 and Newton's Lexington Force sweeping in from the northwest. Once the carriers were within mutually supporting distance, Halsey would feel relief. He already had warned Kimmel at Pearl that he would need the help of every flyable plane on Oahu if he was to hold even close in the coming battle.

Off Kauai, Patrol Boat No. 1 was cautiously edging her way back towards Hanalei Bay, her captain and executive officer congratulating themselves on their fortunate escape from the guns of the midnight American destroyer. On the crest of Hanalei Lookout, both sides were preparing to renew their battle at dawn, the national guardsmen having received reinforcements in the late night hours while the Japanese landing party commander was determinedly preparing for the new assaults he felt would come with the growing daylight.

In San Diego the giant carrier *Saratoga,* sister of the *Lexington,* was hurriedly loading planes, ammunition and other materiels of war, for a flying trip down to Pearl Harbor. But it was a voyage which might never be made depending on the outcome of the battle now building to the west of Kauai. In the Atlantic orders went out to the aircraft carrier *Yorktown* and battleships *Idaho, New Mexico* and *Mississippi* to sail for Panama to transit the canal into the Pacific. But they were weeks away from Hawaii.

Lexington launched four search planes at 0600 with instructions to fly to the northeast before turning eastward towards *Enterprise* search areas. Captain Frederick Sherman personally insured that the pilots were certain where they were going to rejoin the carrier at the end of their final dogleg.

Now the seas and skies north and west of Oahu and Kauai were becoming alive with planes and ships. Some submarines were in the area but no one seemed quite certain where.

All that was certain was that the next few hours would bring all the combatants within striking distance of each other and that the new Pacific war would see the first great carrier battle in naval history.

The weather, which had been marred by heavy rain squalls during the night, began to gloom over with more frequent showers while the clouds started to gather down closer to the surface of the ocean, now making up under the lash of an increasing wind. It was not going to be the pleasant day that had smiled on the Japanese successes of the seventh.

Decreased visibility coupled with the monotonous drone of the engines acted as narcosis on the aircrews so that in spite of the vital importance of their missions, they found themselves fighting to overcome the hypnotic drift towards sleep which enwrapped them all. Flying at considerable height, the rock-like islet of Nihoa slipped under the port wing of *Enterprise's* most easterly plane briefly arousing some interest before the vast emptiness of gloomy seas and skies usurped all visible space again.

It was now nearing 0800 for the *Enterprise* search. The 200-mile mark had passed with nothing to report. But the critical part of the flight was now beginning, causing the pilot and his crewman to stir themselves in their seats.

Then they both saw it at the same time, the shadowy outline of a plane speeding from beneath one cloud shroud to another far below them.

The crewman tapped the pilot on his shoulder, receiving a nod in reply.

It was time to warn the *Enterprise*.

Swiftly the signal went out giving the carrier the course, speed and altitude of the intruder. Suddenly both fliers were wide awake. The pilot adjusted his course to the reverse heading from the stranger, the search for the enemy now growing warm.

Careful scrutiny of the northeast horizon revealed nothing more, however, than the lowering clouds over the gray ocean with splashes of rain speckling the sea as far as the dim horizon.

A few minutes more and the plane was nearing the northern limit of its flight pattern before it would turn into the northeasterly heading along which it would fly for fifty miles before executing its final change of course which would bring it back to the carrier.

Then they saw the prey. Dim shapes on the sea line, hidden intermittently by clouds and rain. Seeking the shelter of a large mass of gray cloud, the plane flashed its message to *Enterprise*.

"Two surface ships bearing 22 degrees, distant 270 miles, course 230 degrees."

A long interval of silence followed while the scout bomber dodged from cloud cover to cloud cover, closing the range with the enemy.

Finally emerging from a long cloud barrier before darting into another, the pilot, staring with disbelieving eyes, sent his shocked report: "Four carriers, one battleship, one cruiser, destroyers bearing 21 degrees, distant 280 miles, course 230 degrees, speed 20."

Enterprise was galvanized by the message. Lexington Task Force 12 was notified directly, then Task Force 3 and Special Task Force 1 and Pearl. The bearing and distance factors were rapidly computed by *Enterprise* in preparation for launching her attack.

Dodging from the shelter of one rain-dark cloud to another, the *Enterprise* scout closed in for a nearer look knowing he was now entering the sky of the Japanese combat air patrols protecting Nagumo's fleet. But what of the first plane they had sighted? Deciding it must have been a delayed long distance reconnaisance aircraft, the *Enterprise* pilot pressed his search.

But he had been seen.

High above him and to his rear, the Japanese was carefully scrutinizing every cloud for his prey. He had also alerted *Akagi* so the fleet fighter cover was now directed toward the area through which the American plane was approaching.

That plane crew's prayers for rain squalls to cover their flight were now answered with huge black rags of cloud hiding them from their hunters. But the *Enterprise* pilot knew from the black specks darting out from the carriers that he must have been seen. Still he pressed his approach.

Then in a clear space of ocean to the north he glimpsed the Nagumo Force with astonished eyes.

His message went out: "Six carriers, two battleships, cruisers, destroyers, bearing 21 degrees, distant 280 miles, course still 230 degrees." Then knowing that he had been seen by at least one Japanese, he flashed: "Am attacking."

In *Enterprise* the air strike had begun to launch. *Lexington* had been alerted but there was no time to plan a concerted attack. It would be delivered by *Enterprise* first with *Lexington* coming in from the west northwest as soon as she could get within striking distance.

At the same time *Enterprise* began the long careful examination of the cloud filled skies for the attack which was now certain to come to her.

But still the Japanese reconnaissance planes, droning their ways to the west and to the south, had not picked up either of the American carriers. The early launch of the

Enterprise search planes had paid off. In her combat information center ears were strained for the first news of the lone attack of her scout bomber.

In the flag plot Halsey and Browning waited tensely for the attempt against the odds.

Suddenly the pilot's voice came over the miles. "Am going after Shokaku class carrier."

Then silence.

It was a time of waiting now.

The *Enterprise* dive bombers and torpedo planes had a good bearing. They should do some work.

High above the *Lexington* her fighters circled Task Force 12 ceaselessly searching the gray seas and skies. Nothing.

At the antiaircraft guns it was the same. Nothing.

Out in the protective screen of cruisers and destroyers, it was the same. Waiting, waiting and nothing.

Lexington was coming within supporting range now, preparing to launch her air strike. Because she had suffered no losses, her blow would be a heavier one. She also had the advantage of the *Enterprise* scouting report. Swiftly she marshaled her attack force. She would hit the Nagumo force with everything she had.

Rolling down her flight deck, her planes circled Task Force 12 then bore off to the eastward. The Americans would not have a coordinated attack but their two blows would be sharp ones.

Both Admiral Nagumo and his Chief of Staff Kusaka received the first report of the sighting of the American scouting plane with apprehension.

"Was it from Oahu or was it from one of the missing carriers?"

That was the critical question.

In their anxieties over delivering an attack in which they did not believe and their fears for the safety of the great striking force under their command, they turned their frustrations on their air staff.

"What was the matter with their air cover? Why had the

American snooper been allowed to approach so close to the carriers?"

While they were venting their spleen, the warning of impending attack vibrated through the fleet. The cloud cover which hung over the force now seemed charged with danger as the protecting fighters searched unsuccessfully for the intruder.

But when he did break out of the gray obscurity the attack came with great swiftness.

The *Enterprise* pilot, upon obtaining his clear view of the entire Japanese formation, immediately climbed higher into the cloud cover which extended over the fleet.

"We're going after the first carrier nearest to us," the pilot told his gunner. "I'm going to drop straight down so guard our tail."

Carefully he positioned himself for the attack while the gunner searched constantly for any sign of the enemy, but there was none, although both flyers were certain that they were out there in the clouds.

Suddenly a break in the cover gave him a glimpse of the intended victim. She was directly below.

Dropping her nose, the scout bomber plummeted down towards the enemy. It was one of their new carriers, the *Shokaku*. Suddenly her dark shape came alive with twinkling sparks, her antiaircraft guns blazing into action.

At the same time, the gunner reported he had two enemy planes on their tail.

It would be a close race to the target.

Down, down, down they dropped through black mushrooms of antiaircraft fire, their two pursuers spitting out the venom of their guns.

The decks of the carrier now broad before him, the *Enterprise* pilot released his bomb. It dropped, a speck of black against the dull skies. With hypnotic fascination the crew of *Shokaku* watched it fall.

Amid clanging alarms the firefighting crews held their places, waiting for the blast of the explosion. It came with a mighty roar just aft of the carrier's island, blowing up several fighters waiting for take-off, but most devastating of all, although it could not be clearly seen, it jammed the forward plane elevator so that when the smoke had cleared, its after edge jutted up some four feet above the flight deck.

Shokaku would not be launching planes that morning.

But the American pilot had no chance to check his work, the two Zeros poured fire into him as he dived towards the sea where a great splash soon marked the kill.

Enterprise had drawn first blood.

It now became vital to Nagumo that his scout planes sight the enemy carrier which had put *Shokaku* out of action.

A tall pillar of smoke hung above the stricken ship while her crew moved in to bring the destruction under control.

Kusaka looked silently at Nagumo. Their judgment had been vindicated. Still they had to eliminate these two great vipers, the American carriers. The need for success was now more urgent than ever.

"Where were they?"

As if in answer the air officer handed Nagumo a message. It was from Kaga's reconnaissance plane.

"Carrier, cruiser, two destroyers bearing 205 degrees, distant 280 miles, course 38 degrees, speed 20."

So they had found one!

Quickly the strike was readied for take-off, but an equally powerful force must be held in reserve for the other carrier.

"Where was it?"

The air officer spoke. "She must either be in supporting distance of the one we now have in view or she must be steaming into that position. In either case our scout planes should pick her up soon."

Meanwhile an American strike must be on the way, but Kaga's plane had forwarded no more information.

He was directed to report "Yes" or "No."

The answer came in shortly.

"No planes in view."

What the pilot did not know was that he had overflown the *Enterprise* aerial strike force while searching for the carriers.

Meanwhile the Japanese strike launch had been completed, the bombers and torpedo planes with their fighter cover winging their deadly way down the bearing towards the enemy.

The battle was about to be joined.

26

The Lonely Beach

KNOWING HE HAD INSUFFICIENT STRENGTH TO PUSH THE Americans down the road from Hanalei Lookout, the commander of the Japanese landing party opened a spoiling action just before dawn in anticipation of an attack in force by the Americans. He was correct, for such an attack was ready to jump off when the Japanese fire disrupted it.

When full daylight came, the fire fight sputtered out with both sides settling back into the stalemate which had lasted through the night.

Only a small number of reinforcements had been sent to Hanalei during the night for the district commander had to guard many miles of shoreline with no indications as to where another blow might fall on Kauai.

He had requested more troops from Oahu but had been turned down after Pearl Harbor had warned the Army that a large sea battle was in the making with all the odds in favor of the enemy. The Navy did promise that surface ships would be sent to shell the Japanese invaders whenever they could be spared.

So matters stood while Patrol Boat No. 1 held position north of Kauai preparing to run into Hanalei Bay at nightfall to take off the landing party which now seemed to have little hope of holding on for another night.

But while the commanders of the Hanalei expedition were disappointed in the results they had obtained in the first night's action, they could not know the great forces they had set in motion by the first major foreign invasion of American soil since the war of 1812.

The intrusion weighed heavily on the calculations of Kimmel and Short for the defense of Hawaii, while at the same time it brooded like a cloud over the preparations Halsey and the other sea commanders were making to bring the Japanese to battle.

But its greatest effect was in the shock waves it sent out to the leaders of the United States government in Washington and to the military and naval commanders charged with the defense of the long American coastline stretching from Alaska to Mexico.

Where would the Japanese strike next? California, Oregon, Washington, Canada or Alaska?

Emergency conferences dragged on throughout the night and into Monday as the nation's leaders wrestled with the problem.

At first they had attempted to keep it as a military secret, but too many people were involved, so the Hanalei landings erupted on the front pages of the nation's press in headlines: "HAWAII INVADED!" "JAPANESE ASHORE IN HAWAII!" "WEST COAST PERIL!"

If there had been dismay in Hawaii at the Kauai landing, there was consternation in the nation's capitol.

Winston Churchill asked Roosevelt for details. He got none for Roosevelt had none.

There was great glee in Tokyo where the action assumed gigantic proportions with the army and navy reviewing all of their widespread attack plans to see if indeed strength could be quickly mustered so all of Hawaii could be captured and attacks launched on the American mainland itself.

Only in the naval general staff and the combined fleet

was the reaction more restrained as Yamamoto and the other admirals awaited the results of the sea battle they knew was building west of Kauai.

San Francisco, Los Angeles, Seattle, Portland, Oakland and San Diego were close to panic as rumor had Japanese divisions landing at various places along the almost undefended coast.

Protecting the West Coast were two Regular Army and two National Guard divisions stationed at Fort Lewis, Washington, and at Fort Ord and Camp Roberts in California. In addition there were harbor defense seacoast artillery units at the entrance of Puget Sound, the Columbia River, San Francisco Bay, Los Angeles Harbor and San Diego Harbor.

Backing up the Fourth Army on the West Coast were the other 26 Regular and National Guard divisions spread throughout the continental U.S.

But on 7 December the 3rd and 41st Divisions at Fort Lewis, Washington, and the 7th and 40th Divisions in California were the only guardians of the coast.

Exposed to naval surface or air attack were the U.S. Navy's major shore establishments at Bremerton, Washington, and Mare Island, Hunters Point, Long Beach and San Diego in California.

It was a long nervous day and night for the commanders of U.S. Army and Navy installations in the West.

But although they could not know it, any threat of a major invasion of Hawaii or the West Coast would depend on the outcome of the sea battle in its opening phases west of Kauai.

On that outcome the commander of Patrol Boat No. 1 felt he could no longer wait. He would enter Hanalei Bay in darkness, assist the special naval landing party with covering fire, then remove its men and weapons from the beach. Even then the evacuation would not be complete until the old destroyer-transport had logged enough sea miles during the night hours to put her out of reach of land based aviation on Oahu. It would be a neat problem in time and space so the captain had made up his mind. He would embark the troops and leave knowing he was cutting short the mission. But in his opinion the landing party had achieved more than could have been expected of it.

27

Sea Battle

ANXIOUS WAITING GRIPPED THE BIG E AS HER PLANES MOVED towards their target. Her crew's ears were tuned to the loudspeakers but they were silent. Nothing came back from their strike which by now must be close in to the area the *Enterprise* scout had reported his attack on the Japanese carriers. Maybe they had been given the slip by the Japanese. With their numbers seriously cut back by their scout bomber losses at Pearl the day before, every plane must make its attack count. If the formation failed to find the enemy carriers it would be all over for the *Enterprise*.

It was an anxious time.

The gun crews at their weapons in the gun platforms jutting over the sides of the big carrier searched the skies ceaselessly for the Japanese attack they knew must be on the way.

But nothing was heard, either from the *Enterprise* strike or from the scout bomber which had sighted the Japanese fleet and then attacked.

Meanwhile the sea had begun to make up with white flecks creaming the sullen waves rolling heavily under cloudy skies. Now intermittent rain squalls were sweeping across *Enterprise* and her cruisers and destroyers. The foul weather would be helpful to the ships in hiding them from the Japanese scouts which by this time must be somewhere up there in the overcast.

It was then *Enterprise* was galvanized by the voices of their own combat air patrol above them, the fighter pilots having sighted the intruder which had already reported their position to the *Akagi*.

"There he is! Below, below!"

"Roger. Let's go!"

Then silence with the ship's gunners waiting tensely.

"Got him! Look at him burn!"

Suddenly the plane dropped like a flaming brand out of the overcast about two miles from *Enterprise*. It hit the water with a tremendous splash, burned for a few seconds, then sank.

The task force watched their first enemy kill grimly. The hounds which he had called in must be very close.

Far to the east the *Enterprise* strike planes had caught their first glimpse of the enemy carriers through the obscurity when the air group commander led them deep into the cloud cover to the north. He had determined to deliver his attack from that direction pouring all of his force at the enemy at once. Hopefully the fighters would keep the Japanese covering Zeros so busy they would find it difficult to interfere with the dive bombers and the torpedo planes when they came in.

The fighters were the first to strike, jumping the Japanese protective air patrol which had chosen to stay just under the clouds while guarding their charges far below. An aerial melee quickly developed, spreading all over the sky.

Enterprise got its first hand reports of the battle from the fighter pilots' chatter to each other during the action.

"Watch out, Joe! On your tail!"

"Got him!"

"Into the clouds! Into the clouds! I think they are surprised!"

On the instant the attack on the carriers developed with great rapidity with the dive bombers leading the way, jumping all six carriers in the Nagumo force.

A huge orange explosion erupted on the flight deck of the already crippled *Shokaku*, steaming astern of the flagship. It was followed by a series of blasts which wracked the new ship now spitting at her tormentors with all her guns.

But her fighter protection had failed her, so two Dauntless dive bombers dropped their deadly cargo on her broad deck. Apparent that she was badly hurt, the following bombers picked other targets.

Their attention focused on the dive bombers which were swarming down on the force, the Zeros failed to react quickly to the oncoming torpedo planes skimming low over the ocean out of the overcast. By luck and by skill, *Enterprise* had timed her strike so the deficiency in the number of her planes was made up for by their convergence on their targets at the same moment.

Filling the skies with black ackack blossoms, the guns of the Japanese fleet roared into continuous action which began to take its toll. Two American TBFs blew up in face of the heavy frontal fire but two others dropped their fish in dead line with the carrier *Soryu* on the northern edge of the fleet formation. The battleship *Kirishima*'s towering pagoda shape flamed like a blazing bonfire with all her guns speaking, even the great 14.2-inch main battery giants which were attempting to splash the gray ocean into the faces of the oncoming torpedo planes.

But the torpedoes were launched at the long span of *Soryu*'s gray hull. Twist and turn as she would, she would not escape.

Almost simultaneously two explosions, one forward and one aft, fountained alongside the carrier but still she came on. The TBFs evaded her protective fire long enough to fly low across her flight deck before attempting their get-away.

For a moment it appeared that *Soryu* would come free of serious harm. Then a huge burst of flame spouted out of her hangar deck aft. The results of this explosion were catastrophic to the carrier. Her speed dropped away while she swung erratically to starboard unable to answer her helm.

At the moment a belated dive bomber laid its bomb on her flight deck just inboard of her island superstructure. A delayed flash was followed by an eruption of debris vomiting upwards over the island.

During this action burning *Shokaku* circled and dodged impotently, unable to launch her planes because of flight deck damage and fires.

All of this further alarmed the two admirals on *Akagi's* bridge. With their air strike already off to attack *Enterprise*, where was the other carrier?

As if in answer, the sky lookouts alarmed the force to new dangers coming out of the northwest. It was *Lexington's* dive bombers shepherded by her fighters sweeping in to join the *Enterprise* attack. Below them there were torpedo bombers boring in with the oncoming force.

The Japanese Zeros were now all over the sky attempting to shield their carriers from this new onslaught. Although they had been unable to fend off the attack on *Soryu*, they had been successful in turning back the thrusts at the other ships.

Many of *Enterprise's* planes would not return.

Crippled *Soryu* and sinking *Shokaku* drew more dive bombers although *Akagi*, *Kaga*, *Zuikaku* and *Hiryu* had their share.

To Nagumo and Kusaka it seemed that all of their worst fears had come to life. Here they had two carriers heavily damaged, one of which might be fatally hurt, with no report of any retaliation on the Americans.

It was then they were told in the noise of the battle that

contact had been made with an *Enterprise*-type carrier and the attack was going in.

"Still nothing on the second one," Nagumo complained.

Kusaka morosely shook his head.

Then came another flash. "*Lexington*-type carrier sighted northwest of first carrier."

"That attack should be going in shortly," Kusaka said.

But the strike force commander and his chief of staff were staggered by the destruction surrounding them. They should have taken their winnings and left. So much for airmen's judgment.

Now everything would rest on the results of the attack on the two American carriers. It was a time to hope.

In *Enterprise* her silent crew stood to their guns while their fighter cover pulled itself up into the overcast waiting for the fury they knew was about to burst on them.

Then the news was flashed that *Lexington* was forty miles to the northwest and was launching her air strike on the Japanese force. A cheer swept through the ship, only to be choked off by the word: "Here come the bandits!"

So high above the ship that *Enterprise* looked like a toy vessel, the combat air patrol leader marshaled his forces to meet the Zeros, Vals and Kates which would soon be upon them.

If the Kates, the torpedo bombers, came in first, half of his force would have to drop almost to the surface to attack them. That would leave the other half to handle the Val dive bombers as well as fend off the Japanese fighters.

Now *Enterprise* was telling them: "Bandits approaching 85 degrees, distance 30 miles."

Then there they were!

It came all at once.

With her fighter cover battling Zeros while coping with torpedo planes and dive bombers, *Enterprise* found herself dodging torpedoes while her gun crews fought off the dive bombers which fell upon her.

First came a near miss on the port side which rocked the

carrier violently, water from the splash pouring down on her signal bridge. The antiaircraft guns filled the skies with fire. Three dive bombers burst into flames but the others came on.

All the while the heavy cruisers and the destroyers of the screens augmented by the cruisers and destroyers of the Special Task Force from Pearl Harbor joined the battle centering over the carriers.

Then came the word.

"Torpedo planes approaching from 15 degrees."

Attention of the screening ships turned to the north-northeast where the black shapes of the deadly-looking Kates could be seen skimming above the waves intent on making a good launch at *Enterprise,* twisting and turning like a huge leviathan attempting to evade the harpoon.

Her own Wildcat fighters were now down on the sea pouring fire into the tails of the Kates. One by one the Japanese torpedo bombers fell before the deadly attack, some blowing up before smashing into the sea while others burst into flames before taking their death plunge. Still they came on to launch their long, deadly fish.

Two looked like they were going to hit, but violent evasive action by the carrier's helmsman pulled her clear.

Then *Enterprise* took a bomb well forward on the starboard side. Violence of her shaking tumbled a plane off the flight deck into the sea while damage control parties rushed along the hangar deck to fight fires set off by the burst.

Still the Big E fought on.

On the signal bridge a seaman pointed off to the northwest where the same drama was being played out over *Lexington.* Binoculars picked out the Japanese dive bombers falling on the huge carrier while her own fighters followed them down in their plunging descent.

Suddenly a plume of dense black smoke towered over the carrier.

"*Lexington's* hit!"

Even men engrossed in their own self-survival could not forbear a quick glance off to the northwest.

It was now apparent to the naked eye that fire was sweeping the Big E's consort.

But attention whipped back to *Enterprise* as she took another hit, this one along her port gun catwalk. Fires broke out along the flight deck but were quickly doused while the corpsmen moved to rescue the wounded.

It was a savage blow but not fatal. *Enterprise* survived, her damage control parties fighting fires in various parts of the ship while she continued to steam with full power, adroitly dodging the bombs and torpedoes which beset her.

Suddenly it was all over, the Japanese were returning to their own carriers. In a grandiose gesture *Enterprise* launched some pursuing fighters, but the main action had ceased.

Now word came from *Lexington* that she was sinking, her crew were being taken off by ships of her screen. *Enterprise* would not only have to take aboard her own aircraft survivors of the strike on the Nagumo force but she would have to provide a haven for the survivors of *Lexington* and her air group. Emergency preparations got underway to receive all returning planes from the battle.

Halsey watched anxiously from his flag bridge where he had been from the first predawn takeoffs of *Enterprise* scouting planes. His vigil was shared by the carrier's Captain Murray on the navigating bridge.

To the northwest Captain Frederick Sherman was directing the abandonment of *Lexington* and transfer of her crew to ships of her screen.

Halsey ordered a concentration of all task forces at sea to bring together in the same general area the commands of Admirals Wilson Brown, John Newton and Milo Draemel.

It was a time to count the losses and care for the wounded while preparing for the morrow.

In *Akagi* the mood was almost as grim.

Nagumo and Kusaka had fretted throughout the day at the pace of the battle. The scouting had been slow and unsatisfactory, resulting in the Americans drawing first blood.

Then the defense of the force had been handled clumsily allowing the enemy to break through the fighter cover. Before midday the Nagumo force had two heavily damaged carriers which might be lost before nightfall.

Yet their orders were clear: "Sink the carriers!"

In his long naval career Nagumo had always held the power over his adversary. Now he was not sure and the uncertainty was pushing him towards flight.

One of the air staff approached the pair almost diffidently handing Kusaka the latest message from the *Lexington* strike commander. The chief of staff held it before him impatiently. It was good news.

"Lexington-type carrier attacked. Great damage. She may be sinking."

Kusaka almost managed a smile when he handed it to Nagumo.

"It appears we may have got one of them."

Nagumo read the dispatch fluttering in the wind.

"That is good news," he said. "I hope it is correct."

Kusaka ordered an immediate recheck.

Nagumo looked at him almost petulantly.

"What of the other?"

Almost as if in reply the air officer was back with a message from the strike force commander.

"Enterprise type struck twice with bombs. She is burning."

"Well things are looking up," Nagumo commented cheerfully.

"The attack forces are returning," Kusaka told him. "We will be able to accurately assess results once they are aboard."

Nagumo nodded. He was feeling more optimistic.

"We may be able to finish them off," he replied tentatively.

Kusaka pursed his lips.

"We will see."

Just then *Akagi* shuddered violently almost in answer to a lookout's call of: "Torpedo off port bow!"

The first shock was followed by another explosion.

Immediately the damage control crews swarmed to the forward port hand spaces of the flagship which continued to take sharp evasive action. In five minutes the ship's captain gave them a report.

"Two ballast tanks ruptured forward but no vital damage."

Luck was with *Akagi*. The American submarine had inflicted critical damage, however.

It was real but invisible, for it was to the spirit of the two admirals. From now on the airmen would have to prove the effectiveness of their projected plans. The fighting spirit was gone. It would not return that day.

Now the first of the strike planes were returning to their carriers, with those from *Soryu* and a few strays from *Shokaku* being directed to the flight decks of *Akagi*, *Kaga*, *Zuikako* and *Hiryu*.

A cheer ran through *Akagi* as the planes touched the deck. The first flyer waved his *hachimaki* in reply. "Be quick!" he warned his flight deck handlers. "We will have to return."

Reports were taken rapidly from each pilot after they had gathered at a table set up on the deck immediately below the bridge of the giant carrier. It was a tale of great damage to both *Lexington* and *Enterprise*.

The gathering fliers waited impatiently the arrival of the strike commander who had hovered over the two targets checking damage inflicted and his own losses in planes and air crews. Now his plane settled easily onto the *Akagi*'s flight deck across which drifted ribbons of smoke as the damage control teams brought her fires under control.

Climbing from the aircraft, he held a hurried conference with his pilots while the rearming and refueling of the planes was speeded by *Akagi*'s crewmen.

He heard the same story from all.

The Americans had shot down many Japanese planes but the U.S. carriers had been hit hard.

Lexington seemed to be sinking while *Enterprise* was smoking from several fires.

In addition it appeared two heavy cruisers had been damaged with at least three destroyers sunk.

After one final round of questions, the air commander bounded up the steel ladders leading to the bridge.

There Nagumo and Kusaka awaited his report.

"We have inflicted great losses on the enemy," Fuchida began. "It would appear that *Lexington* is sinking and *Enterprise* is severely damaged. We must go back to finish them off. In addition three destroyers have been sunk while two heavy cruisers have been badly damaged. It has been a great day."

His elation was not reflected in the cautious faces of the two highest officers. Rather they had him review his report in detail even though every moment was of the greatest import.

Impatiently Fuchida pleaded for another attack. Commander Genda reinforced his plea.

But the two admirals continued irresolute.

From Admiral Tamon Yamaguchi in *Hiryu* came again the signal as it had the day before: "Am ready to renew attack."

The commander of the 2nd Carrier Division was opting for complete destruction of the enemy even though his own carrier *Soryu* was in extreme straits.

But his advice was not to be considered for at that moment air attack alarms sounded throughout the fleet. Looking aloft the startled Japanese could see a lone dive bomber begin his descent on the flagship. The covering Zeros, following him down in his dive, sprayed the American with their fire.

This failed to stop the attack however as the pilot dived for the flight deck of *Akagi*, forcing the conferees to scurry for whatever cover they could find. His bomb arced down, exploding in a near miss with the U.S. plane, now a mass of flame, following it into the sea. There was no damage to *Akagi*, but here again the psychological impact would prove decisive.

Nagumo and Kusaka looked at Genda and Fuchida with accusing eyes.

Kusaka spoke to his admiral.

There should be no more attacks. The safety of the entire Nagumo force was obviously at stake. It was time to end the mission and steam for home.

Nagumo agreed.

Orders were passed to the signalmen. The formation wheeled abruptly to the north. All of the cripples were shepherded into the center of the fleet while the fighter cover over the ships was reinforced.

Even though he had no knowledge of what his lone dive bomber had achieved, Halsey's spirit had prevailed.

In *Enterprise* with fires still burning forward, the fighting admiral knew he had but little choice but to break off the action. *Lexington* was going, *Enterprise* was severely damaged, three destroyers were sunk and two heavy cruisers were barely afloat.

Still the signal came hard. It was time to make for Pearl.

Light cruisers and destroyers with fuel supplies permitting were ordered to range the battle area for survivors while the wounded carrier gathered the rest of the U.S. Pacific Fleet around her for the voyage home.

A destroyer assigned to look in on the situation at Hanalei Bay on its return to Oahu found the Japanese gone, having embarked their landing force survivors shortly after dark with minimal interference from the American ground units.

It was a night as somber as the Sunday night after the Pearl Harbor attack.

The same uncertainties were still there:

Where were the Japanese?

Would they attack again?
But Halsey could take heart in spite of all.
At odds of three to one he had inflicted heavy damage
on the enemy fleet.
He had done all he could with what he had.
He had found his fight!

Part VI

*The brazen throat
of war*

—John Milton

28

A Tough Nut to Crack

ENTERPRISE ARRIVED OFF THE PEARL HARBOR ENTRANCE buoys late Tuesday night. Scarred and burned from her fight, the yard tugs took her in hand to escort her around the devastation of Ford Island to her berth for refueling from a fleet oiler and replenishment for the voyage back to the mainland for repairs and refit.

Damaged as she was she would not be able to mount another attack while the ruined Navy yard had lost the facilities in Nagumo's third raid which would have enabled it to restore the Big E's fighting capabilities. Her lot would be to steam back to a nervous West Coast and drydock.

Meanwhile the Navy Department had decided to hold *Saratoga, Lexington's* sister, in San Diego until the situation clarified. At the same time the carrier *Yorktown* with battleships *Idaho, Mississippi* and *New Mexico* was steaming from the East Coast to Panama for transit to the West Coast.

Two more Army divisions were ordered West to join the four already guarding the Pacific Coast. They would be supported by all the planes the Army and Navy could muster to reinforce the defenses against invasion.

Hawaii, except for whatever aircraft could be spared, would have to meet any further attacks with what it had on hand.

On the other side of the continent all assistance to Great Britain and Russia locked in battle with the Axis powers would be suspended while the United States took care to protect her Pacific flank.

Whatever would happen next, Admiral Yamamoto aboard his flagship *Nagato* in the Inland Sea had changed the course of the European War in a drastic way, the direction of which could not be foreseen by any man.

The damaged Nagumo force, less *Shokaku* which had slipped beneath the waves late Monday afternoon 8 December, nursed the crippled *Soryu* and two damaged destroyers through the dangerous mid-Pacific waters to dockyards on the Japanese main islands where they would undergo repair. Halfway through the voyage the *Hiryu* was detached with the two cruisers *Chikuma* and *Tone* and two destroyers to beef up the 23 December attack on Wake Island where the Japanese had been defeated in their first attack 11 December.

Major Japanese naval attention in the combined fleet and the naval general staff was now directed at what to do with the great Hawaiian victories, for in spite of the loss of one carrier and severe damage to another, the Japanese regarded the action of the day after Pearl Harbor as a shattering blow to American seapower. With no operational carriers in the Hawaiian area, it was felt throughout the naval staffs that the time had come for an all-out invasion attack on Oahu with diversionary thrusts at the West Coast and Alaska.

Capture of Hawaii would assure domination of the Eastern Pacific with small chance of success given any American attempt at its recapture.

It would be difficult to marshal the necessary ground forces and their transport but the Navy felt it could be done without withdrawals from the drive to the south.

The Navy's task would be to convince the Imperial

Army that it could and should provide the needed ground elements for the operation. The combined fleet estimated that with three good divisions and the control of the sea and air surrounding the Islands, success would be assured.

Yamamoto told Navy Chief of Staff Nagano that he would personally undertake the conversion of the army general staff to the operation.

Carefully he and his staff drafted the arguments for immediate action.

Set forth by the Combined Fleet, these were:

1. Capture of Hawaii, coupled with the destruction of American fleet units sent to its defense, would constitute the greatest blow which could be dealt to the United States.

2. The present situation with Japan holding a predominant edge in carrier and heavy ship strength offered a never-to-be-repeated chance to strike this decisive blow in the Eastern Pacific.

3. Hawaii could now be isolated from reinforcement, other than by air, by the submarines of the fleet.

4. Such isolation would contribute to the success of the invasion of Oahu by Japanese ground divisions.

5. Seizure of Hawaii would cut off Australia, New Zealand and the South Seas from any American aid.

Obstacles to the implementation of the plan would be:

1. Need for speed.

2. Need for curtailment or postponement of other operations so the necessary ground forces and sea transport could be provided.

3. Control of the air over the Islands would be difficult because of the size of the area.

4. Surprise in the attack would be most difficult to achieve because of American air patrol units on Midway and Johnston Islands as well as from Oahu itself.

Nevertheless Yamamoto was convinced that the navy should press ahead to exploit the current imbalance of strength in favor of the Japanese.

At most, the Americans could oppose the combined fleet with one carrier, the *Saratoga*, which would probably now be held on the West Coast, plus any reinforcement which would be sent by way of the Panama Canal from the Atlantic Fleet. These forces could include another carrier or two, plus battleships, but Yamamoto felt his assembled forces could overpower any fleet the enemy could throw together, for he meant to hit hard and fast.

So he took his plan first to the chief of the naval general staff Admiral Nagano. It was a short interview which surprised Yamamoto for this time Nagano was in full accord. There would be difficulties but he would put the naval staff at work to surmount them.

A pleased Yamamoto then called on army chief of staff Field Marshal Hajime Sugiyama to secure the assignment of three army divisions needed for the invasion of Oahu.

Here he faced reluctance. The field marshal said it might be very difficult to break loose three divisions with supporting troops and staff, for such a venture.

But Yamamoto reminded him that success could be decisive in the winning of the war. Still Sugiyama was hesitant. The southern operations already had put a tremendous burden on the army. Then there was always the Siberian frontier with Russia ready to exploit any Japanese weakness along that long line.

It was then Yamamoto who changed his tactics.

Why didn't they put it up to the prime minister himself? Let Tojo decide it.

The field marshal looked at Yamamoto, who was flanked by Nagano, the naval chief of staff. Nagano nodded his agreement.

Facing the man who had designed the great victories at Pearl Harbor was too much for the field marshal. Why not indeed? If the prime minister authorized the operation he would find the divisions.

The conference with Tojo was longer in that he wanted a detailed summary of the phases of the proposed operation. But in the end he authorized the planning and preparations to begin.

It was a heady time for the navy. Repair work was rushed forward on the damaged *Soryu* and the submarine forces were ordered to put in place an immediate blockade of the sea approaches to Honolulu and Pearl Harbor.

Simultaneously a joint army-navy staff commenced working out the details of the attack on large operational maps of the island of Oahu. These were very accurate maps for they bore the imprint of the "War Department—Corps of Engineers, U.S. Army."

The joint planning proceeded rapidly for the two services had detailed plans in their files for an attack on the American fortress dating back many years.

All in all it was one of the most harmonious projects in which the army and navy had ever engaged.

Other than the air strength in the Islands, there could be few surprises for the maps were precise and the services had voluminous records of improvements in the installations and armaments that had been made by the American army and navy over the years.

The major question was the attack date, for a great number of factors had to be considered including phase of the moon, the weather, the tides, and the surf and beach conditions.

But in the end the time required to assemble the necessary sea transportation for the troops would be the final determinant.

Along with the air defenses of Hawaii the navy had to put great emphasis on the large caliber seacoast artillery rifles which would have to be knocked out of action and the great number of antiaircraft guns which would have to be suppressed.

Ashore a Japanese landing would confront the U.S. Army's 24th and 25th Infantry Divisions reinforced by units of the 298th Infantry Regiment of the federalized Hawaii National Guard. Other ground elements which would have to be considered would include the Marine detachments at Pearl Harbor, the Ewa Marine Air Station and the naval air station at Kaneohe Bay. Then there would be detachments of the Army's Hawaiian Air Force personnel and the artillerymen of the Seacoast and Anti-aircraft Artillery Brigades.

The two Army divisions had been created by splitting the old square Hawaiian Division in two, so they essentially consisted of two infantry regiments, each with supporting artillery and other arms. Two weak divisions.

These the Japanese knew had divided responsibility for Oahu into North and South Sectors with the 24th Division defending the North Sector and the 25th the South. Both divisions were sparingly manned with supporting troops: tanks, engineers, signal corps, medical and supply units.

Oahu would be a tough nut to crack but combined fleet staff experts were sure that with the proper bombardment preparation from the sea and air that landings could be effected on the island's beaches and the land battle begun. In this battle the navy could be of immense support to the ground troops once they were ashore by laying in heavy bombardment patterns ahead of their advance, either from the air or from the sea.

With absolute command of the battle in the air and on the sea, the naval planners were confident that the outcome would never be in doubt.

29

"My Name's Nimitz"

RAPID AND SAFE RETURN OF *ENTERPRISE* TO THE WEST
coast now became the U.S. Navy's priority task followed by the clean-up of the destruction inflicted at Pearl
Harbor and at the Kaneohe and Ewa air stations.

At the same time the Army's efforts focused on completing preparations for the invasion battle which was to come,
and the transit of long range bombardment aircraft for the
defense of the Islands. Rehabilitation of the wrecked airfields was started immediately so the new bombers would
have adequate bases from which to fly.

Accompanying *Enterprise* to the coast would be a fleet of
cruisers and destroyers both for protection to the damaged
carrier and to allow the men-o-war to effect repairs and
resupply, a burden that Pearl Harbor could not bear.
Meanwhile Pearl Harbor Navy Yard was hurriedly put into
order so that it could support the remaining cruisers and
destroyers which along with the invaluable submarines
would provide the sea defense of the Hawaiian Islands.

Work was rushed on all damaged aircraft of both Army
and Navy so there would be fighters and patrol craft to

supplement the operations of the Army B-17s as they flew into Oahu.

Gasoline was the most critical item of supply so commercial oil tankers were commandeered along the West Coast to be sent helter skelter down on Hawaii with the meagerest of protection from the Navy and the Coast Guard. In the Islands petroleum supplies were sequestered so that all civilian automobiles except those used directly in defense ceased to operate.

The military governor, using his powers under martial law, ordered rationing of supplies of every kind including food.

The blackout which had been imposed the Sunday night of 7 December was continued in force. Bomb shelters were dug by both civilians and military while all travel was restricted to that related to work or defense. Residents of Honolulu having homes or relatives in the country were urged to move out of the city.

All Hawaii was now under a state of siege, chilled by reports of submarine sinkings of merchant vessels caught between Hawaii and the mainland. Ships were torpedoed in Hawaiian waters, their crews coming ashore seared by fire, death and shock. Submarines surfaced off the outside islands to open fire in the darkness on piers and buildings in the outports.

Meanwhile after unfavorable weather delayed their start, the heavy bombers began streaming in from the West Coast to restore the broken air arm. Three Matson liners, *Lurline, Matsonia, Monterey*, their glistening white hulls covered with gray war paint, were hurriedly converted to troop ships at San Francisco to be sent speeding down to the Islands with guns and men.

On Thursday following the Pearl Harbor attack and the battle off Kauai Secretary of the Navy Frank Knox arrived to personally view the destruction at the great base. When he looked at the sunken fleet with Admiral Kimmel at his elbow he put out his cigar and turned away in utter silence.

Three days later upon the return of the Navy secretary to Washington, the unhappy admiral and his colleague at Fort Shafter, the stern visaged General Short, were relieved of their commands, the blame for the great disaster gathering by inference about their shoulders.

Islanders now came to live with the blackout, censorship, rationing and bad news.

All normal life ceased at sundown when everyone but the men at their battle posts faced the alternative of sitting in rivulets of sweat in a tiny blacked out room or simply giving up the effort and going to bed. It was on these nights with the radio drumming out the hymn of defeat that the vast Pacific seemed a world abandoned to shame and misery.

First Guam, then Wake Island after a very stubborn resistance, fell to the Japanese. In the Philippines, MacArthur was fighting for his life, while the British and Dutch were pressed ever backwards in Malaya. The fall of Hong Kong came amidst scenes of rape, pillage and murder on Christmas Day.

Oahu continued to swell with preparations for the attack that was to come. Soldiers in numbers began to arrive to flesh out the two army divisions. Work at Pearl Harbor went on twenty-four hours a day. At night the navy yard was one sheet of incandescent light on a blanket of darkness while the tasks of clean-up and repair were pushed remorselessly.

Still the atmosphere held fearful anticipation of the day the Japanese would be back with the full Imperial battle line. At no point did the Americans seem to be able to hold their own.

It was during these days of doubt that the Americans born of Japanese ancestry in Hawaii came forward to lay their loyalty on the line. They offered their services to the Army for any duty. It was the commencement of a proud record.

So it was on one of these tension-filled days following the attack that a young captain at Fort Shafter headquarters found himself summoned by the Hawaiian Department Intelligence Officer, the G-2.

"General Emmons has need of an aide," he said. "Report to him for instructions."

The captain walked with curiosity through the old G-2 Section towards the chief of staff's office. Delos C. Emmons, Air Force general and American observer of the German blitz on England, had just taken over command of the Hawaiian Department from the ill-fated Short. The captain wondered what sort of a man he would be.

In a moment he was standing in the commanding general's office. A smooth-faced, rather rotund officer with the look of long authority and good cheer about his eyes, was sitting at a large desk—it had been Short's desk.

"Captain," he said, "I am expecting a distinguished visitor in a few moments. I want you to go out front and bring him up here when he arrives."

Acknowledging the order, the captain went below to take up his vigil at the curbside opposite a tin-hatted sentry standing at ease before the headquarters, his bayoneted rifle thrust out before him.

A host of throughts paraded through the captain's mind as he waited, all centering around the near collapse of the entire Pacific defense line from Australia to the American West Coast.

He knew that the fleet was immobilized, to a great extent impotent, and worst of all, it had acquired a characteristic utterly foreign to the United States Navy—it was almost as if it were ashamed of itself.

A long black sedan swung into the palm-lined loop road at the foot of the parade ground. It came rapidly towards the headquarters and stopped. In a moment he would meet the man who was supposed to lift up the American Pacific Fleet and prepare it for battle while holding a victory drunk Japan at bay.

The door of the sedan opened.

A tall, lean man with a raw-boned face and the weather-beaten appearance of a Texas cowhand, took his salute. His keen eyes met the captain's square on. He held out his hand.

"My name's Nimitz," he said. "What's yours?"

30

Operation Hawaii II

HAVING SECURED APPROVAL OF HIS PLANS FOR THE CON-
quest of Hawaii, Yamamoto pressed preparations for
the attack with all of his formidable vigor. Every element of
the Imperial Navy felt the spur of his attention from its
highest officers to the most newly mustered seaman. He
got results.

The Nagumo force would add the carriers *Junyo* and
Ryujo to make good the loss of *Shokaku* to the sea and the
damaged *Soryu* to the repair yards. Now the force was
back to its full power. None of the other ships involved in
the Pearl Harbor raid had suffered other than superficial
damage. By late February 1942 the combined fleet plus the
landing force was ready to sail east for the great shoot out
of the Pacific War.

Transports and train vessels had been assembled even
though they had to be removed from the sailing lists of
other operations.

Even the army had proven a surprise.

With the chief of staff himself pushing for speed,
Yamamoto's needed three divisions were swiftly assigned.
And they were top-flight battle tested units.

Field Marshal Sugiyama had personally assured Yamamoto that he was getting the best on hand.

Where the first Pearl Harbor attack plans had been viewed by many officers in both the army and the navy with doubt and distrust, now there was a ground swell of support which carried all obstacles before it.

What if the Americans had two new commanders in Hawaii, Admiral Nimitz and General Emmons? What could they do to impede the onsweep of the Imperial Way which was now triumphant over all the broad reaches of the Pacific?

It was in this overwhelming spirit of confident power that the various components of the attack forces prepared to sail for what would be the decisive action of the Great Pacific War.

It would be the greatest joint combined arms operation of the war.

Spearheading the attack would be the First Carrier Striking Force commanded by Admiral Nagumo and comprising four of the six fleet carriers used in the Pearl Harbor raid plus *Junyo* and *Ryujo* of the Second Carrier Striking Force. There would be a support group of two heavy cruisers and two fast battleships, a screen of one light cruiser and twelve destroyers with a supply group of five oilers. The fleet carriers would stow more than 350 planes on their hangar decks.

They would precede the main force commanded by Admiral Yamamoto which would include seven battleships, three light cruisers, one light carrier, twenty destroyers, two seaplane tenders and four oilers.

The Oahu Invasion Force under Vice Admiral Nabutake Kondo would have two battleships, eight heavy cruisers, two light cruisers, one light carrier, twenty destroyers, thirty transports, four oilers, two seaplane tenders and a repair ship.

A minesweeper group would round off the surface ship formations.

The Japanese submarine force would be expected to play

a major role in the operation with every available boat scheduled to prowl the waters ahead of the mighty armada or assigned to cut Hawaii's umbilical cord to the American mainland.

Feints against the West Coast would be made by light cruisers and destroyers to give the impression of landing operations on the California and Oregon coasts.

Nagumo was expected to defeat any attempt by remaining American carriers *Saratoga* and *Yorktown* to attack the invasion fleet and its protecting screen while denying the air space over the fleet to land based aircraft from the Hawaiian Islands.

The date for X-Day was set for early March with the carrier force to unleash heavy bombing strikes on Oahu installations. The main force would move in close to the island under the cover of this attack to saturate the heavy-gun seacoast defenses with powerful battleship firepower.

Landings would follow beginning shortly before dawn of X-Day with the expectation they would continue through the day and later as needed. Midway Island would be neutralized by aerial and sea bombardment by a special task group employing heavy cruisers and a light carrier.

Landings would be made simultaneously on Oahu at selected points along each of the four shores of the mountainous island with the two major thrusts to come from the north and south shores. The eastern and western attacks would be restricted to specific military and naval installations in those two pockets. The attack was planned to overwhelm the defending forces with the all-out effort to be completed by the fourth day.

Both the north and south shore offensive commanders would constitute their own reserves to be used in the final battles for control of the island while the eastern and western drives would hold out small maneuvering elements at the beginning of their attack, these forces to be used for exploitation of opportunities as they arose.

Control of the land battle would rest in the hands of a

general with long experience in amphibious landings along the Chinese coast.

In attacking Oahu the Japanese realized they were assaulting the most heavily defended fortress in the world. In so doing they knew that the issue would be decided in their favor by the fourth day or they would have to concede defeat and withdraw.

But Yamamoto was confident there would be no defeat.

Oahu is the shape of a skewed square with its east and west sides slanting roughly parallel in a northwesterly direction while the shorter north side trends slightly to the south of west. The southern side of the island is much longer, stretching the southeastern end out into a mountainous promontory.

Both east and west sides are formed of rough volcanic mountains with only one pass through each range. Lying between the two ranges is the wide central plateau of the island, famed for its pineapple fields and for the Army's major base at Schofield Barracks. Sugar cane blankets the north shore slopes with other sugar fields stretching from the south central area off to the southwest, some of these fields lying directly north of Pearl Harbor.

The city of Honolulu sprawls along the southeastern shores of Oahu.

The eastern side of the island is some thirty-three miles long with the shorter western shore twenty-one miles in length. The north shore is roughly twenty-one miles long while the southern shore, in which is situated the entrances to Pearl Harbor and Honolulu harbor, extends about twenty-nine miles.

The critical central part of the island from Pearl Harbor and Hickam Field to the North Shore is twenty-one miles as the frigate birds fly.

The two mountain ranges rising up to elevations of 4,000 feet were impassible except by difficult mountain trails, but for two roads, the Honolulu-windward side highway over the world famous Pali in the Koolau Range to the east, and a tortuous military road from the leeward side through the Waianae Range to Schofield Barracks in the west.

This topography of Oahu meant that travel was generally restricted to the roads along the ocean except for the highway traversing the central plateau from south to north, and the two narrow roads passing through each mountain range. No real road except the roadbed of an old railroad passes around the northwestern tip of the island which is known as Kaena Point.

From a military defense standpoint this means that any landings on the windward (eastern) shore or the leeward (western) shore would be restricted to the relatively narrow strips of land lying between the mountains and the sea. Only in the central part of the island would attackers either from the north or south shores find ample room for widespread maneuvers for infantry, armor and artillery units.

Although the island was ringed by gun positions, most of the very heavy seacoast artillery from 12- to 16-inch cannon were emplaced along the southern shore for the protection of Pearl Harbor and Honolulu. However with ranges of beyond twelve miles it was possible for the largest guns to drop projectiles all about the island. Range finding instruments located inside the face of Diamond Head at Waikiki, and at other elevated land positions, were so coordinated that fast and effective fire could be brought down at almost any point off Oahu.

All in all there was a total of 127 fixed coast defense guns, 211 antiaircraft weapons and more than 3,000 mobile artillery pieces and automatic weapons available to the Army forces for beach defense.

To man this array of armament the Army could muster 42,850 officers and men. Under the Hawaiian Department's command were the two infantry divisions, a light tank company, four antiaircraft regiments, four coast artillery harbor defense regiments (two incomplete), plus the engineer, quartermaster, medical, chemical and other special units attached to the headquarters.

The Army's Hawaiian Air Force operated Hickam Air Base adjacent to Pearl Harbor, Wheeler Field next to Schofield Barracks in the center of the island, and Bellows Field on the windward side. The Navy had Ford Island in the middle of Pearl Harbor, the Naval Air Station at Kaneohe Bay and the Marine Air Station at Ewa.

Army air strength alone numbered 50 bombers, 61 fighters and 7 reconnaissance planes.

Some of the fighters had been brought down from the mainland after the Japanese raid, aboard *Saratoga* which had made an alarm-ridden run from San Diego. She was now temporarily based at Pearl where she could be reinforced by the carrier *Yorktown* due at San Diego from the Atlantic on New Year's Day. With two carriers at Pearl plus additional Army and Navy planes, Oahu would have some air power to hurl at any new Japanese attacking force.

Work was rushed on the Aircraft Warning Service installations but much remained to be done.

Silently the Japanese submarines were now tightening the noose around Hawaii with more cargo ship sinkings reported daily. Sea traffic off the West Coast came to a halt. A wave of panic hit the large cities. The merchant vessels continued to go down.

In Tokyo the Japanese army and navy were putting the final touches to the invasion plan.

It was a relatively simple one.

One division, the Blue, would land on the north shore of Oahu and drive straight up the long sugar-cane-covered slope towards Schofield Barracks, its objective the destruction of the American 24th Division holding the northern shore line from Kaena Point to Kaaawa village well down the eastern shore.

Another division, the Red, would attack from the south, landing from Kahe Point to Ewa Beach on the western edge of the Pearl Harbor channel, and farther to the east at selected points off Honolulu and Waikiki. Its objective would be the destruction of the 25th Division spread all the way from Waianae past Pearl Harbor and Honolulu to Makapuu Point on the southeastern tip of the island.

The third division, the Gold, would send one brigade onto the beaches of the leeward (west) side to capture the naval ammunition depot at Lualualei, while another brigade was landing at two points across the island on the windward side to seize the Air Force's Bellows Field and the naval air station and coast artillery guns on Mokapu Peninsula in Kaneohe Bay. The remainder of the division would be held aboard ship as a floating reserve.

In spite of the treacherous nature of some of the beaches, the first landings would go in during the dark hours before dawn. It was hoped most of the troop units would be ashore shortly after daylight. All highways would be cut and power stations blown up as the troops advanced.

On the American side, the plan was to pound any Japanese invasion force from the air as it approached Oahu. Then the heavy seacoast guns would go into action when the enemy fleet came within range. They would be joined by the 155-mm field guns, and the 155-mm and 240-mm howitzers of the field artillery regiments, as the range closed.

Then while the landing craft were approaching the shoreline, the lighter artillery pieces would take up the song of death to be followed at closer ranges by the heavy and light machineguns, rifles and mortar fire. Emplacements for the mobile artillery which had dug into their positions during the daylight hours of 7 December had been constantly improved since that time so they were formidable indeed.

All of the gun positions including the huge seacoast artillery pieces did have one common problem, however, in that they had no protection against aerial bombing and strafing attacks other than their attendant antiaircraft guns and whatever cover the camouflage netting would afford. In the case of the big twelve- and sixteen-inch seacoast guns, this would not mean much for the Japanese pilots would have their fixed positions pinpointed on their bombing charts.

If landings were effected then the infantry battalions in that area would immediately launch attacks to eject the invaders. For these efforts they would have the assistance of the fighter squadrons in strafing the landing craft and beach lines if the planes were not engaged in dogfights with the enemy Zeros which would be sure to be protecting the incoming bombers.

Obstacles and mines were already in place at likely landing points, and avenues of approach into the defense positions were so drawn that any enemy thrust would be channeled towards the main battle lines so flanking machinegun and rifle fire would be joined with artillery and mortar fire on the advancing Japanese. Fire lanes were cut for all weapons as necessary while ammunition was stored handy to the guns and mortars for instant use.

All positions were then masked or camouflaged so they could achieve surprise of enemy formations attempting to drive inland. Constant observation of the sea and land areas fronting the positions was conducted by the troops both by day and by night.

Back of the beach defenses which were manned to serve the automatic weapons they encompassed, the main battle position provided for strong points and reserves of infantry so that any penetration of the beach line could be immediately counterattacked.

Signal communications which went in with the first arrival of the troops at their battle positions the morning of December 7th had been improved and added to on a daily basis until by January a network of telephone and radio circuits provided instant contact between all headquarters and their forward units, as well as between adjacent elements strung out around the island.

Because the Army expected simultaneous attacks on all sides of Oahu, each larger formation in the battle line was required to be so self-sufficient that it could continue to function even though the Japanese were successful in putting large elements ashore and a land battle was raging around the defenders.

All planes were sheltered by earth revetments which had been thrown up at the air fields. Many of these had been in existence at the time of Nagumo's first raid, but Short's anti-sabotage alert had gathered the planes together in midfield at the Army air strips so they would be better protected from any sabotage attempts.

Like an over-all umbrella the radars of the Aircraft Warning Service were now in operation from both mobile and fixed sites to provide the around-the-clock coverage which might have given an early alarm to the defenders on the critical morning of 7 December. Complete aerial surveillance of the ocean areas surrounding Oahu still was not possible with the aircraft available, but a much more comprehensive scouting effort was conducted daily from the northern to the southwestern perimeters which were deemed the most dangerous.

U.S. Marine Corps units coordinated their defense positions on naval installations with those of the adjacent Army elements around the island.

Overseeing all of this activity was a new chief of staff, Colonel J. Lawton Collins, Army ground fighting expert who had been sent to Hawaii with General Emmons with the express mission of insuring that Oahu defenses were the strongest that could be attained with the means at hand.

The trim, unsmiling Collins, soon to be promoted brigadier general, sparked the Army preparations with vast tactical knowledge, a caustic tongue, and an intense fighting spirit.

In the city and countryside the military government marshaled the civilian community for the expected air and sea attacks. Organized defense volunteers were mustered in to augment the troops holding the battle lines, aiding them in a hundred ways. The Honolulu police and fire departments dovetailed their activities with the military in the fields of anti-sabotage, traffic and crowd control, and fire suppression. Enforcement of the absolute blackout regulations became a major duty for the police.

The medical community, mobilized at the time of the Pearl Harbor raid, proceeded to organize hospitals, clinics, doctors, nurses, staff and volunteers for emergency action.

So with the military and naval defenses under the single command of Admiral Nimitz, and the civilian community integrated into the overall defense plans, Oahu waited through the long and lonely nights.

31

Battle for Oahu

O PENING PHASE OF THE BATTLE FOR OAHU COMMENCED
far to the northwest of Kauai at 1500 hours on a gray
blustery, cold afternoon in early March 1942, when the
huge Japanese invasion force began its run-down on
Hawaii some 180 miles to the southeast.

Yamamoto had indeed been fortunate, for so far as he
knew, his ships had not been sighted by the enemy. Now
at 3 o'clock on an unpleasant afternoon with a rising sea,
he could with some assurance look forward to twelve
hours of steaming time, with ten of these hours being
under the cloak of darkness, to bring him off the shores of
the great target island at 0300 hours. At that time his
transports would start debarking their troops and the battleships and cruisers would move in to bombard the
known heavy-gun positions of the enemy and certain pre-
selected beach landing areas.

Full daylight would not come to Hawaii until well after
0600 hours by which time the Japanese admiral hoped
many of his troops would be ashore engaging the ground
defenders of the island.

The long morning and afternoon in the wild North

Pacific had been a lonely one for the short, stocky admiral for he alone now bore the responsibility for bringing the Imperial Japanese battle fleet within range of the enemy's shore guns of the largest caliber, and exposing it to air attack from both land and carrier based aircraft.

He had made the decision that the landings would be made with surprise rather than following a heavy sea bombardment of the shore defenses. He alone had again decided to risk not only the core of Japan's carrier fleet but the ships of the main battle line including his flagship *Nagato* in seeking the knockout blow which would bring America to her knees.

He also had decided to risk the daylight run-in, gambling that the long-range aerial patrol sweeps would have reached their turn-around points before his ships entered the radius of danger. So far so good. No aerial, no surface, no submarine sightings had been reported by the wide sprawling fleet.

With less than three hours until full dark on a cloudy obscure night, it seemed that he again would gain surprise. But for how long? He knew only too well that all of Oahu's observers would be searching for his ships before the dawn. In addition he suspected that radar would pick up elements of his force, but here again he was gambling that with ships approaching from all sides of the island at once, the defenders would be confused as to where the main blows were to fall.

So the great fleet steamed on through the cold cresting seas under rain swept skies. His chief of staff, Admiral Ugaki, stood with him on the flag bridge of *Nagato*.

"We have done better than I could have hoped," Ugaki said scanning the gray clouds shrouding the advance of the ships. "Two more hours and it will be dark."

"Yes, we have been lucky," Yamamoto replied. "Fortune favors the bold," he added with a smile. "Our fleet is so large, however," he observed, "that I believe we must be prepared to be discovered some time before the morning."

The remaining two hours of sullen daylight dragged themselves out leaving the darkened fleet moving shadow-like over melancholy seas. Now the rites of preparation were being checked throughout the fleet. The soldiers inspected their weapons for the dependence their lives would have upon them.

Landing craft skippers checked their vessels from stem to stern in the remaining moments of daylight for now the test was nearing and they would have to meet it as they came.

Although it increased the difficulties of the navigators, the rest of the fleet felt great relief with the coming of the night.

In the carriers the plane handlers were already preparing their charges for the morning's work. The first priority would be to put up an umbrella of fighters over the island while the bombers went in to attack the airfields as they had on 7 December.

These attacks, to be delivered at first light, meant the planes would have to be ready long before the dawn. Meanwhile the pilots whiled away the hours in the briefing rooms awaiting any last minute information which might affect their missions. But the air of tenseness, which had enveloped these same rooms on the night before the Pearl Harbor raid, was not there, replaced by a feeling of confidence born of their previous experience in combat. The fliers felt they were not only good, but that they were the very best!

In this battle the carriers with their protective screen would not close the island but hover off the outer perimeter of the attacking forces, furnishing air protection and air attack on an on-call basis after the dawn attack on the airfields.

In the transports the troops stolidly awaited their orders to embark into the landing craft which would put them on the beaches before dawn, while in the main batteries of the battleships, the gun crews could hardly wait for their first taste of action. They well knew they would be sorely tried by the shore batteries, but their confidence was such in their great guns they looked forward to the artillery duel which would open the great battle.

Closer in two I Class submarines, keeping watch over the entrance to the Pearl Harbor channel, had watched a large carrier slip to sea with her escorting cruisers and destroyers but had been too far out to attack her.

This was the *Saratoga*. After delivering fighters and other aircraft to Oahu, she had been ordered to take station east of the Islands to await the attack Nimitz felt was imminent.

She would be joined later by *Yorktown* which had transited the Panama Canal from the Atlantic side, steaming to San Diego to join the battered Pacific Fleet.

The two carriers representing the striking power of the American fleet had to be carefully used, guardians as they were of the entire western continental seaboard. As Pearl Harbor could no longer furnish them a haven for repair in case of damage, they had to be within fair steaming distance of the large Pacific Coast naval dockyards in case they suffered serious damage. Yet they would be expected to send their planes against the Japanese as the invasion unfolded.

Between them and the West Coast were stationed the battleships from the Atlantic Fleet, the *Idaho, Mississippi* and *New Mexico*, with screening cruisers and destroyers as a blocking unit behind the carriers.

It was the ill fortune of the American defenders that no sighting of the enemy armada was obtained during the daylight hours of the afternoon because of the obscure weather conditions and Yamamoto's crafty planning of his time factors in the approach voyage.

First sign of the impending invasion was picked up by the Aircraft Warning Service at Fort Shafter when its information and plotting center began to receive radar plots of surface vessels some fifty miles out from Oahu approaching from the northwest. It was 2400 hours of a sullen night.

The alarm went out immediately to all services while along Oahu's shoreline observation posts stared into the blackness for some sign of the attack they were told was on the way. But the night was so black that nothing could be seen.

All beach positions were now alerted, patrols being most careful not to leave any length of the long shoreline uncovered. Still nothing appeared.

Within minutes of receiving the radar plots from Fort Shafter the submarine base at Pearl Harbor alerted two of the large fleet submarines to slip to sea to positions southwest of Barbers Point where they could move against an attack along the west or south sides of Oahu. Others already at sea in the Hawaiian area were instructed to move in closer to Oahu to harry the invasion attempt.

At midnight a full battle alert was ordered for all forces on Oahu.

Now there was little more to do but wait while the hands of the clock drew on inexorably towards 0500.

First action came from out to the southwest when a cruiser shepherding transports took two torpedoes broadside, erupting in a fountain of scarlet flame which cast brilliant light over a vast segment of sea. Instantly scores of ships were illuminated by the series of explosions. These were the transports preparing to load their troops into landing craft which would ferry them to the southwestern beaches of the island from Kahe Point to Ewa Beach.

The American submarine commander took one look at the awesome sight through his periscope before he dived.

At the same time thousands of watching eyes on Oahu glimpsed the enemy ships steaming toward Oahu.

First blood to the U.S. Navy!

A few minutes later the coughing roar of fighters sounded across the runways at Army and Navy airfields, followed by the noise of their takeoffs.

All of the Air Force, Navy and Marine air installations sprang to life with their pilots and ground crews swarming around the planes already loaded with bombs, ammunition and gasoline ready for the attack.

Then came another strange interval of waiting as utter blackness again cloaked the island brooding in the night.

Suddenly the order was passed for takeoff, followed by the roar of scores of planes as they soared into the air. This mass operation had not been underway for more than five minutes when the mission of the first planes became apparent to both watching Americans and the attacking Japanese.

First there was one brilliant ribbon of light floating down over the Japanese armada soon joined by scores of others as the flares were dropped along a wide arc of ocean.

There were the enemy ships, some illuminated as if in a marine diorama. A low rumble reached the ears of the shore watchers, to be followed by the electric flashes of bomb explosions as hits were scored.

They were joined by the throaty roar of the shore artillery firing rapidly on the momentary sightings. Then came bombs exploding on steel decks or in the seas close aboard the ships.

Yamamoto had been upstaged. It was not yet 0500.

Now the operation unfolded more rapidly than had been planned. The troops must get ashore as quickly as possible.

Japanese planes left the crowded carrier decks to join the nocturnal aerial melee.

Another Japanese ship went up in flame, a submarine off Kaena Point planting a torpedo into a transport maneuvering into position to launch her landing craft. Instantly the Japanese destroyers commenced their counter-attack, depth charging a wide area along the north shore.

The large seacoast rifles in their emplacements along the southern shores did not go into action, however, their huge shell being saved for more certain targets.

Then Oahu's western coast blossomed into view as large star shells fired from the Japanese ships brought momentary daylight to the island. The light was instantly followed by the sullen rumble of naval guns laying down a smothering barrage from Nanakuli around Barbers Point to the Ewa plain.

The southern landing would not be long in coming. Still there was no activity reported from the difficult north shore or the brooding windward side.

But just when the defenders began to believe the Japanese attack would be focused on the south and west sides of the island, Bellows Field, the small Air Force field near the southeastern tip of the island, reported the enemy was landing in Waimanalo Bay, that ground units already ashore were advancing northward towards the airfield.

So while most attention had been centered on the illuminated battle off the south and west shores, the Japanese Gold Division had landed an infantry battalion with supporting weapons on the wide beaches of Waimanalo Bay meeting but light opposition from the beach outposts which had been quickly overwhelmed.

Now the flare of ground fighting shimmered amidst the tall trees which crowded the edges of the beach along this part of the coast. It was apparent from reports to the Hawaiian Department's battle command post deep inside the old Aliamanu Crater west of Fort Shafter that the 298th infantrymen and airmen engaged with the enemy were being pushed slowly up the beach toward the end of the Bellows Field air strip.

If this drive could not be stopped the air field would be denied to American planes while those still on the ground would be trapped by the invading forces. A quick order went out to transfer all aircraft to Wheeler Field while the Bellows Field commander was ordered to hold the air strip as long as possible then blow up all facilities including premined sections of the runway to deny its use to the Japanese.

The hour of 0500 came and went with as yet no action of any kind along the rough North Shore beaches. Observation posts of the 24th Division reported unconfirmed sightings of ships from time to time. A heavy surf running along this rock strewn shore would make all landing attempts difficult.

Yet the reports of action around the island while experiencing nothing to their own front made the 24th Division commanders very uneasy. Where was the enemy? Would he simply by-pass the north shore in favor of other places?

The answer came with stunning surprise in an excited telephone conversation with a 21st Infantry Regiment outpost near the western end of Mokuleia Beach.

"The Japanese are ashore in great strength east of Kaena Point. They have surprised our outposts and are advancing eastward along the highway leading into Wailua town. They are being supported by small field guns and mortars. Blocking positions are being set up in an attempt to hold them out of Wailua and deny access to the Kaukonahua Road."

Kaukonahua Road was one of the two main highways leading from the north shore to the center of the island. It provided direct road access to the huge Army base at Schofield Barracks with its stores, supplies, weapons and munitions.

The 24th Division commander, General Wilson, alarmed at the danger, instructed the 21st Infantry to hold this thrust where it was. He would send reserve elements to reinforce the regiment.

Another message soon followed the first. It was from the command post of the 21st Infantry:

"Enemy identified as elements of the Blue Division. We have slowed their advance."

Officers of the G-3 Operations Section of the Department battle command post in Aliamanu Crater were studying the implications of the North Shore and Bellows Field landings with Air Force officers.

"This means there will be at least one landing strip available to them if we cannot hold these thrusts," one airman said. "We must deny them use of any airfield during the battle."

"The 21st is a tough regiment. They will do the best that can be done. Bellows may be another can of worms. The 298th is strung out all along the east side of the island from Mokapuu to the north end of Kaneohe Bay. It is too long a line. I don't know whether they will be able to hold on. The air contingent is very small."

"Colonel! Colonel!" an operations sergeant called to the G-3 himself. "Landings in force now underway on both sides of Barbers Point. The 25th Division reports the 35th Infantry is heavily engaged."

"Let me have the phone," the colonel replied. "Hello, hello G-3 here."

A quiet voice responded.

"Bill, we have a big show going on down here. The 35th Infantry has identified elements of the Red Japanese Division ashore in strength along both sides of Barbers Point. They took quite a beating but they have knocked us back."

"That rough terrain will favor their advance."

"Yes, I am afraid so. Particularly if they get heavy support from their ships and planes. Will keep you informed."

G-2 and G-3 personnel with Air Force and Navy liaison officers stared at the large wall map of Oahu which dominated the section. Red grease marks on the cellophane covering the map outlined the three enemy landings while blue depicted the defenders' positions.

"They are coming at us from all sides."

"Remains to be seen where the strongest efforts will be made."

"They haven't tried Waianae on the west or Mokapu on the east side yet."

Morning twilight was announced by the heavy thunder of the largest seacoast artillery as the guns took the invasion fleet under fire.

"There go the big boys," someone said. "We will soon see what they can do."

"I only hope some aerial bombs or strafing runs don't put them out of action," the G-3 answered.

A moment later a corporal looked up from his phone.

"They're pretty good. Fort Weaver's sixteen-inchers have a direct hit on a cruiser. She just blew up." He paused. "There they go again. This time a battleship on fire."

"Good," the G-3 replied. "Fort Kam and Fort Barrette ought to be getting into the act."

"They are. There are ships afire south of Pearl Harbor."

"Those coast artillerymen don't get much of a chance to strut their stuff, but when they do, look out!"

"I only hope we can keep them in action."

Now the length of the south shore was thundering to the sound of the big guns—from Fort Ruger at Diamond Head, to Fort DeRussy at Waikiki, to Fort Kamehameha and Fort Weaver—they were all in heavy action. With great accuracy they were scoring direct hits while the largest caliber guns of the Japanese battleships were seeking out these deadly batteries. It was a ship to shore gun duel in the style of the old school.

Enemy landings were now reported to the G-2 Section of the Department headquarters, to be taking place in the Waianae District on the Leeward Coast apparently aimed at capturing the naval ammunition depot at Lualualei, and in the Kailua Bay area on the windward side with this objective the Kaneohe Naval Air Station.

"This latest thrust could also mean a back door land attack on the coast defense guns in Ulupau Crater at Mokapu Point," an artillery officer remarked.

Shortly before 0900 reports came in from the Air Force of heavy Navy dive-bombing attacks on the Japanese carriers which were sending their own aerial strikes against Oahu from far beyond the fringes of the invasion fleet. Up until now the enemy carriers had evaded attacks by high level Air Force bombers. But during one of these attacks the Navy dive bombers surprised the enemy patrols over the carriers with the result that one ship appeared to be burning.

These planes were from *Saratoga* and *Yorktown* far to the eastward which had scored a complete surprise on the

Japanese fleet by eluding the submarine line intended to intercept them between the Islands and the coast.

Nevertheless the invaders had elements of three divisions ashore at five different points on Oahu with two of these intrusions, those on the south shore in the Barbers Point area and on the north shore near Wailua, threatening the north-south central corridor and the very integrity of the island's defense structure.

Up until this hour the city of Honolulu itself had been hardly involved in the battle with the exception of the seacoast artillery forts along its beach front, yet every one of Oahu's men, women and children knew their fate depended on the outcome of the fierce actions raging on all sides of the fortress island.

Rumor and alarm swept through the population like fever for few knew more than that the Americans and Japanese were locked in a desperate battle to determine the course, maybe the outcome, of the Pacific War. The city's hospitals already were beginning to handle the floods of wounded, rushed to them from the battle lines.

But other than offshore bombardment the 27th Infantry Regiment, the famed Wolf Hounds, born in Siberia in the first World War, had little evidence of enemy activity in its sector which extended from Pearl Harbor east to Mokapuu Point at the southeastern tip of the island.

By 1000 the situation seemed to be stabilizing with the Japanese north shore drive stalled in front of the sugar town of Wailua, and enemy south shore units regrouping on the broad Ewa Plain in the face of stiff resistance from the 35th Infantry.

Japanese troops in the Kailua Bay area on the eastern shore were bogged down at the foot of the Mokapu Peninsula while across the island the Marines at the Lualualei Naval Ammunition Depot had succeeded in stopping a Japanese Gold Division combat team at the mouth of the Waianae Pocket surrounded by the frowning cliffs of the Waianae Range.

Honolulu itself had been left to the soldiers and the police with all residents long gone from the shore areas with their attendant battle dangers.

The vacant city stood abandoned and forlorn waiting the tide of battle. Infantry formations of the 27th Infantry taking up positions in the rear of beach defense points prepared demolitions and firing points to be used in building-by-building and house-to-house fighting for possession of the downtown Honolulu dock areas and the long stretches fronting on Waikiki Beach.

During the morning the battle for possession of the air over the island intensified hourly with great destruction of aircraft, both American and Japanese. But though the dogfights were intense and although the outnumbered Americans continued to press their attacks home, there was a noticeable deterioration in the air defenders' ability to counterattack the Japanese aerial offensive.

Before noon General Emmons, realizing what was happening, ordered the Air Force to be prepared to destroy all of their installations, fuel and munitions on order. The gallant carrier pilots, having expended all of the gasoline they could without imperiling their return to their ships, now had to unwillingly break off the action and fly eastward.

It was before noon that one of the most shocking blows to the Island was delivered by the invaders.

Promptly at 1100 hours a long line of landing craft approaching the mouth of Honolulu harbor was taken under fire by the artillery on that part of the island, except the heavy seacoast guns which could not bring their fires to bear on the Japanese assault boats. At the same time the attackers laid down smoke shell on the American positions so that in a few minutes the Honolulu harbor front as well as the city itself was obscured in heavy, dark crawling smoke lit up at intervals by the explosion of white phosphorous setting everything it touched on fire.

Other landing craft deployed over a wide area were approaching Waikiki and its long sandy beaches.

These small unit attacks spreading along the front of the 27th Infantry pinned down the defenders to their beach positions while the mobile units in their rear had to be held out of the action until it could be determined where the enemy would aim his main effort. It was not long in coming.

First ashore were riflemen of the special naval landing forces. Fighting at close quarters with rifles, bayonets, grenades and small mortars, they effected a lodgment on the harbor front at the foot of Fort Street. Then they commenced advancing straight up the long avenue towards the mountains, brushing aside their opponents to either flank.

Destroyers ranged their guns to rake the upper reaches of Fort Street and its companion thoroughfare Nuuanu Avenue which parallels its run towards the high ridges back of the town. This new form of fire support accelerated the Japanese advance so that within an hour it had pushed up near the Punchbowl and gained access to that part of Nuuanu which was the lower approach to the Pali and the other side of the island.

Now occurred some of the most vicious close-in fighting of the day as the 27th Infantry tried to cut off the Japanese spearhead, but their troops kept pouring ashore until the Americans could only assault the shoulders of the long penetration.

By 1300 hours the forces of the 27th Infantry had been divided and the 25th Division split in two. At the same time the Red Japanese Division pressed its western prong of attack on the Ewa Plain to make it difficult for the American commanders to shift their reserve elements eastward to cut off the attack through the center of Honolulu.

At 1300 the Hawaiian Department Headquarters ordered the military governor and his staff to evacuate their quarters in Iolani Palace while the U.S. Engineers were directed to destroy vast stores of equipment and supplies at Punahou School to deny them to the enemy. After some harrowing moments the military governor and his staff were successful in slipping through the streets along the slopes of Punchbowl Crater until they found a clear way around the head of the Japanese advance so they could reach the Department's rear command post at Fort Shafter.

With their hold on communications with U.S. fleet units threatened, the Navy high command was ordered by President Roosevelt to fly out to *Saratoga* and *Yorktown* from which they could exert command of the ships at sea.

At the Aliamanu Crater battle command post, the department staff knew the battle was now nearing its critical point.

Most damaging to the island defenses was the sudden Japanese thrust through the center of Honolulu which had split off part of the 27th Infantry from the rest of the 25th Division, and the inability of the defenders to contain the slow advance of other elements of the same Red Division on the Ewa Plain.

On the north shore the 24th Division by withdrawing its defensive units from all of its sector east of Waimea Bay had managed to stabilize a rough defensive line across approaches leading south in the central corridor towards Schofield Barracks. By frustrating the attacks of the Japanese Blue Division, the 24th Division had so enraged its hot-headed commander that he began throwing away his men in futile assaults easily hurled back by the defenders.

A G-3 officer in the battle command post at Aliamanu Crater summed up the situation for the commanding general as of 1400: "On the leeward (west) side the enemy has landed elements of an infantry brigade of the Gold Division at Nanakuli and penetrated about a half-mile up the Lualualei Naval Road where they have been stopped by the naval ammunition depot's marine detachment. Efforts to flank the Marines from the north have been defeated. At the present time we can say that their advance in the Waianae Pocket to capture the Depot, has been held.

"On the North Shore the 24th Division has defeated all efforts of the Blue Division to seize Kaukonahua Road in the Waialua town area, thereby denying this division's attempts to advance by way of this road on Schofield Barracks. On other parts of the north shore landing attempts have been made by small parties, most of which have been destroyed by the 19th and 21st Infantry regiments. In turning back the Blue Division our 24th Division has had to uncover the coast east of Waimea Bay all the way to Kaawa. However, at this moment it can be said that the northern end of the central corridor remains closed to the enemy."

The officer moved his pointer to the windward side on the east. "Here another partial brigade of the Japanese Gold Division has landed at two points. First at Waimanalo Bay where his advance on the Bellows Field airstrip has forced us to blow up the runway and evacuate planes and personnel. Fighting is continuing."

The pointer moved northward to Kailua Bay. "Here another detachment of the same brigade has landed, evidently with the mission of seizing the Kaneohe Naval Air Station and the coast artillery guns in Ulupau Crater. At this time it has failed in both missions as Marine and Army troops have stopped the attempted advance across the neck of the Mokapu Peninsula."

The briefing officer dropped his pointer to the south shore with its concentration of installations at Pearl Harbor and around Honolulu. "It is in the south sector that the most dangerous penetrations have been made."

His pointer moved to the southwest end of the island at Barbers Point. "This was the area of the enemy's first landing. After getting ashore on both sides of the lighthouse he advanced his troops until they overran Barrette, the 16-inch gun battery west of Ewa. Continuing on they headed north evidently making for the Kunia Road but were stopped in this area by the 35th Infantry with supporting troops sent in by the 25th Division. Maintaining pressure they have advanced slowly northward cutting off the Fort Weaver battery and spilling over towards the West Loch of Pearl Harbor.

"It appears that this drive may become the enemy's main

effort, directed towards Schofield Barracks with the objective to force the 25th Division to commit all of its reserves to stop it. The cutting action of the special naval landing force under command of the Red Division, up through the center of Honolulu, has split the 25th in two with little chance at this time of the 27th Infantry being able to cut through this penetration while repelling other landing attempts all along the Honolulu-Waikiki Beach front area.

"Buildings in Honolulu and Waikiki have been set afire by the shelling and the city is now burning."

He paused. "If the Japanese succeed in capturing the heights above Pearl Harbor they will be able to bring down artillery fire on the navy yard area, Hickam Field, and the Submarine Base.

"At present we have reports of additional troops coming ashore on the beaches south of the Ewa Plain. It would appear that these troops are intended to reinforce the main drive to the north to force a battle of decision along the Kunia Road north of Pearl Harbor."

The Chief of Staff broke in. "We will have to throw them back along a line from West Loch to the Waianae Range." He turned to the commanding general. "The time has come to commit the reserve forces. The 24th Division should be able to release units to assist. It seems to have stopped the enemy in the north sector."

"That can be done," the G-3 agreed while staff officers took notes as the final defense battle plans were shaped.

So stood matters as night fell on the beleaguered island lit up from time to time by explosions of aerial bombs while planes from Wheeler and Hickam Field continued to attack the Kunia Road line and the landing operations along the Ewa Beach shore.

Other explosions shook the American battle positions as the Japanese carriers unleashed their bombers in support of their troops. But gradually the night brought most of these to an end with close-in fighting and infantry fire taking over the burden of battle.

For a while Schofield Barracks was subjected to high

angle fire from naval guns but this was mostly a nuisance with little real damage being accomplished by the Japanese.

Throughout the night reinforcement of the 25th Division continued with units withdrawing from the 24th's North Shore line to undertake the hazardous blacked-out traverse of the island, mostly along obscure cane and pineapple plantation roads to bring help to the exhausted troops deployed along the Kunia Road front.

On the southern beaches the Japanese were moving their forces north and east to gather the power for the morning attack designed to punch holes in the American defense.

Already the commander of the Japanese Blue Division, attacking from the north, had been relieved with a new commander directed to so press the American 24th Division that it would not be able to detach elements for relief of the 25th on the Pearl Harbor front.

Although casualties had been heavy on both sides, the Americans had been able to feed coast artillery and anti-aircraft troops into their lines to make good their losses, while the Japanese had to wait for the arrival of their new units, struggling over the dark and tortuous roads and trails leading inland from the landing areas.

To the eastward *Saratoga* and *Yorktown* were preparing for dawn attacks on the great fleet of ships Yamamoto had assembled around Oahu. It now seemed certain that the second day of the battle for Oahu would be the day of decision.

But first there would be a most uncertain night.

In the Army's battle command post news of heavy civilian casualties was not making the commanders' choices of options easier. The burden of the fate of so many non-combatants bore down harshly on the military officers. It was a factor which would affect command decisions.

Reports of renewed enemy pressure began to be relayed by the two division command posts long before the dawn.

At first the action seemed to be concentrated around the

Waialua village area on the north shore where the new commander of the Japanese Blue Division was intent on breaking the American 24th Division lines barring his way to the south. But this attack soon flamed eastward into the village itself, aimed at the point where the around-the-island road, Kamehameha Highway, swings inland towards Wahiawa and Schofield Barracks.

If the Japanese could stage an advance up this major highway in conjunction with their effort up the Kaukonahua Road to the west along the base of the mountain, the American defenders would find themselves heavily beset.

At the same time reports came in of more troops coming ashore at Haleiwa to the east, to expand the small beachhead the Japanese had established there on the first day of the invasion. From this area forces pressing inland would strike directly at the rear lines of the Americans attempting to contain the original thrust eastward from the Mokuleia beaches.

Naval guns offshore were providing artillery cover for the Japanese offensive, ranging all along the American lines as the dawn crept across the mountain peaks and into the green lushness of the sugar cane fields through which this battle of the north shore would be waged.

Action on the Kunia Road front of the 25th Division in the south sector stirred sluggishly while the naval bombardment roared along the northern lines. First came small patrol fire from the mountain slopes to the west as the Japanese tried to edge around the American right flank, but these efforts were contained by the infantry deployed along this area.

It soon became apparent however, that the major offensive would be directed straight up the Kunia Road and the slopes over which it traced its descent from the high central plateau towards the shores of Pearl Harbor. Here the Japanese were forced to rely on infantry weapons and light artillery for they had had neither time nor opportunity to bring ashore heavy land guns, depending in the initial stages of their intrusion on the overhead fire from the guns of the fleet.

But now with their salient extending some four miles into the island, it was both difficult and dangerous to bring down fire on the forward American lines without hazarding the safety of their own troops.

Full daylight revealed the enormity of the destruction wrought by both sides during the first full day of battle. Corpses and wounded littered the rough terrain of the Ewa Plain where entrenched American automatic weapons and artillery had laid down vicious fire screens through which the invaders had tried to penetrate. They in turn had insured that no structure in the region remained standing. Smoke funneled skyward from the cane fields that had been put to the torch or had been ignited by exploding artillery shell or machinegun tracer ammunition.

Few bodies could be seen along the American lines for the defenders had been able to retrieve the wounded and most of their dead from their front.

The beaches south of the Ewa Plain were littered with wrecked and blasted landing craft used in the most concentrated Japanese attack.

It was on the north shore that the refuse of war was most visible.

From Mokuleia to Waimea Bay the beaches and reefs were littered with corpses and wrecked and overturned boats, marking the ill-fated attempts to land through the tremendous surf and jagged rocks guarding this side of Oahu. Most of the wounded had been gotten off and back to the ships, but the dead, the evidence of defeat, tumbled in the surf as it burst in high combers on the guardian reefs before it angrily spent itself upon the shore.

Here again there was much less evidence of American loss of life as the wounded and most of the dead had been recovered by the defending troops as they were forced ever backward by the pressure of the attack. All structures had been leveled so that little remained of Waialua and Haleiwa villages.

The great cane fields extending inshore up the long volcanic slope of the island towards Schofield Barracks were burning here and there, sending their smoke plumes upwards into the new day. South of Waialua lay swaths of charred cane, black gashes against the green marking the intensity of the first day of battle.

It was in Honolulu that the material devastation of war was most evident. Fort Street and Nuuanu Avenue marked the Japanese advance from the harbor side to the Punchbowl with fire and ashes where they had burned their way through the center of the city. With morning light came more fighting along the entire depth of the salient which had cut the 25th Division literally in two.

There was evidence of the attacks at Waikiki but much less so than in the downtown area. Off the world famous beach small dwelling houses burned here and there where they had been set afire during the fighting of the previous afternoon and night. But as daylight grew it was becoming more apparent that Waikiki would not be a major arena in the second day of fighting.

Strangely enough Pearl Harbor itself, the navy yard, Ford Island, the submarine base evidenced little damage from the first day of battle other than the wreckage which had been sustained during the initial attacks on the island on 7 December. Hickam and Wheeler air fields, however, were again burning and smoking from the bombings when the Japanese carrier planes attempted to suppress Oahu's air power.

The windward side of the island bared the lash of Mars in burning buildings at Bellows Field and at the naval air station at Kaneohe Bay. As the troops committed here by the invader were fed in in much smaller numbers there were only occasional bodies to mar the beauties of the long surflines of Oahu's eastern shore.

The leeward coast appeared little touched for the same

reason, other than fire which had swept across the trees and grass of the wide mouth of the southern side of the Waianae pocket where the Marines had disputed the foot by foot advance of the brigade of the Japanese Gold Division dispatched to secure the destruction of the naval ammunition depot at Lualualei and seizure of the twisting road which climbed up to Kolekole Pass and thence down upon Schofield Barracks.

But the Marines with the help of some Army beach defense units had managed to hold the attacking Japanese brigade to small gains on the first day of the invasion. During the night infiltration attempts were nipped off so that in the dawn of the second day, the Gold Division's brigade had only an advance of half a mile to show for a naval supported offensive which had been hoped to be able to crack the pocket so invading forces could climb the steep Kolekole Pass road with the prize the easy descent into Schofield.

This was not to be, so the early morning hours saw the resumption of a slow grinding advance aimed at the center of the ammunition depot. By 1000 it was apparent that whatever was to happen in the pocket, it would be all for the Americans unless the Japanese came up with an entirely new plan for the seizure of the valley.

About the same hour carrier planes from *Saratoga* and *Yorktown* struck the invasion fleet, roiling the skies with aerial battles in which the land based Army and Navy aircraft joined, taking off from bloody oil soaked runways at Hickam and Wheeler Fields and from beleaguered Ford Island and the naval air station at Kaneohe Bay.

Hits were scored. Transports were set afire and destroyers sunk. But the main Japanese invasion drives were little affected. It was becoming clear that if the Japanese were to be held at all, they would have to be defeated and thrown back on the ground.

Although the Americans had stiffened their defense, and although the Japanese were encountering hard going throughout the morning hours, the defenders had to knock them back with a smashing counterattack if the island of Oahu was to be held. But up until this time they had been hard put to snubbing off the Japanese advances before they could critically damage the defensive structure of the island.

To accomplish a violent change in the pattern of the battle, the Army operations staff was directed to plan for going over to the offensive. This was to be launched as soon as troops could be assembled to strike the enemy at the most critical point. This was determined to be the Japanese drive from the Ewa Plain up the Kunia Road. In this attack the invaders were threatening to crack the 25th Division line, flanking Pearl Harbor and imperiling the security of Wheeler Field and Schofield Barracks.

An advance to the north would also uncover critical Army ammunition depots tunneled back into the cliffs on the sides of Kipapa and Waikakalaua gulches.

"There is no doubt that this is the most dangerous penetration the enemy has made," the G-3 told the chief of staff as they huddled before the large, detailed map in the Aliamanu command post.

"The landings at Bellows and Kailua are troublesome but they are not of major impact. Besides it seems that both of these attempts are not only being blunted but may be on the verge of being thrown back."

He turned his attention momentarily to the Waianae Pocket. "I am certain the Japanese were trying for an end run here, but the Marines and our beach defenses have bogged them down so a successful attack on the Kolekole Pass road would be most unlikely at this time."

"What about the North Sector?" the chief of staff asked.

The G-3's pointer moved north to the Waialua and Haleiwa areas. "These are the critical points on this line," he said. "Up until this time the 24th Division has been able to hold the Japanese Blue Division in check. There is a danger, of course, that if it could pull off a break-through, it could drive right on up to Schofield and Wheeler. But the division commander has not asked for any help so I am hoping that he will keep the enemy contained to the areas he now occupies.

"It is in the south sector that we are having our problems."

His hand swept over the city of Honolulu, past Waikiki and on out to Makapuu Point. "This long penetration in the Honolulu downtown area is presently being held in place. It has however severed the division into two parts. This is a dangerous development but as you know a late afternoon counterattack is planned to cut this salient off at the base. I am told by the commanders fighting along that section of the line that they are inflicting heavy casualties on the Japanese, leading them to believe that they have at last contained this thrust.

"It is here that the battle is going to be decided," the operations chief declared, outlining the Japanese positions and the American defense lines extending from the shores of West Loch in Pearl Harbor westward to the slopes of the Waianae Range.

"If we could drive them back from what has been their most dangerous advance we would stand a good chance of destroying them on the Ewa Plain."

He looked directly at the chief of staff. "I believe this offers us our best chance," he said simply.

The chief of staff spent a long time at the battle map. When he had finished he turned to the G-3. "I agree with you. The time has come to attack with all the forces we can gather. But I would go even farther."

"The 25th Division must withdraw all of the troops it can from the western side of the Honolulu penetration and transfer them to the Kunia Road front. At the same time the 27th Infantry on the eastern edge of this salient must prepare an all-out attack on the penetration with all the strength it can muster. This attack must be made in coordination with the major offensive to be launched west of Pearl Harbor."

The G-3 nodded while his assistants took notes. "Air Force and Coast Artillery commands must give us whatever men they can spare to beef up the 25th Division reserve. The naval forces at Pearl Harbor should attack the Japanese in their rear with a line of departure from the Fort Weaver enclave which is still in our hands.

"The 24th Division should hold their line with a minimum of troops, sending all they can to the 25th."

He looked at his watch. "Let me confirm these movements with the commanding general. We will have to hold where we are until nightfall when the troop movements can get started under cover of darkness."

A sergeant was sent to ask the commanding general to come to the G-3 Section.

Appearing in a few moments he was briefed on the situation and the planned operations sketched out by the chief of staff.

He approved. "The Air Force should be prepared to bomb and strafe the Ewa front lines of the enemy with everything they have. Request the Navy to renew their carrier attacks on the enemy ships at first light and assist in beating off Japanese air attempts to impede our attack."

His listeners, marking his designation of the battle line as the "Ewa Front," knew that they were facing the battle of decision for the mastery of Oahu.

Aboard the flagship *Nagato*, Yamamoto impatiently awaited the arrival of his land force commander, General Sato, from his command ship stationed closer to the shore. He was not in a good humor. Tomorrow would mark the beginning of the third day of the battle with Yamamoto not sure that his forces would be able to compel the surrender of the island.

At the commencement of the operation four days had been allotted from the time of the attack until the clean-up. Now there was no certainty that there would be a fourth day.

The general entered the briefing room where he found the admiral with his chief of staff, regarding a map of Oahu with a baleful stare.

"Ah, Sato," he said turning to his land commander. "I

know that you have been busy. It was good of you to come."

The tall, thin general bowed uneasily.

"I want you to give me your appreciation as to just where we stand in our attack on Oahu."

Sato motioned to a staff colonel who had accompanied him to the flagship.

Carefully the pair of them briefed the admiral on the current status of their landing attacks on the great fortress, the short, white uniformed commander in chief of the combined fleet following their report closely on the Oahu battle map. Once his chief of staff, Admiral Ugaki, began to intervene, but Yamamoto held up his hand. "Let them finish. I want to hear all."

Sato stepped away from the operations map on which he had been pointing out the forward lines of the six Japanese penetrations of the island. "Tomorrow at dawn," he concluded nervously, "simultaneous attacks will be opened from the south and the north shores on the island's central corridor, so forcing the Americans to mass all of their available strength before us. In this attack we hope to destroy them."

"You know you must succeed," Yamamoto warned him almost gently.

"This will be the third day of the assault, and you know that the operation must be concluded within four days."

Sato nodded.

"I know, but the resistance has been far stronger than we had anticipated. I trust that by tomorrow night it will be overcome."

"It must be overcome," the tall Ugaki intervened. "Our fuel and ammunition are being depleted at an alarming rate."

Yamamoto again held up a restraining hand.

"I know the general appreciates the need for a speedy conclusion," he said. "But it must be a successful conclusion. We cannot afford a drawn battle much less a repulse."

Sato inclined his head in acquiesence.

"The battle for the island will be renewed on all fronts before dawn," he pledged his commander in chief. "I trust we will succeed."

Yamamoto had his steward bring a tray of glasses filled with sake.

Waiting until all had been served he raised his glass to General Sato. "His Majesty the Emperor!"

The response came in muted tones. "The Emperor!"

The conference was over.

Part VII

All they that take the sword shall perish with the sword.
                        —St. Matthew

32

It Was Not to Be

O F COURSE, NONE OF THIS HAPPENED.
    What might have been the outcome of the battle for
Oahu will never be known, for because of indecision and
apprehension in the minds of two men, Vice Admiral
Chuichi Nagumo and his chief of staff Rear Admiral
Ryunosuke Kusaka, on the wind swept bridge of the
flagship *Akagi* that sunny afternoon of 7 December 1941,
and because of the failure of Operation Hawaii's planners
to provide for the contingency of overwhelming victory, it
was not to be.

In spite of the pleas of their own airmen, the two admirals, in ordering the signal to withdraw from Hawaiian
waters, doomed their empire to defeat.

In not ordering his planners to completely explore all of
the possibilities of the preemptory first strike attack once it
had been decided to proceed with the clandestine assault,
Yamamoto himself contributed to the launching of Japan
on her long and painful voyage to catastrophe.

Millions of Japanese would die because of the decisions
at Pearl Harbor.

Yamamoto was quick to grasp this when in the early

morning hours of that fateful day, 8 December in Tokyo, while receiving news of the great victory in his flagship *Nagato* and beset with pleas to order a third attack on Oahu, he refused to approve the order drafted by his operations officer, the eccentric Captain Kamahito Kurashima: "Seek out American carriers. They must be destroyed."

Instead he sat as if under a spell, muttering half to himself: "He will not attack again. He will withdraw."

Then turning to his eager captain, with a shake of his head, he said: "Don't send it. . . . Nagumo must fight his own battle. I have complete trust in him."

Complete trust Yamamoto did have.

For six months later the commander of the carrier force spearheading the attack on the Midway Islands and the American fleet by the greatest naval armada ever assembled at that time was Nagumo and his chief advisor, the cautious Kusaka. On that critical 4th of June 1942, Yamamoto was physically nearer to the series of disastrous decisions made on the bridge of the *Akagi*, being himself in command of the entire operation in his new flagship, the superbattleship *Yamato*, three hundred miles astern of Nagumo.

The Midway attack was made necessary to retrieve the timid errors of judgment made by Nagumo and Kusaka the afternoon of 7 December 1941.

Why the same commanders who had failed to reap the results of their great victory that day were again in command in an equally critical spot six months later is not easily explained other than in the measured march of Fate as in a Greek tragedy.

The Midway operation which was to come to a climax in the most decisive sea battle in history commenced with direct ties to that dead Admiral Heihachiro Togo, Yamamoto's idol and the Imperial Japanese Navy's god. For the sailing of the spearhead of the vast armada, Admiral Nagumo's First Carrier Striking Force, was scheduled for 27 May, Japanese Navy Day, the anniversary of that day in 1905 on which the immortal Togo had destroyed the Imperial Russian Fleet at Tsushima.

Two days before the sortie, Yamamoto had invited his senior commanders and their staffs aboard the flagship *Yamato*, swinging to her red mooring buoy at the Hashirajima anchorage in the Inland Sea, to toast the destruction of the American Pacific Fleet in sake cups presented to the admiral by His Imperial Majesty, Emperor Hirohito. It was a ceremony curiously similar to that held by Togo in his flagship *Mikasa* when he had toasted the success of his torpedo boat captains in their surprise attack on the Russian's First Pacific Squadron lying at anchor off the fortress of Port Arthur.

But no toast out of Imperial cups could implant the flaming spirit of attack in the two key admirals entrusted with the destruction of the American naval forces at Midway.

Instead when at last discovering they had been ambushed by an American carrier or carriers, neither Nagumo nor Kusaka could bring themselves to the swift and desperate decision to immediately launch their dive bombers and torpedo planes at the enemy without the fighter cover needed for their protection.

Yet Rear Admiral Tamon Yamaguchi, commanding two carriers, *Hiryu* and *Soryu* of CarDiv 2 of Nagumo's force, had no trouble making up his mind when upset by the indecision in the flagship, he signaled *Akagi:* "Consider it advisable to launch attack force immediately."

This was the same admiral, who on that critical day north of Pearl Harbor while air officers Genda and Fuchida were pleading with Nagumo and Kusaka for a third attack on Pearl Harbor and a search for the missing American carriers, had signaled the force commander: "All is ready for another attack."

At Midway as at Pearl Harbor he was ignored.

The indecision in *Akagi* following receipt of cruiser *Tone's* scouting plane report that it had an American carrier in view ate up two fateful hours from 0820 to 1020 that in the end would irrevocably decide the course of the Pacific War.

At 1024 just when Nagumo had given the order to his carriers to launch their planes to attack the Americans, the blow fell.

33

Why Midway?

WHEN THE HAWAIIAN ISLANDS WERE CAST INTO THE PA-
cific like a cupful of dice, they were spilled out over
sixteen hundred miles of ocean. Where the lip of the cup
hit the living crust of the ancient days lie clustered the
main islands. Then as afterthoughts, little inhospitable
rocks and reefs raise their heads above the lonely seas at
distant intervals along a gentle arc curving away off to the
west-northwest.

At the end of this submarine mountain chain lies the
tiny atoll of Midway Islands enclosing two minute bits of
sand within a barrier reef of coral. These islets, covered by
grubby scrub and ironwood trees, measure two miles in
length for the larger and barely a mile for the smaller.

Yet for these two ragged bits of sand in a deserted sea,
the fate of the world's oldest empire and her greatest
republic were to be at hazard.

One man, a smooth-faced stocky man of short stature,
pondering the matter in the quiet of his command quarters
high in the superstructure of battleship *Yamato*, had decided it. He must have those two tattered islets. He
wanted them because the threat of their loss would force a

tall, red-wristed Texan to gamble all his remaining naval strength to hold them.

And the stocky man with the solemn face knew that plane for plane, gun for gun, ship for ship, he held the master cards. This would be the stroke which would break haughty America to the whiphand of Japan.

The warning order went out on 5 May 1942 when Admiral Isoroku Yamamoto, commander in chief of the combined fleet of His Imperial Japanese Majesty's Navy, began assembling the armada which would crush Midway as a man would crush a fly. It would then proceed to the far more crucial task of destroying the remnants of the American Navy in the Pacific.

There was to be a double-barreled aspect to the gigantic operation. To mislead Nimitz the Texan into displacing his meager forces toward the north, Yamamoto would hurl two carriers guarded by three heavy cruisers and support ships against the American base at Dutch Harbor in the Aleutians. The naval station crushed, the Japanese would then proceed to their first conquest of Alaskan soil with the capture of the islands of Adak, Attu and Kiska.

When the bombs screaming down on Dutch Harbor signaled "Battle Stations!" for the greatest fleet Japan had ever sent into any action, the main units of the armada would be seizing Midway in preparation for the destruction of the canny Nimitz.

Yamamoto felt good those sunny days in May in spite of the losses suffered in the Coral Sea. With Midway under the Rising Sun, an aerial harassment of Pearl Harbor and the Hawaiians could begin, preliminary to an assault on Oahu itself.

There was great confidence in the admiral's flagship. Around it at Hashirajima were anchored other men-o-war, visible evidence of the mighty Japanese power which had moved so relentlessly across the Pacific world. How could Nimitz, denuded of carriers and heavy ships, hope to meet and repel the conquering fleet which Yamamoto proposed to unleash upon him? Pearl Harbor had ushered in a long series of astonishing Japanese victories. Now Midway was to become the jeweled name, the greatest battle of them all.

Outside the concrete battlements of his headquarters at Pearl Harbor's naval base, the penetrating blue eyes of the silvery haired admiral scrutinized the effect of his pistol fire on the small paper target. He was hitting but he was not perfect and he demanded perfection.

Chester Nimitz, the sailor who had been detailed to salvage the burning, bloody wreckage left by the treachery of Pearl Harbor, had so far admirably fulfilled his task. Neither he nor the Navy indulged that overblown self-confidence which had been a prewar stamp; instead they had substituted grim resolution and a desire to get at the jugular of the Japanese fleet.

But now he was "on target" for the most savage thrust of all. It was to come at him fast. To meet it he would have to round up a scratch team vastly inferior to the enemy in every weapon. Nimitz looked at the end of the pistol barrel then shook his head wryly at his Marine orderly. You couldn't be expected to put them all in the black all of the time.

Back in his headquarters he resumed the weighing of certain intangibles which now monopolized all his thinking hours. By the most secret of operations he was being furnished with information rivaling that of the Magic which had been so misused in the months and weeks and days preceding Pearl Harbor. Naval combat intelligence at Pearl had broken into Japan's top secret naval codes, and this calm admiral with the straight-lipped smile was reading portions of their dispatches and orders.

But could he be sure the Japanese did not intend he should read them? It was a difficult question.

In war commanders can only be certain of uncertainty.

But Nimitz in weighing his intangibles was coming to some conclusions. On 14 May 1942, they resulted in the ordering of a state of "Fleet Opposed Invasion" for the Hawaiian Islands and the vast ocean areas surrounding.

Simultaneously orders were flashed to all available vessels including those in the Coral Sea to hurry home to Pearl. Without fanfare or public notice, the Army began tightening the already taut defenses of Oahu.

Gradually silent tension began to enwrap Hawaii. No one was quite sure why, but something ominous was in the air. The days of Pearl Harbor were coming back. Would enemy bombers roar over Oahu again? This question loomed most menacingly in the black hours of the blackout when men and women were forced to ponder what must be done when the sirens screamed again.

On the tiny target of Midway itself, Marines were throwing up more strongpoints and gun positions on their beach lines of resistance. More ordnance was secured and more aircraft began moving up from Oahu. The Marines would be ready, they told themselves grimly. This would be a tough nugget for the Jap to grab. The trade winds soughed through the trees with a somber whistle and there was little comfort to the sentries in the whiteness of the surf line against the mysterious obscurity of the Pacific night.

On the tiny atoll, the only question was: "When?"

Yamamoto knew but he was not telling just then—even in code.

He had in fact already made his opening moves. Three large minelaying submarines loaded with tons of gasoline and oil slipped away from Kwajalein atoll in the Marshalls to cautiously proceed northward to the spreading arc of the Hawaiian chain—their objective: French Frigate Shoals.

In the lee of these almost awash reefs, they were to refuel two big 31-ton four-motored Kawanishi flying-boats which were to wing up from the Marshalls to the shoals. Refueled, the planes would then take off for a careful night reconnaissance of Pearl, checking the location of the American fleet. But when these submarines arrived off the rendezvous on 30 May they were chagrined to find two American seaplane tenders already there before them. They loitered around but to no profit to the Emperor. The

Texan at Pearl Harbor had successfully parried Yamamoto's first move.

While the big I Class submarines were slithering futilely about the reefs at French Frigate, the Aleutian attack fleet was steaming out to its task. The following day, anniversary of Togo's victory at Tsushima, the First Carrier Striking Force, key of the whole Midway operation, sortied into the Pacific from the Inland Sea.

The voyage to the Hawaiian area would be a return visit for most of these ships, planes and men of the force, for was it not they who had started the war with their glorious destruction of the American fleet at Pearl Harbor? Memories of the earlier thrust—only six months before, but how long ago that seemed now—swept through the mind of Nagumo as he stood on the command bridge high in the island of *Akagi*. This battle would drive home the final blows required to finish the job which he had begun so well back in December.

Two days later Commander in Chief Yamamoto steamed away from the Empire in flagship *Yamato* with her giant 18.1-inch rifles. What could the battered American fleet offer to stand up to her? Officers and men were cheering and singing upon departure for this "last battle," but Yamamoto was more solemn than usual. Perhaps it was his stomach pains which depressed his spirit.

Sunny weather favoring the start of the voyage was reflected in the fleet. The crews were eager. They had the strength. And as the huge mass of overwhelming naval might moved eastward, it picked up additional reinforcements from Saipan and Guam.

More than two hundred war vessels including eleven battleships and eight carriers, twenty-two heavy and light cruisers, sixty-five destroyers, twenty-one submarines, seaplane carriers, minesweepers, patrol boats, oilers and twelve transports loaded with five thousand men of the Midway Occupation Force swept on towards the sand patches of the atoll in battle array. The first bombs would fall on Dutch Harbor on 3 June. Immediately thereafter the

Imperial Combined Fleet using Midway as the bait would first snare then crush the Americans. It would be Tsushima on a scale of which Togo had never dreamed. The enemy would be driven back upon his own Pacific Coast.

At Pearl Harbor a nervous apprehension gripped all hands. As each day fled into the next with so much left undone, labor went on around the clock. Meanwhile the interminable calculations of the staff ground on and on, measuring with utmost delicacy the comparative strengths of the two contenders.

On 26 May, *Enterprise* and *Hornet*, too late to join the battle for the Coral Sea, returned to Pearl and immediately began emergency preparations for their sortie into the coming battle. The following afternoon battered *Yorktown*, survivor of the Coral Sea attacks where she had left her consort *Lexington* sunk, entered Pearl's channel. Rear Admiral Aubrey Fitch, tactical air commander in the battle, estimated it would take three months to put her back into fighting shape. Pearl Harbor navy yard was to prove him wrong.

Without *Yorktown*, Nimitz would meet Yamamoto with but two carriers, the only capital ships he had, against the overpowering forces of the Japanese. *Yorktown* wouldn't even the odds by a long shot, but her presence in the battle would be vital.

So as she slid into the wall-sided graving dock, more than fourteen hundred of the navy yard's civilian workers swarmed over the crippled carrier to begin the arduous tasks of battle repair. All through the long twilight the work went on and when night came it continued without halt under the hot glare of the floodlights.

It was still clattering on when *Enterprise* and *Hornet* stood grandly down the narrow channel on 28 May bound out for the action which would decide the mastery of the Pacific. It continued on right up through Friday night of the twenty-ninth even while the carrier was sucking in her oil and taking on replacement air crews. Finally at nine o'clock Saturday morning of Memorial Day the weary mechanics and technicians watched her edge out into the stream and slowly square herself away for the channel.

As *Yorktown* commenced to get underway, she was fondly observed through proud and misty eyes. What had been estimated at a ninety-day job had been completed in two.

And Nimitz had three carriers.

34

In the Fog

FAR TO THE WESTWARD BUT DRAWING NEARER TO MIDWAY with every turn of the screws, Nagumo nervously walked the bridge of *Akagi*. The carrier striking force was groping its way through heavy seas and fog. The fog was admirable cover from Yankee aircraft but it could hide enemy submarines and it was so dense it became a hazard to the fast steaming carriers and their escorts. Ships found it hard to hold station even in the daylight hours and the nights were filled with alarms and terrors which began to exert a subtle effect on the spirits of their crews.

The confidence of the sunny days off the Japanese coast began to distill into a grim appreciation of the great risks which surrounded them. Men became touchy and look-outs unreliable.

Six hundred miles farther to the west, Yamamoto, the man who had planned Pearl Harbor and rammed through the decision to sink the American fleet at Midway, was feeling the depressive effects of the weather. Still all was going according to the plans drafted in the staff cabins of the supership *Yamato*, and there was no indication the enemy held any suspicion of his forthcoming doom.

Meanwhile *Yorktown* and her Task Force 17 under Rear Admiral Frank Jack Fletcher, officer in tactical command of the battle, fueled from the oilers *Cimarron* and *Platte*. The larger Task Force 16 with *Enterprise* and *Hornet* as its carrier strength had refueled the day before. There was gossip in the wardrooms about this sister task force's new commander.

"Spruance will have a tough time filling Halsey's shoes," one flier predicted, bemoaning Halsey's relinquishment of command to enter the hospital.

"I don't know," another countered. "He did a good job with the Bull's cruisers."

On the bridge of *Enterprise* Rear Admiral Raymond Spruance, substitute commander of Task Force 16, pondered Nimitz' orders: ". . . you will be governed by the principle of calculated risk."

No flier himself, this slender admiral with the intense face listened carefully to what his aides had to say then went right on thinking. The crew of *Enterprise* began to feel they were in the hands of a cool and clever fighter.

Monday the first of June faded into night with the Japanese forces still groping through heavy, obscure weather to the west. In mid-morning on the second visibility was so bad *Akagi* lost contact with the rest of her task force. The time had come for the turn southeast towards Midway. This involved a wide swinging movement of the entire force. Yet visual signals, even searchlights, could not be seen through the gloom.

Nagumo held a worried conference. Wouldn't it be better to steam on course until the weather broke, in hopes of trapping the American fleet? Staff officers told him no. The orders were inflexible, the carrier striking force must hit Midway first to prepare the way for the landing forces.

Nagumo shrugged his shoulders. They would have to use a weak radio signal within the force itself then—this in spite of the fact it was almost sure to be picked up by the Americans. But there was no escape, radio silence was broken and the turn was made. This signal was heard aboard Yamamoto's flagship six hundred miles to the west. If it could be heard that distance, the enemy surely must have picked it up. Japanese spirits became even more depressed.

Yet by a quirk of war this signal was not heard by American ears.

So night came to the Pacific with the Japanese Imperial Navy on the threshold of its long desire—the complete destruction of American seapower.

Two more days and it should all be over.

Earlier that afternoon the two American task forces under Fletcher and Spruance had rendezvoused at "Point Luck" and were steaming some 325 miles north and east of Midway as ordered by Nimitz. The canny Texan had placed them there beyond search range of the Japanese forces, estimating and hoping that the long-range patrols from Midway would find the enemy before the enemy found his carriers.

Nimitz was correct.

Just before 0900 on 3 June, Ensign Jack Reid in his twin-motored PBY flying-boat was at the turn-around of his search mission some seven hundred miles west of Midway. He let the big plane fly on for a few more minutes over the empty ocean. Then suddenly the cockpit came alive.

Reid sat staring at long lines of black ships crawling over the surface of the sea.

"My God, aren't those ships?" he shouted. "I believe we have hit the jackpot."

"You're damned right they are!" his co-pilot replied.

From then on there were busy times in the lumbering patrol craft. Sallying in and out of the clouds, she shadowed the Japanese formation for more than two hours, sighting eleven ships steaming eastward at 19 knots. Finally avoiding fire from the hostile force and with one eye on the fuel guages, Reid winged around for his long return to Midway.

In *Yorktown*, Admiral Fletcher, receiving the report as a

sighting of the Japanese "main body," correctly interpreted it to be instead the occupation force with transports full of troops for the seizure of Midway. He decided to keep the carriers hidden to the northeast until their Japanese counterparts showed their flight decks.

During the long nervous afternoon Army flying fortresses sent to Midway from Oahu flew out to bomb Reid's fleet but they got no hits. Four Navy patrol planes, each lugging a torpedo, then took off after nightfall to find the enemy transports in bright moonlight. Before they turned for home, one of them had hit the oiler *Akebono Maru*. Twenty-three crewmen were killed or wounded but the ship returned to her station to continue her voyage.

The Americans had drawn first blood.

With the reports of these actions the American carriers had turned on a southwesterly course which would put them about two hundred miles off Midway by dawn so they might ambush the Japanese carriers after they had flown off their planes to attack the island. Meanwhile Nagumo, running up his speed to twenty-five knots, was coming down on Midway from the northwest, his striking force straining to arrive at its fly-off position.

While Midway planes were searching for these attacking forces, the northern prong of the vast oceanic assault launched its planes against Dutch Harbor in the early morning of the third of June, bombing and shooting up the installations extensively. Admiral Kakuta was most anxious to acquire a good bag in this initial action of the battle for the Mid-Pacific. Bombing results were fair but no surface craft were sunk.

Playing hide and seek with the Americans in the damp mists and fogs of the Aleutians, the Japanese feint intended to draw Nimitz' strength to the North Pacific had gone off as scheduled, but the admiral at Pearl only smiled grimly and fixed his eyes on Midway. The Nips were doing just what they had said they would in their most secret codes.

Now the fourth of June was growing older. In the Midway area *Enterprise, Hornet, Yorktown* and their cruisers and destroyers were watching the sun slice the eastern rim of the horizon at 0457. At Pearl the same sun which had already been up an hour found Nimitz and his staff tensely waiting word from their marine ambush. Would it work?

They should soon know.

35

The Ambush

THE VERY EARLY MORNING HOURS OF THURSDAY THE fourth of June were ones of intense activity aboard the four large carriers of Nagumo's striking force. With their crews routed out at 0130, the work of arming aircraft with bombs for Midway was rushed in the mounting tension of pre-battle.

Commanders Fuchida and Genda of Pearl Harbor fame, although now both sick, watched anxiously as preparations for the great strike went forward. As at Pearl, Nagumo was going to hit with a heavy hand. When the planes bouncing off the flood-lit decks at 0430 formed up in the darkness, they were a formidable air fleet.

Behind the leading plane of Lieutenant Joichi Tomonaga of the *Hiryu* were 107 dive and level bombers, and fighters. Midway was distant 240 miles to the southeast. Its Marines would soon have plenty to do.

Meanwhile the American ambush carriers had been equally as industrious in the pre-dawn hours. At 0300 the wardrooms saw the pilots already at breakfast. Some were tingling with the expectancy of the battle while others, outwardly at least, seemed icy calm.

347

Soon they were filing into the ready rooms to be briefed on the carrier's position, her course, wind and much other data. When the briefing was completed there was nothing to do but wait.

Four o'clock dragged by. The Japanese must be getting ready to launch somewhere out there in the blackness. Everyone came to an edge of suspense they feared they could hardly sustain another moment. Yet time dragged by, minute after each painful minute.

At five o'clock the sun was but three minutes over the disc of the sea. A light breeze from the southeast was playing over the ambush carriers. Visibility would be good and the temperature was mild. It was going to be a beautiful tropic day. At first light, one-half hour before, *Yorktown* had launched ten scout dive bombers to fan out two hundred miles to the west and north, searching the lonely seas for signs of the enemy.

It was at the same time Nagumo's Midway-bound planes had roared into the morning darkness.

So far as Yamamoto in the flagship knew everything was proceeding on schedule. The Dutch Harbor bombing had come off and the Midway strike was airborne, the occupation force was moving in, and his own main fleet was in good position to go in to pulverize Midway or the American fleet as needed. His big question was: Where was the American fleet? He supposed it was still in Pearl but because the Americans had beaten his submarines to French Frigate Shoals, he had never been able to get off the Kawanishi flying-boat reconnaissance which was to have made sure. Never mind, the attack would be driven home.

But there were three factors of which Yamamoto did not know but which already were operating heavily against him.

Admiral Nimitz was reading his codes; the Japanese submarines which were establishing a double cordon between Midway and Oahu to snare the American ships when they did sortie from Pearl had taken position two days too late to catch their prey; and three large United

States carriers were silently laying a trap for Yamamoto off to the northeast of Midway Islands.

The United States Marines on Midway didn't know any of these things either. They just knew they were due for one hell of a fight and the ground troops would have to take the Japanese attack head on. Marine and Army aircraft on the island were instructed to give first priority to the enemy carriers when they did appear.

At thirty-four minutes past five o'clock the waiting American carriers got the word.

"Enemy carriers!"

The message was an intercept from a searching Navy PBY flying-boat reporting to Midway. At four minutes to six the air raid sirens on the two tiny islets began to wail their ominous cry of coming destruction. Three minutes earlier the listening carriers heard another pilot tell Midway: "Many enemy planes heading Midway bearing 320 degrees distant 150."

Now the deadly game of seek and find would begin in earnest.

Three minutes past six o'clock a patrol Catalina reported: "Two carriers and battleships bearing 320, distance 180, course 135, speed 25."

Fletcher waiting in *Yorktown* to recover his search planes dispatched earlier, signaled Spruance: "Proceed southwesterly and attack enemy carriers. Will follow as soon as search planes recovered."

Enterprise and *Hornet* began to show white water at their cutwaters as they swung away with their task force.

The trap was ready to spring.

36

Devil's Dilemma

WHILE THE PILOTS SAT IN THE READY ROOMS AWAITING their attack orders, Midway battened down to the wailing of the sirens as they rose and fell in baleful malediction over the lonely stretches of coral sand. At 0553 *Midway's* search radar took the enemy in contact some 93 miles out.

The Marine fighter squadron roared off Eastern Island while all along both of the islets Marines stared skyward and fiddled with last moment adjustment of their guns. They would be waiting.

Thirty miles out the Marine fighters sighted the sky-filling Japanese formation. Climbing to 17,000 feet the 26 Marine fighters dropped onto the enemy flying at 12,000. A great dogfight splattered through the sky, but the Japanese, leaving their Zeros to handle the outnumbered Marines, disengaged their bombers to send them winging in over Midway. It was 0630.

For twenty minutes of hell, the bombs rained on command dugouts, observation posts and gun positions. But the island was spitting back. Oil tanks on Sand Island blew up in flames. The powerhouse was hit and the hospital and storehouses were fired.

Marines remarked with irony that the runways were untouched. Maybe the enemy was saving them for his own planes once the island was secured. The sea soldiers looked, cursed, and went right on fighting. At 0650, except for a "tail end Charlie" attack by two planes minutes later, the great air assault on Midway was over.

Meanwhile six Navy torpedo planes and four Army B-26s armed with torpedoes slung under their bellies were searching out the Japanese carriers. They found them at 0710 and immediately attacked. One torpedo plane dived on *Akagi* after it had been hit by gunfire, roared across the flight deck and fell into the sea. But Nagumo's squadron was too good. It massacred the Americans without taking a hit.

Only one torpedo plane and two of the Army bombers lived through the rain of fire thrown up by the carrier force and its combat air patrol.

Things were going according to Japanese plans. These attacking planes were all from Midway. The American fleet had put in no appearance. Nagumo had 93 planes poised on the flight decks of his four carriers ready to roar off with bombs and torpedoes in case that fleet should be found. Earlier he had sent off seven float planes searching for American ships. Six of them which had launched beginning at 0430 reported negative. The seventh from the cruiser *Tone* had trouble with her catapult, delaying her fly-off a half-hour to 0500. This was to prove one of the most costly half-hours in Japanese history.

Then at 0700 Lieutenant Tomonaga had radioed Nagumo from over Midway: "There is need for a second attack."

Nagumo walked about the bridge trying to make up his mind. There had been no reports of any surface contacts. The enemy torpedo planes striving futilely to get at him were eloquent proof that Midway needed further working over. Dare he take the chance?

At 0715 he made his decision. He "broke the spot." He would hit Midway again.

Planes spotted on the flight decks were ordered returned below to the hangar decks where the unwieldy torpedoes were removed and replaced with bombs for the land installations at Midway. The plane crews made ready for an hour of sweat resulting from the admiral's order.

While this work was being rushed, cruiser *Tone's* tardy search plane No. 4, having reached the 300 mile limit of its eastward course, had turned north to fly the 60-mile base of its dogleg flight before homing back to the force. At 0728 the observer in the float plane saw black specks on the ocean far off on his port hand.

Shortly after, the jittery admiral in *Akagi* was jolted by this message relayed to the flagship by the *Tone:*

"Ten ships, apparently enemy, sighted. Bearing 010 degrees, distant 240 miles from Midway. Course 150 degrees, speed more than 20 knots. Time 0728."

The position of these ships would be some two hundred miles to the east.

Surface craft speeding to attack him! If they had planes he was already within their range.

But the dread word "carrier" did not appear in the search report so the irritable Nagumo let the preparations for the second strike on Midway go ahead unhindered in the hangar decks below.

Then at 0745 the Japanese carrier striking force commander appropriated a feminine prerogative. He changed his mind.

The signal flashed out to his carriers: "Prepare to carry out attacks on enemy fleet units. Leave torpedoes on those attack planes which have not as yet been changed to bombs."

He then ordered *Tone's* scout plane: "Ascertain ship types and maintain contact."

At 0809 that "ten o'clock scholar" came through with this reply: "Enemy is composed of five cruisers and five destroyers."

A tremor of relief ran through the command group on the flagship's bridge. But it was short lived.

For at 0820 *Tone's* observer reported: "The enemy is accompanied by what appears to be a carrier."

It was a most conservative misestimate.

Actually what the scout plane was looking at and what Nagumo had been waiting to find since before daybreak was Spruance's Task Force 16 with two carriers, six cruisers and nine destroyers. *Enterprise* and *Hornet* had been launching planes since two minutes after seven o'clock, the same time Tomonaga had advised Nagumo that Midway would require a second strike.

While these less than adequate intelligence reports were being received by the harried Nagumo, his force had been subjected to a glide-bombing attack by 16 Marine Corps dive bombers followed by a high level bomb drop by 15 Army flying fortresses. A moment later 11 Marine vindicators had dived on him but Nagumo's luck was riding, none of his ships took any but minor damage.

He had lost about forty aircraft but in turn he had heavily bombed Midway and shot down more than half her planes. But the vice admiral with the cropped head was uneasy despite the early advantages he had scored.

If *Tone's* search plane report was true, he could expect an attack by carrier-based aircraft at any moment. Moreover he had to keep his flight decks clear to receive the Midway strike planes which would begin coming aboard at 0837. By "breaking the spot" with his abortive decision to rearm his reserve planes for a second slash at Midway, he had put himself on the spot and in spite of the cocky demeanor of his officers and men, Nagumo was extremely apprehensive.

It was then his commander of CarDiv 2, Rear Admiral Tamon Yamaguchi who had urged him to renew the attack on Pearl Harbor, sent him a signal from *Hiryu:* "Consider it advisable to launch attack force immediately."

But this would mean the dive and torpedo bombers

would have to go out without adequate fighter protection. Nagumo refused. He would attack when he was ready. Meanwhile he tried to speed up the recovery of the returning Midway strike planes. But little could be done. It took just so much time to land each plane. No more, no less. Nine o'clock had just passed when he ordered the carrier force to turn to the east northeast. It took 17 more minutes to get the last of the Midway strike planes aboard. It was then *Akagi* made the signal: "We plan to contact and destroy the enemy task force."

The action was rising toward crescendo but first there must be a bloody prelude.

On decks crowded with aircraft the tasks of rearming and refueling began. No one needed to spur the crews to their work. Already word of their danger was spreading through the ships.

Spruance leaving Fletcher to recover his search aircraft in *Yorktown* had turned to the southeast to begin launching planes at 0702. The slender, quiet admiral, acting on the advice of his chief of staff, Captain Miles Browning, ordered the early launch—two hours ahead of plan—in an attempt to catch Nagumo's carriers when they were taking their Midway strike planes back aboard to rearm and refuel them. Browning had calculated 0900 was the magic hour, but Nagumo, who was proceeding exactly as Browning estimated he would, was some 23 minutes ahead of the schedule the Americans had worked out for him.

Spruance had launched everything but his combat air patrols. It was a big launch of 116 dive bombers, torpedo planes and fighters. It had taken just better than an hour with the last planes soaring off *Enterprise* and *Hornet* at 0806. When they were on their way the task force turned southwest in the direction of the enemy.

First carrier planes to find Nagumo's expectant force were the torpedo bombers of the *Hornet*. Having lost their fighter cover, which missing the enemy on the southeast heading were forced to ditch at sea, Lieutenant Commander John Waldron's planes swung north to sight smoke and the enemy about 0925. The fifteen fat bellied torpedo planes, catching Nagumo after his shift toward the northeast, went in strong through a hell-fire of anti-aircraft bursts, great wave splashes made by the lobbing of enemy shells into the water ahead of them, and swarms of Zero fighters. Fiery fingers plucked the luckless TBDs out of the sky in flaming death. Still the survivors pressed on toward the twisting, turning carriers.

Now there were only two left. Suddenly there were none. The first attack had failed but it had been driven into the dragon's teeth.

A few minutes later *Enterprise* torpedo planes winged about the great circle of Japanese ships all spitting fire into the sky. Fourteen planes went in, four came out—no hits were made.

It was 0930 and Nagumo was to have thirty minutes of respite.

In the ready rooms of *Yorktown* the order had come: "Pilots man your planes."

The launching which had started at 0838 had been completed at 0906 with 35 planes in the air and a second echelon on the flight deck ready to take off on order.

Anxiously all eyes aboard *Yorktown* had watched them assemble in formation then moving speck-like against the clouds, fly off to the southwest where the battle was raging in all its fury.

Shortly after ten o'clock *Yorktown's* twelve torpedo planes drove into the frantically twisting Japanese formation. Again the hail of steel. Again the flaming bombers. Five were able to launch but got no hits. Only two planes flew out of the hell pit but both were forced to ditch on their return.

So the torpedo bomber attacks of the three American carriers failed. Not a single hit was registered by these brave men. Forty-one planes went out. Four returned. They had flown off their flight decks knowing they had but little chance of coming back, yet each had pressed home on the enemy with unbelievable tenacity.

No hits.

But they had given Nagumo no surcease. Their attacks had kept the carriers and their escorts turning and dodging at high speeds, making it impossible for them to launch more planes. Flying low to the water, the torpedo planes had pulled the Japanese combat air patrols and the antiaircraft guns of the ships, down to the very surface of the sea.

These men died without the satisfaction of seeing their torpedoes go home. Yet it was because of their devotion and courage that the most important moment of the Great Pacific War had come.

They had set the stage.

37

Five Terrible Minutes

ENTERPRISE GOT HER DIVE BOMBING SQUADRONS AWAY shortly before eight o'clock. After a monotonous flight to the estimated position of Nagumo's fleet, they found only empty ocean. It was 0922 with the planes reaching beyond their fuel range. Still their persistent commander, Wade McClusky, hung to the assigned southwest heading with his 33 dive bombers.

Then at 0935, still over vacant peacefully rolling seas, he turned northwest. Twenty minutes later from his lofty vantage point, 19,000 feet in the cloud flecked sky, he saw off to his starboard hand a Japanese destroyer running at high speed toward the north. Deciding she was a laggard trying to catch up with Nagumo's force, McClusky laid a new course off of hers, then flew over and beyond her.

This was the destroyer *Arashi*, delayed by her attack on a U.S. submarine, and now striving earnestly to regain her station in the task force.

In the cockpits of *Enterprise's* dive bombers one fateful minute dragged into the next. Nerves and muscles were raw with expectancy. Where were Nagumo's big carriers?

Things were now looking up for the Japanese. They had

repelled every attack sent against them. The big strike force of 102 dive bombers, torpedo planes and fighters had been brought up and set into position on the flight decks. Take-off time was set for 1030.

Nagumo was getting off his spot. To hurry things along he passed the word at 1020 for the carriers to launch when ready. In a very few minutes the falcons would be unleashed on the American carriers. These were the conquerors of Pearl Harbor.

At this moment, coming in high and undetected from the sun, McClusky's dive bombers took three of Nagumo's powerful carriers in view. There they were—the famous names of the Japanese navy—*Akagi, Kaga, Soryu,* thrashing and twisting in their desperate efforts to shake free of the last ill-fated American torpedo plane attack. *Hiryu* was unseen, hidden by cloud.

The guns of Nagumo's force were depressed, beating off the fatal runs of *Yorktown's* torpedo bombers. Zero fighters were down low for the same game. Nimitz' carefully laid trap was ready for the springing.

McClusky triggered it off!

Quickly assigning targets he led his dive bombers down for the kill. One by one they peeled off from the formation. Blazing downward from 15,000 feet they plummeted on their prey at better than 280 knots.

Still the Japanese did not see them.

Akagi, the flagship, had just turned into the wind. At 1024 the white signal flag for take-off fluttered in the wind. The first Zero gathered speed down the flight deck. At that moment a sky lookout yelled "Hell Divers!" to the men amid the massed aircraft on the broad deck below.

The enemy carriers were coming up fast in the bomb sights of the American dive bombers. The planes waiting take-off on the flight decks grew larger. For an instant the bombers hung strung down from the sky in an artistic pattern above the fleeing ships.

Then hell burst upon the despoilers of Pearl Harbor.

Akagi took a near miss, then a hit which blasting her 'midships elevator exploded amongst bombs and torpedoes piled high in her hangar deck. A third bomb crashed into the midst of forty planes massed on the after portion of the flight deck. Annihilation had caught up with *Akagi*. In an instant she was a sheet of flame.

Kaga's death strokes came with equal swiftness. Four hits blossomed in scarlet rage along her flight deck, the first throwing burning gasoline over her island superstructure. Explosions wracked the great ship, tore her vitals, then vomited them skyward in great billows of fire. Her captain blown to shreds, their shipmates dead, many of her crew leapt into the sea.

Soryu fell victim to *Yorktown's* dive bombers as *Akagi* and *Kaga* were commencing their death throes. Squadron commander Maxwell Leslie had wasted no time in finding the Japanese. Although starting much later, he arrived over Nagumo simultaneously with McClusky of the *Enterprise*.

Soryu was just preparing to launch when her crew observed *Kaga* shivering to the great explosions tearing her frame. Then *Soryu* took her own reward. Leslie's bombs erupted along her flight deck setting off great fires. Explosions of bombs and shells in the magazines sped the destruction, igniting the carrier into a blazing funeral pyre.

So in the space of five minutes Nagumo lost the heart of his striking force and three of Japan's greatest carriers were burning furiously on the sea over which a few moments before they had reigned.

The devastating swiftness of the attack left the conqueror of Pearl Harbor dazed and distraught. Dragged from the smoke fogged bridge by his aides, he slid awkwardly down a rope to the destruction of *Akagi's* flight deck. Dead were scattered all about. Sheets of orange flame roared skyward amid bursts of fire from the flagship's antiaircraft batteries, firing automatically through the smoke.

Ignominously Nagumo was forced to scramble from the burning carrier into a small boat which carried him to the light cruiser *Nagara*. It was just 1046.

The fourth Japanese carrier *Hiryu* which had escaped the fate of her three sisters beneath the fortunate cloud cover which hid her from American eyes was now sharpening her claws. At 1040 a search plane reported the position of *Yorktown* and the rest of Fletcher's task force. Desperate Japanese were not slow in responding. *Hiryu* immediately launched dive bombers and fighters to the attack.

Meanwhile far to the westward, the bridge of *Yamato*, flagship for Admiral Yamamoto, had witnessed a dramatic counterflow of emotion. All through the morning Yamamoto and his staff had confidently followed the operations of Nagumo against Midway. They had tensely marked the reports of the carrier striking force's successful efforts at beating off the early American attacks. Now they were waiting for news of Nagumo's strike against the American surface forces discovered northeast of Midway.

Then at 1050 Yamamoto got the word.

Rear Admiral Hiroaki Abe of the support group, but now temporarily in command of the battered carrier striking force, while Nagumo crawled from his burning flagship, flashed it: "Fires raging aboard *Kaga*, *Soryu* and *Akagi* resulting from attacks by enemy carrier and land based planes. We plan to have *Hiryu* engage enemy carriers. We are temporarily withdrawing to the north to assemble our forces."

The world fell in on Yamamoto as he scanned the bitter words.

If Japan was not to sustain the most crushing defeat in her long history, he must gamble everything he had and quickly.

Out went the orders.

Kakuta's carriers, *Ryujo* and *Junyo* which had blasted Dutch Harbor, must come running south to the rescue.

Kondo's battleships and cruisers supporting the Midway occupation force must race northward. Yamamoto himself would bend on speed with the main body and its mighty battle line. He had been hurt but he still was master of the greatest fleet the world had ever seen. With it he would hammer into extinction these small American forces which had stung him so badly.

Meanwhile the invasion of Midway would have to wait.

Aboard *Yorktown* men thrilled to the snatches of combat reports intercepted by the carrier on her attack frequencies. But this running radio account was confused and fragmentary. So all eyes watched westward for the carrier's returning war birds.

First to appear were four of her fighters and two damaged dive bombers all of which were landed safely. Fighter commander John Thach was hustled to the bridge where he gave Fletcher his first eye-witness account of the blasting and firing of *Akagi, Kaga* and *Soryu.*

Even in this moment of triumph Admiral Fletcher wondered grimly if a search mission of ten scout bombers, sent off shortly before, would have any luck with finding the *Hiryu* which Thach reported running in safety from the devastation which had destroyed her three sisters. Would his planes find the *Hiryu* before her planes found him? Fletcher had not long to wait for his answer.

As he talked with the fighter squadron commander, *Yorktown's* radar officer reported enemy planes approaching. In the meantime Leslie's dive bombers circled their carrier in their landing pattern. But it was not to be for the Japanese were upon her.

Eighteen Japanese dive bombers flanked by fighters appeared over the rim of *Yorktown's* task force where the sky was already blotched with smears of black ackack bursts. Up there in the melee they could see *Yorktown's* fighters working over the enemy. One Jap blew up. Another went screaming down in a ribbon of fire. Another. And another. Eleven in all.

But the survivors dived swiftly toward their target. Destroyers blew two of these right out of the air. But the rest pressed on. One, blown open as she swooped low over *Yorktown*, spilled out her bomb, which landing on the flight deck, lay there an instant before exploding with a terrific blast. Wounded and dead were hurled about and flames danced in fury.

Another bomb hit the stack. Burning debris fountained over the ship, two boilers were damaged while fumes and smoke forced fireroom crewmen up the ladders. One boiler was kept going by crews in gas masks but *Yorktown's* speed fell off rapidly until at 1220 she went dead in the water. The attack was over but thick columns of smoke mushroomed above her in the faint airs.

Fletcher signaled the cruiser *Astoria* for a boat which took him off the stricken carrier, the *Astoria* becoming the flagship for Task Force 17.

Yorktown planes in the air were ordered to land on *Enterprise* and *Hornet* which were in sight of the action.

While the heavy cruiser *Portland* attempted to take the carrier in tow, radar reported another enemy attack on the way.

Then suddenly after *Yorktown* had lain motionless for about an hour she sprang back to life. Her yellow breakdown flag with its blue crosses was hauled down to be replaced by another signal: "My speed five."

A cheer rose from the ships of her screen. Then it changed to: "My speed ten". . . .and then "My speed nineteen".

By then enemy torpedo planes were in sight.

Eight of ten fighters on her flight deck managed desperately quick take-offs behind their commander Thach who making a violent turn shot down one of the incoming Japanese before he could drop his torpedo.

Black splotches were blossoming against the clouds as the task force fired everything to save the wounded *Yorktown*. Ten "Kate" torpedo planes guarded by six Zeros raced towards her barely above the surface of the sea.

Enterprise and *Hornet* fighters plunged in to the rescue. Japanese began falling out of the sky.

The cruisers protecting *Yorktown* were exploding eight-inch shells in the sea before the approaching torpedo planes. High fountains of water leapt up to shield *Yorktown* but still four of the "Kates" drove on until they were close enough to launch. *Yorktown* avoided two of the fish but the other pair were marked for her. They exploded with a great roar in her port side. The carrier lost way and came to a stop listing badly to her stricken side.

It was 1442 of a hot tropic afternoon.

At this same moment, the ten search planes which had left *Yorktown* before noon to fruitlessly hunt for *Hiryu* were some 110 miles west by north of their wounded carrier. They knew nothing of what had happened to her but they were to avenge her mightily. It was then Lieutenant Samuel Adams of *Yorktown's* scouting five saw stretched out on the ocean before him the hated *Hiryu*, two battleships, three cruisers and four destroyers, all steaming to the north.

Word flashed into the ether sparked great activity in *Enterprise*. Their talons already bloodied with their morning's work on Nagumo's other carriers, twenty-four dive bombers, fourteen being *Yorktown's* own planes, rose rapidly from the Big E to fly swiftly off to the north.

At five o'clock on this Thursday afternoon they found their vengeance.

Hiryu was squirming frantically below them, traveling thirty-four knots and belching all guns. But the Americans were coming in despite her. For the dive bombers there came the graceful wing over, then the deadly plunge downward and the release. Four devastating hits twinkled over her flight deck and she too was enwrapped in the same fiery robes her sisters had worn that morning. Smoke funneled upwards so densely Lieutenant Earl Gallaher leading the way back to *Enterprise* was certain they had left another "kill."

Earlier, shortly before three o'clock with the *Yorktown*

listing 26 degrees, Captain Elliott Buckmaster ordered her crew to abandon ship. But she would not sink. Only when the enemy sub I-168 fatally torpedoed her two days later would she give up her gallant ghost.

With his carrier gone Fletcher relinquished command of the American forces to Spruance.

Now both Nimitz at Pearl and Spruance in *Enterprise* were confused as to just what the situation was. They knew they had hurt Yamamoto badly but how badly? That was what they could not know. Spruance fearful of running his night blinded carriers into the powerful Japanese battleships pulled away to the eastward. He had firsthand reports of *Akagi, Kaga, Soryu* and *Hiryu* burning but had those fires been doused? Were the carriers still afloat?

In the fog of battle he could not be sure.

Yamamoto, far to the westward in his great flagship, had a much more detailed picture. It was not a pleasant one. He knew *Akagi* had been abandoned and would be sunk by a Japanese torpedo during the night. *Kaga* had slipped beneath the waves just before sunset, her heat reddened hull hissing steam as it slid into the cool twilight surge.

Soryu burned like a funeral pyre all afternoon, then blew up and sank at about the same time *Kaga* was going down. *Hiryu's* crew was fighting a losing battle with the flames. She would be the last of the four fleet carriers to sink, plunging to her death at 0900 the following morning, taking with her her stout-hearted Admiral Yamaguchi who had done everything he could to exploit victory at Pearl Harbor and avert disaster at Midway.

It was after Yamamoto had ordered all his fleets to close on the main force that he had received his first accurate report of the strength of the American forces opposing him. Three large carriers! And Japan had lost her four big ones! Samurai hearts sank. They had lifted a little at news of the hot strikes on *Yorktown* but then had come the word on *Hiryu*.

All of Nagumo's carriers gone!

There was a hollowness in Japanese stomachs. The great

Togo had not built the Imperial Japanese Navy for a night like this.

Almost in disbelief Yamamoto urged his huge force eastward to Nagumo's aid. Then to quicken Japanese spirits he radioed all force commanders at 1915 hours: "The enemy fleet which has practically been destroyed is retiring to the east. Combined fleet units in the vicinity are preparing to pursue the remnants and at the same time to occupy Midway. The main body is scheduled to reach Latitude 32 degrees 08 minutes North, Longitude 175 degrees 45 minutes East on course 90 degrees, speed 20 knots, by 0300 5th. The mobile force, occupation force and advance force (submarines) will immediately contact and attack the enemy."

But Nagumo knew better. There followed an interchange of messages between the battered admiral and his commander in chief during the night which showed the conqueror of Pearl Harbor apprehensive with alarm. Vice Admiral Nobutake Kondo, finally swept into the area with his battleships and heavy cruisers, prepared for night attack.

It was fifteen minutes to midnight.

Thursday the fourth of June was dying. It had been a full twenty-four hours of battle.

It had been history's most decisive day upon the sea.

It had been a day in which the wisdom of a calm admiral in his war room at Pearl and the devoted skill and courage of officers and men in planes, ships, submarines and in the sandbagged redoubts of Midway had seen the American navy reborn and the Japanese invaders flung back in defeat.

Shortly after midnight Yamamoto cancelled a last chance bombardment of Midway. At 0255 he ordered all surface units to retire to the northwest.

Japan was never to return to the central Pacific again. By dawn the huge Japanese armada was in full flight for the homeland.

The great battle was over.

38

The Admirals Wept

YAMAMOTO AND HIS GREAT ARMADA SLUNK BACK TO THEIR home ports in Japan to land their wounded under cover of night. No word of the shocking defeat was permitted to escape. Rather the Japanese proclaimed the action a victory for the Empire. Even many naval officers were not sure just what had happened and many were not to learn until after the war was over.

Two bleak rocks in the Aleutian Islands, Attu and Kiska, invaded by the northern force under Vice Admiral Moshiro Hosogaya, were displayed to the Japanese public as major trophies of the battle.

Not a word, not a whisper was permitted of the staggering losses in carriers, planes and men.

To regain the initiative of conquest Yamamoto moved rapidly in the South Pacific seizing the Solomons island of Guadalcanal. On it he would build an airstrip from which air cover could be flown for the combined fleet's operations in the southern ocean from Fiji to the north coast of Australia to ultimately isolate the Commonwealth from her great Pacific friend.

But Admiral Nimitz decided to make a fight for it. So the

bloody land, sea and air battles raged about the Solomon Islands which were eventually to drive the Japanese out of them by February of 1943. Admiral Nagumo and his chief of staff Admiral Kusaka, both of Pearl Harbor fame, conducted early carrier operations against the Americans in this area from their naval headquarters at Rabaul on the island of New Britain.

But Nagumo and Kusaka were to be no more successful in turning the tides of war than they had been at Midway. The Japanese finally had to retreat north from Guadalcanal.

It was then Yamamoto decided that he must personally tour the South Seas bases to bolster the morale of his officers and men serving in these difficult and dangerous advanced posts.

A top secret tour was set up for him to fly south from the great base at Truk where his new flagship *Musashi* was anchored, to Rabaul, then on to Buin on Bougainville Island in the northern Solomons, then finally back to his superbattleship at Truk.

The trip was to be made in two Mitsubishi twin-motored bombers, his chief of staff Admiral Ugaki of the "Waterloo speech" fame in the second bomber. They were to take off from Rabaul at 0600 on 18 April 1943 for Buin escorted by six Zeros.

Details of the flight plans were sent in top secret coded messages to officers along their route on a "need to know" basis. One of the recipients, which from the Japanese standpoint did not "need to know," was an American radio interceptor station at Dutch Harbor in the Aleutian Islands. Here the message was routinely sent on to CINCPAC at Pearl where Navy code experts broke it down and delivered it to Admiral Nimitz who relayed it to Frank Knox, Secretary of the Navy, with a recommendation.

This resulted in the planning of Operation Vengeance the target of which would be Admiral Yamamoto, commander in chief of the Japanese Combined Fleet, the architect of the attack on Pearl Harbor. With the commanding general of the Army Air Forces H. H. Arnold, Admiral Halsey, commander of the South Pacific, and Navy Secretary Frank Knox, all concurring, it was decided to send a squadron of Air Force P-38s from Henderson Field on Guadalcanal to intercept Yamamoto and shoot him down.

After arrangements had been made to fly up long-range gasoline tanks from the Air Force base at Milne Bay in New Guinea, the following order was radioed across the Pacific for Major John W. Mitchell commanding a P-38 squadron at Henderson Field, Guadalcanal:

> Washington Top Secret. Secretary Navy to Fighter Control Henderson. Admiral Yamamoto accompanied chief of staff and seven general officers Imperial Navy including surgeon grand fleet left Truk this morning eight hours for their trip inspection Bougainville bases stop Admiral and party traveling in two Bettys escorted six Zekes stop escort of honor from Kahili probable stop admiral's itinerary colon arrive Rabaul 1630 hours where spend night stop leave dawn for Kahili where time of arrival 0945 hours stop admiral then to board submarine chaser for inspection naval units under Admiral Tanaka stop Squadron 339 P-38 must at all costs reach and destroy Yamamoto and staff morning April eighteen stop auxiliary tanks and consumption data will arrive from Port Moresby evening seventeenth stop intelligence stresses admiral's extreme punctuality stop president attaches extreme importance this operation stop communicate result at once Washington stop Frank Knox Secretary Navy stop ultra-secret document not to be copied or filed stop to be destroyed when carried out stop.

Mitchell, for the utmost effort, decided to take eighteen P-38s on the long flight. The gasoline tanks arrived from New Guinea and were fitted to the planes that night.

The next morning Yamamoto's party took off for Bougainville with their escorting fighters.

They were flying in low for the Kahili airstrip when Mitchell and his fighters approached the coast. Immediately the P-38s gained altitude before diving to the attack. In spite of the Zero escort the admiral's bomber was hit, exploded and crashed burning into the palm trees. Admiral Ugaki's plane was shot down into the water where he was rescued, injured but alive. The P-38s wheeled away from the island for their long flight back to Guadalcanal.

The creator of the Pearl Harbor raid was dead.

In the Truk lagoon his flag was lowered from the masthead of the *Musashi* for the last time while admirals and seamen wept.

Much later Admiral Nagumo, then commanding the defense forces for the islands of Saipan and Tinian in the Mariannas, would commit hara-kiri in a cave on Saipan while the island was being overrun by United States Marines.

Admiral Kusaka, chief of staff to Nagumo at Pearl Harbor and Midway, would live out the war to see the surrender of Japan.

Their American opponents Admiral Kimmel and General Short would be retired from active service to live out their lives amid a swirl of controversy over the Pearl Harbor disaster which continues to this day.

Out of the wreckage of Pearl Harbor, the great fleet admiral Chester W. Nimitz was to shape the Navy, Marine, Army and Air Forces under his command into a vast machine of destruction which would end its course only with the surrender of Imperial Japan.

39

The Bitter End

WHERE IN ALL OF THE INTRICATE PLANNING AND TESTING and drafting of the Pearl Harbor operation did Admiral Yamamoto and his most capable staff advisors go astray?

What robbed them of the fruits of victory which could have been theirs if they had just reached out for them?

In reviewing the chronology of the events preceding, during and after Pearl Harbor, one cannot but be struck with two aspects of the operation which have never been adequately explained.

First, in the planning one is surprised by the lack of options provided the commanders in meeting conditions not visualized when the original plans were drafted. Although much was left to chance, and the Japanese were most favored in this regard considering American stupidity in not properly evaluating the intelligence they had collected through the reading of the Japanese diplomatic codes, some provision should have been made for bringing the U.S. carriers to battle in case they were not in Pearl Harbor the morning of the attack.

These were the great prizes the Japanese sought. They

already knew the aircraft carrier had supplanted the battleship as the major power element in modern navies. Yet we are witness to the almost frantic frustration of the air officers when their eleventh hour reports revealed that neither *Enterprise* nor *Lexington* would be victims of their raid on Pearl Harbor.

Nagumo and Kusaka who were not airmen were provided no direction as to what actions they should take to seek out and destroy these two mighty ships.

One such course of action which would have accomplished this has been suggested here. There were others all within capabilities of the Japanese navy. But as a matter of fact *Enterprise* and *Lexington* were hunting the attacker both on the afternoon of the raid and the day after.

Of this unparalleled opportunity the Imperial Japanese admirals took no advantage, choosing instead the course of safety and running for home, while denying the pleas of their own airmen to seek out and destroy the American carriers.

But most important of all, the plans included no options for victory in that Nagumo was not forced to conduct at least a third attack on the vast shore installations of the Pearl Harbor naval base, a blow which would have inflicted much more vital damage to the future operations of the U.S. fleet than the loss of the battleships.

Then there is the matter of the selection of the two top officers to conduct this most daring raid.

Admiral Nagumo never was in favor of the operation. In fact he was silently opposed to it. His chief of staff Admiral Kusaka was even more opposed, going to Yamamoto himself to cite reasons why the Pearl Harbor attack would fail.

The result was they seemed almost terrified by the success of the two air strikes and would waste no time in fleeing from Hawaiian waters after they had recovered their planes.

In stark contrast was the opposition to their decision to retire, by Rear Admiral Yamaguchi, commanding carriers

Hiryu and *Soryu* of CarDiv 2, who was to pay with his life for Nagumo's indecisiveness at the battle of Midway.

If the Japanese task force had renewed the Hawaiian attack it is almost a certainty that it would have sunk either *Enterprise* or *Lexington*, if not both, considering the number of planes, 350, that Nagumo could have hurled against the maximum 144 of the two American carriers combined.

Such a victory would have opened the way for a later follow up assault on Oahu.

One version of such an invasion operation has been suggested here. What the final results would have been cannot be determined with certainty because of the imponderables of war. Nevertheless the Japanese would have held all the major advantages if they had returned to attack Oahu within the first twelve weeks of the conflict.

Instead they spent their time in debating the next major use of their great carrier striking force only to arrive at a decision which would waste this mighty power against aging British men-o-war in the far off Indian Ocean.

But their great opportunity had not been overlooked.

Belatedly in mid-January 1942 Yamamoto assigned the task of developing plans to exploit the Pearl Harbor victory to Admiral Matomi Ugaki, his chief of staff, who after deliberating for four solitary days in his guarded cabin in the flagship *Nagato* emerged to present his chief with three possible courses of action.

They were to attack Hawaii, Australia or India.

When Yamamoto asked him for his recommendation, he unhesitatingly declared for Hawaii. This attack, he said, would result in the destruction of the remainder of the U.S. Pacific Fleet including the carriers, and by seizure of Oahu would deliver the most devastating of all possible strokes against the enemy.

Immediately a hornet's nest of argument and activity erupted within Yamamoto's staff.

Inevitably the ubiquitous, eccentric operations officer Captain Kamahito Kuroshima came up with his own plan—the capture of the island of Ceylon off the southern tip of India.

In Tokyo the naval general staff drafted a still different recommendation—Australia.

In the staff cabins of Nagumo's flagship *Akagi*, the man who knew most about the Pearl Harbor raid and the American carrier fleet, Commander Genda, the carrier fleet's operations officer, was polishing his own plan which he had developed while the carriers were returning to Japan—an attack against the islands of Midway and Kingman's Reef south of Hawaii to bring the American carriers out to do battle with the Japanese.

But in the end no immediate decision was made. The Nagumo force put to sea again 5 January 1942 bound for Truk and the South Seas where it pounded the shores of New Britain, New Ireland and New Guinea prior to their invasion by Japanese troops. Then back in Truk again, the Japanese naval airmen were electrified by the news that American carriers were raiding the Marshall Islands to the east.

It was their old antagonist Halsey in *Enterprise*, who with Fletcher in the newly arrived *Yorktown*, worked over Japanese forward bases in the Marshalls and the Gilbert Islands on 1 February 1942. So soon after Pearl Harbor had the counter blows started to fall!

The Nagumo force sortied out of Truk to attack Halsey but gave up the futile chase when after the second day it was a certainty that the Americans were no longer in the area.

Retracing his course westward Nagumo received orders from combined fleet to detach the two newest carriers, *Shokaku* and *Zuikaku*, for patrol duties in the Pacific off the eastern coasts of Japan itself, while the intrepid Yamaguchi who had reinforced the second attack on Wake Island, was directed to join *Akagi* and *Kaga* at Palau en route to an attack on Port Darwin, Australia, on 19 February. Then followed other miscellaneous tasks in support of the invasions of Java and Sumatra in the Dutch East Indies.

Finally on 26 March with Carrier Division 5, *Shokaku* and *Zuikaku* rejoined Nagumo was ordered to attack Ceylon and the British Far Eastern Fleet in the Indian Ocean. This was done 5–9 April with overwhelming results. Then at last the carrier striking force, less Carrier Division 5 dropped off at Truk to cover the New Guinea invasion, was ordered to steam for home.

It was now mid-April during which time the Imperial Japanese Navy had let run through its fingers the most precious hours and the most precious days in its proud history.

On 18 April 1942 Colonel James Doolittle led a flight of sixteen Army B-25 medium bombers off the flight deck of the carrier *Hornet* escorted by *Enterprise*, for the first aerial bombardment of Japan including the capitol city of the Emperor, Imperial Tokyo.

At the moment the returning Nagumo force in the Bashi Strait south of Formosa was ordered to proceed full speed to the attack area in an abortive attempt to catch the carriers from which the planes had come. It was all too late.

It was also too late for the planners of the combined fleet and the naval general staff as they rushed to complete work on preparations for "Operation MI," the ill-fated attack at Midway.

For now, depleted as his forces were, Nimitz had organized them around his carriers so the task forces would be highly effective instruments of naval warfare if and when the two fleets confronted each other.

On Oahu the great fortress had undergone immense strengthening in planes, in guns and in men. The Aircraft Detection Service was in effective operation, functioning on an around-the-clock basis every day of the week with alert aircraft ready to take off within minutes of warning.

The civilian communities on all of the islands had been organized to push the war program and assist the armed forces in the defense of Hawaii.

Over all there was a single commander, Admiral Nimitz, so the old days of split command with its opportunities for delays and misunderstandings, were gone.

The American nation, now fully aroused to its danger, was putting all of its vast energies into the effort to defeat Japan in Asia and Germany and Italy in Europe.

It would be a long, tough ordeal for the fighting men in the Pacific but for America there would be no turning back.

For Japan at the full flush of victory on the seventh of December 1941, it would be the beginning of a painful ordeal of suffering and death which would bring her people to the brink of mass destruction.

So it was that those hours following the flashing of the "Tora! Tora! Tora!" signal by the leader of the Pearl Harbor air strike were such critical ones for both nations.

So it was that those minutes of argument on the bridge of the *Akagi* between Nagumo and Kusaka and their airmen Genda and Fuchida were so fraught with destiny for two great nations.

So it was that when chief of staff Kusaka informed his admiral: "I will order the signal to retire."

And Nagumo responded: "Please do."

It was the most disastrous decision ever made by a victorious commander in the history of war upon the sea.